the
Tuscan
Diary

BOOKS BY ANITA CHAPMAN

The Florence Letter

The Venice Secret

ANITA CHAPMAN

the
Tuscan
Diary

bookouture

Published by Bookouture in 2024

An imprint of Storyfire Ltd.
Carmelite House
50 Victoria Embankment
London EC4Y 0DZ

www.bookouture.com

Storyfire Ltd's authorised representative in the EEA is Hachette Ireland
8 Castlecourt Centre
Castleknock Road
Castleknock
Dublin 15 D15 YF6A
Ireland

ISBN: 978-1-83618-004-3
eBook ISBN: 978-1-83618-003-6

For Siena, the fairytale city that inspired this novel

PROLOGUE

The woman entered the bedroom and pushed open the shutters, welcoming the view of the Tuscan hills. They were painted in various shades of green and yellow, narrow roads twisting and winding in between them, one leading to a farmhouse surrounded by cypress trees, protecting it from the tramontana; the wind coming from the north. Taking a moment to appreciate this beauty, even though she woke up to it every day, she made out a German tank, edging its way along one of those roads, the sound of its engine reverberating around the valley and bringing her back to reality. Her gut lurched in that way it often did these days. She was exhausted by the horrors of war, her beloved Tuscany occupied by the enemy, and how this had greatly impacted her and her neighbours. How she longed for it all to be over soon. Would it ever be over? Every morning and night, she would pray, and she continued to attend Mass every Sunday. Before too long, she hoped to live some kind of ordinary life again, one that wasn't filled with fear for every single minute of every day.

Despite it being almost autumn, the air was thick, and she wiped the film of sweat on her forehead with the back of her hand. The man behind her lay in bed, the white cotton sheets dotted with dark-red blotches from where his blood had seeped through the bandages wrapped round his shoulder – she would ask the maid to change the bedding if and when he was able to move. Standing over the bed, she looked down at him sleeping, his breathing soft, lips slightly open; grateful that his face, a handsome one at that, had not been impacted by what occurred the previous night. With his thick, dark-brown hair, and tanned skin, no doubt from the summer months, he could easily pass for an Italian. The lower part of his face was covered with a dark beard and, apart from the slight smile creases around his eyes, the skin that was visible was smooth with youth. He appeared to be several years her junior, and she hoped he'd make a full recovery under her care and have many good years ahead of him.

The night before, after the physician had left, she'd prayed by his bedside, her rosary running through her fingers as he drifted in and out of consciousness. As she pressed a cool, damp cloth to his forehead, he mumbled words that she mostly couldn't comprehend, apart from 'Mother', which she knew to mean mamma. Of course, at a time when death was a real probability he would call for the woman who'd brought him into the world – it was only natural.

She couldn't begin to imagine how much pain he must be in, and wanted to do all she could to attend to his needs. Taking the chair from underneath the dressing table, she placed it beside the bed, and found herself studying his hands. He had long, elegant fingers, but she could see that his nails needed cutting, and they had dirt underneath them.

He started to talk – she couldn't make out what he was saying, not only because he spoke in a language she barely understood, but also because he was mumbling.

Then he shouted, in Italian, 'Please, you must do this for me. I implore you.'

She jumped out of her skin. Madonna!

Placing her hand on his, she said, softly, also in Italian, 'Don't worry, I am here. You are safe in my house.'

She squeezed his hand, gently, and he brushed one of her fingers with his thumb. This small gesture told her he was reassured by her words.

He opened his eyes, and she was surprised to see they were a blue-grey colour, and they were mesmerising. Italian men usually had brown eyes. He looked up at the ceiling, and seemed to be studying the fresco – for it was rather beautiful, with angels forming a circle, and she hoped they would play their part in saving him. He turned his head to the left, in the direction of the window with the view of the countryside. Sighing, he then turned his head to the right, and set those eyes on her. Instantly his face broke into a smile, revealing a perfect set of white teeth – he was glad to see her, and this brought her joy.

'Buongiorno,' she said.

'Buongiorno.'

'Would you like a glass of water?'

He nodded, and said, 'Si.'

She got up and approached the bedside table, picking up the jug brought earlier by the maid, and poured a little water into a glass. Edging the chair closer to the bed, she sat back down and lifted the glass to his lips. He positioned his head in order to be able to drink, and, when he'd had enough, gently pushed the glass away with his right hand, sighing, 'Grazie, Signora.'

'Prego,' she said. For he was most welcome, and she found herself wanting to do all she could to aid his recovery. She hoped this might take a little time, if indeed he survived, as she found herself comforted by his presence – for she'd been so very lonely recently – and longed to get to know him better.

Putting the glass down on the bedside table, she took his hand once again, and they looked at each other, but didn't speak. There were no words. He was alive because of her, and surely, he knew that. By the way he assessed her face with those eyes, he was curious to know her as well. It was still early, and he may not live – the physician had said the wound in his shoulder was a serious one – and she needed to ensure it didn't become infected. But she endeavoured to do her best and would continue to pray for him.

CHAPTER 1

ELEANOR

It had been a quiet afternoon at Thorpe's. Working at a stationery shop wasn't exactly my calling. My legs ached at the end of each day with no opportunity to sit down, apart from in the back room at lunchtimes. There we'd eat sandwiches brought from home, and share a pot of tea.

Immensely bored, I was rearranging items inside a display case when a man walked in, the bell jangling as he came through the door. He took off his hat and placed it on the stand. Instantly, I recognised him as my best friend Mabel's older brother, Peter. He was as handsome as ever, thick dark hair flopping over his face on one side. We hadn't seen each other for several months because he'd been living in barracks while training with the British army.

The duty manager, Mrs Dobson, a stern woman with pince-nez resting on her nose, approached him.

She said, 'Good afternoon, sir,' but he mumbled something and walked straight past her in rather a rude fashion, heading in my direction. He must have recognised me too, and he came to stand next to me – I sensed his presence as he waited for me to close the display case. Locking it with the key attached to the chain in the pocket of my dress, I composed myself before turning to face him.

'Well, I never, Peter Hill. I haven't seen you in quite a while.'

'I'm actually here to see you, Miss Wade,' he said, his lips turned up at the corners. We shook hands. 'Mabel called the house earlier, and, seeing as I was going to be in the vicinity this afternoon, I offered to pass on a message.'

Soon I would be leaving to work as a land girl in the North Riding. Mabel had told me about a girl dropping out, and I'd be taking her place. Having recently turned twenty, I was obliged to do my bit by working for one of the auxiliary services, and being with a friend would hopefully make it a less daunting experience. I hadn't spent much time in the countryside before and had no idea what to expect. But I looked forward to getting away from the fear of being bombed at any moment, and the hustle and bustle and fumes of central Leeds, that was for sure.

'Oh yes?'

'She asked me to tell you that next week, when you arrive at the station, the farmer's son, Jack, will collect you in a horse and trap. You won't be able to miss him – he has a large shrapnel scar on one side of his face.'

'Oh dear, poor chap. Thank you, Peter, for passing that on.'

He looked at me awkwardly, and drummed his fingers on the counter, as if in deep thought.

'I wonder if you might be able to assist me with something?'

As he looked down at me, I couldn't help getting lost in those misty blue-grey eyes of his. It wasn't the first time, seeing as we'd shared a drunken kiss a few years back. It had been a balmy summer evening and we were swigging whisky nicked from his father's drinks cabinet in the garden at his house. He returned to university shortly afterwards, and that was that –

although I couldn't help being a little in love with him at the time. Ever since then, he'd acted a little nervous in my presence. He opened his mouth to speak, but swiftly closed it again. The cat seemed to have got his tongue, and I felt uncomfortable on his behalf. Smiling, I lifted my eyebrows, encouraging him to try again. He swallowed, got a ten-shilling note out of his trouser pocket and placed it on the counter. Surely it wasn't me having such an impact on him?

Clearing his throat, he said, 'I'm leaving for war tomorrow, and...' He hesitated.

His voice was as deep and husky as I remembered it, so masculine. I was utterly captivated. Having him come into the shop had quite made my day – his vulnerability was most endearing. But I dreaded to think what might lie ahead for him.

'And?' I prompted.

'And... I'm actually looking for a new notebook to take with me.'

I reopened the display case and removed a selection of our bestselling notebooks, in an array of colours, all made from leather. I laid them out on top of the case – red, tan brown, black, all manufactured in Manchester by the luxury brand Cookson. He picked up the tan-brown one and ran his hand over its smooth cover. It was a beauty, with COOKSON embossed in gold capital letters on the front. His hands were as I remembered them, the skin creamy and smooth, and he had elegant long fingers with nicely rounded fingernails. He put the notebook down and I placed my hand on it.

'We always sell out of this one at Christmas, and it's my personal favourite. Real leather, of course,' I said. Opening the cover, I lifted the thin black ribbon. 'And it comes with its very own bookmark, so you don't lose your place. If you smell it, you'll know straight away that it's real leather because of its sweet, earthy scent.'

I handed the notebook back to him, our fingers brushing,

and he raised it to his nose and inhaled. Nodding, he turned it over and checked the price label on the back. His eyes widened.

'What do you suggest I do with such an expensive note-book?' he said, with a smile. His eyes twinkled, creases forming at the edges as he studied me, and now it was my turn to feel awkward. My face warmed, and I looked away in order to compose myself.

'Well, why not use it as a diary? My father did just that during the Great War and said it stopped him from going off his rocker.'

'What a marvellous idea,' he said, handing it to me. 'I'll take it.'

'Very good.'

He watched as I went through the rigmarole of folding cream tissue paper round the notebook and placed it inside a red Cookson box with the same gold letters embossed on the lid. Then I wrapped the box in the dark-green paper of the highest quality that we liked to use at Thorpe's. I took a roll of satin ribbon out of a drawer and decorated the small parcel using a criss-cross pattern, then created a bow at the centre and curled the ends with a pair of scissors. There was a palpable tension in the air, and I could hear Peter breathing quietly as he stood on the other side of the counter, studying my every move with admiration. That was probably the greatest skill I took away from Thorpe's, apart from learning how to persuade customers to spend money on expensive things they didn't need. I supposed Peter was searching for distractions that afternoon, anything to take his mind off the journey he was to embark on the following day. Anything to lift his mood even a trifle.

I picked up the ten-shilling note, opened the till, calculated how much change he was owed and dropped the coins into the palm of his hand followed by the receipt. Our hands brushed again as we did this exchange, and he seemed to take a breath, as if this had sparked something within him.

'As this is my last day in Leeds, I'm going to Raymond's for fish and chips later – who knows if and when I'll get chance to eat them again?' he said.

Was this a roundabout way of asking me to join him?

'Oh really?'

'While you were wrapping my new notebook so beautifully, I found myself wondering if I should ask you to come with me. After you finish work, perhaps you could meet me there, if you have nothing better to do?'

I couldn't think of anything I wanted to do more at the end of my shift. Although meeting the man I'd been a little in love with since that kiss as he was about to leave for war wasn't the brightest idea.

'I finish in an hour, and will need to tidy up, so could meet you at half past five, if that's all right?'

He beamed, as if he were greatly surprised at my accepting. 'It will be my treat.' He proffered his hand once again, and I shook it and his grip was firm.

'I'll see you at Raymond's at five thirty prompt then,' he said, sliding the notebook into the inside pocket of his coat and then going to take his hat off the stand. Placing it on his head, he gave me a nod.

'Good day, Miss Wade.'

'Good day, Mr Hill,' I said, watching him leave. The bell jangled once again as he went through the door, and closed it carefully behind him. Then he turned to look at me through the window, and I thought he threw me a wink, but couldn't be certain.

CHAPTER 2

JESSICA

It was the end of the summer. Me and Mum had spent the morning picking apples in the orchard and arranging them neatly into boxes so they could be stored away for the winter. It was one of those lukewarm almost-September afternoons, and the sun was shining after a recent bout of rain. We were in the kitchen taking a break – me, Mum and Gran – with a pot of tea and a Victoria sponge that Mum had just finished filling with freshly whipped double cream and sliced strawberries soaked in a sugar syrup.

'Fill up the pot, will you, Jess,' Gran said.

Getting up, I reached for the kettle on the stove, and through the window saw an unfamiliar car pull into the yard, splattered with mud from the country lanes surrounding Birch Farm.

'We have a visitor,' I said, as a man got out of the car. We'd often get people knocking on our door in the summer, lost while exploring the Yorkshire Dales and needing directions. His hair was dark brown, and he was relatively tall. He wore beige cargo shorts with pristine white trainers and a t-shirt. From a distance he seemed quite good-looking and appeared to be around my age, maybe a little older. He was carrying a black briefcase and I wondered if he was here on official business. Was he a lawyer or debt collector or something? The farm did have a lot of financial problems – Dad often talked about being on the verge of bankruptcy. But then wouldn't the man be wearing a suit?

'Who is it?' Mum said.

'I don't know. It's a man, seems quite young. He has a briefcase. Were you expecting anyone?'

'Not today,' she said.

He shook his head and seemed to be talking to himself as he stepped around all the puddles in the yard – we'd had a downpour the previous evening – and a couple of geese honked at him as he approached the back door. Then Cassie, our sheepdog, jumped up at him, barking with the usual enthusiasm she greeted visitors with. He seemed unfazed by this, and gently stroked her head, speaking to her softly. She cocked her head to one side, looking up at him, tail wagging. But then he stepped right into a muddy puddle, and seemed to be swearing to himself as he studied the state of his trainers.

'Oh dear,' I said.

'What's the matter?' Gran said.

'He's just trodden in a muddy puddle in his new-looking trainers, and doesn't look too happy.'

'You'd better go and help him clean up then,' Gran said.

I passed through the porch, where we kept wellies and coats, and hats in all shapes and sizes, and opened the back door. And there he stood, an exasperated look on his face. But then he lifted his eyebrows and studied me with the loveliest dark-brown eyes. I didn't know what to say. My outfit of skimpy shorts and tiny vest top left little to the imagination, and I caught him glancing at my legs, nicely tanned from being outdoors. Our eyes met and we exchanged a smile.

'Hi,' I said.

'How are you doing?' he said in an American accent.

'Oh, you're American?'

'I am, from New Jersey.'

Looking down at his feet, I said, 'Would you like me to sort out your trainers?'

'You can do that?'

'There's a sink right here. Why don't you take them off?'

I gestured for him to step over the threshold, and he entered the house, closing the door behind him.

'Okay, thank you, ma'am.'

I'd never been called ma'am before. Was this an American thing?

He crouched down and untied the laces, doing his best to remove the trainers without getting mud on his hands. Picking them up, I filled the Belfast sink with hot water and washing-up liquid and set about removing the mud with an old nailbrush. Within minutes, they were as good as new. I put the trainers on the shoe rack and gave my hands a thorough wash with a bar of soap. When I was done, he approached the sink and did the same.

'So, I'd ask if you're looking for directions, but you seem to have a briefcase with you. Are you here on official business?' I said, drying my hands on a towel before passing it to him.

'I'm actually looking for a woman called Eleanor. I doubt she still lives here, but maybe you might know where she could be, or if she's even still alive?'

Gran was called Eleanor. I bit my lip. What did this mysterious, handsome man want with her? She didn't really know anyone outside of Little Vale, having lived here since the war. Me and Mum kept her company most of the time, that's when she wasn't at Camellia Cottage on the other side of the orchard, where she lived. Perhaps some distant relation had left her money? But who did she know in America, apart from Auntie Mabel?

'Actually, she does live here, and she's very much alive. Eleanor is my grandmother.'

'Oh, really? What a stroke of luck. I'm here on behalf of my grandfather, Benedetto Sabatini. He was friends with a man called Peter, who Eleanor knew during the war.'

Gran had never mentioned a Peter before.

'You'd better come in,' I said.

He followed me into the kitchen, and I told Mum and Gran what he'd just said.

'I'm Eleanor,' Gran said, 'and this is my daughter, Mary, and granddaughter, Jessica.'

'Pleased to meet you,' he said, reaching forward to shake Mum and Gran's hands. 'I'm Alessandro, but most people call me Al.'

Al as in Pacino. *The Godfather* was one of my favourite films. Never had such an exciting person rocked up on our farm.

'Why don't you sit down and join us for tea,' Gran said. 'Jess, can you get another cup and saucer and a side plate.'

I did as she asked while Alessandro put his briefcase on the floor next to the table, pulled up a chair and sat down, next to Mum and opposite Gran and me. We exchanged a look.

I poured him a cup of tea and cut a slice of cake and placed it all in front of him. Did Americans even drink tea?

He looked pleased with the offering, and smiled and said, 'Thank you, Jessica,' his eyes meeting mine.

I liked the way he said my name in his American accent.

'So, what may I ask are you doing here, young man, and, more importantly, what's in the briefcase?' Gran said.

Dear Gran, always to the point.

'I've brought you something that my grandfather has been keeping for years,' Alessandro said. 'Sadly, he's dying of cancer, and when he found out I'd be working in London this summer he asked me to bring it with me and try to find you.'

Gran frowned, the lines on her forehead deepening. 'What on earth is it?'

Alessandro picked up the briefcase and placed it on the table as if he was in an important business meeting in some boardroom. He clicked open the latches before reaching inside and taking out a tan-brown notebook. The front cover looked as though it was damaged, with a hole at the top right-hand corner, and it appeared to be quite old.

Gran gasped as he passed it to her across the table. The look on her face said it all. She'd seen this notebook before. Turning it over, her hands began to shake, and she let out a long deep sigh.

'Well I never... Peter Hill,' she said.

CHAPTER 3

ELEANOR

A few minutes before five thirty, I crossed the road outside Thorpe's and walked along the street until I reached Raymond's – the most famous fish and chip shop in Leeds, founded in the 1920s, complete with wooden panelling and chandeliers, and a thick cream carpet. It was very posh indeed, and I was grateful that fish and chips were not subject to rationing as Churchill liked to call them 'the good companions'. Sadly, the Dog and Duck, the public house next door to Raymond's, had been badly damaged during the Leeds Blitz the previous spring, a stark reminder of the war going on around us. Through the window, the restaurant appeared to be relatively busy with men and women who, like myself, had probably just clocked off from work. Opening the door, I went inside, and instantly spotted Peter sitting in a booth by the window, large enough for four people. I went over to join him. He wore a shirt and tie – I hadn't noticed what he was wearing in the shop because he'd had his coat on. Immersed in the pages of the *Yorkshire Citizen*, spread out on the table before him, he didn't see me approach.

'Hello,' I said.

He looked up and smiled. 'Good afternoon, Eleanor. Do sit down.'

Carefully, he folded up the newspaper and put it on the banquette next to him. I took off my coat and hung it on the stand in the corner before taking the seat opposite Peter. I placed my gas mask and handbag beside me. We looked at each other, but didn't speak. Despite being wartime, everything seemed calm and still. Who'd have thought that I'd end up having supper here with him when he walked into Thorpe's that afternoon?

A waitress came over.

'Well, I'm having cod and chips. How about you?' Peter said.

'Good choice. I'll have the same, please.'

'And a pot of tea for two?'

I nodded.

She scribbled everything down on a notepad. 'Anything else?'

'Oh, and bread and butter on the side,' he said, handing her the menu.

Before long, she'd brought over a pot of tea with cups and saucers, a jug of milk and a bowl of sugar lumps. Peter gestured for me to take the pot, and I filled a cup before putting it down on his side of the table. I added a sugar lump to my tea, and gave it a thorough stir. Sugar was a luxury, and to be savoured at every opportunity.

A double-decker bus passed the window, and people filled the pavement as they made their way home.

'So, you're leaving for war tomorrow?' I said.

'I am indeed.'

'Do you know where they're sending you?'

He shook his head. 'I have absolutely no idea.'

It struck me that, even if he did know where he was going, he wouldn't be allowed to tell me.

'I have a confession to make,' he said.

'What's that then?'

'I wasn't planning on buying anything in Thorpe's today but, well, I felt a need to impress you.'

'Impress me how?'

'By spending an obscene amount of money on a notebook when I have several cheaper ones at home.'

'Oh,' I said, a butterfly sensation in my gut.

'Were you impressed?' he said.

'I was a little. They are rather nice notebooks, after all. You do have impeccable taste.'

'And now that I've bought it' – he picked up the paper bag next to him with 'Thorpe's' written on the side – 'I'll have to use it, won't I?'

'Indeed, you'll have to record every single day, even if you only write a short paragraph each time.'

'You'll hold me to that, will you?'

'I shall expect updates by post.'

'We'll be exchanging letters?'

Shrugging, I said, 'If you'd like to, I don't see why not.'

The waitress brought over our fish and chips along with a small plate piled with bread, sliced into triangles and spread with butter. I put salt and vinegar on my fish and chips, and Peter squeezed the slice of lemon over his cod. I unfolded the white linen napkin and placed it on my lap, and we tucked in.

'Weren't you still at university at the beginning of the war?' I said.

'Yes, I was studying English literature at Oxford, and after that I was a schoolteacher for a short time,' he said.

'And what will you do when the war ends?'

'Assuming we win, and I make it home in one piece, I'll probably teach again. My dream is to write novels, but I doubt that would be very lucrative.'

'You enjoy writing?'

'Oh I enjoy it, but I'll admit I've tried and failed to write a novel. It is harder than one might expect. And will you miss working at Thorpe's?'

'Not particularly. I'm so glad that I'll get to be a land girl with Mabel – going somewhere in the countryside all on my own would have been quite daunting.'

'Mabel seems to be enjoying it.'

'She did say in one of her letters that she's met a few American soldiers based nearby down at the pub – hopes to court one of them. I'm sure that's one of the reasons.'

'Is that what you're hoping to do?' he said.

'You're asking if I'm hoping to court an American soldier?'

He looked me in the eye, the corners of his mouth upturned. 'Yes.'

'Oh no. Mabel is far more adventurous than me.'

He laughed, and wiped his mouth with a napkin. Stroking his chin, he said, 'You prefer British men?'

Unable to meet his gaze, I found myself struggling not to smile. He was being quite flirtatious. Picking up the teapot, I refilled my cup.

'What will you do after the war, Eleanor?'

'I have absolutely no idea.'

'Well, what do you enjoy doing?'

Racking my brain, I struggled to come up with much. I wasn't the ambitious type.

'I'm very fond of baking. I used to help Mother in the kitchen making delicious cakes for us to eat, working my way through the family recipe book, passed down from her mother. But with rationing, I don't get to do that much these days.'

'Maybe you can open a bakery one day?' he said.

'I'd prefer a tea shop if I had my own business. One of those quaint places you see in old villages, with lace tablecloths and matching napkins. Oh, and with cups and saucers and plates with pretty patterns on them in blue and pink.'

'There it is, you do have a dream, after all. I just had to prise it out of you.' He smiled, his eyes twinkling.

I did like the idea of owning a tea shop. Baking all day and talking to customers would be a nice way to pass the time.

'Here's to you writing your novels, and to me opening my own tea shop one day,' I said, lifting my cup of tea.

He did the same, clinking it against mine, and we laughed.

'And what will you call your tea shop?' he said.

'I don't know... I guess maybe Eleanor's?'

'Very well. Eleanor's it is. Here's to us and our dreams.'

CHAPTER 4

JESSICA

'This diary belonged to a man called Peter Hill,' Gran said, putting the notebook down on the table. She ran a hand over it, and her eyes glazed over for a moment. 'I sold it to him when I worked in Thorpe's, a shop in Leeds. He took it with him when he went to fight in the war. Sadly, not long after he left, his mother received a telegram to say he was missing in action. I've always wondered what happened to him.'

Gran seemed so sad, and I couldn't believe there was this whole part of her life we didn't know about. Who was this man called Peter? Had he been a boyfriend or something? It seemed that she'd cared about him a great deal and must have been devastated to hear about his disappearance. Missing in action wasn't the same as killed in action, and perhaps she'd been secretly wondering all this time if he was still alive.

'Well, I can tell you this,' Alessandro said. 'He was captured in Tunisia and taken to Italy, where he was held as a prisoner of war. When the Italians changed sides, he was released and joined the partisans – the Italian resistance fighters – in Tuscany with my grandfather, Benedetto, and they were friends. Benedetto held him as he lay dying, and Peter's last

THE TUSCAN DIARY 21

request was that he give this diary to Eleanor on Birch Farm in Little Vale, Yorkshire.'

Gran closed her eyes and opened them again. Then she said, 'I hope you don't mind my asking, but why has this taken so long?'

Alessandro nodded.

'I completely understand why you'd want to know that. Benedetto blamed himself for Peter's death. Peter had warned him about one of the partisans, saying he believed him to be a traitor. Benedetto didn't listen. They were waiting for a supply drop from the British army near Siena, on the edge of some chestnut woods, and he was shot by German soldiers.'

'So where has the diary been all this time, Al?' Mum asked.

'In a drawer in Benedetto's study. He'd always planned to gather the strength to bring it to you one day, but never got round to it. He asked me to try and bring it to you, to fulfil both Peter's dying wish and now his own.'

'Better late than never, I suppose,' Gran said, looking down at the diary again.

'I am sorry if this is all a shock, Eleanor.'

'It's not your fault – you're only the messenger, after all, and I appreciate you driving all the way up here. It's not the shortest journey,' Gran said.

Alessandro looked at his watch. 'Yes, I have to get back to London, I'm afraid. As you say, it's a long drive.' Standing up, he leant over to shake hands with Gran and then Mum, before removing a business card from the pocket of his shorts. He got out a pen and wrote down a phone number on the back, before placing it on the table. He threw me a smile.

'If you ever want to come to Siena, give me a call on this number and I can ask Benedetto to show you where Peter died – there's a wooden cross where he's buried. But I'd do it fairly soon as we don't know how long my grandfather has left.'

'I'm not sure whether I'd be up to doing that, but thank you all the same,' Gran said.

'If you change your mind, I'll be in Siena for another couple of weeks, then I'm heading back to New York. You can still contact me there, and I'll put you in touch. It might be better if I'm in Siena though, so I can act as your interpreter. My aunt Isabella does speak enough English to get by, but she works long hours and might find it difficult to spare the time.'

'Thank you, Al, it's very kind of you to offer. Show the young man out, will you, Jessica,' Gran said.

He said goodbye to them both, and I got up and led him back to the porch, where he took his trainers off the rack and put them on.

'Do try and persuade your gran to come out to Siena,' he said, tying the laces. 'It seems like it may be the closure she needs after all these years.'

'Okay,' I said, doubting very much that she'd have any interest in going.

'You could come with her?' he said. 'It's a beautiful city with an interesting history, and I'm sure you'd love it. If I'm still there, I could maybe show you around.'

I liked the idea of visiting Italy and of seeing him again, but Gran would need some persuading, and I could hardly go on my own, could I?

'That's something to think about. Thanks, Alessandro,' I said.

He gave me a nod, and I stood there on the threshold, watching him walk across the yard, this time being careful to avoid the muddy puddles. He got into his car and looked through the window at me. I smiled, and he threw me a wave before starting the engine and driving away. As I watched him progress up the drive, zigzagging his way around potholes filled with rainwater, I inhaled, surprisingly bowled over by the man who'd just walked into my life. I smiled to myself as it struck me that I really wanted to see him again. Maybe somehow it would happen...

CHAPTER 5

ELEANOR

When we'd finished eating, Peter picked up the bill left by the waitress and dropped a few coins onto the table. I thanked him for his generosity.

'Where do you live, Eleanor?' he said.

Although we'd known each other growing up, he'd never been to my house – I'd only seen him when dropping in on Mabel.

'It's a ten-minute bus journey away.'

'Shall I accompany you?'

It was now dark outside, and I appreciated him asking. I didn't particularly enjoy negotiating the streets of Leeds at night alone, especially during blackout.

'That would be most kind, thank you.'

We put on our coats, and Peter placed his hat on his head, and we left Raymond's and went outside into the crisp night air. The bus stop was only a few feet away, and we joined the queue of people waiting.

On the pitch-black bus journey, we didn't talk and the other passengers didn't say a word either. But I sensed his presence next to me. I could hear him breathing lightly and found myself inhaling his cologne, sweet like vanilla. I wondered if he could smell the rose-scented perfume I'd doused myself with in the back room before leaving Thorpe's.

When we reached my stop, I nudged Peter and said, 'We're here.'

He got off the bus with me and we walked to my front gate. My parents were out that evening at a music recital, and I knew they wouldn't be home until after midnight as they were going to a friend's house for drinks afterwards. It was too dark to see the time on my watch, but I calculated it would be around eight o'clock.

'Would you like to come in for a cup of tea?' I said. 'My parents are out and won't be back until the early hours.'

'Well, all right then.'

I reached into my handbag for the keys and unlocked the front door, and we went inside. He took off his coat and hat and put them on the stand, and I undid the buttons on my coat and hung it up.

I led him into the kitchen and filled the kettle and put it on the stove.

'This is a nice house,' he said. 'Remind me, what does your father do for a living?'

'He's a solicitor. My mother is a housewife, but also heavily involved with the Auxiliary Territorial Service. She helps out at the ATS canteen, and does a great deal of work with the local church.'

'Oh, I see,' he said.

'I recall you lost your father?' Mabel had told me this.

He sighed. 'Yes indeed, my father was killed at the end of the First World War. I don't really remember him – he left when I was three years old, and didn't return.'

'I'm sorry.'

I imagined how difficult it must be for Peter having to go and fight when this was how his father had met his fate.

'Thank you,' he said. 'My mother worries about losing me as well, understandably.'

'I'm sure she would,' I said.

A moment of silence fell between us as the reality of what he was facing had become apparent. The kettle whistled. I filled a teapot and took the bottle of milk out of the larder, and we sat down at the table.

'Like your mother, she's been volunteering in order to do her bit.'

'Mabel told me. And she still teaches?'

'Yes, at the local primary school. It hasn't been easy for her looking after young children who find the war terrifying.'

'That must be some responsibility. Do you get your love of books and writing from her?'

'She encouraged me to read from an early age and would take me to the library every Saturday. Mabel was never that interested in books though, as I'm sure you know.'

Mabel didn't like to sit still for long. Being a land girl would probably suit her, with all the physical work.

'Yes, you and Mabel are indeed like chalk and cheese,' I said.

He looked at me across the table. He was so handsome, and my heart sank as I wished he wasn't leaving the following day. Why did it have to be wartime, and why did he have to choose today to come into Thorpe's? All I could do was hope he'd return – perhaps we'd meet again and have a chance to get to know each other better.

He stirred sugar into his tea and picked up the cup to take a sip.

'I wish we'd spent some time together sooner,' he said, as if reading my thoughts.

'I feel the same,' I said.

'If there wasn't a war on, do you think you might have allowed me to kiss you again, like that time in the garden?'

I nodded. It was a memory I often returned to.

'Yes.'

'That's an awful shame,' he said.

He placed the cup in the saucer and a silence fell between us. After a moment, he smiled slightly and said, 'Well, I'd best be off then.'

'Already?'

'I need to finish packing, I'm afraid.'

Peter stood up, and I did the same, and we walked down the hall towards the front door. He took his coat off the stand and pushed his arms through the sleeves, stealing a glance in my direction as tension hung in the air between us – there were so many things being unsaid. The thought of never seeing him again was too much. How I wanted him to kiss me.

Taking the hat off the stand, he hesitated and said, 'I know I'm leaving tomorrow, but how about I kiss you just once before I go. Give a man a morale boost, if you will, to send him on his way?'

There were no more words needed. I nodded, butterflies fluttering in my stomach, and he leant forward and pressed his lips gently to mine. Kissing Peter was even better than I remembered. It went on and on, and I didn't want it to stop. Then he pulled away and stepped back, and placed his hat on his head. He checked his appearance in the mirror above the console table.

'Thank you, Eleanor. I'm glad I came into the shop today,' he said, quietly.

'Aren't we going to write to each other?'

He picked up the pen on the console table and wrote down his details on the telephone pad.

'Why don't you give me your address?' he said.

'I'll give you this one, but don't forget that from next week I'll be on Birch Farm.'

'Mabel has already given me that address,' he said.

I wrote down my parents' address and tore off the sheet of paper before handing it to him. He folded the piece of paper carefully and placed it into his coat pocket.

He scratched his head as he stood near the door. 'Actually... would you mind if I stayed just a bit longer, Eleanor?' he said. 'I don't feel ready to leave you yet.'

I smiled, so pleased he wanted to see more of me. 'As I said before, my parents won't be back for hours.'

He removed his hat and coat, and put them back on the stand, and we exchanged a look.

We went into the kitchen, and I refilled the pot of tea, and we talked for a while, and then he leant across the table and kissed me again. I asked if he'd like to look at the books on the shelf in my room, and upstairs we sat on my bed and talked some more. When he leant in to kiss me, I did something completely out of character. The fact that he was leaving made our time together especially exciting, and adrenaline pumped through my veins. The war made you want to savour any precious moment you could grab hold of. It made you do things you wouldn't consider appropriate during peacetime.

'You will write to me, Eleanor, won't you?' he murmured, caressing my neck.

'Of course I will. I already promised, didn't I?'

That night when I gave myself to him, it was my first time, but it wasn't his. He was a complete gentleman, asking more than once if I was sure. I almost had to persuade him to take me to bed...

Afterwards, I gave him a small photo, recently taken, to keep in his wallet, and we kissed goodbye on the doorstep. I went inside, and back up to my room, where I lay on my bed, smiling to myself, reliving our time together in my head as if it were playing at the pictures. All I could do was pray he'd come back to me as soon as he possibly could, because I knew in that moment that my heart belonged well and truly to Peter Hill.

CHAPTER 6

ELEANOR

A week after my night with Peter, I took the train from Leeds to the North Riding village of Little Vale. I remembered the reason Peter had come into the shop was because he was delivering a message on Mabel's behalf about who would collect me from the station. When I stepped down from the train, carrying my suitcase, I spotted Jack instantly, the scar on one side of his face making him easy to see. Mabel must have given him a description of me, as he came straight over and said, 'Miss Wade?'

'Yes?'

He studied me for a moment, and smiled, but it was nigh on impossible not to find myself staring at the scar. He must be used to this reaction when meeting someone for the first time, but I looked away, hoping I hadn't made him feel uncomfortable.

'I'm Jack Foster from Birch Farm. My father asked me to collect you as it's a bit of a walk like.'

'Hello, Jack. I'm Eleanor,' I said.

We shook hands.

'Delighted to meet you, Eleanor. Let me carry that for you,' he said, taking the suitcase from me.

'Thank you.'

He walked ahead of me and held out a hand to help me up into the horse and trap. I sat beside him, and he took the reins, and we moved forward, away from the hustle and bustle, along a quiet country lane bordered by hedgerows. The only sound was of the birds singing, the clippity-clop of the horse, and the rumble and squeaking of the wheels on the road. Jack did his best to negotiate the vehicle around all the potholes. The road was steep, and over the hedgerows, green fields stretched ahead for miles, with hills in the distance. I saw a cluster of houses ahead, a church spire rising above them, and presumably that was the village of Little Vale.

We reached a sign saying BIRCH FARM and Jack took a right, and then continued along a drive that went on for at least half a mile until we reached an old stone farmhouse. I imagined that it would be immensely dark at night, and no doubt they'd get snowed in every winter for weeks on end. Jack pulled into the yard. A middle-aged woman, presumably his mother, Mrs Foster, stood outside the back door, an apron tied round her waist. Jack helped me down from the horse and trap and carried my suitcase into the house.

'You must be Eleanor,' Mrs Foster said. Her cheeks were rosy and her demeanour friendly.

We shook hands.

'Pleased to meet you, Mrs Foster.'

'Come on in, my love.'

She went inside, I stepped over the threshold, and she closed the door behind me. We passed through a porch filled with an assortment of wellington boots, coats and hats, then went through a door into a cosy kitchen dominated by a large table and chairs. Mabel and another girl were sitting there.

They were dressed in brown jerseys and wore their hair in plaits.

'At last, Eleanor,' Mabel said. 'Just in time for tea.'

Standing up, she came over and gave me a big hug.

'Well, you know Mabel already. You being old friends saved us from being in a bit of a fix, Eleanor. This is Nora,' Mrs Foster said. 'They're both excited to share their tasks with you. Diane left in rather a hurry last week, and they've been managing just the two of them ever since.'

I'd last seen Mabel when we met for tea and cake at our favourite café, Sally's, on the day before she left for Birch Farm only weeks earlier. Having been firm friends since the age of five, we'd always spent a lot of time together, and it would be good to have her company again.

'You'll be milking cows tomorrow morning,' Mabel said. 'I've been upgraded to tractor duties.'

'All right, that sounds fun,' I said. Surely it couldn't be that difficult?

Nora gave me a warm smile and said, 'Pleased to meet you, Eleanor. You'll feel at home before long, I'm sure.'

I reciprocated, and said, 'Hello.'

'Although I hope you're an early bird? You'll need to get down that milking barn at six o'clock sharp,' Nora continued.

That didn't bother me at all as I was used to getting up early from working at Thorpe's.

'You'd better sit down for tea and get your strength up – you'll need it tomorrow,' Mabel said.

'They're only teasing, it's not so bad,' Mrs Foster said, putting a cup and saucer in front of me. 'Have some tea and cake, dear.' She cut a slice of fruit cake and placed it on a side plate.

'Peter rang before he left, and told me that after he delivered my message you both went to Raymond's for supper?' Mabel said.

'Indeed, we did.'

'And you managed to sell him an expensive notebook to use as a diary too?'

Nodding, I said, 'Yes, he was delighted with it.'

'I do hope he was a gentleman and that he saw you home?'

'He accompanied me on the bus and walked me to my door. Then we parted ways. He needed to finish packing his belongings,' I lied. There was no way Mabel could know about what we'd done. This was her big brother we were talking about.

'And he said you gave him a photograph of yourself?'

'I did because he wanted to keep one in his wallet. He asked me to write, to help keep up his morale and all that.'

'So, are you sweethearts now?'

'I'd like to think so,' I said.

'You take good care of him then,' she said, giving me a look.

'Of course I will.'

This conversation did make me worry that my liaison with Peter might have driven a wedge between me and Mabel. If it had been another man, I would have told her everything about that night. But how could I? And what if things didn't work out with Peter? Would Mabel hold that against me? I couldn't imagine losing her as a friend, and would be devastated if that happened.

After tea, Mabel showed me to our room. Jack had carried my suitcase up two flights of stairs, for we were on the top floor. The room had three single beds, and I wasn't thrilled to be sharing with two others after having a room to myself at home. We had a bathroom to share next door.

'It gets cold up here at night,' Mabel said, 'but you'll get used to it before long. Seeing as I have a few more jobs to do before supper, I'll leave you to unpack.'

Sitting on the bed, I studied the room with its floral wallpaper and matching curtains. A window looked over the yard, and I went over to sit on the vast windowsill. Mabel walked across the yard in the direction of a barn. Life would certainly be very different here. A wave of sadness swept over me as I thought back to my night with Peter. He'd been on my mind ever since, and I wondered when we'd see each other again. Would he be all right, wherever he was? I hoped that life wasn't too arduous for him, and that before long he'd come home on leave and let me know he was in Leeds. Would Mrs Foster give me time off to go and see him? How I hoped she would.

We had supper at eight o'clock – all of us, Mr and Mrs Foster, Jack, Mabel, Nora and me. Mrs Foster had made a lamb stew and mashed potatoes and it was delicious. Before long, we were heading upstairs to bed, as we had to get up at a quarter past five in the morning. Mabel and Nora – clearly tired from the physical work they'd done that day – fell asleep straight away, but I lay there, freezing cold, and got out of bed to put on my jumper over my pyjamas and pull socks onto my feet. Once again, my thoughts returned to Peter. Would he keep his promise and write in the notebook every day? I wondered what he would have to write about. I would send him a letter as soon as I could to tell him about life on the farm. Was he lying in bed right now thinking about me? Which country was he in? No doubt he was sharing a room with many other soldiers, or perhaps a tent. Who knew what his sleeping situation was? Was he in a trench? He could be fighting right now, firing shots at the Hun. I wondered what he'd eaten for dinner and doubted it was anywhere as nutritious as what I'd been lucky enough to consume... I couldn't wait to see him again.

The next morning, Mabel woke me up and we all got dressed rather swiftly – it was still damn cold in that room – and we went downstairs to the kitchen, where Mrs Foster waited for us. She'd already put breakfast on the table and the kitchen smelt of fresh bread. Being hungry, I was glad to see a loaf on a chopping board, and there was a pot of tea complete with cosy, and jug of milk. There was also a jar of strawberry jam and a block of butter. We ate and drank our tea and then I went to the milking barn. Jack and his father had already brought the cows in from the field, and I wondered what time they'd had to get out of bed.

'Good morning, Eleanor,' Jack said, grinning at me.

A little nervous, I was glad that he was at least friendly.

'Morning, Jack.'

'Shall we get started then?'

I nodded.

He showed me to a stool. 'You sit down there and watch me, and then you can have a go.'

Taking a teat in each hand, he, squeezed each one in an expert way, and I watched, wondering how on earth I was going to do the same thing.

'Now it's your turn,' he said.

We swapped places, and I grabbed the teats and attempted to squeeze them, but no milk came out. The cow mooed and stamped her hoof, almost kicking me in the face. I yelped, and moved out of the way in the nick of time.

'I can't do this,' I said, frustrated. Thorpe's suddenly seemed like an appealing place to be, and I wished I was walking through the door there right now.

'It takes a few goes to get the hang of it,' he said.

He placed his hands over mine and showed me what to do until milk came and started to fill the pail beneath. He was so close to me, and I could hear him breathing, and was able to smell the tobacco on his breath as well as the spicy, orange scent of his cologne. It was an intimate experience and, with Peter being my sweetheart, this seemed inappropriate. He removed his hands and I carried on by myself, at last getting the hang of it.

'Well done that girl,' he said, looking at me with a broad smile.

'Thank you, Jack,' I said.

He took a stool and went to milk the cow next to me, and we made our way through them all. By eight o'clock, I was worn out and ready for a break.

'Right, you're dismissed. Go back to the house and have a cuppa. I'll fetch you when it's time to feed the chickens.'

I made my way back to the house, where Mabel and Nora sat at the kitchen table.

'How was it?' Mabel said.

'Not so bad.'

'And Jack?'

'What do you mean?'

'You know he's looking for a wife? I'm sure he's got his eye on you,' Nora said.

Jack did seem friendly, but that didn't mean he wanted me to be his wife.

'Don't be ridiculous.'

'We've told him we're not interested. Who would want to marry a man with such a dreadful scar on his face?' Nora said.

Although Nora was speaking the truth, it seemed cruel to actually say the words out loud.

'You're being rather unkind.' I frowned. 'Besides, I'm corresponding with Mabel's brother, Peter, and would like to think we'll be courting when he comes back.'

'Well, let's hope he does come back,' Mabel said quietly, her eyes meeting mine.

CHAPTER 7

ELEANOR

Over those first few weeks at the farm, I knew something about my body felt different. I was nauseous a lot of the time, but put this down to the change in diet. Meals consumed were rich with butter and cream, and Mrs Foster was generous with portion sizes due to all the physical work. Even though I went to bed early in order to milk the cows at six in the morning, no amount of sleep seemed to be enough. After lunch, I'd often feel the urge to take a nap, but there was more work to be done. The chicken houses needed to be cleaned and the eggs collected. The geese were to be fed, and the horses mucked out. Then at five in the afternoon it was time for another round of milking the cows, once Jack had brought them all in from the field. It was always a twelve-hour working day, even at weekends. Although I longed for a break, I had to accept this was my life now, until the war was over, and who knew when that might be?

When December came, and I didn't need my usual rags, I didn't want to admit to myself that I was pregnant. How could it be possible after only one time? What was I supposed to do?

Mother would be furious with me for being so careless. The number of times she'd warned me not to succumb to a man's advances before marriage. I'd probably have to go and live in one of those homes for unmarried mothers. How did one go about making such arrangements? More sleepless nights followed as I tossed and turned, dithering over what on earth to do.

One morning after no sleep whatsoever, I decided to confide in Nora while we were getting dressed, after Mabel had gone down for breakfast. We'd only exchanged small talk since my arrival, but I needed to ask someone for advice, and she was my only option. I could hardly tell Mabel what was going on when her brother was the man responsible for my situation.

'I'm in a bit of a fix, Nora,' I said.

'What's troubling you, Eleanor?'

Gritting my teeth, I told her about my night with Peter.

Her eyes widened. 'Oh dearie me. Are you saying Aunt Flo has not been?'

I nodded. 'Promise me you won't breathe a word to Mabel?'

'Of course I won't. It's understandable that you wouldn't want her to know.'

'What shall I do, Nora?'

'Have you written to your chap?'

'Shouldn't I wait to tell him in person?'

'There isn't time for that. Write to him today, and say you expect him to marry you next time he comes back on leave. I'm sure he'll return, and you'll get married. Everything will be fine, you'll see.'

'You're right, I'm probably worrying about nothing,' I said, certain that Peter would support me when he found out the news. When we'd lain in bed together after our love-making, he'd said such flattering things – how beautiful I was, with the face of an English rose, and how much he enjoyed being in my company. He wasn't the kind of man who'd say those words without meaning them, especially after we'd already done the deed, was he?

'I'm sure you are. Now get that letter written and posted as soon as you can. Maybe he can arrange to come back a bit sooner than originally planned, seeing as you're in a spot of bother.'

'Let's hope so.'

That evening after supper, I wrote to Peter in the sitting room, in an armchair by the fire, Charlie the farm cat curled up on my lap. I prayed that he'd come back soon and marry me before I started to show. There were only so many weeks where I could claim I'd put on weight because of Mrs Foster's outstanding cooking. If the vicar couldn't accommodate us at the church, we'd need to have our ceremony at the register office. Peter could rent somewhere for me to live, or I could always stay with my parents until he came back. I reassured myself that he'd reply to my letter before long, telling me he was delighted about the baby and yes, of course we'd get married – it had been his intention to propose anyway.

But a couple of weeks went by, and I heard nothing. Was he shocked by the news, and didn't know how to reply? Perhaps he hadn't received the letter at all... And so I wrote again, just in case, this time adding that soon I'd have to ask Mrs Foster about arranging to go into one of those awful homes for unwed mothers. There was no way I could ask my own mother for help – she'd be absolutely horrified by my predicament. After sending the second letter, all I could do was wait and hope and pray that he'd reply with news that I wanted to hear. That I *needed* to hear...

CHAPTER 8

JESSICA

After Alessandro left, I went back into the kitchen and joined Mum and Gran at the table. They both wore serious looks on their faces, as if they'd been deep in conversation. Something was wrong, but what on earth had happened in the few minutes that had passed since I'd gone to show Alessandro out? Mum and Gran were always bickering about one thing or another, but it was just the way their relationship worked. Me and Mum on the other hand had a much calmer relationship. Growing up I'd seen the way she challenged Gran and how it affected her. So, I'd often let things go with Mum for an easier life and to keep the peace. The tension hanging between them now was annoyingly putting a dampener on the fantastic mood I'd been left with after waving Alessandro off.

'What's going on?'

'Apparently your gran has something important to tell us relating to that diary,' Mum said.

Whatever Gran had to say couldn't be that big a deal, surely? But why did she look so down?

'Well, what is it?' I said, curious to know what was going on.

Gran looked across the table at us, and let out a long sigh.

'Come on, Mother, you've got us both on tenterhooks,' Mum said.

Gran wrung her hands. 'There was no need to tell you this before, but now Peter's diary has turned up like this, well – Mary, love, what I'm about to say might give you a bit of a shock, I'm afraid.'

I looked at Mum, whose eyes were all scrunched up.

'On that day when Peter bought this notebook from me, we went to Raymond's for fish and chips. Afterwards, he accompanied me on the bus back to my parents' house. I'd been a little in love with Peter for years – he was the older brother of my schoolfriend, Mabel, and we spent a lot of time together growing up.'

Surely Gran wasn't talking about the same Mabel who lived in North Carolina with the American she'd met while he was living on a base nearby during the war?

'Hold on, are you talking about Auntie Mabel?' I asked.

'I am indeed.'

We'd met Auntie Mabel many times. She'd fly back to England to visit her mother in Leeds a couple of times every year, and would often stay with us for a night or two. She and Gran remained firm friends and wrote to each other regularly. We'd always called her Auntie Mabel because she was Gran's best friend, and she was also Mum's godmother.

'Anyway,' Gran continued. 'What with the excitement of Peter going off to war the next day, and the possibility of us never seeing each other again, one thing led to another...'

'What are you saying exactly, Mother?' Mum said.

Gran took a deep breath. 'Peter Hill, who this diary belonged to, is your real father, Mary, rather than my late husband, Jack. And your real grandfather, Jessica. And Mabel is your real aunt – or great-aunt.'

'But how can that possibly be true?' Mum said, her face all flushed. 'And if it is, why haven't you told me before?'

Gran started to blink really quickly.

'My agreement with Jack was that we wouldn't tell anyone about you not being his child, including you, Mary. When he died, five years ago, there was no reason to suddenly turn your life upside down – I must admit, I thought about telling you then, but after much consideration I decided against it. I didn't want to spoil any of your memories of him when, in all the ways that mattered, he was your father. I'd only discovered that I was pregnant a few weeks after Peter left, and wrote to tell him. A couple of weeks later, I wrote again, saying if I didn't hear from him my only choice would be to go to one of those homes for unmarried mothers. To this day, I have no idea if he ever received those letters. A week or so after I wrote the second letter, his mother received a telegram to say he was missing in action.'

'Mother, how can you keep something like this from me for almost forty-seven years?' Mum said. 'I should have known... it was so obvious Dad always preferred Prue to me.' She gulped. Prue was her younger sister.

Gran placed her hand on Mum's and said, 'I am so sorry. And that's not true, he loved you in his own way.'

Mum removed her hand from underneath Gran's and got up, her chair scraping the flagstone floor.

'I need time to think about all of this.'

She put her empty cup and saucer and side plate on the worktop, and left the kitchen, banging the door shut behind her. This was how Mum tended to deal with news she didn't want to hear. I wondered how she'd get past Gran keeping this information from her for so many years – a huge secret that would impact the way she looked back on her whole life. I couldn't imagine how she must be feeling. Everything until now had been a lie.

Gran looked at me. 'Oh dear, Jess. I handled that badly, didn't I?'

'It's understandable that Mum would be upset,' I said. 'I couldn't imagine how I'd react if she told me Dad wasn't my real father. And especially at her age too.'

'I know, you're right. Jack wouldn't allow me to tell her – we made a pact. I could have continued to keep it quiet, but who knows what Peter has written in this diary? What if he received my letters and wrote about them? I wouldn't want your mother or you to read the diary and find out the truth that way.'

She picked up the tan-brown notebook and ran her thumb over the hole in the top right-hand corner.

'I can't bear to read it, and your mother isn't going to any time soon. It's down to you, Jess, to take this diary and read every word, get to know your real grandfather. This is your field of expertise, after all, what with you being a journalist. You've had a curious mind ever since you were a little girl, and this is the perfect project for you, my love.'

Yes, I was a journalist, albeit a local one who didn't get to report on very exciting things. I'd been feeling disheartened with my job lately, and over the summer had started to think about whether I'd ever achieve my dream of being a travel writer. I hadn't exactly done much about it, so only had myself to blame. Mum wasn't exactly encouraging – she liked to keep me close to home. I'd even lived with my parents while studying at the polytechnic nearby. She was keen on me keeping the farm when she and Dad retired, and marrying a man who could help me run it – ideally my boyfriend, Tom.

Gran handed me the notebook across the table. It was beautifully made and must have cost a small fortune when Peter had bought it.

'And you can tell me if he mentions my letters... that at least I would like to know. I've always wondered if he knew about your mum.'

'Of course I can do that,' I said.

Gran was like a second mother to me. We spent a lot of time

together, often sitting in front of the fire at Camellia Cottage in the evenings. I worried about her getting older, and couldn't bear to think about her not being around for ever.

'Thank you, Jess, love.'

She stood up and started to dry cups and saucers in the washing-up rack with a tea towel.

The diary had the word COOKSON embossed in capital gold letters on the front. There was also a thin black ribbon that could be used to keep the page. I lifted the cover, and there in beautiful cursive handwriting, in royal-blue ink, were words written by my real grandfather, Peter.

25 *November 1942*

Today I had to deliver a message to my sister Mabel's friend from school, Eleanor Wade. We'd shared a kiss in the back garden once on a balmy summer night, while swigging a bottle of my father's whisky. I must admit that I'd been a little in love with her for many years. I found that I didn't want to leave the shop after delivering the message, and stood there dithering for a minute, trying to think of a reason to stay. Then I decided to try and impress her and buy an expensive notebook. This bought me more time so I could stand there and look at her while she wrapped it up, a real exercise it was. She has hair the colour of honey, and beautiful big green eyes, a colour you don't often see, and the loveliest face with fair skin – an English rose, one might say. And then I found myself inviting her to join me at Raymond's for a fish and chip supper. I'd planned to go there anyway one last time before leaving for war, to read the news-paper. She said yes, and we arranged to meet later on after she'd finished her shift.

I would read every single word and tell Gran what she needed to know. What had Peter been like? I was curious to know whether he'd been aware of Gran's pregnancy, and how he might have reacted when he received her letters. Where had he been when he wrote the words in this diary? And what had he been doing? Was his life in real danger? Where was he when he wrote his last entry? Had he died shortly afterwards? Looking down at the beautiful tan-brown notebook in my hands, I realised I was holding a part of history, and it belonged to my family. It was a privilege to be in such a position, and I should treasure it always. Presumably the diary belonged to me now? When Gran sold it to Peter that day in Leeds, she'd set off a chain of events – them going for supper and what that led to afterwards. Then Peter took the diary off to war. And now Alessandro had brought it to us, opening a real can of worms. Where would this diary take us all next? I would read one page every day, and savour it. Surely there wasn't any rush, especially after all this time?

CHAPTER 9

ELEANOR

Two more weeks passed, and I had still heard nothing from Peter. I was at my wits' end. The nausea persisted, and I had little appetite, but still forced myself to eat the food put in front of me by Mrs Foster as, with all the physical work and a baby growing inside me, I needed to stay healthy and strong. My thoughts were constantly consumed by the situation I found myself in as I deliberated my options. What a fool I'd been going to bed with Peter that night. What was I thinking? But we'd both been swept away by the moment, and the prospect of him leaving the next day had added real excitement and passion to our encounter.

One afternoon, I was carrying bales of straw into the barn and had one of my dizzy spells – these were becoming more frequent and really, I shouldn't be doing physical work at all. I'd started to worry about what bending down and lifting heavy items would do to the baby growing inside me. Sitting down on one of the bales, I put my head between my knees, attempting to pull myself together. I took a few deep breaths, inhaling and exhaling over and over again. Fortunately, no one on the farm had witnessed one of my dizzy spells yet.

Nora was the only person who knew of my pregnancy. In the kitchen that afternoon, we were having a cup of tea when I told her what had happened in the barn and that I didn't know what to do.

'You can't carry on like this, Eleanor. Why don't you come up with a fake injury, so you don't have to carry heavy things?' she said.

This was an excellent idea, and so later that day I told Mrs Foster that I'd done my back in when milking the cows. She was kind, and gave me her admin to do until I was feeling better. Nora and Mabel would have to pick up the slack and I felt bad about that, but what was the alternative? They both took it rather well, and thankfully, Mabel didn't seem to have an inkling about what was really going on.

My days from then on were spent sitting at the desk in Mrs Foster's cosy study, a fire crackling beside me. Charlie the cat would be curled up in an armchair and I'd go through paperwork, sorting out bills and tallying up receipts. Life became easier after that, but still I had no idea what to do. Time was running out before I'd need to speak to Mrs Foster about going to a home for unwed mothers.

When I was four months pregnant – I was counting the days in my diary – I still hadn't heard from Peter. Either he was dead, or he had no interest in marrying me. But my khaki trousers were becoming unbearably tight. I'd already moved the buttons at the waist, but it wouldn't be long before I'd need to wear a larger size. It was time to confide in Mrs Foster, and I went to the kitchen to find her. But when I got there, she and Mabel seemed to be having a serious conversation, and I felt as though I was interrupting. Mabel held a letter and was dabbing her eyes with a handkerchief. Mrs Foster had a hand on her shoulder as if she were providing comfort. By the looks on their faces, I knew what Mabel was about to tell me.

I clutched my throat. 'No!'

Mabel nodded, and then she came over to embrace me. We stood there for who knew how long, clinging to each other. I began to sob – hot, thick tears. How could I ever tell her about the baby?

'Can I see the letter?' I said, feeling light-headed all of a sudden. I grabbed the edge of the kitchen counter to steady myself.

Mabel handed it to me.

Dear darling Mabel,

I am writing to tell you that I received a telegram yesterday to say that your dear brother, Peter, is missing in action. I am absolutely devastated, as I'm sure you will be. I couldn't bring myself to deliver this horrific news over the telephone, but perhaps we can talk next week when we've both had a chance to take it all in. All we can do is go to church and pray for his safe return. Let us hope that he is still out there somewhere, being kept safe by members of the French resistance or something along those lines. We still have hope, if nothing else.

All my love,

Mother

How I hoped that Mrs Hill was right, and that Peter was safe and well somewhere. Had my letters reached him before he went missing?

'I'll put the kettle on, and we can sit down and have a nice cup of tea,' Mrs Foster said. 'I made ginger biscuits this morning, and they will help to lift the spirits.'

'I need to go for a walk, if that's all right?' I said, edging towards the door, in desperate need of a place to sit down and process this devastating news.

'You take as long as you need, dear.'

CHAPTER 10

JESSICA

That evening, after Gran had given me the diary, I took it upstairs to read in bed with a cup of tea. Mum hadn't come back into the kitchen, and Gran had quietly disappeared off to Camellia Cottage.

'Best give her some space until she comes round,' Gran had said as she left, kissing me on the side of the head.

Neither she nor Mum wanted anything to do with the diary, but Gran had chosen me to read it on their behalf. I changed into my pyjamas and climbed into bed. My room was chilly, despite the temperature being warm outside. The farmhouse was over a hundred years old with little insulation and I could never seem to get warm on the top floor. But as a teenager I'd asked to move up there, as it was exciting having a whole floor to myself with my own bathroom. I lifted the cover of the diary, then closed it swiftly. How was I going to approach this? It felt like such a responsibility as there were so many emotions involved for both Gran and Mum. Although Peter appeared to be my real grandfather, I would be able to read the diary with more emotional detachment. What if he had written something that I needed to pass on to Mum and Gran? It didn't seem fair that I was being tasked with delivering news they wouldn't want to hear.

Jack had been the best grandpa a girl could have and, when he retired, he'd showered me with attention, always encouraging me to follow my dreams. I'd been his only grandchild, and so he'd made a fuss of me. He'd take me on adventures – rambling on the Yorkshire Moors, climbing Ingleborough, to the seaside at Morecambe, where we'd get a bag of chips and cover them with salt and vinegar and walk along the promenade, the sea breeze brushing our faces. Then we'd go on the pier, and he'd give me coins to spend on the penny machines and we'd get candyfloss to eat on the way back to the car. People would stop in the street to look at him, with that big scar on his face, but he didn't seem to mind. Although it made him look scary, I knew that my grandpa had a heart of gold.

Grandpa had died five years previously, when I was in my first year at the polytechnic. He'd slipped when attempting to climb Ingleborough late one afternoon, banging his head badly. He lay there all night until a rambler found him the next day. He was rushed to hospital, but it was too late. Grandpa always had an adventurous side, and that day he'd decided on a whim to go off on his own. Gran had obviously been devastated when a policeman turned up at the door to tell her the news. We'd all had to rally around and look after her in those first few months after his death. What would Grandpa think about Peter's diary turning up? It was understandable that he wanted everyone to see Mum as his daughter – at the time, this would have been best for everyone. If he was still alive, he wouldn't have been pleased about the diary turning up, but he wasn't here any more. Alessandro bringing the diary to the farm had set wheels in motion and our lives were surely about to change. The relationship between Mum and Gran was bound to be impacted, and I hoped Mum would forgive Gran in time – for none of it was her fault. She could hardly have gone against her husband's wishes and told Mum the truth when he was alive. And it was understandable that, when he'd died, she'd considered revealing all and then changed her mind. Why rock the boat?

As a writer, the whole idea of receiving a diary almost fifty years after it had been written, by an unknown ancestor, was all quite exciting. But the fear of finding something out that Mum and Gran wouldn't want to know meant I wanted to approach it with caution.

Sitting up in bed with a couple of pillows propped behind me, I read Peter's first diary entry after he had left Leeds.

25 January 1943

Our fate's been decided by Churchill and Roosevelt during their meeting in Casablanca, and we're on a ship headed for Tunisia. Conditions are cramped but I have enough to eat at least. I expect this is nothing compared to what we have to come. My mind has been wandering back to the fish and chip supper at Raymond's on my last night in Leeds. I accompanied Eleanor – the girl from Thorpe's where I bought this very notebook – back to her house and she invited me in for a cuppa. Her parents were at a music recital. I spent a few precious hours in her bed, and after we'd made love I held her in my arms. I hope that she'll write to me.

Gran seemed to be his main focus so far, and clearly he'd liked her a great deal. It struck me at that moment that I was more than likely the first person to be reading his words, for Benedetto couldn't speak English, and I doubted very much that Alessandro would have bothered to read it – why would he? It was tempting to flick through the pages and find out if Peter had known of Gran's pregnancy straight away, but this would take the joy out of slowly reliving his journey from Leeds to Tuscany all those years ago. Closing the diary, I put it on my bedside table and went to brush my teeth. This diary turning up, and being delivered by such a handsome Italian-American man, seemed significant in some way. I climbed into bed and pulled the covers over me, and switched off the lamp. Then I lay there in the dark replaying Alessandro's arrival in my head. Seeing him through the kitchen window, watching him cross the yard and tread in that muddy puddle, the tension that hung in the air as I cleaned mud off his trainers while he stood there waiting for me to finish. The way he'd looked at me across the table. As I watched him walk back to his car, somehow I'd felt in my gut that we'd meet again. Surely that couldn't be our one and only meeting? Hadn't he suggested that I go to Siena with Gran to see where Peter was buried, while he was still there? Did this mean he'd like to see me again?

Lying there in the dark, I considered where I was at in my life. After completing an English literature degree followed by a postgraduate diploma in journalism at Lancashire Polytechnic, I'd started working for the local newspaper, the *Dales Echo*, and would drive to the office in Lupton on weekdays. Being a local journalist was all right as jobs went, but I'd expected to find it more exciting, and to be given more opportunities. Being the most junior person in the office, I was sent to report on local stories that weren't particularly exciting, such as when a cat was stuck in a tree or someone's washing machine had flooded all over their kitchen floor. It wasn't that I wanted to report on serious news, more that I wanted to write the kind of feature that appeared in supplements for national Sunday newspapers. Writing for one of their travel weekend sections was my ultimate dream. Or even having a column in a travel magazine would be an achievement. Writing was my thing and I'd kept diaries for years. And this was why seeing my real grandfather's diary was particularly exciting. I'd thought about penning a travel-writing book one day. And I liked to take photos with the camera left to me by the man who I'd thought was my grandfather. He'd been a keen photographer and would disappear onto the Yorkshire Moors for hours on end and take wonderful nature photos. Sometimes I'd go with him, and we'd take sandwiches and a flask of tea. It would be a lovely day out, and I had fond memories of those days with my grandpa. Every now and again, he'd get one of his photos printed in the *Dales Echo* and would receive a small fee. That was how I'd got the job there. He'd asked his contact if I could do some work experience after my A levels, and after that I'd work there in the summer holidays. Then, after I graduated, the editor offered me a full-time position. But recently I'd found that being a local journalist wasn't fulfilling enough for me.

The other problem was Tom, son of neighbouring farmer Mr Gilbert, Grandpa's schoolfriend and best man at his and Gran's wedding. Tom and I had been together since slow-dancing at the end of a mutual friend's eighteenth birthday party. I liked him, but wasn't sure I loved him. Lately we hadn't spent much time together, as he always seemed to be working. I had considered asking him if we should take a break but, without knowing how he'd react, hadn't yet plucked up the courage. He was my first boyfriend, and I wasn't sure what real love felt like. Did I want to spend the rest of my life with the first man I'd met? How would I know without experiencing being with anyone else? Mum was keen on Tom because his family owned the farm next door, and she saw him as perfect marriage material. When she and Dad retired, he could take over the business and run our farm alongside his. Meeting Alessandro had got me thinking, though. Maybe there were other options out there for me. I wanted to go to Italy and see where my real grandfather had spent his last moments. I wanted to go to Italy full stop. I'd never been abroad. Dad didn't believe in holidays. We hadn't even taken a holiday in England, never mind abroad. This was my chance. Could I persuade Gran to come with me? We were bound to have fun, and it might be an opportunity for her to do something different. Her life seemed a little dull, with most of her days spent sitting in our kitchen, reading the newspaper and doing the crossword. She'd chat away to Mum while she prepared meals and made cakes. Sometimes I'd look at Mum's life – a farmer's wife, a mother, more often than not a dogsbody – and think it wouldn't be enough for me. I wanted to make something of myself, and to earn my own money instead of relying on a man to give it to me. It was down to me to break the cycle of women in our family having decisions about their future made for them.

Checking the time on my radio alarm clock, I saw it was half past eleven – time to sleep. I needed to get up for work in the morning. Rain pattered against the window, a flash of light came through the curtains, and thunder rumbled in the distance – another storm. Tomorrow evening, I'd go over to Gran's after supper and see if I could persuade her to go to Siena. If she said no, could I go on my own? Would she mind if I did? All I could do was make the suggestion and see what she said.

The following evening, me and Gran were in the sitting room at Camellia Cottage. The temperature had dropped since the thunderstorm the previous night, and I'd built a fire for us. We were facing each other in armchairs by the hearth. Gran was doing the crossword in the newspaper, and I was drinking a cup of tea, pondering my future.

'Gran, I've been thinking about what Alessandro said.'

She put down the newspaper and looked at me over her glasses. 'What's that then, love?'

'You know how he said that, if we went to Siena, he'd take us to the spot where Peter died. Would you want to come with me if I went?'

'I've never been abroad in my life, Jessica, you know that. I haven't even been to London.'

'There's no time like the present,' I said.

'Well, I suppose it would be a chance for me to step out of my comfort zone and see the world outside of Little Vale while I'm still young enough.'

I hadn't expected Gran to agree so readily, and decided to seize the moment before she changed her mind.

'Shall I go to the travel agency tomorrow during my lunch break, see if I can book flights and a hotel?'

She took a sip of her tea, then put the cup down on the coffee table.

'Why not? I'll pay for it. We can go for a few days, if it's not too expensive.'

'Really, Gran? You'd do that?'

'Yes, I think it would be good to close the chapter of Peter and me, and I'm sure we could have a lovely time while we're at it.'

The thought of going to Italy was exciting, and to see Alessandro again, and look into those deep-brown eyes, would be the icing on the cake. I couldn't wait to get something arranged.

CHAPTER 11

ELEANOR

Leaving the kitchen, I passed through the porch, going through the back door into the yard. Outside, it was freezing cold with a thin sheet of ice covering the windscreen of Mr Foster's truck. Where could I go to collapse in a heap? I saw Manor Barn filled with hay, and went to find a corner amongst the bales. There I lay on my side and bawled my eyes out. It was more than likely that the father of my unborn child was dead. Even if he wasn't, there was no way to contact him. My only option was to ask Mrs Foster to arrange for me to go to a home for unwed mothers. But this wasn't the day to do that. I would ask her first thing in the morning. Shivering, I crossed my arms and wrapped them around myself, wishing I'd brought a coat. But the thought of going back inside to get one didn't appeal – I just wanted to get away from everyone.

Hearing footsteps, I looked down to see Jack enter the barn, carrying hay bales. He was a big burly man like his father, and seemed to be so strong and capable. I tried to remain as still as I could in order not to alert him to my presence – the last thing I needed was to talk to him – but as he arranged the bales neatly, I couldn't help sniffling. He looked up, instantly spotting me.

Oh no. How was I supposed to explain my presence? I'd just have to say I was upset about Peter being missing, leaving out the real reason for this.

'Whatever is the matter, Eleanor?' Jack said.

Tears streamed down my face, and I couldn't bring myself to speak. He came and sat down beside me, taking a handkerchief out of his pocket.

He handed it to me. 'Don't worry, it's clean.'

It was as white as a handkerchief could be, and beautifully pressed. I wiped my eyes.

'Thank you, Jack.'

'Is there anything I can do to help?'

'Unfortunately not. Peter is missing.'

'Peter who?'

'You know, Mabel's brother, and, well, he was my sweetheart – I hoped we might get married when he returned.'

'I'm really sorry to hear that, Eleanor. Perhaps he's just lost contact with the British army, and is in hiding somewhere behind enemy lines.'

'It's a possibility, I suppose.'

'There's no rush to get married at the moment, is there?'

He looked at me with kind eyes, and I found his presence a comfort.

'I'm with child,' I said, and instantly regretted blurting out my secret. What would he think of me?

He frowned, his thick eyebrows knitting together.

'What?'

'I'm going to have a baby, and I don't know what to do.'

He scratched the stubble on his chin. 'Oh, dearie me. And this Peter, he's the father, presumably?'

I nodded.

'I'm so sorry, Eleanor.'

We sat in silence while I sobbed quietly. I was making a fool of myself but my emotions had taken over and it was impossible to control them. Having only lived at Birch Farm for a short time, I didn't know Jack well, and dreaded to think what he made of me expressing my feelings so openly.

After a few minutes, he turned to look at me and carefully brushed my face with a hand. I did my best to ignore the scar on his left cheek, but it was impossible not to notice it. Without the scar, he would be rather handsome. I couldn't imagine how hard it must be for him having to live with it.

'You don't have to answer right away' – he put a hand on my shoulder – 'but I could marry you?'

I sat up, slowly. This proposal was a shock. What was he thinking? We barely knew each other. Was he really willing to take on another man's child?

'What are you saying, Jack?'

He sighed.

'It's not ideal, I know, but look at me. Do you think I don't notice people staring at this hideous scar? I used to be quite a catch before this injury, you know. But no woman wants anything to do with me now.'

'I'm sure that's not true.'

'Believe me, it is.'

'I appreciate your proposal, but can't accept. It wouldn't be fair to you.'

'We'd be helping each other. Father is ready to retire. He and Mother want to live at Camellia Cottage – they're just waiting for me to find a wife. They'd be delighted if we got married. I know Mother is particularly fond of you already.'

We'd be making a kind of business deal, and I wasn't sure how I felt about it. But what was the alternative? Give up my baby to strangers? Was I prepared to do that? Didn't I want the chance to be a mother to the child I was carrying, who I already felt a connection to? The more I thought about Jack's idea, the more it seemed like a plausible solution. And surely all the worrying I'd been doing wasn't helping the baby either. Still, I didn't want to make a hasty decision, and needed to mull over his proposal. There wouldn't be much time to play with even if I did accept. We'd have to make wedding arrangements straight away.

'That is a very noble and kind offer. Thank you, Jack. Do you mind if I have a day or two to think about it?'

Standing up, he brushed the hay off his trousers, and held out a hand to help me up. I took it and we climbed down from the bales and stood at the entrance to the barn, looking at each other. He took my hands in his and squeezed them gently. Anyone passing would have thought we'd been up to no good, and the irony of this brought a slight smile to my face.

'I have to bring the cows in now, so I'll leave you to ponder. Why don't you sleep on it and give me your answer tomorrow?'

'All right,' I said.

'How far gone are you?'

'Four months.'

'So, the baby would be due in August or September. I would suggest a March wedding – that would give my mother time to prepare – and we could get married at St Mary's in the village. Mother could have a word with the vicar to get us a spot.'

I smiled, weakly. The thought of a rushed wedding to a man I barely knew was quite overwhelming.

'All right, thank you, Jack.'

We parted ways and I went back to the house, and, as I sat there at the table drinking tea, and eating the ginger biscuits Mrs Foster had made, Mabel and Nora talked around me about an American soldier they'd met at the Old Hare the night before, called Richard. They were both sweet on him, but he'd asked Mabel out for a drink. She was delighted by his invitation. Not only was he handsome, but also he'd promised to get her as many pairs of silk stockings as she wanted.

'I'm sorry to hear about Peter,' Nora said.

Mabel looked to be in a right state, her face shiny from crying, and I probably did too.

'All we can do is hope he's out there somewhere, still alive,' I said, refilling my cup and stirring in a sugar lump.

'I'm sure he is,' Nora said, reaching across the table and taking both our hands. 'We'll go to St Mary's tomorrow – put on our Sunday best and pray for his safe return.' And then when Mabel got up to refill the kettle, Nora looked over at me, and mouthed, 'Are you all right?'

I nodded, slowly. Later, I'd tell her about Jack's proposal and ask for her advice. Oh, I was really in a quandary...

CHAPTER 12

ELEANOR

The day of the wedding came in March, and I was understandably nervous. I'd put on a few pounds by then, and worried that guests would be able to tell this was a shotgun wedding. Even if they suspected this, it wouldn't be obvious that the baby was Peter's. That was a secret to be kept strictly between me and Jack, Nora – who'd vowed to keep it under her hat – and Mr and Mrs Foster, who were aware of the situation but did not say one word about it to me. I wore Mrs Foster's wedding dress – thankfully she'd been bigger than me on her wedding day, so it was a matter of taking the dress in rather than making it larger. I'd stood on a stool in the sitting room at Birch Farm the previous week while Mrs Foster, armed with her pincushion, marked changes to be made. When it came to pinning the front of the dress where a small bump was evident, she didn't utter a word, instead making small talk and saying she hoped it wouldn't rain on our big day. I appreciated her discretion, but also, she was sure to be relieved that her son had found someone willing to marry him and take over her role of farmer's wife.

It hadn't struck me until that moment, standing on the

stool in the sitting room, that this was now my destiny – my future had been decided for me by Peter's baby. From now on, I would have no choice about how I lived my life. But there was no alternative, and I accepted my fate – for I had given in to my feelings for Peter that night. I took responsibility for my situation – for it was all my doing. I'd had a choice during that fleeting moment and, being young and in love, had not properly considered the consequences of my actions.

Mrs Foster arranged for us to get married at St Mary's. I was sure that during our meeting with the vicar, Mr Bradley, shortly after Jack's proposal, he'd cottoned on that I was with child, especially as my future mother-in-law made it clear that getting married was a matter of urgency. He skimmed his diary for a suitable date, trying to fit us in as soon as he could. It was more than likely that he was used to seeing couples in our situation.

My parents came from Leeds and stayed in a room at the Old Hare. They had no idea about those few hours I'd spent with Peter in my bed. I'd convinced them that I was marrying Jack because then I wouldn't need to be a land girl any more – the physical work being exhausting – and that he'd fallen in love with me at first sight. I also told them that Mr Foster had a bad back and wanted to retire as soon as possible (and this was true), and therefore I needed to support Jack by being a farmer's wife. They were satisfied that their daughter was marrying a man who had a secure income and a bright future. As Mother brushed my hair in my room at the Old Hare beforehand, she said, 'Do you think you ought to have waited to find a man without such a horrific scar on his face?'

'Mother, really,' I said.

'Well, it's only the truth.' She wasn't a woman who minced her words. 'Don't you think you could have found someone a little more handsome? You do realise you'll have to look at that face for the rest of your life?'

'But, Mother, I don't see it in the same way you might do. I love him.'

'Very well, it is your life, after all,' she said.

And that was that. We never spoke about Jack's face again. She didn't seem to have any idea about the real reason I was marrying him, and for that I was grateful. She would have been horrified that I was carrying an illegitimate child.

There were only a few attendees at the ceremony, and we kept the service as short as we could because there was work to be done back at the farm. The cows weren't suddenly going to start milking themselves. Mr and Mrs Foster of course attended, along with my parents, Mabel, Nora, and a handful of friends and acquaintances of the family.

Being early March, spring hadn't yet arrived, and the morning started with a frost, but then the sun shone, and it was one of those crisp winter days with a deep-blue sky. I arrived at the church five minutes or so late, as was expected, in a Rolls-Royce, borrowed from Mr Foster's accountant – also a friend of his – for the short drive from the Old Hare to St Mary's. Mabel and Nora had done a fine job decorating the Rolls with white ribbons at the front and a young lad who worked as a farmhand, Bill, acted as our chauffeur.

When Father and I arrived, the door to St Mary's was wide open and I could hear members of the congregation chattering away, their voices echoing around the church walls. Nerves struck my gut at that very moment, as it occurred to me that Peter might still come back. What would happen if he did? Doing my best to shut this thought out of my mind, I picked up the skirt of my dress as we walked up the steps and passed through the main entrance. I carried a simple bouquet of daffodils – selected by Mabel from the garden, rather aptly as they represented rebirth and new beginnings. Jack stood at the altar with his best man and schoolfriend, Reg Gilbert, from the neighbouring farm. Standing there, waiting to walk down the

aisle, Father looked across at me and smiled, and I pulled the
veil over my face, trying to hold it together as the enormity of
what I was doing hit me. It was then that Jack set eyes on me,
and he beamed, for I don't think he could believe his luck.
Perhaps he'd thought I might change my mind. He didn't seem
to care that he was taking on another man's child – the reality of
what he was doing hadn't yet hit him.

    The organist played 'Here Comes the Bride', and there was
a rumble as members of the congregation stood up. All eyes
were on me, in Mrs Foster's dress, and it was quite unnerving to
be the centre of attention. I slipped my arm through Father's
and we walked down the aisle. It was impossible not to feel
overwhelmed by the thought that my life was about to change
forever. My eyes welled with tears, and I blinked them away.
Was I doing the right thing? Well, it was too late to change my
mind, and there were no other options available to me, not if I
wanted to keep Peter's child. I could have disappeared to one of
those homes for unmarried mothers and allowed a couple who
were unable to conceive to adopt my child. But I wasn't sure I
could have lived with myself. My dream of owning a tea shop
would probably not come to fruition, for now I was a farmer's
wife, Eleanor Foster instead of Wade.

    After the ceremony, a photographer took a few photos of us
standing on the steps of the church, then we headed back to the
farm – Bill drove me and Jack in the Rolls, and for that short
journey I felt like a princess.

    In the car, Jack took my hand in his, and said, 'Thank you,
Eleanor, for agreeing to be my wife.'

    'Thank you for saving me,' I replied.

    'We are saving each other,' he said.

    And he was right. It was a mutually beneficial arrangement,
and I hoped that in time I'd grow to love him, and that he might
love me.

    Mrs Foster laid on a stupendous buffet in Manor Barn – the

barn where Jack had proposed to me that day when he found me crying. She was a wonderful cook and generous too. There was an array of sandwiches with a variety of fillings including cheese and tomato and ham, and she'd made us a wedding cake – one tier, but beautiful all the same, a fruit cake with icing as white as snow, and with a tiny plastic man and woman on top in wedding attire. Father made a toast and gave a short speech to say how delighted he was to welcome Jack into our family, and then there was a wonderful surprise: a barn dance! Mrs Foster had arranged for a local band to play the music and tell us all what to do – the Gordons, three middle-aged brothers, too old to go and fight, who travelled around the area performing at various events, keeping everyone's spirits up.

The wedding guests danced their socks off that night – although I had to be careful not to overexert myself and harm the baby – and it was so much fun. Me and Jack went to the Old Hare afterwards, and our room had a four-poster bed. It was a romantic setting, and our wedding night was not worthy of it. Now here I was, obliged to make love to a man because he'd married me, a man who I'd surely never love as much as Peter. And while Peter's baby was growing inside me. Doing my best not to think about this, I gave myself to Jack that night with as much enthusiasm as I could muster, feeling this was my duty. Carefully, he undid the buttons on my wedding dress – there were oh so many of them, going all the way down my back – until it fell to the floor. He removed his own clothes and we lay there together on the majestic bed, complete with its red velvet curtains. Smiling as he looked down at me, he gently stroked my cheek, and said,

'Don't worry, Eleanor, I'm sure we'll find a way to love each other with time.'

And then he pressed his lips to mine. I closed my eyes, and didn't open them again until it was over. Being with Jack couldn't have been more different from my experience with

Peter: more methodical than passionate, more mechanical than tender. Jack just seemed to want to get the job done as if it were one of his daily tasks on the farm.

After we'd consummated our marriage, I was relieved when Jack fell straight to sleep. And then, I lay awake, thinking... about Peter, and our unborn child – would it be a boy or a girl? Was Peter dead? What if he did come back? Would he be happy about the decision I'd made? Wherever he was, I hoped he'd understand.

CHAPTER 13

ELEANOR

Mary was born at the beginning of September. She was a beautiful baby with a head of dark hair, just like Peter's. The colour of her eyes changed from brown to blue to brown again, then eventually settled to a blue-grey colour, just like her father's. I'd stopped working as a land girl as soon as we got married. Now I was on a different path from Mabel and Nora. They remained civil but, seeing as I now outranked them, as Nora put it one morning over breakfast, they no longer wanted to spend as much time with me. Another land girl called Sarah was brought in to replace me, and the three of them were as thick as thieves.

I felt quite lonely, even though Mrs Foster was kind to me and taught me everything a farmer's wife needed to know, both in the kitchen and in the study when I had questions about paperwork. Mr Foster still helped Jack out on the land but reduced his duties somewhat, and he developed an interest in making home-made cider using apples from the orchard. We all still ate together, and, seeing as I had a young baby, Mrs Foster would help me prepare the meals. After supper the men would retire to the sitting room, where they'd listen to the wireless, read the newspaper and talk about farm-related things. I'd remain in the kitchen, helping Mrs Foster to clear up. Then we'd all go to bed relatively early. Mabel, Nora and Sarah would sometimes sneak out to the Old Hare. Mabel was now courting the American soldier, Richard, and he'd introduced the others to a couple of his friends. They'd go to dances in the village hall, and get all dressed up in their best frocks. Sometimes, they'd ask me to help them decide what to wear. I'd feel excluded, and sad to be missing out, envy filling my insides. They seemed to have so much fun together, always returning late at night giggling as they scrambled up the stairs to their room. Because of those few hours with Peter, I'd never get to live the same experience. But my only option was to shut these thoughts out of my mind. Now I had a child and a husband to care for, and that was that.

One afternoon, I was in the study doing some bookkeeping. Mrs Foster preferred looking after Mary to doing this, and it gave me a break from mothering duties. Mabel came in with a cup of tea and a slice of Victoria sponge.

'Thought you might like this,' she said.

'That's very kind of you, Mabel. Thank you.'

I expected her to leave, but she perched on the armchair beside me. Things had been tense between us since the wedding, and I worried that our friendship wasn't what it once was. A conversation was due, and I knew this.

'Eleanor, I hope you don't mind my asking... it's a little awkward, but, well, seeing as you were so much in love with my brother, I did wonder why you married Jack so swiftly.'

The time had come. I'd rehearsed my lines over and over while lying in bed at night.

'I know what you're implying, Mabel, and I might as well come out with it. Yes, I was pregnant on my wedding day. Jack and I, we had a moment in the barn that afternoon I found out Peter was missing.

'You did?'

'Yes, he comforted me – I was so upset. We'd had some chemistry before that, I must admit. He'd expressed an interest in getting to know me.'

I was telling so many lies now, but it was the only way to get through all this. Under normal circumstances, I was someone who prided myself on being honest, but I tried not to think about how I was letting myself down.

'You do move on quickly, Eleanor, but I appreciate your candour. Now it's set my mind at rest, at least.'

'What do you mean?'

'For some reason, I thought Mary might be Peter's daughter – silly of me, I know.'

'What a ridiculous thought. Nothing happened with Peter that night in Leeds. He just saw me home, that's all.'

'And yet, you allowed Jack to make love to you shortly after you found out your sweetheart was missing.'

'Yes, we all make mistakes, don't we, Mabel. My emotions were heightened after hearing the news about Peter. I heard you've been going to bed with Richard, so you're lucky if you haven't fallen pregnant yet.'

I was sinking so low now, but it was for the best.

Mabel drew in her breath.

'Despite everything, Mabel, I would like Mary to call you Auntie, seeing as you are my oldest friend. And, I was hoping you might agree to be her godmother when we have the christening in the new year?'

She smiled at me.

'That would be an honour, Eleanor. Thank you for asking.'

Standing up, she put a hand on my shoulder, and gave it a squeeze.

I hoped that me and my best friend could go back to the way

we'd been. Surely it would only be a matter of time? I was determined to mend whatever was broken, and would do my best to maintain our friendship, whatever it took. Making Mabel Mary's godmother was a good start, as we'd always have a connection for the remainder of our lives. And this was a way for Mary to have her real aunt in her life.

D-Day came in June 1944, and Mrs Foster suggested we host a game of rounders in one of the fields and throw a party afterwards to celebrate. Other farmers in the area were invited, along with villagers, who included shopkeepers, members of the WI and churchgoers; all acquaintances of the family. It was a day to remember, organised expertly by Mrs Foster. Mr Foster and Jack borrowed tables and chairs, and lined them up in the farmyard. They built a barbecue in the corner using bricks and a rack from the oven. Jack cooked chicken thighs and drumsticks, and a shoulder of lamb. Jugs of home-made cider filled the table, and we all got quite tipsy as it was an especially potent batch. Mrs Foster prepared bowls of salad using lettuces and tomatoes from the kitchen garden, and guests brought desserts – trifles and pavlovas and apple pie for everyone to share.

When I saw an empty chair next to Nora, I sat down. I'd been meaning to speak to her, but until then not found the right moment. Although she'd promised to keep my secret, I was still worried she might tell Mabel the truth – if she hadn't already.

'Nora, do you mind me asking if you ever considered telling Mabel about the baby?'

Looking at me, she said, 'What, you mean that it's Peter's?'

I nodded.

'Eleanor, you can trust me to keep your secret, don't you worry.'

'That's good to hear, thank you.'

'You see, I wouldn't tell anyone, because I know how it feels.'

'What do you mean?'

'I've been there, Eleanor. Last year I had to go and live in one of those homes for unwed mothers. It was a horrendous time, and I wouldn't wish it upon anyone – I'm so glad you didn't have to go through that.'

'Oh Nora, I'm so sorry. You had a baby?'

She blinked as she looked at me, and I could see a tear in her eye. Nora always seemed so strong and bold, and I wasn't used to seeing her vulnerable side.

'I did indeed – gave her up, she was a real beauty too. For the rest of my life, I'll always wonder if she's happy, if I should have found a way to keep her like you did with Mary.'

'So you think I did the right thing?'

She cleared her throat.

'Of course you did. And look how happy Jack is. He's got the wife he wanted. There's something in it for everyone, isn't there?'

Nora was right, and I was relieved that she hadn't told Mabel – I just couldn't do that to Jack – but by being Mary's godmother she would be part of her life, and that was all I could do.

Life as a young mother and farmer's wife was immensely busy. I spent countless hours breastfeeding during those first few months of Mary's life. But before long, she was crawling and eating solid food, and then she was walking – we had to move things out of the way so she wouldn't damage them or hurt herself.

After the war, Mabel married Richard, the American soldier, and went to live in North Carolina. Nora returned to her home city of Southampton, and Sarah went back to the East End of London.

After they had all left, the house seemed very quiet. Mrs Foster would come over and sit in the kitchen with me during the day, and I liked her company. Jack was never around. He was either out on the land, in the sitting room with Mr Foster, asleep or down at the Old Hare. He didn't seem particularly interested in knowing me. He'd wanted a wife to keep the house nice for him and his choice had been limited because of the scar on his face. So, we'd both got something out of the deal that we'd made. Sometimes, I'd reminisce about that night with Peter in Leeds. Had I been foolish to give in to my feelings like that?

But how could I not love Mary? She was a beautiful child with a gentle nature – and then, not long after she turned two, I fell pregnant with Prue, and it wasn't long before Mary had a sister to play with. It was lovely to see them together, and Jack seemed delighted that at last he had a child who was biologically his. He started to spend more time with me and the girls. He was far more interested in spending time with Prue than with Mary, and, though I tried to make sure that wasn't obvious, I'd often catch a look on Mary's face that showed she had noticed – her blue-grey eyes would be blinking back tears. She'd ask me why Daddy offered to take Prue riding or to pick apples in the orchard, but he never suggested spending time with her. There wasn't much I could do, apart from give her all of my love. I did consider broaching the subject with Jack, but wasn't sure how he'd react. Instead, I thought about how to make life better for Mary, and so I enrolled her in ballet classes and arranged violin lessons – although the damn thing made a dreadful sound when she practised, as playing a musical instrument wasn't her forte. These activities at least gave her a distraction, though, and she seemed to enjoy them.

Sometimes, I'd allow myself to think about Peter. I would write letters to him, attempting to alleviate my grief, but then tear them up and throw them in the bin. Would I have felt any different if he hadn't made me pregnant? Would it have been easier to forget him? I was sure this would be the case but couldn't be absolutely certain.

And so my life became that of a mother and a wife. Was I happy? I was content, and that's all one could wish for under the circumstances. I was grateful to have found a husband, as it was expected that women got married and had children in their early twenties, and the pool of men after the war was limited. If one left it too long, family members would say you were 'on the shelf', even if you hadn't yet turned thirty. This didn't seem fair at all.

The years passed. Prue married James, her childhood sweetheart, at the age of nineteen, and Mary married the youngest son of a farmer in the next village, Phil Thomson. And then, for those last twenty years of his life, it was finally Mary's turn to be Jack's favourite. Prue didn't have children – she and her new husband struggled to conceive, and in the end they gave up trying. But Mary provided Jack with a granddaughter, Jessica, who he adored from the moment she was born. He was so overjoyed to be a grandfather and they shared a wonderful bond. Everyone said how much Jessica looked like me in my youth, with the same green eyes and caramel-coloured hair, and this was indeed true. I think it added to us having a special grandmother–granddaughter relationship that brought me so much joy in those later decades.

I never thought I'd see Peter's diary again, so you can imagine my surprise when the young American man turned up with it that day. There hadn't been a need to tell Mary before, but now I was left with no choice in the matter, as it was more than likely Peter would have written something in there about my letters. Mary was shocked, understandably, while Jessica was more curious, as it didn't impact her in the same way. She'd been fond of Jack and he'd encouraged her to embrace her sense of adventure, but she wanted to know more about Peter, her real grandfather. I told her all I knew about him.

When Jessica suggested we go to Italy together to see where Peter had been when he was shot by the Jerries, I agreed. This would be my chance to go abroad before it was too late as I wasn't getting any younger. On my next birthday I would turn seventy, and Mary was already asking if I wanted a party. And it would be good for Jessica. She didn't seem to be getting anywhere in her job at the local newspaper. And then there was the boy next door, Tom, who Mary was fond of because she hoped that, if Jessica married him, she and Phil could retire and live at Camellia Cottage. I'd have to move elsewhere, but they deserved to spend their retirement there, as me and Jack had, and Mr and Mrs Foster before us. But I wanted Jessica to be able to choose who she married, and what she ended up doing with her life. Neither me nor Mary had had that option. I hoped that going to Italy might fire something up inside her, make her realise that the world was bigger than Little Vale, that it could be her oyster if she wanted it to be. And so that was why I agreed to go to Italy. She thought she was going for me. But we were going for her.

CHAPTER 14

JESSICA

The following week, Gran and I flew to Pisa from Manchester airport, then took the train to Siena. It wasn't the easiest journey, lugging our suitcases – I had to carry them both as Gran wasn't up to it – and there were a number of steps to navigate. Gran fell asleep on the train, and I looked out of the window at the Tuscan countryside as it whizzed past. Fields in shades of yellow and green, rows of vines, old-looking towns perched on hills with buildings in a reddish-brown colour, farmhouses surrounded by tall thin trees. I thought about Peter's diary, and how it had brought us here, wondering what life had been like for him in Tuscany. Being occupied by the Germans, daily life must have been immensely hard, and I imagined he would have spent all of his time in hiding. The diary would no doubt tell me all of this. It seemed apt that I would be near to the location where he'd made those last entries.

I was mesmerised by the beauty of the scenery, and so excited to be in Italy for the first time. This diary had brought me on an adventure. And tomorrow, I'd get to see Alessandro again.

When we arrived in Siena, we took a taxi to our boutique

hotel in the centre. After checking in, we slept for a couple of
hours, exhausted from the journey. That evening we ate in the
hotel bar, as we were too tired to explore – that would happen
the next day.

The next morning, we'd arranged to meet Alessandro at his
grandfather's apartment, as agreed on the telephone. After
breakfast, I went to the tourist office nearby and asked for a
map, then worked out how to get to Benedetto's apartment on
Via San Marco at the other side of Siena.

After breakfast, me and Gran set off. The buildings in Siena
were medieval and tall, and the streets were narrow and cobble-
stoned. We passed through the centre where there was a
wonderful view of the red-brick shell-shaped square through an
arch on a tiny street that had lots of steps leading down to it. I'd
been reading the guidebook and the Mangia tower rose above a
vast building called the Palazzo Pubblico. There were shops
with stylish things in the windows – beautiful shoes and bags
and stationery – and a bookshop with some English titles in the
window, no doubt for tourists. We continued to quieter streets
leading away from the centre, uphill and round a corner,
passing through a tiny square with a fountain, and then,
checking the map, I found we were close to the address.
Looking up, I could see the building in front of us.

'Are you ready for this, Gran?' I asked.

Nodding, she said, 'Now is as good a time as any.'

I rang the intercom and Alessandro answered.

'Hey, come on up – we're on the third floor,' he said, and I
couldn't help being happy to hear his voice.

He buzzed us in, and we went through the grand old
wooden door, passing through a musty-smelling lobby with
pigeonholes. There many flights of stairs to climb – this
took Gran a bit of time as she had arthritis in her knees – and we
reached the third floor, where Alessandro stood waiting at an
open door. He had a huge smile on his face, and once again he

wore shorts and a t-shirt. I was glad to see him, and thought back to when he'd turned up on the farm out of the blue. It was a bonus that he was part of this whole adventure that had come about because of my grandfather's diary.

'How are you doing, Jessica? Eleanor?'

'Hi,' I said.

We all shook hands, and he led us into an apartment with dark wooden flooring and paintings on the walls, down a dimly lit hall, until we reached a vast living room with tall sash windows and views of the terracotta rooftops and church spires of Siena. There sat an elderly man, presumably Benedetto, and a woman of around the same age.

'Let me introduce you to everyone,' Alessandro said. 'This is my grandfather, Benedetto, and my grandmother, Sofia.'

Benedetto sat in an armchair by the window, and he was thin and frail, understandably considering he didn't have long to live. He wore a pair of jeans and a navy-blue polo shirt and his thick hair was completely white. Sofia sat beside him, wearing a dress with a floral pattern. Her grey hair had blond highlights at the front and was scraped into a bun. She wore a little make-up, blusher brushed across her high cheekbones and her thin lips painted in a pale shade of pink.

Me and Gran said, 'Hello,' and they both nodded and smiled, and said, 'Piacere.' Sofia's hand was resting on Benedetto's, and they seemed to be very much in love, despite the number of years spent together. I swallowed. This sight moved me, especially as they both knew this era would end before long.

Sofia spoke to Alessandro in Italian, and he turned to us.

'My grandmother is delighted to meet you both. She remembers Peter well, and will always be grateful to him for saving Benedetto's life on the day they met. He was a good man, she says.'

Gran looked at me and smiled. I couldn't imagine how it

must feel to be hearing about the man she'd had a liaison with all those years ago, long after he'd gone.

'Tell your grandmother it's good to hear that about Peter,' Gran said.

Alessandro spoke to Sofia in Italian, and she smiled before replying.

'My grandmother says you must both come for dinner tonight.'

Gran looked at me, and I nodded. It might be helpful for her, and an opportunity to spend more time with Alessandro was too good to miss.

'We'd be delighted to accept your grandmother's kind invitation,' she said.

Alessandro interpreted. Sofia clapped her hands together, and said, 'Perfetto.'

He then approached Benedetto, and helped him get up out of the chair.

'Right, shall we go then?' Alessandro said.

Sofia stayed at the flat, but the rest of us went downstairs and squeezed into a Fiat Uno parked in the street. Alessandro drove, and suggested I sit beside him. Gran and Benedetto went in the back. He started the car and drove along the narrow streets of Siena, the car rumbling on the cobblestones, until we reached one of the city gates. Then we descended – Siena was on a big hill – and the Tuscan countryside stretched out before us. It was so beautiful. A patchwork of fields dotted with trees and farmhouses and roads that twisted and wound around. I stared out of the window and savoured it all.

The sky was a deep blue with wisps of cloud. Benedetto mumbled something in Italian, and we took a right down a single-track road. Birds darted in and out of trees and wildflowers grew on the verges. Benedetto spoke again, and

Alessandro pulled over by the side of the road, next to a small church. We all got out of the car, Benedetto with his stick, and he linked his arm through Alessandro's as he pointed to a path that ran down the side of the church. We followed, slowly, as Benedetto seemed very weak. Cicadas chirruped, and the path was overgrown with long grass and wildflowers brimming with bees. We continued for a few minutes until we reached a small clearing, beyond which were presumably the chestnut woods Alessandro had told us about. Benedetto mumbled something, and Alessandro leant in to listen.

'My grandfather says this is where he and his friends used to go hunting for wild truffles. They're delicious grated over pasta and risotto dishes,' he said.

'Wonderful,' I said, never having eaten truffles before. I'd heard they were very expensive and often served in fancy restaurants.

'Anyway, he says, this is the spot where my grandfather and Peter were when they waited for the British army to do a supply drop. They'd come here when receiving a message, but sadly, on the night Peter died it didn't work out as someone tipped off the Germans. He is very sorry that he couldn't do more to save Peter,' Alessandro said. 'But he's glad you're here as it brings him and hopefully you some kind of closure.'

'Indeed it does,' Gran said.

She gripped my arm, and I saw her hand was shaking. It must have been a poignant moment for her.

Benedetto pointed in the direction of some undergrowth and spoke in Italian.

'My grandfather says that there is a cross here where he sent one of the partisans, Francesco, to bury Peter after he was sure the Germans had left. Every now and again, he would come and clear this area, until recently. Since his illness, he hasn't been able to.'

'Oh.' Gran burst into tears, and I supposed reality had hit, making Peter's death very real indeed. Feeling sympathetic – it must be so hard to digest – I threaded my arm through hers and squeezed her to me. She took a handkerchief out of the pocket of her trousers and blew her nose, then forced a smile through her tears. Good old Gran, always strong in the face of adversity.

Alessandro bent down and set about clearing the undergrowth, revealing a wooden cross.

We all stood there for a few minutes without speaking – for there were no words. Benedetto made the sign of the cross with his hand then closed his eyes and spoke in Italian. It seemed that he was saying a prayer.

'Thanks for bringing us here,' I said, not really knowing what else to say.

'You're welcome. I'm sorry that it must all seem strange as well as long overdue.'

'Better late than never,' Gran said. 'I'm ready to go back now, if that's all right.'

'Sure,' Alessandro said.

He drove back to Siena and none of us said a word. When we reached the flat, he parked, and we all got out of the car.

'I hope that was the right thing to do?' he said, scrunching up his eyes.

'Yes, it was helpful to go there, but I do feel unexpectedly overcome with emotion,' Gran said.

Of course she would be. I needed to be there for Gran on the rest of this trip in case she wanted a shoulder to lean on. I wasn't used to seeing her like this – Peter's diary had certainly brought out her vulnerable side. She'd always been so stoic, and wasn't the kind of person who talked about her feelings often. I guessed it was a generational thing – living through a world war must have been incredibly difficult, and she'd dealt with so much at quite a young age. She must have been greatly impacted by what had happened, but always carried on with her life as best she could.

Alessandro proffered a hand, and she shook it. And then he shook mine.

'Well, I'll see you both later,' he said. 'Sofia said come at eight o'clock this evening for dinner.'

Benedetto put his arm through Alessandro's, and they disappeared through the front door of the apartment building.

'What shall we do now, Gran?'

'Why don't we find a lovely café and get a nice coffee and some cake. Maybe you can buy a postcard to send to your mum and dad?'

'That's a lovely idea,' I said.

We walked back to the centre of Siena, and I bought a postcard with a field of sunflowers on the front. And then we found a cosy bar in a side street behind the shops with tables outside, and sat down. I ordered cappuccinos for us both, with pastries dusted with icing sugar. When I bit into mine, it was filled with custard and deliciously sweet. Writing the postcard, I decided that I really liked being in Siena, and it had been so good to see Alessandro again. I couldn't wait to see him at dinner that evening.

CHAPTER 15

JESSICA

It was still fairly warm when we left the hotel that evening to walk back to Benedetto's apartment. Now dark, there was a sliver of moon in the sky, and a few stars were visible. Me and Gran progressed towards the centre, streetlamps and displays in shop windows lighting our way. People filled the streets, dressed up for the evening, and Siena had a relaxed atmosphere. Once again, we walked uphill and past the small square with the fountain until we reached the flat. I pressed the button for the intercom, and the door buzzed almost straight away. We stepped into the lobby and climbed the stairs. But this time when we reached the top, Alessandro wasn't waiting there. Instead, the door was ajar, and we went inside, following the hall until we reached the living room, where Sofia called out, 'Buonasera', when she saw us.

'Buonasera,' I said in reply, the only Italian word I knew, apart from buongiorno. In the guidebook, I'd read buonasera was often used from lunchtime onwards, meaning both good afternoon and good evening.

Benedetto smiled and lifted his arm to gesture for us to enter. He and Sofia sat on a sofa. The windows were pushed up as far as they'd go. It was quite warm and the thin white curtains danced in the breeze created by a fan whirring in the corner as it moved from side to side. A woman stood by one of the windows, and she wore leather trousers and a white shirt and high heels. She was glamorous, with dark hair pinned up, and she had a mobile phone pressed to her ear. She held a long, thin cigarette in her hand, and flicked ash out of the window. Even though I couldn't understand Italian, it was clear she was exasperated by the conversation she was having by the tone of her voice.

'Prego,' Sofia said, gesturing for us to sit down.

Me and Gran took the armchairs opposite her and Benedetto, and I wondered where Alessandro was. Would he not be at the dinner after all? The woman continued to talk on the phone, and she looked over and threw us a wave. It was a little awkward sitting there, unable to speak Italian – how would we communicate without Alessandro there to interpret? I looked around the room. The walls were painted a deep red colour and filled with paintings of the Tuscan countryside – fields of sunflowers, olive groves, vineyards, and also there were still lifes of bottles of wine and bowls of fruit and vases of flowers. And then there he was. Alessandro stood by the door, holding two flutes filled with an orange drink.

'Hey, there you are,' he said, bringing the flutes over and handing them to us.

'What's this?' Gran said.

'It's a Bellini, made from peach purée and prosecco. My Uncle Enzo brought over a box of peaches from his garden this afternoon, and Nonna didn't know what to do with them, so I suggested we make Bellinis.'

I took a sip, and it was delicious – cool and refreshing with the sweetness of the peaches, and the prosecco was so bubbly it fizzed up my nose.

'This is really good,' I said.

'Glad you like it. I'll get the rest of them.'

He disappeared and came back with a tray of flutes for Sofia and Benedetto, the woman on the phone, and himself.

'Cin cin,' Sofia said, raising her glass.

'That means, "Cheers",' Alessandro said.

'Cin cin,' me and Gran repeated.

The woman said, 'Ciao ciao,' and placed her phone on the coffee table. 'Buonasera, I am Isabella,' she said to us, shaking our hands.

'Isabella is my aunt – I call her "Zia" – she's Benedetto and Sofia's daughter, and my mom's sister. And Uncle Enzo, who I call "Zio", is their brother – he couldn't be here tonight, which is why he wanted to send the peaches,' Alessandro said.

'Pleased to meet you,' I said.

'Isabella speaks English as she lived in London for a while, didn't you, Zia?'

'Yes, I studied at Imperial College for a short while and lived in Kensington, many years ago now,' she said, lighting another cigarette. She inhaled and blew a cloud of smoke sideways, saying, 'It was behind a big round red building, come si chiama...? Ah yes, the Royal Albert Hall.'

She sat on the sofa between Benedetto and Sofia and started talking to Gran, leaving me and Alessandro able to speak to each other without anyone listening in.

'So, what do you think of Siena?'

'It's lovely,' I said.

'I like it.' He took a sip of his Bellini. 'I could easily live here.'

'I could too.'

A maid came into the room wearing a black dress, a white apron tied round her waist.

'Cena è pronta,' she said.

'Dinner is ready,' Alessandro said. 'That is the maid, Carla, who has been helping out more recently as Isabella works long hours and needs help looking after Benedetto and Sofia since they moved in a few months ago. They've just hired an au pair as well who will be starting soon.'

He got up and led us into a dining room, where there was a long table covered in a yellow cloth with place settings, open bottles of red wine and mineral water. Candles ran along its centre, and there were a couple of small vases of flowers, and a basket of bread.

Sofia spoke to Alessandro, and he told us where to sit. She and Benedetto were at the head of the table with Gran and Isabella on one side, and me and Alessandro opposite. I was glad to be sitting next to him.

Carla brought in bowls of steaming ravioli with Parmesan grated on top, and we all tucked in. Alessandro went round filling our glasses with wine and water. When we'd finished our starters, Carla cleared the bowls and Alessandro helped her, and then they brought in plates of grilled chicken, bowls of potatoes cut into cubes and green beans with slices of garlic on top. After the main course, we ate tiramisu.

'Have you had tiramisu before?' Alessandro said.

I shook my head.

'In Italian, it literally means "Pick me up", deriving from "tirare", meaning to pull, "mi" me and "su" up.'

'Oh, why's that?'

'Because it's made from sponge fingers soaked in coffee and a liqueur, usually Marsala wine.'

'So, it's supposed to give you some kind of kick?'

'Exactly. So what do you know about Siena? Have you heard about the Palio?'

'No.'

'It's a horse race around the Piazza del Campo and it takes place twice a year in July and August. Siena is divided into seventeen districts called contrade. Every contrada has its own flag with an animal symbol, and a motto. They each have a horse competing and the jockey wears their colours.'

'That sounds really interesting,' I said. How I'd like to find out more, and maybe write about it. 'Which one is this flat in then?'

Carla brought in espressos and put them in our places.

'Chiocciola, meaning snail. The flag is red and yellow.'

'Have you seen the Palio?'

He shook his head. 'Oh no, this is my first time in Siena. My mom wanted me to come and meet my grandfather before he died. But I'd like to see it, maybe next summer. Maybe you could come out and see it too?'

Smiling, I shrugged and said, 'That sounds amazing, but I can't really see it happening.'

'You could always come and do an Italian course, like Sofia's au pairs.'

'That's an idea,' I said. Studying Italian appealed to me, but I hadn't studied a language since school when taking French. However, Alessandro had planted a seed in my head by suggesting I do something way out of my comfort zone. I'd mull it over, perhaps.

'I've thought about doing one as I can speak Italian, but can't write it that well – it would be a good excuse to spend time in Siena. They run every three months,' Alessandro said.

Gran was in conversation with Sofia and Isabella was interpreting. They were discussing the diary.

Sofia spoke to Alessandro, and he said, 'Nonna liked Peter and is sorry it took Benedetto so long to get the diary to you. They'd talked about it many times over the years. She knew Peter a little as she used to handle the documents for the partisans. When Siena was occupied by the Germans, she lived here in this very flat. It was a frightening time, with her constantly fearing they'd find out she was working with the partisans.

Thankfully she wasn't caught. If she had been, she would have been shot.'

I couldn't imagine what life would have been like for Sofia and Benedetto during that time. They must have been left with terrible memories.

'One good thing to come out of the war,' Alessandro continued, 'is that's how my grandparents met, when Sofia helped Benedetto out with a document for one of the partisans.'

'Ah, it sounds like they've had a happy life together.'

'So, are you reading the diary then?' he said.

'Yes.' I explained that neither Mum nor Gran wanted to read it, so it was up to me to find out whether Peter had known Gran was carrying his child.

Alessandro sat up in his chair.

'What? She was pregnant with his child?'

I nodded.

'Yes, so you bringing the diary to our farm changed everything for us. That was the day my mother found out Peter was her real father.' I went on to explain about Gran marrying Jack, and how he hadn't wanted anyone to know the truth.

'Oh dear. I am sorry.'

'It's not your fault. You were only the messenger. And I guess it needed to come out. Poor Gran has had to keep it to herself all these years.'

'And your mom, how is she?'

'My mum isn't too happy about being lied to for all that time. She has been sulking a bit.'

'Yeah, that kind of sucks, but hopefully she'll come around with a little time?'

I nodded. 'Yes, you're probably right. I'm sure she'll get past it when she realises Gran was just doing what she had to do. Marrying my grandpa meant she didn't have to give Mum up for adoption. And part of the condition of their marriage was that no one knew he wasn't her father.'

Gran looked across the table at me.

'We ought to go, Jessica. I'm sure everyone is ready for bed. Alessandro, can you please thank your family for this delicious meal?'

He spoke in Italian, and I liked the way he sounded when speaking such a beautiful language, the words rolling off his tongue. It was certainly an attractive trait, and I admired how clever he was, and so lucky to be able to speak another language. Sofia's face broke into a warm smile. Benedetto nodded. He could barely keep his eyes open, and looked to be in need of some rest. Getting through the trip to Peter's grave as well as dinner with us must have been draining for him in his condition. Hopefully now he'd have some closure when it came to the diary he'd been keeping all these years, and he could rest in peace knowing he'd fulfilled Peter's dying wish in the end.

Isabella said, 'You are most welcome.'

Alessandro saw us to the front door.

'Well, goodbye, it was so nice to see you again,' I said.

'Bye, Jessica. I hope we can stay in touch?'

Meeting his eye, I said, 'Of course, I'd like that.'

'And maybe I'll see you at the Palio next year?'

I laughed. 'Yes, well, we'll see.'

'Promise me you'll think about it?'

'Okay.' I nodded. 'I promise.'

'Well, if you do decide to take a class, write to me at the address of the auction house where I work, Pimsy's – it's on the business card I gave you. Then maybe if I'm here in Siena at the same time, we can meet up.'

He worked at an auction house? This made him even more intriguing and I was impressed. The prospect of seeing him all alone, just the two of us, in a bar with coffee or a refreshing drink was a lovely thought.

He kissed me on both cheeks, and I breathed in the smell of him, detecting hints of sandalwood on his neck.

Gran shook his hand. 'Thank you, Al, for all you've done today.'

'It's a pleasure, Eleanor.'

We started to walk down the stairs, and Alessandro stayed by the door, throwing me a wave just before I disappeared out of sight. I hoped we'd stay in touch, and that I would indeed see him again.

CHAPTER 16

JESSICA

The next day, me and Gran had a lovely breakfast in the hotel garden. There was a buffet with just about everything you could want – slices of orange melon, pastries, cereal, fresh bread, juice, coffee. We sat there for a while as it was such a relaxing place to be, our table set amongst trees and surrounded by old terracotta pots brimming with flowers in bright colours. It was our last day in Siena, and I didn't want to leave. Three nights didn't seem like long enough, but it would have been expensive for Gran to pay for longer. Besides, we hadn't known it would be such a lovely place.

'This is the life, isn't it?' Gran said, biting into the croissant she'd just cut in half and lathered with jam.

'It really is.'

'All these years I've missed out on doing things like this,' she said. 'Your grandpa – Jack – had no interest in going on holidays. Besides, money was always tight, what with trying to keep the farm afloat.'

'I'm sorry, Gran.'

'I think he was so traumatised by his experience abroad during the war, when he ended up with that terrible scar on his face, that he never wanted to leave the country again, once he was safely back in England.'

'Everyone used to stare when we went out, and I felt so bad for him,' I said.

'I know, he never made a fuss. He was very brave.'

'He was.'

Gran dropped a lump of sugar into her cup of tea and gave it a stir.

'Now it's up to you, Jessica, to seize the moment and make sure you get to do things like this. Make up for what me and your mother never had.'

Refilling my cup with the cafetière of coffee, I said, 'Well, coming here has certainly inspired me. I'll try my best.'

She looked across the table at me and gave me a warm smile, then placed her hand on mine and gave it a squeeze.

After breakfast, we ambled around the centre of Siena, browsing the shops – looking at handbags and jewellery and books and stationery. Gran bought a pack of notecards with pictures of Tuscan places on the front – Pisa, Florence, Siena, San Gimignano. Being in Italy had inspired me to write about my travelling experience, and I bought myself a notebook with pink pages. Afterwards, we stopped in a fancy-looking café in the Piazza del Campo. I ordered cappuccinos for us both, and as we sat there in silence – I never felt the need to fill every second with conversation when spending time with Gran – I studied my surroundings. Our table gave us a wonderful view of the whole square. There were people walking around – tourists, and Italians going about their daily business, some with phones clutched to their ears – but it was a calm place to be.

'Are you glad we came on this trip, Gran?' I said.

'Yes, I think it was the right thing to do.'

'Do you feel that you can put the story of Peter to bed now?'

'Well, I need to bring your mum round – she is rather upset, as you know, but I'm confident that she'll get there. It's a big thing for her, and she's always been a sensitive sort.'

'Alessandro suggested I come here and study Italian, can you believe it?'

'What, really? How long for?'

'He said it's possible to do a three-month course.'

'And what do you think, Jess?'

'It's kind of ridiculous, don't you think?'

'Not really, you always did like French at school, and it was a shame your mum and dad couldn't afford to send you on that trip to Normandy. I offered them the money, but your mum wouldn't accept it.'

Gran was right. I had always liked French, perhaps because I'd always had an adventurous side wanting to get out. I probably wouldn't find studying Italian that difficult, and it would be fun to do something different. And I really did love the sound of the language – it was so beautiful. I was bored with my life at home, and the change of scenery might do me good. Besides, I could use the opportunity to write travel articles, perhaps give the whole thing a go. It had been my dream for a while after all, and I'd put it to one side for far too long.

'I wonder how much it would cost. And I'd need to get time off work.'

'Don't you have some money saved?'

'I do, but not that much. Enough perhaps to get me through three months here.'

'And then you'd have no savings left. Why don't I check my bank balance when I get home? Perhaps I could make a contribution.'

'What? Oh Gran, that would be so kind and generous of you.'

'Coming here would do you the world of good. You've never

known life outside our part of the country. Even when you were studying in Preston, you still lived at home.'

'You're right. I'll mull it over.'

'I'd like to see you spread your wings, get out of Little Vale. Do consider it carefully. These opportunities don't come along very often and you're still young. Grab it while you can, Jess, you really have nothing to lose.'

Gran was right. So what if I lived in Siena for three months and it was a disaster? I could just return to my old life knowing I'd tried something else and it hadn't worked out.

CHAPTER 17

JESSICA

After returning from Siena, I found myself doing a great deal of thinking. The seed that Alessandro had planted when suggesting I study Italian was beginning to germinate. This could be an opportunity to pave my way to becoming a travel writer. I could write freelance articles while living in Siena, and try to sell them. And with Gran contributing money towards the fee for the course, I wouldn't have to spend all my savings.

There were two people who wouldn't be happy about me going to Italy: Mum and Tom. Mum had always liked having me close to home, and she would miss me, especially as she'd been a bit low since discovering Peter was her father. She'd been doing a lot of soul-searching, and this was understandable, seeing as her identity was completely different from what she'd thought it was. Mum was having weekly sessions with a counsellor, who'd recommended she write a letter to Peter to tell him how she felt. This exercise would supposedly help her deal with the situation and to grieve for the father she'd never known. The counsellor also suggested she take part in activities that took her away from Dad and the farm. She'd signed up for a yoga class at the village hall and joined the local WI. In a way, it seemed that the diary turning up was the kick she needed to break out of her comfort zone. She was enjoying the yoga and had started to do it at home too sometimes. And the kitchen was filled with jars of home-made jam and cakes for all the WI coffee mornings she was now taking part in. Gran would often help her, and it was a fun activity they could partake in together. I did feel bad about abandoning Mum when she liked having me around so much, but perhaps now was the time for her to start living her own life rather than just being my mother and Dad's wife.

And then there was Tom. I hadn't seen much of him since the summer as he always seemed so busy with work, even at weekends, when he was still immersed in tasks to be done on his farm. We had begun to grow apart, and I hadn't done anything about this. Once, I would have made a fuss and complained about us not going on dates. Instead, I'd left it to him to suggest when we saw each other, and that wasn't very often. Sometimes we'd end up down the Old Hare in the village for a couple of drinks on a Friday night. But often his friends would be there, so it wasn't really a date. Still, I knew he liked having me around, and often promised to spend more time alone with me when work on the farm calmed down, but it never seemed to. And I wasn't that bothered really. Our relationship was one of those that had started in our late teens and carried on because neither of us had met anyone we liked more. We had split up a couple of times over the years but got together again quite quickly.

When calling the language school, I found out there wasn't any availability until March, and so I decided to give myself a little time to come to a decision. Autumn became winter, and it got very cold on the farm. Christmas came and went, and then in the new year, after a particularly frustrating day at work, I made up my mind once and for all. Struggling to get to sleep, I found myself imagining what my life would be like if I lived in Siena for a short time. Would I manage all right on my own? I'd lived at home when studying at the polytechnic in Preston, not embracing student life at all.

The next morning when I woke up, I was brushing my teeth when it struck me – I had to do this! What was stopping me? When would this chance come again? I was still young and had no commitments. That morning at work, I knocked on the door of my boss Mr Carter's office and plucked up the courage to ask if it would be possible to take time off from March to June. He said I could take a sabbatical and he'd keep my job open.

And so that lunchtime I called the language school in Siena, and the receptionist said she'd post the paperwork to me. When I asked about accommodation, she said she would send a list of landlords to contact in order to book a room in a shared flat. It all seemed quite daunting, arranging to live in shared accommodation abroad with someone I didn't know, but she reassured me that I could request to live with other female students at the language school, and so I'd do that. The thought of uprooting my whole life and going to Siena was disconcerting but also so exciting. It was the beginning of a new era for me as well as Mum and Gran, the diary having impacted all three of us. Now I needed to think about what to take – would I need summer clothes? – and book my flight to Pisa.

CHAPTER 18

JESSICA

A couple of weeks before I was due to leave, it was Valentine's Day, and Tom turned up at the farm with a dozen red roses and a box of luxury chocolates in heart shapes. He'd always been good at grand gestures, but sometimes I felt that they were to make up for what was lacking elsewhere – spending quality time together and a closeness emotionally that I craved but didn't quite get from him. Then he suggested we drive to the coast. This was often something he did when we hadn't seen each other for a while. I got into his Land Rover, and we set off along country lanes towards Lancaster and then took the road to the coast.

When we reached the seaside town of Morecambe, it was pouring with rain, and Tom parked with a view of the bay and went to get fish and chips while I stayed in the car. Five minutes or so later, he got back in and handed me my cod and chips, wrapped in newspaper, along with a cardboard fork and a can of Coke.

'Can you get some napkins out of the glove compartment, Jess love?' he said.

I opened the glove compartment and reached inside. Sitting

there in the centre was a blue jewellery box in the shape of a cube – there was no doubt in my mind about what was inside. What on earth was Tom thinking? A wave of nausea swept over me, and I took out two napkins, handing one to Tom before clicking the glove compartment firmly shut. Dumbstruck, I ran through what to say in my head, but came up with nothing.

'Didn't you see anything else in there?' he said, breaking the ice.

'What do you mean?' I said, to stall him while working out how to respond. Our relationship had been on the rocks for months, and he thought this was a good idea? I'd been thinking about ending it before leaving for Siena, and on the drive had even considered initiating a conversation about whether we had a future together.

'Come on, Jessica, you must have seen the jewellery box?'

I was all ready to leave for Siena, to try out a new life, and here was Tom putting a spanner in the works.

'I didn't see anything,' I said to buy myself more time. How should I respond to this without upsetting him?

'Go on, have another look then,' he said.

Opening the glove compartment again, I took out the blue jewellery box and held it in my hand. In shock, I froze, not knowing what to do. This was such a big moment, but I wasn't ready for it. Why hadn't Tom dropped any hints so I could be mentally prepared?

'Open it.'

Gingerly, I lifted the lid, and there sat an engagement ring with a gold band and huge diamond at the centre. It had probably cost Tom a small fortune, but how did he not know this ring was far too over the top for me? I couldn't imagine walking around with that on my finger – I'd feel self-conscious and would worry about losing or breaking it. But still, I didn't want to hurt his feelings. Tom had always been good to me, and I had nothing to complain about when it came to our relationship – it just didn't excite me as much as it should. This was supposed to be that fairytale moment most women dreamt of, but it wasn't at all. Sadness consumed me. I felt bad for Tom because I was so disappointed by his grand gesture rather than as delighted as he'd want me to be. Turning to look at him, I did my best to smile and look enthusiastic.

'Will you marry me then?' he said.

Closing the lid on the box, I said, 'But Tom, you do know I'm going to Siena soon?'

'Yes, of course, but I thought it would be a nice idea to give you that before you go so you have it with you.'

'Look, Tom, this is a lovely gesture, it really is. But we haven't talked about getting married at all yet, and this is such a surprise. We've hardly seen each other for several months now.'

'You know my dad has been giving me more responsibility because of his bad back. It will calm down soon, I promise, once the dust has settled.'

I took a deep breath. Tom had always been a workaholic, and I doubted that would change any time soon.

'When you said you were going away, it got me thinking. What would I do if you didn't come back? What if I lost you to someone else? I need you to come back, Jessica, and be my wife. I'm expanding the business and need a good woman by my side.'

At only twenty-four years old, I wasn't sure if I was ready for any of that, although it was quite common for farmers in our neck of the woods to marry at that age, or even earlier. Dad was almost ready to retire and, me being the only child and a girl, he and Mum thought the best way to keep the farm going was for me to marry a farmer who was keen to take it on. The Gilberts had been after our land for years, as they wanted to expand their riding school and build a cluster of holiday cottages for ramblers to stay in.

Tom saw me as a kind of business deal and, although Gran

had been part of something similar, and even Mum, I didn't want to feel obliged to follow the same path. Times had changed. Why should I accept that my future was to be a farmer's wife? Maybe I would end up being one, if it was my calling, but I was keen to explore other options first.

I looked out of the car window at the rain, the Irish Sea a brown-grey colour – it was all so miserable, and I couldn't wait to be in a place where the weather was bound to be brighter.

'How about you decide when you get back? I can keep the ring until then if you want?' Tom said.

'Don't you want to know now?'

'It's only for a few months, isn't it?'

I nodded.

'In that case, I can wait. I'll be busy with work and the time will fly by. Before I know it, you'll be back, and hopefully you'll have got whatever this is this out of your system and be ready to settle down.'

'All right, I guess... Thank you for understanding why I can't give you an answer right now. And thanks again for asking, it's really... a lovely offer, and I appreciate all the effort you've gone to, finding such a phenomenal ring.' I unwrapped the newspaper on my knees and tucked into the fish and chips – they were thankfully still warm and delicious, covered with salt and vinegar, and a comfort as the wind howled outside, the waves crashing against the shore. We didn't speak as we ate, and I tried to process what had just happened. I couldn't imagine me and Tom being married – and even if we were, he'd need to get me an engagement ring that was more understated. Perhaps in time I'd change my mind, but first I needed to go to Siena.

On the way home, we stopped at Tom's cottage on the farm next door and slept together for what felt like the last time. I just couldn't see a future with him, but was torn between these feelings and what Mum would expect from me.

In the car on the short drive back to Birch Farm, I said, 'Tom, about the ring...'

'I caught you off guard, and I'm sorry about that,' he said. 'But it is what I want, and, deep down, I think it's what you want as well.'

'I'm sorry for not saying yes, for not taking it with me.'

'Just go and do what you have to do. And when you come back, I'll have the ring waiting for you to put on your finger.'

'Tom, would you mind very much if we have a break while I'm away? We don't need to write or call each other, do we?'

He scratched his nose and glanced across at me before fixing his eyes back on the road.

'If that's what you want. We can have a break, and pick up from where we left off when you return.'

He pulled into the yard, and I kissed him gently on the cheek before getting out of the car. He sped off down the drive, the Land Rover bumping in and out of potholes as he went. He seemed so disappointed by my reaction to his proposal, but who could blame him? The diary turning up was bringing out a more selfish side of me, but I kind of liked it. I'd been a people-pleaser for far too long, and I needed to start putting myself first if I was ever going to live a life that fulfilled me.

I went into the house and found Mum in the kitchen. She was sitting at the table, drinking tea.

'Hello, love,' she said. 'Come and join me.'

Taking a breath, I wasn't looking forward to telling her about the proposal. She'd have wanted me to say yes, and would no doubt try to persuade me to accept when I returned from Siena.

'Tom just proposed,' I said.

Her face lit up. 'What?'

I repeated myself.

'Well, that's wonderful news. I'll tell Dad to go down the offy and get some sparkling wine to celebrate. Well done, Jess, you did it!'

'I didn't say yes.'

'Please tell me you're joking?'

'No, I'm not.'

'But you didn't say no? Surely, you told him you'd think about it?'

'I did.'

'Oh what a relief. For a minute there... of course, you'll say yes, won't you?'

I looked at her across the table, and her face dropped.

'Jessica, what is wrong with you?'

'Nothing. It's just why shouldn't I get to choose what I do with my life?'

She shrugged. 'But what's the alternative, exactly? If you don't get a man soon, they'll all be married and then your only choice will be someone much older, looking for his second or third wife. And he won't want children with you because he already has them.'

'Oh come on... isn't that a little narrow-minded?'

'It's true. In a few years, all the eligible men will start to disappear off the market – you'll see. And then you'll be on the shelf.'

I sighed. Mum's views were so outdated – how did she not realise that?

'I'll just have to take that risk, won't I?'

'It is a risk, indeed, and I hope you know what you're doing.'

'So do I. It just feels like the right thing to do. That diary turned up for a reason – it's made me rethink my whole life.'

'Don't be ridiculous.'

'Mum, it's just how I feel, that's all.'

'Let's hope that when you get back from this grand adventure you'll come to your senses. You won't find another man like

Tom, who's willing to take on our farm. And it would be so easy too what with his farm being next door.'

'Easy for you and Dad, but perhaps not for me.'

Mum got up, her chair scraping the flagstone floor. She took a bag of potatoes out of the cupboard and started to peel them. She filled a saucepan with water from the tap and more or less slammed it down on the hob, making me start.

'I need to get on with making supper now. Why don't you have a sit-down in the other room? I'll bring you another cup of tea.'

I was being dismissed. This was something Mum did when upset and she wanted to be on her own. Getting up, I made to leave the room, and she stood at the counter, looking out of the window, her eyes glazed over. Guilt did its best to consume me, but I couldn't allow it to. I understood her position, but also didn't feel she was being entirely fair. Hopefully in time she'd come round and start to see things from my point of view.

That night in bed, looking for inspiration as well as some kind of distraction from how Mum had made me feel, I read Peter's diary.

1 February 1943

My battalion's been captured by the Jerries in Tunisia, and we've been sent to a prisoner-of-war camp near Laterina in Italy. We're crammed into small huts and my head itches from the lice which live amongst us. There isn't much to eat and we're losing a great deal of weight. The guards provide us with two meals a day, but most of the time we can't identify what they're feeding us. We're grateful for the Red Cross parcels we each receive once a week. They contain tins of food, soap and most importantly cigarettes, which we use to barter for the food we like most. Being in this camp is tedious and the days drag on and on. I'm haunted by memories of comrades dying in Tunisia and I often think of home to get me through. I received two letters from Eleanor. The first says she is carrying my child and could I take some leave and go back to England to marry her. I can't deny it left me feeling rather confused. She is a lovely girl, and I enjoyed the few hours we spent together, but to be forced into marriage like that – well, it's not what a man wants, is it? The second letter says that if she doesn't hear from me soon, she'll have to go to one of those homes for unwed mothers. There is no way of contacting her now, or of taking any leave. I'll just have to hope she finds a way to manage her situation. No doubt, she'll go and stay in one of those homes and have the baby before giving it up for adoption.

Fury raging through me, I dropped the diary onto the floor beside the bed. After reading that paragraph, I was suddenly so glad that I'd been able to see the diary first and protect Mum and Gran from Peter's words. I had felt so sure he mustn't have known about Gran's situation, and the truth was almost too difficult to handle. Poor Gran. How could he write such hurtful things? Clearly, he'd misled her into thinking they had a future together, when in reality, he'd only been interested in going to bed with her before leaving for war. I felt so angry on Gran's behalf. Showing this to her would cause a great deal of upset, but hadn't she wanted to know if he'd received her letters? I needed to consider telling her, but decided to say nothing unless she asked. She hadn't brought up the contents of the diary since giving it to me that day in the kitchen, after Alessandro's visit, and so I wondered if she really did want to know the truth. No doubt the diary would come up at some stage – if it did, maybe I'd have to tell a small lie in order to protect her, and say he'd been delighted to find out about the baby, that he couldn't wait to come home and make an honest woman of her. I doubted she'd want to see what he'd written with her own eyes as it would be too much for her. For now, though, I would take a break from reading the diary. I'd hoped to find some connection to Peter in its pages – some inspiration for going off to Italy and discovering where he'd spent his final days. I'd thought that living my best life in Tuscany would perhaps make up for the time he'd lost. But now I couldn't bear to discover anything else Gran wouldn't want to know. I would take the diary to Siena with me though, for when I was ready to read it again.

CHAPTER 19

JESSICA

In March, I went back to Siena, full of nervous energy – it was a bold move for someone like me. I was just a girl from a small Yorkshire village and had never really done anything so adventurous before, even though I'd always hoped to. Before leaving, I'd sent a postcard to Alessandro's office. It had a picture of the Yorkshire Dales on the front, and I told him my address in the city, suggesting we meet up if he was there too. I didn't know if he'd be in Siena, but thought I'd write just in case he had decided to do the course, or if he visited Sofia. Gran had paid for a three-month Italian course at the language school and I was grateful. This meant I'd still need to pay for living expenses and rent was quite expensive so I would have to dip into my savings. I had my camera and a couple of notebooks, and was ready to write articles to submit to newspapers and magazines. I'd be sharing with one other female student. I had no idea who she was and hoped we'd get on.

Mum and Gran drove me to the airport and we had one last coffee before they waved me off as I went through departures.

'Good luck, dear,' Gran said.

'I'll miss you so much,' Mum said.

I hugged them both, and Mum squeezed me tightly. She didn't want me to go, but I'd told her I would be back before long. She'd said that she understood why I was doing this, although I wasn't sure if this was true.

'I'll write,' I said. And I would. I loved writing letters, and sending them home from Italy was an exciting prospect for me.

This time my suitcase was bigger and heavier than when I'd visited with Gran, and it included summer clothes as well as jeans and jumpers. I had no idea what the weather would be like when I arrived. At home, it was still frosty in the mornings and there was talk of snow before spring arrived.

I took a taxi from Siena station to Via Vecchia, a street off the Piazza del Campo. The driver took me along narrow streets with tall medieval buildings, shutters flanking the windows, the car rumbling on cobblestones. It struck me that I was actually going to be living in Italy, and my life was about to be very different for the next few months.

After paying, I got out of the car, and there before me was a beautiful door made from a dark wood. It looked so worn and old that it could have existed in medieval times. This was where I'd be living until June, and it couldn't be more different from Birch Farm. The air was mild, a warm breeze brushing my face, and I felt too hot in the jumper put on that morning when dressing in my chilly bedroom at home. A moped buzzed past and opposite, I saw, there was a bakery called Pasticceria Luigi. Next door was a greengrocer with boxes of peaches and oranges and enormous tomatoes and courgettes and huge lettuces. Next to the flat was Bar Lorenzo, with a couple of tables outside the front. Glancing inside, I could see it was cosy, with Italian radio coming from speakers behind the bar. It was the kind of place I could probably go to on my own with a book or pen and paper. I pressed the button on the intercom for number twenty-one.

'Pronto?' a female voice said. Oh, was the girl I was sharing with Italian?

'Hi, I'm Jessica, here for the flat.'

'Oh, at last,' she said in a posh English accent. 'Do come in. We're on the top floor.'

The door clicked and I stepped into a lobby, filled with pigeonholes. It reminded me of Benedetto's building and there was a musty smell. And before me were a lot of stairs, old and crumbling. Picking up my suitcase, which was getting quite heavy by now, I walked up the stairs, floor after floor, stopping for breaks. When I reached the top, there stood a girl around my age, tall and slim with blond hair in a longish bob.

'Jessica.' She held out a hand rather formally, and I shook it. 'Pleased to meet you. I'm Harriet, but most people call me Harry.'

'Okay.'

'Welcome to number twenty-one. Come in and let me show you around.'

I stepped into the hall and ahead of me was a kitchen. There was a small table and chairs next to a tall sash window overlooking the rooftops of Siena. The window was pushed up and a light breeze came in. In the distance stood a big old church, and beyond was Tuscan countryside with a patchwork of fields, vineyards and rolling hills.

'Wow,' I said.

'You need to see the back. It's really impressive.'

I picked up my suitcase and Harriet led me down a hall to a vast bedroom with a big old wardrobe and two single beds.

'We're sharing?' I asked.

'Unfortunately, yes, most students share in Siena. It seems to be the done thing. Perhaps to discourage bad behaviour,' she said with a laugh. 'Although my boyfriend, Fabrizio, has his own room at a place in the countryside, so I stay at his every now and again. Then you'll get this place to yourself.'

Approaching the window, I could see that Harriet was right. What lay before me was magnificent – an uninterrupted view of the Tuscan countryside beyond the terracotta-tiled rooftops and church spires. It was possible to see for miles, and I picked out a farmhouse with a lane leading up to it flanked by what I now knew to be called cypress trees from reading the guidebook.

'Beautiful, isn't it?' she said. 'And it's especially lovely when you're sitting in bed reading at weekends.'

'It really is wonderful.'

Inspired, I felt an urge to write. Perhaps I would produce some really good words in this place.

I put my suitcase on the floor.

'I expect you're tired after your flight? Why don't you have a nap and maybe you can come out with me later to Bar Atlantico. Fabrizio's band, Azzurro, is playing.'

'That would be nice,' I said.

'I'll bring you a bottle of water – we have loads in the kitchen in case you're thirsty.'

'Thanks.'

After taking a shower in the bathroom next door, I climbed into bed, made up from sheets and a blanket, and with the view, it was a nice place to be. I opened Peter's diary. I hadn't looked at it since the day Tom proposed, but now in Siena, I felt inspired to read it again. I still hadn't told Gran that he knew about her letters or his reaction. Having had a break from it, I was ready to read his words again, to find out more about him and his thoughts about Gran and her baby if he had any before I reached the end.

20 May 1943

Fifty of us are being kept as prisoners of war in an old castle between Florence and Siena and we're guarded by ten Sardinians who are friendly towards us. Life here is blissful, compared to the camp at Laterina. The guards provide us with bread and meat and they've given us a plot of land for growing

vegetables. We still receive the Red Cross parcel once a week, so
we have more food than in Laterina and my strength's return-
ing. We have space to move around in and being transferred
here has boosted morale considerably. The Italian lieutenant in
charge has been kind to us because he's married to an English-
woman and before the war he worked in a bank in London. He
speaks good English and he gave us a ball so we could have a
kick-around in the evenings, after supper. A recently widowed
countess with land nearby visited today. The lieutenant told us
the Germans shot her husband because they believed him to be
helping the partisans, who hide around us in caves and in the
woods, when they're not carrying out ambushes. The countess
has beautiful dark hair which runs down her back and the
figure of a woman Botticelli might have asked to sit for him.
After spending months in the company of men, it was rather
nice to set my eyes upon a member of the fairer sex. She doesn't
speak English, and only communicated with the lieutenant.
When she asked him if we needed anything, he told her about
the worn-through soles on our boots. She said she'd try to bring
us more pairs belonging to her late husband. She didn't even
notice me as I stood there admiring her, and next time she
visits, I hope to catch her attention even if it's only for a mere
moment. How I would like those big brown eyes to be looking
at me.

So, it was possible that Peter had found another woman
when living in Italy. I wondered if he had got her to notice him
when she visited another time. By now I expected he'd forgotten
all about Gran and the unborn baby she'd written to him about.
I still felt annoyed with him on her behalf – and my mother's.
No doubt he assumed she'd given the baby up for adoption and
that was that.

Putting the diary on the bedside table, I decided to close my
eyes for a bit. It had been a tiring journey and, if I was going out

with Harriet later, I'd need to take a nap. I turned on my side to face the window, and looked out at the rooftops of Siena. The window was open, and I could hear the sounds of Italy – a woman clanking pots and pans next door and talking in Italian, the rumble of a car on cobblestones, the buzz of a moped, church bells. And I closed my eyes, and drifted off to sleep.

CHAPTER 20

JESSICA

'Jessica?'

I woke up to find Harriet standing over me. At first, I didn't know where I was and felt all confused and groggy. Then I remembered – I was in Siena.

'What time is it?'

'It's only seven o'clock, but I thought you might want a bite to eat and some time to get ready so you can come to Bar Atlantico to see Fabrizio's band.'

I'd been asleep for almost two hours, and felt totally dazed.

'I'm sorry, I'm not sure I'm really up to going out tonight,' I said.

Putting a hand on her hip, she said, 'Oh come on, Jessica. It's your first night in Siena! You'll love it, I promise. And I can't wait to show you around.'

So, ten minutes later, I found myself sitting in the kitchen with Harriet, and she'd made us both a bowl of penne with tomato sauce and basil leaves ripped over the top. She handed me a hunk of Parmesan and the smallest grater I'd ever seen. I grated the cheese over my pasta and tucked in with a fork. It was delicious and instantly I felt more energised. She poured us both a glass of local wine, Chianti, and it was smooth and rich and went down very easily. Before we knew it, we'd polished off the whole bottle.

'That was really good pasta,' I said.

'Fabrizio taught me how to make it. I'll show you, if you like.'

Harriet seemed like a kind person, and I was sure that living with her would be okay. I smiled.

'Thanks. So, how long have you been living here for?'

'Since September when my classes started. But what brings you to Siena then?'

'A few things. It all started with a diary.' I told her about Alessandro bringing Peter's diary to the farm that day.

'Ooh, and what was this Alessandro like?'

My face warming, I said, 'He's quite nice-looking, actually. Italian-American, from New Jersey. Works in New York. Calls himself Al as in Al Pacino.'

'Yum,' Harriet said. 'And did you stay in touch?'

I told her about visiting Peter's grave back in September. And how Alessandro had gone back to work at an auction house in New York.

'Well, never mind. Perhaps he'll come back to Siena, and you'll bump into him. Imagine!'

This reminded me about the postcard I'd sent to Alessandro's office, and I wondered if he'd received it.

'That would be nice, but I don't even know if he's coming back to Siena. His grandparents do live here though, so there's a chance he might visit them, especially as his grandfather hasn't got long to live.' I went on to tell her about the postcard.

'Well, let's hope he received it and comes to find you. Even if you don't see him, there are lots of gorgeous Italian men to choose from here. I can ask Fabrizio to introduce you to his single friends if you like. I'm sure you'd get on well with the drummer in his band, Giuseppe. I've already told him that my new flatmate is arriving today and he wanted to meet you. Having an Italian boyfriend is a great way to learn the language too.' She winked.

'That's very kind, thanks, but...'

'But what?'

'I was really hoping to just see Alessandro. Although I feel that I shouldn't...'

'What, do you have someone at home?'

'Yes.' And I told her about Tom's proposal, and that we'd agreed to take a break.

'Oh, well, I guess while you're here you'll have to decide whether you want to spend the rest of your life with him. Although, I'd highly recommend seeing someone else before doing that. How will you know if he's the right man for you otherwise?'

Harriet was echoing my thoughts. I'd soon find out if I missed Tom. If I didn't, surely we weren't meant to be together?

Harriet stood up, put our bowls in the sink, and gave them a rinse with the tap.

'Well, I'm off to get ready. We leave at a quarter to nine prompt – the band starts playing at nine and I have something in mind for us to do en route.'

At quarter to nine, we left the flat and walked along Via Vecchia. I wore jeans and a green top with a cardigan tied round my waist. By now it was dark and Siena, with its medieval buildings, shutters flanking the tall windows, terracotta pots outside front doors and old-fashioned streetlamps, was quite magical. The temperature had dropped since earlier in the day, but it was warmer than at home – the equivalent of an evening in late spring. We passed a restaurant where people sat outside, talking quietly, with glasses of wine, bowls of pasta and baskets of bread. Before long, we reached the square and I instantly knew where we were from my visit with Gran – the Piazza del Campo, in the shape of a shell. It was truly beautiful. I recognised the Palazzo Pubblico with the Mangia tower running along one side. The remainder of the square was edged with restaurants and bars, with tiny streets leading uphill in between them.

People ambled, all dressed up for the evening, and the murmur of voices echoed around the buildings. The tables outside bars and restaurants had candles on them, and some of the waiters wore black tie. Young people sat on the red bricks of the square itself. A small group sat by a man with a guitar and passed round a bottle of red wine, pouring it into white plastic cups. I'd thought we were only passing through the square, but Harriet led me to a fountain. It was a rectangular shape with white statues, the Madonna and Child at its centre.

'Okay, Jessica, it's time for you to stand with your back to this fountain, the Fonte Gaia. Throw a coin over your shoulder, and make a wish.'

I hadn't expected this, and was caught off guard.

'I don't have any coins with me, besides I wouldn't know what to wish for,' I said.

'Everyone has things they wish for. And this is a rite of passage – you have to do it on the day you arrive in Siena – well, that's what me and my friend, Clara, who moved out, decided. So' – Harriet reached into the pocket of her jeans, and pressed a coin into the palm of my hand – 'here you go.'

I stood there and looked at her, without any idea what to wish for. The man with the guitar sang 'Sweet Caroline' and the girls sitting round him joined in, their voices gradually getting louder as the song went on. It was distracting and I tried to focus. What did I really want? To be a travel writer who was successful enough to support myself with my earnings. To write travel-writing books in the style of Peter Mayle's *A Year in Provence*. A writer living somewhere scenic and observing the way the locals lived as well as getting to know them and embracing their lifestyle. Gran had given me a copy of that book – she'd always been an avid reader and had built up quite a collection over the years. Although she hadn't been abroad – until visiting Siena with me – she had done a lot of 'armchair travelling' by reading travel-writing books in order to see the world. She also loved television programmes that took her to interesting locations and was particularly fond of Michael Palin.

I'd only been in Siena for half a day, but already knew that three months wasn't going to be enough for me. I needed to find a way to stay for longer, although that seemed like an impossible dream. I couldn't afford to support myself after the course ended in June. Maybe I could get a job, although I wasn't sure how easy it would be to do that with a British passport. Were there visa rules? I needed to find out. The receptionist at the language school had mentioned that I needed to go to the police station and get a permesso di soggiorno that lasted for three months. Was there a way to extend that three months? And I wanted to read the diary while I was here, get a feel for what Peter had lived through during the war, and experience Tuscany in the way that he'd never been able to.

So, that was what I'd wish for – a way to remain in Siena for longer. At least another three months, so I could stay for the whole summer and see the Palio, the horse race in the square that took place in July and August. After what Alessandro had told me that night at dinner, I really wanted to experience it for myself and maybe even write an article to send to a magazine.

'Come on, get on with it, we'll be late. The band starts playing at nine,' Harriet said.

'All right,' I said.

'Don't forget to close your eyes as well.'

I turned my back to the fountain. 'Hold on, which hand?'

She shrugged. 'Well, in Rome it's traditional to throw a coin into the Trevi fountain with your right hand over your left shoulder if you want to return, so perhaps try that?'

Getting into position, I did as Harriet suggested, the coin creating a gentle splash. And I made my wish to stay in Siena for longer than three months – it was done.

'Right, let's go,' Harriet said, and she led me towards one of the tiny streets that went up a steep hill to the Banchi di Sopra, a busy street at the centre of Siena.

Before long, we arrived at a bar with a sign saying BAR ATLANTICO. Inside, the place was bustling, with cocktail waiters shaking their shakers, and loud music played through the speakers and there was the hum of people talking. We went to the bar and Harriet got us pina coladas – gratis apparently as she was friends with the barman. A gregarious type, she seemed to be friends with everyone. I'd never had a pina colada before; I had spent my late teenage years drinking half-pints of lager in the Old Hare, or vodka and orange on special occasions. It tasted of coconut and pineapple and had the consistency of a milkshake. I drank it fairly quickly without realising how strong it was. And before long I felt a little tipsy. And then it struck me – I was living in Italy for the next few months and this was going to be my life. We took our seats at the front, 'Riservato per Harry'.

'I'm their favourite groupie,' she said into my ear as the band started playing 'Don't Stand So Close to Me' by the Police.

They were good, and I was enjoying myself, tapping my foot to the beat and nodding along, mouthing the words, which I knew off by heart. And that was when I saw him, casually leaning on a pillar next to the guitarist, a bottle of beer in his hand, and he was looking directly at me.

Alessandro.

So he was here. He nodded very slightly when our eyes met across the room, and butterflies fluttered in my stomach. Why was he having this effect on me? I gave him a little wave, then self-consciously put my hand back down on my leg, feeling stupid. Was a wave too enthusiastic? He smiled. I looked at the band, pretending to be immersed in their performance, when all I could think was Alessandro had come back after all.

Before long, Fabrizio announced that the band was taking a piccola pausa, and Harriet and I went to the bar and I bought us bottles of beer. Fabrizio came over and double-kissed her, and then me, even though we didn't know each other.

'This is Fabrizio, Jessica,' Harriet said, proudly.

He was blond and nice-looking, and said, 'Ciao, Jessica.'

And then the drummer stepped forward. He had dark hair tied back in a ponytail and, as Harriet had mentioned, seemed to be expecting me.

'Jessica, this is Giuseppe.'

He double-kissed me as well. 'Ciao, Jessica,' he said. 'You come to our place in the country and I make you pasta, okay?'

Nodding, I said, 'Okay.'

'We'll go over one day this week,' Harriet said. 'Their house is in the most beautiful setting right in the heart of the Tuscan countryside. You'll love it.'

Now *this* would be a great experience to write about.

Fabrizio and Giuseppe headed back to the set, and I was about to follow Harriet to our seats when someone tapped me on the shoulder.

Turning round, I saw it was Alessandro.

'Oh, hi,' I said, trying to play it cool. 'So you came back then?'

'I was about to say the same to you,' he said.

'I'm doing a three-month Italian course.'

'No way, I'm actually doing the same, although for six months, until September. The auction house where I work, Pimsy's, has given me study leave as I wanted to learn how to write Italian as well as speak it. Then maybe I can work at the Rome office.'

'So you're going to be here the whole time I am,' I said, the prospect of this giving me a warm feeling inside. 'Are you living with your family?'

He shook his head. 'Oh no, I'm sharing with a roommate, an Australian guy called Matt. What about you?'

'You didn't get my postcard?'

'What postcard?'

I explained.

'Oh, well, post does sometimes get stuck in the internal mail, but I was probably already here when you sent it.'

Thank goodness that I'd managed to bump into him, and on my first night in Siena too. My backup plan had been to leave a note for him in Sofia's pigeonhole too, just in case.

'I'm in Via Vecchia, sharing with a girl called Harriet. Her boyfriend is in the band.'

He took a receipt out of the pocket of his jeans, and asked the barman for a pen. He wrote something on it, tore the receipt in half and handed it to me along with the pen.

'Here's my address. Why don't you write down yours on this half.'

I wrote it down and passed him the piece of paper. He glanced at it and folded the receipt carefully before placing it in the front pocket of his jeans. There were no landlines in flats for foreign students – it was more or less impossible to get one without an Italian passport. The landlord had told me this on the phone when I asked for the number to give to my parents.

'You should come over some time,' he said.

'And you're welcome at mine too,' I said.

His eyes met mine and he smiled.

The band started playing, and I said, 'Well, I'd better get back to my seat.'

'Sure, good to see you, Jessica.'

'See you later.'

I went back over to my seat, sneaking a glance over my

shoulder at him. He was still watching me, a faint smile on his lips, and I sensed my cheeks were warming. Did he like me? And did he really want me to go to his place? I'd like to, but wasn't sure if I would be brave enough to turn up unannounced. Hopefully, he'd make the first move and come over to see me 'some time', as he put it, instead.

CHAPTER 21

JESSICA

The next day, Harriet drove us to Fabrizio and Giuseppe's house in the countryside. It was warm enough for shorts and a t-shirt. Harriet wore a sundress and sunglasses with white frames. She drove us along a narrow street, the car rumbling on the cobblestones, until we reached an arch, a gate in the city wall, which looked very old and descended to the countryside – fields stretching for miles and dotted with farmhouses. We stopped at a supermarket en route to get a few provisions – freshly baked Italian bread, tomatoes as big as your hand, a giant lettuce with frilly leaves, a selection of cheeses, ham and salami, and a couple of bottles of Chianti. There were many vineyards, marked by neat rows of vines and olive groves along the way. We passed through a village, and Harriet took a right through a big arch and uphill along a single-track drive.

We progressed along the lane, bumping up and down on the uneven surface, tall cypress trees on either side swaying gently in the spring breeze. Cicadas chirruped, and birds sang, and it was all quite idyllic.

Harriet pulled up outside an old stone farmhouse with steps going up one side. There was a terrace, covered with plants, and a table underneath, the perfect spot for a long lunch or dinner party.

We got out of the car, and Fabrizio appeared at the top of the steps.

'Ciao, ragazze,' he said.

He came towards us, and Harriet kissed him on the lips, and then he double-kissed me and the two of them spoke in Italian and I had no idea what they were saying, but heard Giuseppe's name mentioned.

And then Fabrizio shouted, 'Giuseppe,' and he appeared at the top of the steps and walked down them, a guitar slung over his shoulders with a strap.

'Ciao,' he said, approaching us and doing the double-kiss.

We went inside, and Fabrizio and Harriet cooked lunch while I sat at the table with a glass of wine and Giuseppe sat by the hearth, strumming his guitar. He seemed like a passionate person. He sang a few Italian songs with great intensity, and every now and again Fabrizio sang along with him, while chopping items for a salad at the sink.

Before long, lunch was ready, and we sat at the table outside with glasses of Chianti, a basket of bread and a huge salad bowl filled with lettuce and slices of tomato and red onion, and basil leaves. And then Fabrizio put steaming bowls of spaghetti carbonara in front of us and a huge piece of Parmesan was passed around the table with a small grater. It was by far the best pasta I'd ever eaten.

'This is delicious,' I said.

'Fabrizio has taught me how to make so many Italian dishes,' Harriet said. 'I'll show you how to make this, Jessica.'

We finished eating, and then Harriet disappeared with Fabrizio to his bedroom, and Giuseppe went back to strumming the guitar in the chair by the hearth. We couldn't speak much as my knowledge of Italian was virtually non-existent and he didn't speak much English apart from words learnt from songs.

He'd jumble them together so his sentences didn't make a lot of sense, and anyone observing us would have found our interactions entertaining. He broke into singing 'More than Words' by Extreme, and looked at me as he sang, 'Saying I love you...' He was clearly trying to seduce me. Smiling to myself, I looked away as he worked his way through the song, putting his whole heart into it. When he'd finished, he put down the guitar and came over to me.

'Jessica, you have beautiful green eyes. Can I kiss you?'

Shaking my head, I said, 'No, although I do appreciate your singing.'

Scrunching up his eyes, he said, 'You love someone else?'

I wasn't in love with Alessandro, but certainly I wanted to spend some time with him and see how things went.

'Not exactly.'

'Well, he is lucky man, whoever he is.'

'Thanks, Giuseppe. That's nice of you to say.'

Harriet came out of Fabrizio's room, finally, while Giuseppe was singing an Italian song I hadn't heard of.

On the drive back, I found myself thinking about Alessandro as I looked out of the car window at the Tuscan countryside whizzing past. I wished it had been him complimenting my eyes, and asking to kiss me, although not while playing the guitar and singing to me. It had felt like a cheesy attempt at seduction, and I found it hard to take Giuseppe seriously. But he seemed like a decent enough bloke who was just trying his luck, and I hoped he wasn't too offended by my turning him down after all his efforts.

CHAPTER 22

JESSICA

It didn't take long to settle into a comfortable routine in Siena. I'd get up at around eight o'clock and go to Bar Lorenzo downstairs for a cappuccino before making my way to class, a five-minute walk away. I was in the beginner's class with students from all over the world. Many of them were American, Australian and English with Italian roots. Everyone was friendly and we'd all have coffee and a pastry during the mid-morning break before returning to class. At lunchtime I'd head back to the flat, stopping at the bakery on Via Vecchia for fresh bread, and then at the greengrocer. Everything was presented beautifully in crates outside the shop. The salad leaves were fresh and crisp, and the tomatoes enormous and sweet. There were oranges that when you sliced them in half were red inside, and red onions, which were much sweeter than white ones. The quality of all the fruit and veg was outstanding, and it was a treat to be able to buy it so easily. I'd never eaten so healthily. There was a small supermarket a few streets away, and I'd go there with Harriet to stock up on cheese and meat and pasta, and of course wine. The selection of local wine was vast, and it was all so reasonably priced compared to at home.

After lunch I'd usually have a nap and then later, after dinner, Harriet and I would go out to a bar nearby and sometimes to a nightclub.

Although I was enjoying living the student life abroad, I was disappointed not to hear from Alessandro. Would I see him again? What had been the point of making such a fuss about exchanging addresses? I guessed that he'd changed his mind about wanting to see me. Either that or he'd lost his piece of paper. As the weeks passed, we still didn't bump into each other, and although I'd look out for him every time I went to Bar Atlantico, there was no sign of him.

Then one morning, during the break from class, I spotted Alessandro at the other end of the bar we often went to for coffee and a bite to eat. He was standing with the bloke he'd been with at Bar Atlantico. They were at the counter with espressos and pastries wrapped in napkins. He hadn't seen me, and I felt certain I couldn't go over to him when he hadn't bothered to get in touch. Why had he asked for my address but done nothing with it? There was a slim chance he'd popped by when I was out, but then wouldn't he have left a note in my pigeonhole? The main door downstairs was usually open during the day, and this was surely what someone would do if you weren't at home.

I was sitting at a table in the corner, tucking into a delicious focaccia sandwich with ham and cheese and some kind of mustard mayonnaise dressing, chatting away to one of the students in my class, when someone tapped me on the shoulder. I turned round to see Alessandro standing there.

'Oh hi,' I said, trying my best to sound nonchalant, although obviously I couldn't have been more pleased to see him again.

'Hey, Jessica. How are you doing?'

Shrugging, I said, 'I'm okay, thanks.' Conscious that I might have some of the sandwich on my face, I wiped round my mouth with a napkin.

'I meant to come by after we saw each other at Bar Atlantico that night, but, well, Benedetto died shortly afterwards.'

Now I felt bad...

'Oh, I'm really sorry, Alessandro. That's so sad. How are you?'

'Thanks, Jessica. His funeral was yesterday. I think everyone in the family is kind of relieved, seeing as he was so unwell for such a long time. He wasn't really living any kind of life. For the past few months, he's been bedridden, unable to do anything for himself. Nonna had to hire a live-in nurse as it was all too much for the au pair to deal with.'

His eyes were filled with sadness, and how I wanted to put my arms round him and give him a big hug. But I didn't know him well enough to do that.

'Oh that's awful. It must have been really hard for your family,' I said.

'Yes, it has been a difficult time. I'm glad I got to know him a little, seeing as we hadn't met until last year. And, well, I do have something to tell you relating to your grandfather, but I'm not sure what you'll think. I was planning to come and see you in the next few days.'

What on earth could Alessandro know about Peter?

'That sounds intriguing. What is it?'

'Nonno told me something on his deathbed. I was the only person in the room at the time, and he wanted me to tell you.'

'What did he say?'

'I'm not really sure how to tell you this, but... Well, he said he wasn't entirely sure your grandfather actually died that night in the woods. It's a whole story, really! Apparently, when Benedetto asked Francesco to return to the scene and bury Peter's body, he felt a faint pulse and carried Peter to a countess's villa. Because Francesco wasn't sure whom he could trust, he planted a fake cross where Peter was supposed to be buried, but didn't tell

Benedetto until years later when he was drunk one night. He claimed that when the Germans shot Peter, the bullet was caught by the diary in the breast pocket of the jacket he was wearing.'

'That would explain the hole in the top right-hand corner, but—.'

'Well, there you go. The diary might have saved his life then, reducing the impact of the bullet. Still, Benedetto wasn't sure whether to believe Francesco, hence why he stuck with the original story when showing you and your grandmother the grave.'

Looking at Alessandro, I didn't know what to think. This was a lot to take in. There must be some mistake, surely? Me and Gran had stood and looked at that cross on the edge of the chestnut woods only months earlier, believing Peter was buried there. What would she think about this revelation? Would she want to know? Should I tell her? And could I trust that Alessandro was telling me the truth? I barely knew him, after all. But then, why would he lie?

'The thought of him surviving is quite bizarre though.'

I reminded Alessandro that Gran had been pregnant with Peter's baby – I'd told him at dinner when visiting Siena with Gran.

His eyes widened.

'Oh yes, now I remember. Wow, the diary really has changed everything for you guys. But how would he have known she was pregnant?'

'She sent him two letters, and he wrote in his diary that he received them. He wasn't sure how to respond. My gran couldn't bear to read the diary herself and so she gave it to me and asked me to tell her if he'd known. I haven't been able to bring myself to yet though.'

'Yikes. I can see why. That must be hard for you, being put in that position.'

'But say he did survive, what could that mean? Surely he would have contacted his mother?'

'Perhaps she might still be around, and you could ask her?'

'I'm not sure how old she'd be if she is still alive. If she was, say, in her forties during the war, it's possible, I suppose.'

'It sounds like you have some research to do.'

'Oh, and he has a sister called Mabel, Gran's friend from school. She lives in America and I've met her a few times. He would have contacted her too.'

'Do you have her address?'

'No, but my gran is still in touch with her. I need to finish reading the diary. Perhaps there's more information in there. It is quite hard going though, and I've been taking my time because I feel so much empathy for my gran. And now, with the possibility of him being alive, well, she'd be devastated to find that out.'

'Yeah, I can imagine,' Alessandro said.

'Maybe I'll wait until I go back to England to tell Gran in person. Perhaps she might want to visit Peter's mother if she still lives in Leeds.'

'Jessica, I'm so sorry to reveal all this to you. I have to get back to class now, but maybe I can drop by some time for coffee and help you come up with a plan?'

'Yes, do that. I'd appreciate the help.' And any opportunity to see him, obviously. Perhaps I could use this as an excuse to spend time with him. Seizing the moment, I added, 'How about Saturday morning?' Harriet would probably stay at Fabrizio's on Friday night, so I'd have the flat to myself.

'Sure, see you then.'

As Alessandro left the bar, I watched him go, struggling to make sense of what he'd just told me. Could Peter still be alive? If he was, how I'd love to track him down and confront him about what he'd done to Gran. But would he want to meet me?

CHAPTER 23

JESSICA

On Saturday morning, I was fast asleep in bed when the intercom buzzed, making me jump out of my skin. Who on earth was it? The buzzing came again, the sound going straight through my head as me and Harriet had been out until three in the morning. We'd drunk a lot of Chianti at the flat, followed by cocktails at Bar Cambio round the corner, and we'd danced for hours. Harriet had gone back to Fabrizio's afterwards, and I'd been looking forward to spending the morning lazing around in bed, writing in my diary and pottering. Climbing out of bed, I went to pick up the handset, my head hurting from all the alcohol consumed the night before. I needed coffee and painkillers.

'Is that you, Jessica?'

Damn, it was Alessandro's voice. My gut leapt. Of course – we'd agreed that he would drop in this morning. I'd wondered if he would actually turn up.

'Oh hello, Alessandro,' I said, my voice all croaky, 'Come on up.'

As I buzzed him in, it struck me that I was wearing a night-dress and hadn't washed yet. After all that dancing the night before in a crowded and sweaty room, I probably did not smell very good at all. There were plenty of stairs for him to climb, and so I raced into the bedroom and pulled on a pair of shorts and a t-shirt, then went into the bathroom to swirl mouthwash, spray myself liberally with perfume and dab foundation on the reddish parts of my face. As I heard his footsteps on the last flight, I quickly applied mascara to my eyelashes. It wasn't my best look, but still a vast improvement, and now I felt able to face him, at least.

A knock came at the door, and I went to open it. He stood there, and oh it was so good to see him, Alessandro, about to step over the threshold into my flat. It was impossible to deny how attractive he was – so tall and dark, and he just had a presence that could be quite intimidating, even though he was grinning at me in a friendly way.

Grinning back, I said, 'Hi.'

'How are you doing?'

'I'm okay, a bit hungover though,' I said, leading him into the kitchen. Harriet and I weren't great at clearing up after our meals, and the counter was littered with dirty dishes. 'Sorry about the mess.' I put the dishes into the sink and gave the table a wipe with a damp cloth, and gestured for him to sit down. 'I was just about to make a fresh pot of coffee. Would you like some?' My voice was all husky from the booze consumed the night before, and I got a bottle of water out of the fridge and swigged it.

'Sure, that would be great.'

He sat down at the table. I filled the base of the silver Italian coffee maker with water, and spooned ground coffee into its centre, then twisted on the top and put it on the hob. Harriet had taught me how to do all this – I'd never seen an Italian coffee maker before, but had become accustomed to drinking espresso every morning.

I stood there, awkwardly, leaning on the counter, while the coffee gurgled away.

'Sorry, I haven't quite woken up yet,' I said.

'Oh?'

'Me and Harriet had a late one. She's at her boyfriend's place but we were up until three and I must admit I was still asleep when you buzzed the intercom.'

'Glad to hear you're enjoying your time in Siena,' he said with a laugh.

When the coffee was ready, I poured espressos for us both and placed the tiny cups with floral patterns on them on the table with a bowl of sugar and teaspoon. I joined him, and our chairs faced the window with a view of the rooftops of Siena and the Tuscan hills beyond. The window was open, and church bells rang in the distance. I really was enjoying living in Italy – it didn't seem real, and every day I felt as though I was living in a Merchant Ivory film.

He stirred a spoonful of sugar into his espresso and knocked it back. 'So, did you find out any more about Peter?' he said.

Shaking my head, I said, 'No, I haven't been able to bring myself to read the diary lately. I feel quite furious with him. But I ought to get back to it soon.'

'I understand. Maybe you need some time?'

'Yeah, I think my gran would probably want to know the truth. It would hurt her though, but also, would it be right not to tell her?'

'I guess you'd need to get your facts right before deciding anything.'

'You have a point, of course. It won't be long before I'm back home anyway. I only have a few weeks left in Siena.'

'What, you're leaving so soon?'

Taking a sip from the bottle of water, I said, 'Yes.'

'Are you ready to go back?'

'No, I love it here. I only wish I could find a way to do

another three-month course and stay until September. I can't afford it though. And if I wanted to earn money, how would I find a job that quickly anyway? I don't think I'm even allowed to work, or whether I need some kind of visa.'

'I'm lucky – I have an Italian passport as well as an American one,' he said.

'So you can live here for as long as you want?'

'I can indeed.'

'How fantastic is that! I'm so jealous.'

'Pretty fantastic,' he said with a grin. He scratched his head. 'Maybe I have an idea...'

'What?'

'Sofia is looking for an au pair.'

'Really? I'm not sure I'd be any good at that. What would it involve, exactly?'

'You'd be more of a companion than anything else. Maybe you'd need to do a little housework when she and Isabella go to their place on the coast. The girl she usually has is going back to the UK in June until September, as her father is unwell. The maid, Carla, works in the mornings and so she keeps Sofia company then. So you'd get until lunchtimes to do what you wanted on weekdays. I think at their place on the coast you get siesta time off instead.'

Standing up, I took the coffee pot off the hob and refilled our cups.

'Are you suggesting I apply for the job?'

'She and Isabella have been interviewing candidates for the past week, and Nonna is rather picky.'

'What's so special about me though?'

'She knew your grandfather and liked him. He saved Benedetto's life on the day they met, remember? So, you kind of have a head start. And she liked you and your gran when you visited.'

'My Italian still isn't that good. How would we talk to each other?'

'You'd be fine. I could help with your Italian if you wanted. And Sofia used to be an Italian teacher in a school, so she could probably help you too. Besides, Isabella's English is quite good seeing as she lived in London when she was a student.'

The thought of Alessandro helping me with my Italian – another excuse to spend time together – was a boost.

'Do you think Sofia really would be interested in employing me?'

'There's no harm in asking. Why don't you leave it with me?'

'I mean, only if you don't mind... My permesso di soggiorno runs out soon though, so I'm not sure if I'd be allowed to stay in Italy for longer?'

'I'm sure you can renew it, but I'll check with Isabella, if she and Sofia are interested in giving you the job. They might invite you over for an interview.'

'That would be very nice of you, thanks.'

'Okay, well, in that case I'd better be going. I'm supposed to be having lunch with Sofia and Isabella today, so I'll mention it then.'

He got up, and pushed his chair under the table. I went with him into the hall.

'See you soon, Jessica,' he said, opening the door. 'I'll be in touch.'

I watched him go down the stairs to the level below, and gave him a little wave, and smiled to myself. Imagine if I got the au pair job? That would mean I wouldn't have to pay for food or board, and I could stay in Siena until September, as long as Alessandro was right about being able to renew my residence permit. It was exciting, but I mustn't get my hopes up in case Sofia wasn't interested – and even if she was, would I be up to such a job?

CHAPTER 24

JESSICA

Harriet stayed at Fabrizio's for the rest of the weekend and, although I'd enjoyed having the flat to myself at first, by Sunday morning I was bored out of my mind. I'd spent the previous evening in Bar Lorenzo – it was the kind of place where I could go alone and write in my diary with a bottle of beer by my side. It would never occur to me to do this in a pub at home but in Italy it seemed socially acceptable to sit in bars alone and spend as long as you wanted there.

I made a pot of coffee and took it back to the bedroom. Filling an espresso cup, I went to stand by the window and looked out at the Tuscan countryside – the view beyond the rooftops of vineyards and countryside in shades of yellow and green never failed to inspire me. I got back into bed and started to write in my diary. Since arriving in Siena, I'd done this daily, recording everything I did. Whatever my mood was like beforehand, I always finished feeling uplifted. The simple act of writing down words on paper, pouring whatever was in my head onto the page, provided a mental release, enabling me to embrace the day. My thoughts turned to Alessandro, and I pictured us the day before, sitting in the kitchen. I'd be quite happy if he dropped in daily to drink coffee and talk to me. His company was undemanding, and I liked being around him. It was interesting how my grandfather's diary had brought us into each other's lives. This seemed significant to me. Were we supposed to know each other? And would he end up finding a way for me to stay in Siena for longer? I couldn't wait to hear what had happened at his lunch with Sofia and Isabella.

I picked up Peter's diary off my bedside table. Since arriving in Siena, I'd kept it there as some kind of companion – it had brought me here, after all. Despite this, I hadn't read much of it since leaving Yorkshire. But now Alessandro had told me about Peter being taken to the countess's villa after being shot, I needed to go back to it. If Peter had survived, had he stayed with the countess? Would the diary tell me if he'd got to know her better before the night in the woods? So far, I only knew that he'd admired her from afar. Had anything happened between them during those difficult wartime months? It would be painful to read that he was seeing another woman while Gran was pregnant with Mum, but I found myself wanting to know the truth. And what if he was still alive? Would visiting his mother and writing to Auntie Mabel open a whole new can of worms that should be left alone?

I opened the diary and lifted the black ribbon from the page where I'd stopped reading the previous time.

9 September 1943

This morning, the lieutenant told us the Italians have joined the Allies and we're free to leave. He advised us not to set off along any roads as the Germans still have a significant presence. The Allied forces are in the south of Italy and he suggested we keep a low profile until they move further north, so we can attempt to join them. He and the other guards have gone, leaving us to fend for ourselves, and we're daunted by

what lies ahead. I asked a local man, Francesco, how we should
go about leaving the castle and he offered to introduce us to a
group of partisans. His friend, Benedetto, is a founding member
of the local group. The partisans are made up of communists,
escaped prisoners of war and fugitive Italian soldiers. They
carry out ambushes with whatever ammunition they can get
their hands on, the downside being the Germans carry out
reprisals in return. He said he'll give me a map and a list of key
Italian phrases, so we'll be ready when it's time to move on.

All this told me was how Peter ended up joining the partisans. I wondered if he'd had any more contact with the contessa
since last writing about her.

That afternoon, I went for a wander around Siena to stretch my
legs, as I'd been doing quite a lot of sitting down while Harriet
was at Fabrizio's. Had Alessandro asked Sofia about the job?
Would she want me to work for her? If she did, would I be able
to do it? As I walked, I decided that if she offered me the position I'd accept and hope for the best – it would mean I could
stay in Siena and see the Palio, and submit an article to the
magazine for expats, *Italian Dreams*. It could be my big chance
to get a piece of travel writing published. Besides, the thought of
spending more time with Alessandro was also an exciting
prospect. When I got back to the flat, there was a note in my
pigeonhole, and I unfolded it. A business card fell onto the floor,
and I picked it up. It had the contact details for Isabella Sabatini
on it, including her mobile phone number – she was a dermatol-
ogist at the hospital.

Jessica,

You've got the job!

Starts at the beginning of June.

Isabella said it wouldn't be a problem to renew your permesso di soggiorno. She'll give you the number of her contact at the police station. Give her a call to make arrangements.

Congratulations!

Al

I'd got the job without an interview? What on earth had Alessandro said on my behalf? Whatever he'd said to Isabella and Sofia, I was grateful to him. Had he helped get me the job so he could see more of me? I wanted to think this but doubted it very much. Surely he was just being nice...?

CHAPTER 25

JESSICA

At the beginning of June, I moved out of the flat in Via Vecchia. Sad to leave the place I'd called home for the past few months, I carried my suitcase down the stairs. Harriet came with me to Bar Lorenzo, where I called a taxi.

'Well, J, I shall see you at the Palio,' she said.

Harriet had taken to calling me 'J' in recent weeks, and I quite liked it.

'I hope you have an amazing time travelling around Italy, lucky you,' I said.

Harriet was going on tour with Azzurro – they'd be playing at bars and clubs around the country – and she'd also spend a few weeks at Fabrizio's family home in a small town on the Amalfi coast. I did envy her getting to see more of Italy, and the Amalfi coast was supposed to be especially beautiful. I'd have loved to travel around, but couldn't afford it, and now I would be working full time anyway. Maybe one day, but for now I was grateful to have the chance to stay in Siena. At least I'd get to see the Tuscan coast, known as the Maremma, on the Tyrrhenian Sea, when I went to Sofia and Isabella's villa in Castiglione della Pescaia.

We'd agreed to go to the August Palio together – Isabella had said we'd be at their villa on the coast when the July one took place.

'And I hope you get it on with Alessandro,' Harriet said.

'Oh stop it!' I said, my face no doubt reddening.

'Come on, I know something is going to happen with you two.'

'I'm happy to be friends with him...' I said.

This wasn't entirely true, but I didn't want to admit it even to myself. What kind of future did we have even if he did like me? Before long, he'd be back in America and I would be stuck in Little Vale. We'd be miles away from each other, and flights were bound to be expensive even if we did embark on a long-distance relationship. There were so many obstacles to us being together, it all seemed impossible. But I needed to stay optimistic. Who knew what might happen over the summer months?

The taxi arrived and the driver put my suitcase in the boot.

I gave Harriet a big hug, and got into the back of the car and waved goodbye. She was such a fun friend to have, and I liked the way she took me out of my comfort zone. I'd never known anyone with such a zest for living. She was the kind of person who made the most of every moment and I found this inspiring. We'd talked about me going to stay with her in London when I got back to England.

The taxi driver took me to Via San Marco at the other side of Siena. When I arrived, Carla, the maid, answered the intercom and let me in. I went through the big old door and climbed the stairs. When I reached the top, she was standing there, and couldn't have had a more unfriendly look on her face. It wasn't the best welcome.

'Buongiorno,' I said.

'Buonasera,' she replied.

Of course, it was after lunch, and I'd forgotten the appropriate greeting. It felt as though she was telling me off. She gestured for me to follow her. Leaving my suitcase by the front door, I went with her along the hall into a kitchen-diner, where Sofia sat in an armchair watching television. The vast sash windows were pushed up to the top. Washing hung on a line outside, sheets billowing in the breeze.

'Buonasera, Jessica,' Sofia said.

I approached her and said, 'Buonasera.'

Isabella came into the room. She wore a pale-grey trouser suit, and looked very stylish.

'Jessica, you are here,' she said. 'We are glad to welcome you to the family.'

It was helpful that Isabella spoke English. My Italian wasn't that impressive after three months of classes where we'd mostly practised asking where the bank or the beach was, or learnt how to buy a coffee.

'Come with me, Jessica,' she said, leading me down the hall to a small bedroom near the front door and away from the rest of the flat. It was opposite the utility room where the washing machine shook during its spin cycle, but I was glad to have a room of my own again after sharing with Harriet. Through the window, I caught sight of a small square with its own church, a fountain, the soporific sound of trickling water, and a cluster of trees with benches in the shade underneath. I'd enjoy sitting on the vast windowsill and watching life go by. On the opposite side of the square was a bar with tables outside and terracotta pots brimming with brightly coloured flowers. I pictured myself going there for coffee and pastries.

'This will be your room,' Isabella said. 'I'll leave you to unpack for half an hour or so, then come into the kitchen and I'll give you your tasks for the day.'

'All right. Grazie, Isabella.'

I went to get my suitcase from by the front door, and hung my dresses in the old mahogany wardrobe, which had a mottled full-length mirror on the front. There was also a chest of drawers and a single bed – with folded-up bedding – running alongside the wall, and a bedside table and lamp. I looked forward to sitting in bed with the window open when writing in my diary. Unfolding the bedding, I put on the sheet and duvet cover and pillowcase, then lay down and closed my eyes for a moment. People walking past below chattered and there was the usual buzz of mopeds and rumble of cars on cobblestones. The church bells rang twice to mark two o'clock. Although I liked this room, would I be all right here in this flat? Already, I felt a little trapped, as if the freedom I'd gained when living with Harriet had been taken away again. I was almost worse off than at home. But I mustn't forget the reasons why I'd wanted to stay in Siena for longer – to see the Palio, to get to know Alessandro, and to avoid having to face Tom. I'd written to Mum to explain that I'd be staying in Siena until September, and asked her to pass on the information to him. And I'd called work to ask if they could keep my job open for longer. Mr Carter had said he'd do his best, but couldn't guarantee anything. It was a risk, but losing my job would force me to try to get work doing the travel writing I really wanted to do.

I got off the bed and returned to the kitchen, and Isabella pointed to the ironing board. On it was a basket filled with washing taken off the line.

'Allora, Jessica, there is the ironing for today. Sofia will stay in here with you. The main part of your role will be to keep Mamma company and get her anything she needs. Please can you give her pills at five o'clock – they are on the side there.'

Ironing? There had been no mention of my least favourite task ever when we'd made arrangements on the phone! Oh well, I'd just have to get on with it and remember why I was here. And give Sofia pills? – that seemed like such a big responsibility.

'Are you sure you trust me to give your mother pills?' I said.

'Certo. There is a note in English, explaining which ones

and how many. At six o'clock, I'll be back, and then you prepare dinner. I give you instructions later. Now I have to go back to the hospital for my afternoon shift.'

Isabella gave me a wave goodbye, and I was left alone with Sofia. I wasn't sure what we'd talk about as my Italian still wasn't good enough to have much of a conversation. I would go through the book I'd been given while studying and try to improve my grammar and learn more vocabulary. Looking over at the sofa, I saw Sofia had dozed off, and so I plugged in the iron and lifted the pile of clothes out of the basket. I began to press one of Isabella's shirts, starting with the arms. Hopefully I'd get to see Alessandro every now and again, and that had to be a perk. I'd found myself lately wondering what it would be like to kiss him. Did he like me in that way? He looked at me as though he did, but still I wasn't entirely sure – maybe he was like that with all the girls he met. Some men were, weren't they, especially nice-looking ones like him? He and his flatmate Matt probably went out every night and had girls falling all over them. Why would he want to know me when he had all the girls in Siena at his disposal?

CHAPTER 26

JESSICA

Within just a few days, I'd settled into a new routine with the Sabatinis. As Alessandro had mentioned, I didn't have to work until midday because Carla came in the mornings, so I'd get up early and make the most of my time off. By nine o'clock, I'd be dressed and ready to leave the flat for three hours of me-time in Siena, and I loved every second of it. I'd amble down the hill towards the centre and find a bar in a small side street. There I'd order a cappuccino and a pastry – I'd become fond of brioches, which were a little like croissants but the same shape as a pain au chocolat, filled with custard or marmalade and dusted with icing sugar. They were absolutely delicious. I would find a table outside and write letters to Mum, Dad and Gran. Sometimes I'd buy a postcard with a beautiful photo of Siena or the Tuscan scenery and send that instead. Then I'd write in my diary. I'd play around with ideas for articles about living in Siena as a twenty-something English woman. And then I'd wander the streets, stopping at a bookshop near the square and skim the shelves for books written in English. Sometimes I'd go and sit down on the red bricks in the Piazza del Campo. There would often be people sitting, in groups or alone, watching life go by.

I'd just soak up the atmosphere – and couldn't remember the last time I'd felt so relaxed and at peace with life.

After this lovely morning I usually walked back to the flat, ready to take over from Carla in the kitchen. She would prepare lunch and I'd serve it up for Sofia and Isabella, who'd return from work for a break until her afternoon shift. The only thing missing was Alessandro – I hadn't seen or heard from him, and hoped he'd drop round at least to see his relatives soon.

One evening, I was reading Peter's diary in bed – I was almost at the end – and found a mention of Benedetto and that fateful night. Or was it a fateful night? I still didn't know.

20 September 1943

I'm living in the woods with the partisans, a group of around seventy escaped prisoners of war of various nationalities including Americans and South Africans; and fugitive Italian soldiers. We're not far from the castle. A man called Benedetto's in charge, a competent leader. We get food from foraging, farmers and the countess. The countess helps our group in every way she can and provides us with information on the whereabouts of the Allies. However, she still hasn't noticed me, seeing as she mostly communicates with Benedetto. I live in hope that one day she might set those eyes on me.

I'd grown used to an almost leisurely lifestyle in the castle, but after days of sleeping rough I'm exhausted and hungry and I fear for my life every minute I'm awake. After the armistice the Italians were under the impression the war was more or less over. But the Germans have such a foothold in their country that the arrival of the Allies will be the only way to get rid of them. We live in hope that the Allies will land on the Tuscan coast or that they'll advance north before the Germans get to us.

Writing has stopped me from going insane, as it did for Eleanor's father in the trenches. It helps to clear my mind so I

*can sleep. I must note down a concern which gnaws at my
insides. There's to be a drop of much-needed ammunition
tomorrow by the Allies and Benedetto wants me to accompany
him. A man named Luigi gave Benedetto the information this
morning. Francesco warned me last week that he has reserva-
tions about Luigi. Some say he's a spy and that he used to live
in a house with a group of fascists. I passed this information on
to Benedetto, who tried to reassure me Luigi can be trusted. My
gut tells me Francesco is right, as Luigi can't look another man
in the eye. However, the opportunity to get more guns and
shells is too good to miss. I do hope my gut is mistaken.*

So, Peter seemed to have a hunch that the supply drop in
the chestnut woods would go wrong. Perhaps it had been a trap
so the Germans could attempt to shoot him, and Benedetto,
who'd clearly managed to get away. Oh, why hadn't Benedetto
listened to his concerns? They must have been in desperate
need of ammunition, and he thought trusting Luigi was worth
the risk. I liked that Peter had found solace in writing down his
thoughts and feelings as I did when keeping my own diary.
Despite my fury with him for abandoning Gran in her hour of
need – and his obvious infatuation for the countess – I liked it
that we shared this urge to write every day, a passion passed
down from one generation to another.

The next morning when I went to the kitchen to make a cup of
tea, Isabella was leaning on the counter, an espresso in one hand
and a cigarette in the other.

I filled the kettle and switched it on.

'Buongiorno, Jessica,' she said. 'Seeing as it is Sofia's eight-
ieth birthday party this evening, Carla will stay on after lunch to
prepare the food. You will need to assist her with whatever she
needs.'

Carla wasn't that friendly towards me, so I didn't relish the thought of working more closely with her. But it struck me that Alessandro had been invited to this party. I knew this because I'd written the invitations using a list given to me by Isabella. As far as I knew, he hadn't RSVPd. Did he think it wasn't necessary as he'd obviously attend his grandmother's special birthday party? I wasn't sure, but really hoped he'd turn up.

'Va bene,' I said.

That afternoon in the kitchen, Carla clicked her tongue as I poured out the prosecco. The bubbles raced to the top of the flutes, fizzing onto the table, and I blotted the mess with a tea towel.

'Madonnina!'

'What is it?' I said.

Carla dropped a courgette flower, stuffed with ricotta and dipped in batter, into the deep-fat fryer and it hissed. She wiped her hands on her apron and took the bottle from me. Holding the bottle the way I had, with one hand at the base and the other round the neck, she wagged a forefinger at me.

'You don't do it like that.' Instead, holding the bottle at its base with both hands, she filled an empty flute. 'You do it like this.' This method worked perfectly, and I hated to admit it, but she was right. She plonked the bottle on the table and returned to the hob.

'Thanks,' I mumbled, and opened another bottle, holding a tea towel on top of the cork and twisting it the way Carla had shown me earlier. The cork popped and the prosecco burst out of the bottle like a fountain, drenching the table around it.

'Oh no, I don't believe it.'

Getting tea towels out of the drawer, I mopped up the prosecco, which was now running along the table and dripping onto the floor. I'd never really done much to help at home – Mum preferred to do everything herself – and I wasn't cut out for all this.

Shaking her head, Carla retrieved a courgette flower from the deep-fat fryer with a pair of tongs, then placed it in a basket lined with a napkin.

'Mamma mia!' she said.

In need of a break, I went over to the open window and leant out of it, taking in Siena. Being June, it was now baking hot all of the time, and humidity hung over the city like a wool blanket. Every single window along Via San Marco was open and I listened to the voices of Italians in their kitchens, preparing their dinners. The aromas of onions, garlic and tomatoes filled the air. A moped buzzed past with a couple squeezed onto its seat, the girl tightening her grip round the boy's waist as they bounced over the cobblestones a little faster than they ought to.

I had no idea why Carla disliked me. I'd expected the maid to be on my side – we were the hired help, after all – and it was disappointing to find out she wasn't. The previous week, she'd sent me to the shop over the road with a fifty-thousand-lire note to get basil, black peppercorns and Parmesan. When I got back, I handed her the groceries with the change and receipt, but she told Isabella that I hadn't given her all of the change. After some discussion, I ended up giving Isabella twenty thousand lire of my own money, almost half of what she paid me every week. This had left me with a bad feeling, and it meant that I needed to have my wits about me when around Carla.

The thought of going to the Palio as well as seeing Alessandro again had kept me going. When I walked around Siena each morning, I always hoped to bump into him. I knew where he'd be during morning breaks from his class, but couldn't exactly go to that bar now I wasn't studying at the language school any more. Wouldn't it be too obvious that I was looking for him? I'd considered walking down the street where the bar was located when he'd be arriving or returning from his break, but hadn't yet plucked up the courage. If he turned up at the party, it would really make my night.

Sofia shuffled into the kitchen. Glancing at the clock on the wall, I saw the party was due to start in twenty minutes and she was still in the nightdress she wore for her afternoon siesta. Oh dear. When I'd finished filling the flutes, I needed to set the scene in the living room – light candles and put on music before the guests arrived. Why wasn't Sofia getting ready?

'Have you seen my teeth, dear?' she said.

Oh no, not again. They seemed to disappear all the time, as Sofia liked to take them out when she was sitting down and relaxing. Looking round the kitchen, I spotted them, floating in a glass of water on top of the television.

'There they are,' I said.

Sofia used a hand to fish them out and slotted them into place.

'Grazie, cara.' She liked to call me 'cara', meaning 'dear' in Italian.

Lowering herself onto the sofa, she picked up the remote control. 'Can I smell courgette flowers? Ask Carla to bring me one, will you.' She pressed a few buttons on the remote, then said, 'Help me with this, cara. I wonder if *Columbo* is on tonight.'

She handed me the remote control, and I put it on the table and sat down beside her.

'But you need to get ready for your party, Sofia.'

Shrugging, she said, 'Mah, what party?'

'Your birthday party. The guests will arrive soon. Some of them are driving back from the coast, especially for you.'

'They're not doing it for me. The guests are all Isabella's friends.'

'You must have some friends coming?'

'All of my friends are dead, cara, or have lost their minds.'

I racked my brain, trying to remember who was invited.

Sofia must at least like one of the guests. Liliana, a beauty thera-pist in her fifties, was one of her few contacts with the outside world. She came to the flat once a month to give Isabella a facial, then Sofia would have a mani-pedi. She looked forward to Liliana's visits, and I guessed she liked having someone listen to her talk for a whole hour.

'What about Liliana?'

'Oh, is Liliana coming?'

'I think so. And possibly Alessandro? Surely you'd like to see your grandson?' I said in a matter-of-fact voice, as though his presence would make no difference to me whatsoever.

Beaming, she said, 'Of course, how could I forget bello Alessandro? He rang this morning, and spoke to Carla.'

Standing up, I made a thing of plumping the cushions on the sofa, doing my best to hide that this newsflash pleased me a great deal.

'There you are then. You really ought to get ready.' Holding out a hand, I said, 'Come on, I'll help you.'

'I can't wait to see my grandson again,' Sofia said, her eyes shining, but she remained firmly seated. Getting her ready for the party was clearly going to be one of those tasks.

Isabella tip-tapped into the kitchen in a pair of heels several inches high. She wore a fitted white dress that clung to her incredible suntanned figure. Looking at her, it occurred to me that she was only a few years younger than Mum, but so glam-orous, and she really seemed to have her life together. And there was Mum stuck in a kitchen all day, cooking and cleaning for Dad and Gran, with nothing of her own. However, she was a much warmer person. I didn't want to become like either of them, but wouldn't mind being somewhere in between, with a thriving career and still being able to wear a dress like that in my forties.

'Mamma, why isn't Jessica helping you get ready?' Isabella said.

Sofia shrugged and said, 'Mah.'

'We were about to get started,' I said.

Isabella rolled her eyes. 'You need to hurry up, Mamma. The guests will be here soon.'

I couldn't help noticing her dangly earrings, the tiny diamonds – knowing Isabella, they would be real – catching the early-evening sunlight coming through the window.

'Can't you help me get ready, cara?' Sofia said to Isabella.

Isabella lit a cigarette and took a long, deep drag. She did seem to be stressed all of the time, and this was understandable, considering the long, intense shifts she did at the hospital, often performing surgery. And then when she came home she had her mother to deal with. But sometimes I found her unnecessarily cold, and wondered if she had a nurturing bone in her body.

'Tiziano's waiting for me in the living room, so Jessica will need to do it. She is more than capable of dressing you, for good-ness' sake. And Jessica, before I forget, Tiziano's having a dinner party in Follonica on the day of the Palio in August. We'll have to stay at the villa in Castiglione della Pescaia, and you will need to be there to look after Mamma.'

What? Isabella was breaking her promise. I'd stressed on the phone when discussing the job how important it was that I get to see the Palio so I could write an article about it for *Italian Dreams* magazine. And Harriet was coming back to Siena too, so she could write about it in her dissertation for university. We were already missing the July one because we'd be at the coast, and that couldn't be changed because Isabella was having work done on the pool and wanted to be there.

'You agreed that I could take the afternoon off to see it,' I said.

'Well, that won't be possible now,' Isabella said, flicking cigarette ash out of the window.

'Don't any of you want to see the Palio?'

'Oh no, we've seen it many times, and like to get away from the crowds.'

I needed to find a way to persuade her to let me go, but this wasn't the time.

'I'd like to discuss the matter further, although not now, obviously.'

'We can discuss it tomorrow, if we must. Can you get Mamma dressed right away, please, Jessica.'

Being spoken to like this was getting a bit much. Now there was a chance I'd miss the Palio, the thought of seeing Alessandro was all that kept me from walking out and getting the first flight home, even though that would mean facing Tom and my life there. Approaching the sofa, I held out my hands and helped pull Sofia up.

'I'd like you to help me get dressed, Isabella,' Sofia said. 'I need to look bellissima for my own party.'

'Mamma, I need to greet the guests though.'

Did she care about her mother at all?

'Jessica is more than capable of looking after them,' Sofia said.

Isabella squashed her cigarette in the ashtray, and shook her head.

'Va bene. Let's go then, Mamma.'

Sofia gripped her arm, and they began to move slowly down the hall.

CHAPTER 27

JESSICA

Candles flickered on the mantelpiece under Benedetto's portrait, and the opera *Cavalleria Rusticana* came from the speakers. The music was beautiful, although it was intense and didn't suit what was meant to be a happy occasion, but Isabella had passed me the CD and told me to put it on. Guests filled the living room, the scent of their perfume and aftershave mixing with the vanilla-scented candles. Fans whirred in the corners, but they did little to reduce the temperature. Alessandro was nowhere to be seen, and I hoped he just hadn't arrived yet rather than decided not to come after all. Scanning the room in case I'd missed him, my eyes met with those of Sofia's son, Enzo. His belly bulged so much, the buttons on his shirt looked as if they were about to pop. He ran a hand through his dyed hair and winked at me and I turned away, feeling sick. He'd dropped in to the flat a few times since I'd started working for the Sabatinis and, he always looked at me for longer than was appropriate. I didn't like him at all.

Many of the guests were smoking, fumes floating up to the ceiling, and so I went over to the windows and pushed them up as far as they'd go. Dusk hung over the city, and the streetlamps had now come on. Singing came from the Chiocciola contrada headquarters nearby. No doubt they were holding one of their dinners in the run-up to the Palio. The anthem for all the contrade used the same tune, but each had different words. I really had to find a way to persuade Isabella to let me stay in Siena for the Palio so I could write my article. Going round the room emptying ashtrays, I saw that Sofia was sitting next to Liliana on the chaise longue. Liliana was showing Sofia a photograph and they leant towards each other as they spoke, as if they were up to something. Sofia had selected a black dress from her wardrobe, and her white curls were scraped into a bun. She wore a necklace with an emerald pendant, and I was glad that Isabella had helped make her look glamorous for the occasion after all.

Approaching them, I said, 'Can I get you anything, Sofia?'

She looked up. The skin on her face was usually pale, because she stayed out of the sun, but Isabella had applied blusher, a little too much, and she wore bright-pink lipstick on her thin lips. She smiled as though she was enjoying herself and I was pleased for her.

'This music's too sad. We need something more lively. What shall we put on, Liliana?' she said.

'Something from *Rigoletto*?' Liliana said.

'What a wonderful idea. Jessica, put on "La donna è mobile". Pavarotti sings it beautifully.'

'Va bene. If I can find it,' I said.

Sofia sipped her prosecco and stuck out her tongue. 'Jessica, I can't bear this fizzy wine. Fetch the bottle of grappa, will you, cara?'

Grappa was the spirit that Harriet referred to as paint stripper. It was very potent indeed. I went to change the CD, as instructed, then filled two shot glasses with grappa and handed them to Sofia and Liliana. Sofia knocked hers back in one go, and beamed, while Liliana eyed her glass with suspicion.

'Is that really Pavarotti? I can't hear him at all.' Sofia adjusted her hearing aid, and then held out the empty glass. 'Turn it up, cara, and bring me another.'

I went over to adjust the volume on the stereo and picked up the bottle of grappa again. But then when I turned round, there he was. Alessandro. He had his back to me, and he was talking to Sofia and Liliana. A queasy feeling overwhelmed me. The thought of us interacting filled me with dread, and so I turned round and snuck off to my bedroom, taking the grappa with me.

In my room, I sat on the bed. It was baking hot even with the window open and a fan switched on. Mopping my brow, I took a swig from the bottle of grappa, telling myself that Alessandro had no idea I found him attractive. Plus, I was being paid to do a job here. I returned to the party. My confidence was boosted by the booze and I tried not to giggle to myself – it felt quite rebellious getting tipsy when I was supposed to be working.

Carla was placing espresso cups in front of Sofia and Liliana as they sang along to 'Nessun Dorma', swaying from side to side. One shot of grappa had clearly been enough for both of them. I picked up a plate of calamari and passed it around, and then there was Alessandro, heading in my direction. I needed to compose myself. Pushing my shoulders back, I did my best to wipe the grappa-fuelled grin from my face.

He picked up a ring of calamari from the plate I was holding. Wearing a white shirt that brought out his suntan, he looked especially handsome. His sleeves were rolled up to the elbows and the collar was undone a couple of buttons, showing the hair on his chest.

'How are you doing, Jessica?' He bit into the calamari with a crunch.

'I'm all right, you?' I took a piece of calamari as well, feeling the need to soak up the grappa.

He swigged his bottle of beer. 'I'm okay. Are you enjoying the new job?'

What could I say? It wasn't that easy, but the Sabatinis were his relatives. Sofia was all right, but Isabella and Carla were cold and mean a lot of the time. I enjoyed my mornings ambling around in my daydream world, but was paid hardly anything and couldn't go anywhere without Isabella's permission from lunchtimes onward. In order to reply, I swallowed the calamari too quickly, and a piece of batter got stuck in my throat and I started to cough.

He patted me on the back.

'Are you okay?' Handing me his bottle of beer, he said, 'Here, have some of this.'

I took a swig and washed the piece of batter down. 'Thanks.'

'Has it gone?' he said.

I nodded, my eyes watering slightly and cheeks no doubt the colour of beetroot. Keen to move the conversation on, I asked, 'So, where are you living?'

'By the Duomo.'

'Right in the centre then. Handy.'

'It is, although not so great on a Sunday morning when the bells ring non-stop and your head hurts from the night before,' he said.

I laughed. 'Oh dear.'

He grinned and moved closer, then spoke into my ear. 'You see that woman with Sofia?' He nodded in Liliana's direction.

When he spoke, his breath brushed my neck, and a rush of longing caught me by surprise. I tightened my ponytail in order to do something with my hands.

'That's Liliana, her beauty therapist.'

'Well, she wants me to ask her niece on a date so I can help with her English.' He lifted his eyebrows.

The niece was probably an Italian beauty with dark hair, and huge brown eyes with eyelashes like spiders' legs. Nodding,

I forced a smile, envy tugging at my gut. Was he telling me this to make me jealous?

'Good for you.'

'She even showed me a photograph.'

So that was what Sofia and Liliana had been planning. What did he want me to say? Go for it, fall in love with some Italian beauty when I'm standing right here?

He put his empty beer bottle on the side. I took another one out of the ice bucket, lifted the cap with a bottle opener and handed it to him.

Smiling, he took it.

'Are you trying to get me drunk?'

That wasn't a bad idea. Then at least we could have a frank conversation about why he wanted me to know so much.

'Of course not. What did you tell Liliana then?'

'I said classes are keeping me busy, with all the assignments.'

'You're not going to meet her?'

He looked me in the eye. 'She doesn't interest me.'

How I wanted to be the girl who did. Picking up an empty glass from on top of the piano, I said, 'Of course. Well, I'd better do some work before Isabella tells me off.'

'Sure.'

I headed for the kitchen, unable to wipe the huge smile from my face.

CHAPTER 28

JESSICA

At midnight, Isabella switched on the lights like a pub landlady at closing time, instantly brightening the room. She had to get up early for a shift at the hospital, but the party was in full swing. Quite a few couples were dancing to the song 'Volare', and everyone seemed to be enjoying themselves. Sofia hadn't moved from the chaise longue all evening, and a queue formed as guests lined up to say goodbye and exchange double kisses. I collected glasses from around the room and placed them on a tray. But as I carried the tray into the kitchen, Carla pushed past me, armed with a pile of plates, and the glasses rocked. I managed to steady them with my hand, and a wave of relief swept over me. What a disaster that would have been. Looking over my shoulder, I saw Carla shaking her head as if she'd wanted me to drop the tray. But then I bumped straight into someone coming from the other direction and this time I couldn't stop the glasses from crashing to the floor.

'Oh noooo.' I said, looking at the broken glass and spilt left-over drinks splattered across the white marble floor. All eyes were on me and the room fell silent, apart from Modugno singing, 'blue, painted in blue,' in a cheery voice. I couldn't have felt more stupid as I squatted on the floor, picking up the larger shards of glass while trying not to cut my hands. Tears pricked my eyes.

'I'm so sorry.' Alessandro's voice came from above me. Of all the people I could have bumped into. He joined me on the floor and helped place the bigger pieces of glass on the tray.

'It's my fault. I wasn't looking where I was going,' I said.

He didn't say anything. Some of the guests had formed a circle around us, but Alessandro stood up, ushering them away.

'Tutto va bene,' he said.

Carla looked down at me, and smirked as she stepped over the broken glass and went into the kitchen. How dare she! Isabella came over, a cigarette dangling between her fingers.

'What happened?' she asked, her face all scrunched up.

I was about to apologise, but Alessandro said, 'It was my fault, Aunt Isabella. Can I replace them?' He threw me a leave-this-to-me look, and so I carried on clearing up the glass as best I could.

I didn't know what to think. Did Alessandro like me or just feel sorry for me?

'It doesn't matter, Alessandro,' Isabella said, throwing him a smile. 'Carla bought them in the sale this morning. Jessica, why don't you fetch a broom and pan.'

Following her instructions, I went into the kitchen. Carla hummed 'La donna è mobile' as she scraped leftovers into the bin.

Battling with fury as it raced through me, I said, 'Why did you do that, Carla?'

Turning her back to me, she bent down to put some cutlery into the dishwasher. 'Do what?' she said, standing back up.

'You pushed past me on purpose so I'd drop those glasses.' My voice was shaking, and I told myself to take a breath.

She wagged a finger at me, her lips pursed. 'You au pairs

think that because you study, you are better than me. Some of you steal husbands.'

Pulling out the top drawer of the dishwasher, she started to load it with glasses. 'Isabella's life is over because of a girl like you.'

'What are you talking about?'

'Her husband ran off with the Swedish au pair who worked for this family.'

I couldn't believe Carla was judging me based on this other au pair's behaviour. There were no words to say. And how had this not been a problem with the au pair who'd gone back to England for the summer? It couldn't have been if she was coming back in September, surely? Carla slammed the dishwasher door shut and ran a damp cloth over the marble worktop. It had only been a few weeks, but I wasn't sure that I could stick living with the Sabatinis for much longer, especially now Isabella was saying I couldn't go to the Palio. But I wasn't ready to go home yet either.

Carla removed her apron, got her handbag off the sideboard and pulled it over her shoulder. As she left the room, it struck me that she was going to do all she could to get rid of me. Was I ready to go into battle with her? And was it worth it? I'd have to find a way to go to the Palio to make it worth putting up with her.

I went back to clear up the rest of the glass, using the broom to sweep it into the pan, savouring the silence now the guests had left and the music had stopped playing. Sensing someone was behind me, I turned round, bracing myself for Isabella or Carla. But it was Alessandro.

'Are you okay?'

I stopped sweeping and leant on the broom. 'I'm all right,' I said with a laugh. 'Thanks for what you did.'

'No problem. Are they giving you the mornings off like they're meant to?'

Did he want to meet up with me?

'Yes, as Carla's here.'

'What do you do?'

'I wander round Siena and stop at a bar to get coffee. Then I look in the bookshop on Via Banchi di Sopra.'

'Would you like to—'

Isabella appeared. *Great.* I went back to sweeping up the glass.

'Alessandro, you must go and see your nonna before leaving. She is complaining that she hasn't seen you all evening.'

'Sure, Zia. See you later, Jessica.' He gave me a nod and followed Isabella into the living room.

Isabella had ruined our moment. I hoped he'd find another way to ask me to meet up with him. I didn't hold out much hope that anything would happen between us, and couldn't wait to go to bed and forget about the disastrous end to the evening. Perhaps tomorrow would be a better day.

CHAPTER 29

JESSICA

The next morning, I did my best to forget the night before and followed my usual routine. After a cappuccino and brioche, I went to have a browse in the bookshop. I picked up *Summer's Lease* by John Mortimer and skimmed the blurb: 'Part social comedy, part murder mystery set in a Tuscan villa'. Isabella paid me so little, I needed to save my cash for cappuccinos and pastries, so couldn't afford it. I read the blurb again and ran my hand over the smooth cover. The words didn't sink in because I kept replaying the party in my head. Alessandro had taken the blame when it was me who'd broken the glasses – although he had played a part in the whole fiasco by bumping into me. It seemed like he didn't want me to get into trouble and lose my job. He cared about me and didn't want me to go anywhere. Was that what his actions meant? Surely the way he'd looked at me when he told me Liliana's niece didn't interest him suggested he liked someone else romantically. Could it be me...? Feeling his breath on my neck when he'd whispered in my ear had reminded me how attractive I found him. And then when he took responsibility for the broken glasses, we were a team, united against everyone in that room. Before Isabella interrupted us, had he been about to ask me to meet him? I found myself thinking about Alessandro a lot of the time. Tom had never monopolised my thoughts in the same way. He'd often appear in my head at unexpected moments when I was carrying out mundane tasks around the flat such as sweeping or ironing, or scrubbing pasta sauce off saucepans at the sink.

'Jessica?'

A hand touched my shoulder, making me jump out of my skin, and I shrieked like a small child. Alessandro was the only person who said my name like that, in his sexy New Jersey drawl. I turned round to see him standing there, a newspaper tucked under his arm. I made a meal of squeezing the novel between two other books on the shelf.

'Oh hi,' I said, trying to act as though he hadn't been in my thoughts only moments earlier.

He wore a white t-shirt that was so creased it could have been slept in, and the lower half of his face was covered in stubble. The just-rolled-out-of-bed-look suited him. Hold on, had he remembered that I came to the bookshop every morning?

'Have you recovered from yesterday?' he said.

I had now. I slid my hands into the pockets of my skirt.

'Yes. Thanks again for what you did.'

He adjusted the sunglasses pressed into his hair. 'You're welcome.' He had huge bags under his beautiful dark-brown eyes.

'Did you have a late night?' I asked.

'Me and Matt went to a club after Sofia's party.'

I pictured him and Matt standing on the periphery of a dancefloor, holding bottles of beer. Imagining them chatting up girls, a pang of jealousy swept through me.

He glanced at his watch. 'I've got ten minutes left of my break. Do you want to get a coffee?'

My answer was of course yes, but I needed to play it cool.

Matt came over, and I hoped he wasn't about to spoil the special moment we were having. People needed to stop interrupting when Alessandro was asking me to spend time with him.

'Are you ready, Al?' Matt said.

'I'll see you back in class,' Alessandro said.

Matt looked at us and threw him a knowing look.

'See you later, mate.' He slapped Alessandro on the back and winked at me.

I could feel my face warming and hoped it hadn't gone the colour of beetroot. Clearly, they'd talked about me.

'Okay, buddy.' Alessandro rolled his eyes and I squashed a smile.

Matt left the bookshop, and I was glad that it was just the two of us again.

We sat at a table overlooking the Piazza del Campo. A waitress went round the room, collecting empty cups and saucers and putting them on a tray. Through the open window, I could see tourists milling about in shorts and t-shirts, some of them with skin sunburnt lobster pink. The Mangia Tower opposite dominated the skyline, and no doubt it could be seen for miles. A tour party followed a guide who held a stick with a flag attached. Pigeons flew out of their path, squawking and flapping their wings. The guide stopped and pointed her stick at the bell tower, her voice resonating off the buildings as the party gathered around her.

Alessandro bit into his sandwich. He ate it with great enthusiasm, no doubt to soak up what he'd drunk the night before. I took in the view, content just to be properly alone with him for the first time in a while.

When he'd finished eating, he wiped his mouth with a napkin.

'This bar would be a good place to get a beer before the Palio.'

I'd forgotten Isabella's broken promise. I needed to speak to her, once she'd calmed down about the broken glasses. It might be worth giving it a day or two.

'I'm not sure if I'll be able to go,' I said.

'Why not?'

'Isabella's boyfriend, Tiziano, is having a party at his place on the coast, and she wants me to be at their villa nearby to keep an eye on Sofia.'

'Doesn't Isabella want to see the Palio?'

I shook my head. 'She prefers to get away.'

'That's a pity,' he said.

'I was hoping to write an article about it to submit to a magazine, so I need to change Isabella's mind.'

'You're a writer?'

'Yes – well, I'm a journalist. I was working for a local newspaper before coming here, but I want to be a travel writer. I'd like to write freelance for magazines and, ideally – and I know it's a dream – the national press.'

'Sounds like an exciting plan,' he said.

'So, you're going back in September?'

'Yes. And then I'll see if I can organise a transfer to Pimsy's Rome office next year. It will probably take a while and the right position would need to come up.'

'That's exciting. Hope you get what you want.'

'I hope you get what you want too.'

We shared a nice little moment right then, supporting each other's dreams. And I liked it. Tom couldn't care less about my ambitions. His only concern was whether I could be useful to him as a wife on his farm. This made me think. Shouldn't I be with someone who rooted for me and my goals rather than made it all about him?

The barman whistled along to the radio while polishing glasses with a tea towel.

'My mom saw her contrada, the Chiocciola, win the Palio a couple of times.' he said. 'They won the year she moved to the US, just after she left, with a horse called Beatrice, the same name as hers.'

Red and yellow Chiocciola flags bedecked the streets around where the Sabatinis lived.

'Did she live where Isabella and Sofia are now?'

'Yes, she grew up in Via San Marco. That apartment's been passed down for generations. After Mom emigrated, Isabella got married and lived there with her husband. Sofia and Benedetto moved into their house in the countryside outside Siena. When Benedetto was taken ill, they both moved back in.'

'It would be amazing if the Chiocciola won this time,' I said.

'I know. My mom's real excited about me seeing the Palio.'

How I wished I could go with Alessandro. What a bonding experience that would be. I finished my cappuccino and used a teaspoon to scoop the froth out of the bottom of my cup.

'So, you'll be supporting the Chiocciola, if they get to compete that is, even though you live in a different contrada?'

'What do you mean, if they get to compete?' he said.

I'd already read a lot about the Palio for research.

'Only ten contradas out of the seventeen get to take part. In the August Palio, seven of the ten contradas are the ones that didn't take part in the July Palio. The other three are drawn by lots.'

'Oh, that's a real pity. It would mean so much to my mom if I saw them race,' he said, his face dropping.

'I'd support them too. Imagine that square filled with thousands of people, cheering on the horses. The atmosphere must be electric.'

'If you manage to get Isabella to change her mind, we could go together.'

I pictured the two of us cheering on the Chiocciola contrada, Alessandro's arm round my shoulder as we waved the red and yellow scarves. I'd bought mine already from a shop in the Piazza del Campo one morning.

I used a napkin to wipe the froth from round my mouth.

'I'd like that.'

Then I remembered Harriet. We'd agreed to go together too.

'Harriet is coming back to Siena especially though, so she'd be there too.'

I watched a group of tourists huddle around a souvenir stall. A man squeezed his arms round his family as a passer-by took their photo, the children swirling contrada flags.

'Matt will want to be there too,' he said.

I pictured the four of us meeting in this bar beforehand. Harriet wouldn't say no to spending the day with Matt.

'I'm sure he and Harriet would get on,' I said.

'Grandma said the winning contrada has a street party,' he said.

Picturing a Chianti-fuelled kiss with Alessandro under an old streetlamp, I just had to do all I could to change Isabella's mind.

'That would be worth gatecrashing,' I said.

He dropped his napkin on the floor beside my chair, and leant forward to pick it up. He was so close, I caught the scent of gel in his hair, sweet like almonds. His proximity took me back to Sofia's party when he'd whispered in her ear. Our eyes locked and he sat back in his chair.

'Can I ask you a question?' he said.

Nodding, I hoped I could answer it.

'I know you want to stay for the Palio, but I get the feeling you're avoiding going home?'

'I'm not ready to go back yet.'

'You don't get on with your family?'

This wasn't the time to tell him about Tom.

'There isn't much to do where I come from. You've seen the farm. It's not the most exciting place to be. And Siena is such a magical place to be.'

'So, you're escaping?' he said.

It sounded dramatic when put like that, but this was true. I brushed a stray hair out of my face with my hand.

'You could say that.'

He looked out of the window.

'Like me, I guess.'

Did he have someone at home too? I didn't have the courage to ask. He seemed to be in deep thought, his eyes glazing over.

'Why did your mother go to live in America?'

'Sofia and Benedetto sent her to New Jersey for a few months because she was hanging out with the wrong guy.'

'What was wrong with him?'

'He had a motorcycle, and was a good few years older than her. Benedetto had a cousin who ran a restaurant in Little Italy. She worked there as a waitress for the summer and fell in love with the chef, Enrico, who happens to be my father.'

The way his parents had met was so romantic, and I wanted to know more about their story. The bell rang in the Mangia Tower, as if to announce that Alessandro's break from class was over. But I wasn't ready for him to leave yet.

'So, your dad asked her to get married?'

'He proposed the day before she was due to come back. She accepted and called Sofia and Benedetto, thinking they'd be happy for her. They didn't approve of my dad either, because they wanted her to marry a doctor. Benedetto used to be a surgeon at the hospital. Sofia and Benedetto begged Mom to come home and marry a guy they had lined up for her, but she refused.'

'What did your father's parents think?'

'They wanted him to marry a nice girl from Sicily, where he's from, of course,' he said, rolling his eyes.

'Did Sofia and Benedetto attend the wedding?'

'No. My parents got married at City Hall in Jersey City and stayed with my dad's uncle for a while. After a few months my dad's parents accepted Mom. She moved into their house until she and my dad could afford their own place.'

'Did Sofia and Benedetto see her after that?'

'Benedetto didn't speak to Mom for years. He was embarrassed, as the guy they had lined up was the son of a work colleague. Everything was arranged for when she returned. Sofia wrote Mom letters secretly and she wrote back, sending them to Sofia's friend. When Benedetto was on his deathbed, Mom came to Siena and they were reconciled the week he died.'

Beatrice had chosen love over her parents and I wondered if it had been worth it.

'It's a shame your mum missed out on all that time with her parents.'

'I know. Before he died, Benedetto said he regretted the day he sent her to New Jersey. Their pride kept them apart all those years.'

'When you said you were escaping, what did you mean?' I said.

'I needed to get away from someone. My mom didn't make me come here, but she gave me the push I needed.'

Beatrice was more or less doing the same to Alessandro as Benedetto had done to her. Except, he seemed to want to get away too. The *someone* just had to be a girl his mother didn't approve of.

'Who are you getting away from?'

He ran a hand through his hair. 'It's complicated.'

If he'd been in a relationship, I hoped it had ended before he came to Siena.

He stood up and dropped some coins onto the table. 'I have to get back to class.'

He'd run over his break by ten minutes, but it wasn't long enough. The way he'd opened up to me was touching – clearly, he trusted me. Our short time in the bar had brought us closer, but I wanted more.

'When are you next coming to dinner?' I said, boldly.

He looked down at me. 'Do you think Isabella would give you tonight off?'

Sofia and Isabella were going to Enzo's for dinner. Whenever I saw Enzo, he drooled over me in such an obvious way, I'd excused myself from the evening by saying I needed to meet an imaginary friend. Not wanting to appear too keen, I rummaged in my rucksack for a packet of chewing gum.

'They're going to your uncle's, and I haven't made any plans,' I said, casually.

'Do you want to do something?'

I offered him a stick of chewing gum and he took it.

'That would be great.'

'I could pick you up, or do you think we should meet somewhere else?' he said.

He was implying we shouldn't tell Sofia and Isabella, I guessed. And he was right. The last thing I wanted was them quizzing me.

'That's a good idea.'

'By the fountain in the square at eight?'

'Okay.'

The Fonte Gaia, where I'd made a wish on my first night in Siena with Harriet. I'd forgotten about that wish, and all the other ones that had flashed through my mind while coming to a decision. I'd been granted a way to stay in Siena for longer, as requested, and I was grateful.

'See you then, Jessica.'

He went down the stairs, throwing me a wave as he went.

Would we go for drinks or dinner? I'd have to go to the cash machine and check my bank balance. I could hardly expect him to pay.

'Bye,' I called after him as I mentally went through my wardrobe. I'd need to look my absolute best for our date.

CHAPTER 30

JESSICA

That afternoon, I was daydreaming while bringing the washing in from the line outside the kitchen window. Soon, I'd need to wake Sofia from her siesta, and I thought about what I'd wear that evening. It would be muggy as it had been recently in Siena, the humidity intense even at night, so trousers were out of the question. Last time I'd made the mistake of wearing jeans in the evening, they'd stuck to my legs within minutes of me walking down the street. I would wear a summer dress. It was green with a halter neck and a slight dip in the front. It didn't show too much, but just enough for a first date – which I was hoping this was... I unpegged one of Sofia's house dresses and pulled it towards me. My arm brushed one of the geranium flowers in the window box and I thought nothing of it, but then it began to really hurt. I dropped the dress into the washing basket and looked down at my arm to see a red bump. I'd been stung by something. Looking at the geraniums, I could see a bee on one of the flowers and another dead one on the soil. It had to be a bee sting.

Isabella came into the kitchen, her heels clicking on the floor, ready to return to the hospital for her afternoon shift.

'What's wrong, Jessica?' she said.

'I think I've been stung by a bee,' I said.

'Really? Let's see.'

She walked towards me, and I showed her my arm.

'Ah yes. It looks as though you're having some kind of reaction – this happens sometimes.'

The bump seemed to be getting bigger with every second that passed, and it was painful.

'You wouldn't want that to get any worse. I'll get you something for it,' she said.

Being a medical professional, she was bound to have everything in her bathroom cabinet.

'Okay, thanks,' I said.

She returned a couple of minutes later with a box of pills, pushed one out of the foil and pressed it into the palm of my hand. I'd been expecting some kind of cream, but trusted she knew what she was talking about.

'Take this with a glass of water and you'll be fine in no time.'

'Grazie.'

I went to the fridge to get a bottle of water, filled a glass and swallowed the tablet.

What a relief that she'd had something to make the bump go down. I wouldn't want anything to spoil my date with Alessandro.

Later, I approached the Piazza del Campo, the waft of takeaway slices from a pizzeria reminding me I'd hardly eaten all day. My watch said eight o'clock, but I didn't want to arrive first, so I admired the handbags on display in a shop window on Via Banchi di Sopra. I especially liked the brown leather one with a pocket on each side and straps long enough to go over the shoulder.

A letter from Mum had been waiting in the Sabatinis'

pigeonhole when I got back that morning. She was disappointed that I was staying in Siena for longer and said how much she missed me. An old schoolfriend, Helen Petersen, had apparently set her sights on Tom – Dad had seen them together down the Old Hare. This grated as Helen had once been a good friend, but we'd lost touch after leaving school. Deep down, I'd always known she had a thing for Tom. It wasn't that I cared about him being with someone else, it was more that she'd once been a good friend, and was breaking the friendship code. Mum worried he wouldn't wait for my return and that I'd miss out on my big opportunity with him. She finished by saying that she hoped I'd do the right thing for the family. It didn't seem fair that she was putting so much pressure on me to follow her agenda. I inhaled, deciding to push her words out of my mind.

My thoughts returned to meeting Alessandro. Would we have enough conversation to fill an evening? I checked my reflection in a shop window and smoothed down my hair with a hand – the humidity made it a little frizzy, which wasn't helpful at all. Standing up straight, I imagined that I was Alessandro seeing me for the first time that evening. Would he like the citrus-scented perfume I'd sprayed myself with liberally? It was called Eau de Vivre, and Harriet had given it to me as a parting gift, suggesting I wear bolder scents. I took Vicolo San Paolo, a steep slope leading to the square, treading carefully so as not to get my heels caught in the cobblestones. They were already rubbing my feet and I could have kicked myself for not wearing flat sandals instead. A waiter dressed in black tie served clientele at an outside table in a bar. The man who by now I knew was called Maurizio sat cross-legged in the square, strumming a guitar as young people gathered around him, singing along to 'Roxanne'. Some of them sipped wine from plastic cups. People walked around the edge of the square as part of their passeggiata, the evening stroll Italians would often take, leaving a trail of perfume, cologne and cigarette smoke as they went.

And then I saw him. Alessandro was leaning against the railings that ran in front of the fountain.

Composing myself, I approached and said, 'Hi.'

'Hey, Jessica.'

He moved away from the railings and leant down to kiss me on both cheeks, something he hadn't done before. The skin on his face was smooth, and he'd clearly shaved on my account. I breathed in the scent of him, the almond gel in his hair and the hint of sandalwood on his neck.

Glancing at my dress, he said, 'You look great.'

I'd chosen the right one, after all. 'Thanks, you don't look bad yourself. Where are we going?'

'I've booked a restaurant some guy in class recommended.'

He'd gone to the trouble of making a reservation?

I'd envied the clientele at L'Osteria Giancarlo while peering through the window on the way back from class at lunchtimes. It was situated down a narrow side street along with a handful of shops, and at the end was a small square with a fountain where I'd sometimes sit with a bottle of water. I'd really wanted to dine in that room with its tassel-shaded lamps, but its prices were beyond the average student budget. Ivy grew around the door and the window boxes were filled with hot-pink geraniums. I'd studied the menu in the glass case outside a few times, and there were local dishes like home-made wild boar ravioli and Livornese fish stew.

Alessandro gestured for me to step inside first. A waiter showed us to our table and Alessandro suggested I take the banquette with red velvet cushions. A Frank Sinatra song played, and there were candles pushed into bottles on each table, wax dripping round the necks. It was the perfect setting for a romantic evening. I'd asked Isabella to pay me a couple of days early and somehow she'd agreed. This was an expensive place and I hoped to have enough money for my half of the bill.

'My mum loves Sinatra,' I said.

'I grew up in the same place as him.' Alessandro said.

'Really?'

'He was born in Hoboken around the corner from where my folks live. There's a street named after him.'

Mum loved the Rat Pack and would find this snippet of information interesting. But I doubted she'd like me going on a date with Alessandro when she had her heart set on me ending up with Tom.

We ordered and I chose gnocchi with gorgonzola sauce as a starter. The home-made pasta dumplings made with potato were delicious, but so filling I couldn't look at the steak when it came.

'You don't have to finish that if it's too much,' Alessandro said.

When I cut into the steak, which I'd asked to be cooked medium, blood oozed onto the plate. I'd forgotten that in Italy if you asked for medium you'd often end up with rare. Not wanting to make a fuss on our special date, I hadn't said anything when the waiter brought it over. We were halfway through a second bottle of Chianti, and so far I'd made the mistake of glugging it down to ease my nerves. The waiter had brought us a complimentary Bellini with our starter because it was the manager's birthday, and I was feeling quite tipsy. Really, I should be pacing myself. During the starters we'd exchanged small talk, and I hoped the conversation would get a bit more interesting. There was so much I wanted to know about Alessandro and his life. Most importantly, did he have a girlfriend back home or not?

'Why are you really in Siena?' I said.

He put down his knife and fork. 'Like you, I shouldn't have ordered a pasta starter with steak as a main,' he said.

I smiled. He hadn't answered my question, probably because he didn't want to talk about the girl he was avoiding.

'You were mysterious this morning,' I said.

He looked away, adjusting the watch on his wrist, before meeting my gaze. 'I came here to get away from my girlfriend, Gabriella.'

So he did have a girlfriend. A wave of nausea swept over me. What was I even doing here?

Wiping my mouth with the napkin, I said, 'Oh really?'

'She wants us to buy a place together, and get married next year, but I'm not ready for any of that.'

'Have you told her?'

'We agreed to take a break while I'm in Siena, but I need to figure out how to tell her it's over. We've been together since school, so it's a big deal.'

So, he was a free agent? Or was he just telling me this? For all I knew they were engaged, and she was wearing a ring with a big fat diamond on it. The waiter came over to ask if everything was all right with the food. Alessandro looked across the table at me and lifted his eyebrows.

'I'll get through it,' I said.

'You don't have to eat it all.'

I couldn't bring myself to finish the steak, what with the way the alcohol was making me feel. But I'd been brought up to consume everything on my plate, especially in a fancy restaurant.

'My parents would be appalled,' I said.

'Well, they aren't here, are they?'

He was right and I shrugged.

Alessandro asked the waiter to take the plates away.

'I saw the maid push you at the party, by the way. She's got it in for you, right?'

'She hates au pairs because Isabella's husband ran off with one, apparently,' I said.

'Yeah, that guy was a walking cliché. Still, she can't judge you on someone else's behaviour.'

'The thing is, I don't understand why it wasn't a problem for the au pair who's gone back to England for the summer. Otherwise, why would she be coming back in September?'

'Ah, they got on really well, I think because her parents were from Puglia like Carla, so they had that in common, and would chat away in the same local dialect.'

'That explains it. Carla's clearly determined to find a way to get me into trouble. Can I ask – why did you take the blame for the broken glasses?'

'I couldn't let Isabella yell at you when it wasn't your fault.'

Wasn't there more to it? He'd found me in the bookshop that morning, brought me to this place, and made a reservation too.

'It was nice of you to do that for me. Thank you,' I said.

He picked up the bottle of Chianti, and refilled my glass. 'Do you have a guy back home?'

So he did want to know. How much should I tell him? There was no way I was going to mention the ring. The alcohol was making me so woozy, I didn't feel capable of editing our story.

'Not really.'

He grinned. 'What does that mean?'

My head was hurting, and I didn't feel like telling him about Tom.

'I'll be back in a minute.'

Getting my bag from underneath the table, I went to the bathroom. Using the sponge in my compact to dab my face with powder, I hoped Alessandro would forget about the question he'd asked. Did he really plan to dump his girlfriend or was he saying that to get me into bed? Surely then he wouldn't mention her at all if that was the case. As I approached the step leading out of the bathroom, I tripped up and grabbed the door frame to steady myself. The alcohol seemed to be having more of an effect on me than usual. I needed to slow down.

But back in the restaurant there were two espressos, two shot glasses filled with what looked like dessert wine and a plate of biscuits on the table.

'I get that you don't want to talk about home,' Alessandro said.

'Do you mind if we leave it for another time?'

'Sure.' He handed me one of the shot glasses. 'Vin Santo?'

Okay, this would be my very last drink for the evening. We clinked glasses, said, 'Cin cin,' and I downed mine in one.

He laughed. 'You're meant to dip the biscuits in the dessert wine, and sip it slowly.'

'Oh.'

Giggling like a drunken fool, I drank the espresso, hoping it would sober me up.

'Never mind,' he said, rolling his eyes, but also smiling as if he somehow found my behaviour charming.

The lights came on, the brightness too much, and the music stopped playing. Looking around, I saw we were the only people remaining in the restaurant. The staff had changed into jeans and were eating at a table next to the kitchen. The head waiter brought the bill, and I picked up my bag. Alessandro leant forward, touching my leg with his as he did so, and removed his wallet from a pocket in his trousers. He dropped his credit card onto the plate.

'I'll get this.'

When I shook my head to protest, he took my hand and said, 'Put away your purse. When you get your big cheque from the Palio article, then maybe you can take me out to eat.'

Usually, I liked to pay my way, but didn't mind him insisting. And he was right, I could pay him back when I made some decent money. He kept hold of my hand, those eyes locked on mine. If we kissed, where would we go? He couldn't stay at the flat, and he was sharing a room with Matt. All we could do was snog in the street like teenagers.

'Thank you, Alessandro,' I said.

'You know you can call me Al, like all my other friends?'

We were friends? Him saying this gave me a warm feeling.

'I know, but I like your full name.'

'What's that mark on your arm?'

He brushed the bee sting lightly with a finger, and it sent a small spark right through me.

'Oh I was stung by a bee today.'

'You were?'

'I brushed it with my arm when getting the washing in. There's a window box on the sill, and the bee must have been sitting on one of the flowers.'

'Did you put anything on it?'

'Isabella gave me a pill because the sting was swelling up.'

He sat back in his chair. 'Well, that explains everything.'

'What do you mean?'

'Now it makes sense why the Vin Santo has had such an effect on you, apart from the fact that you downed it in one go. You are slurring your words a little, and I'm sorry for ordering it, Jessica.'

Resting my elbows on the table, I put my head in my hands. What a complete imbecile.

'You're not supposed to drink when taking antihistamine, and I'm guessing Isabella gave you something a bit stronger than what you'd find at the pharmacist.'

How could Isabella not tell me such vital information? Because of her, I'd got far too drunk in front of the man I fancied. He must think so little of me, although perhaps now he knew the reason for my inebriation he'd understand.

Alessandro signed the credit card slip, and put a handful of lire notes on the table.

'I'd better walk you home.'

We got up to leave, and he placed a hand on the small of my back as we made our way towards the door. Clearly, he was concerned for my welfare, and that was a nice feeling indeed.

The waiter, probably glad to see the back of the drunken *stranieri* at last, threw us a smile that didn't reach his eyes, and said, 'Buonasera Signore', as he closed the door firmly behind us.

Now the air was cooler, and daylight had been replaced by a dark sky and a sprinkling of stars. The only light came from shop windows, a sliver of moon and the glow from a streetlamp. My teeth chattered, and I wished I'd brought a cardigan. My feet were really sore, and it wasn't that easy to walk, more of a hobble. I stepped out of my heels and bent down to pick them up, blood rushing to my head.

'Everything's spinning,' I said.

Alessandro took my hand and guided me to the doorstep of a *tabacchi*, where we sat down. He wrapped his jumper around my shoulders, and I leant into him, closing my eyes. I liked the way being close to him made me feel. That Vin Santo had tipped me over the edge.

CHAPTER 31

JESSICA

The next morning when I reached for the bedside lamp, my hand met a wall. It was pitch black but glimpses of light were visible through the slats in the shutters. The smell of bacon took me back to Birch Farm. Where was I, at Alessandro's? My head hurt and my eyes were clogged up with mascara. Thinking back to the night before, I remembered sitting on a doorstep, and Alessandro putting his jumper around my shoulders, pulling me to him. I'd breathed in the scent of him, that sandalwood cologne he wore. But what had happened after that?

Carefully, I lifted the sheet and turned sideways. I stepped onto the floor, my bare feet touching cool tiles, and ran a hand along the wall until I located the light switch. Flicking it on, I found myself in a room with two single beds, a chest of drawers and a wardrobe. The walls were painted white, and the tiles were a terracotta colour. Catching a glimpse of myself in the full-length mirror on the wall, I was horrified to see that I was still wearing my green dress. Although at least that meant we hadn't slept together. Of course I wanted to, but not when I was apparently so inebriated. There were black smudges under my eyes and my hair was a tangled mess.

Alessandro couldn't see me like this. On top of the chest of drawers I spotted a bag of cotton wool and a bottle of cleanser, and I removed my make-up. I found a tortoiseshell butterfly clip in my bag, put my hair up and instantly felt a bit more normal.

I pushed open the royal-blue shutters, like the heroine in a romantic film, and sun streamed into the room. The Duomo tower, with its black-and-white stripes, rose above the red-brick buildings. What a magnificent sight to wake up to. I leant further out of the window, and watched people amble that way they did in Italy, their voices echoing around the buildings. Despite the sore head, I couldn't have felt more high on life and I had no desire to be anywhere else but right here in this moment.

'Oh, you're awake.'

Alessandro stood at the door, wearing boxer shorts, his bare chest tanned and toned. I inhaled sharply at the sight of him. He must think so little of me.

'Hi.' I adjusted the butterfly clip in my hair. 'Did anything...?'

He shook his head.

'I tried to walk you home, but it would have taken quite a while, so I brought you here and made coffee. You fell asleep on the couch, and I picked you up and carried you to Matt's bed.'

Like Gregory Peck and Audrey Hepburn in *Roman Holiday*. My favourite film ever. How very romantic.

'Where is Matt?'

'He's in Florence, staying with a girl from back home.'

I supposed Alessandro hadn't told me this in the restaurant in case it sounded presumptuous.

'I made you a fried breakfast,' he said.

It was nice that he'd gone to so much effort – the best way to deal with a hangover was to eat my way through it.

'Thanks, I'm starving.'

He opened a drawer and got out a t-shirt and tracksuit bottoms.

'Why don't you put these on and come through when you're ready?'

I sat at the table, studying Alessandro's broad shoulders as he dished up our food with his back to me. His t-shirt smelt of that now-familiar cologne and I liked wearing his clothes. I thought back to when he'd paid the bill and leant forward, pressing his leg against mine. He placed a plate of food in front of me.

'Here you go.'

Bacon, sausages, mushrooms, fried bread with an egg in the middle.

'This is how my mom makes her eggs,' he said. 'You're in for a real treat.'

He poured us espressos from a coffeemaker and slid a bowl of sugar over to my side of the table.

'This all looks amazing.'

We didn't speak while we ate, a comfortable silence falling between us. The bacon tasted different, and it was paper thin. But its saltiness combined with the fried bread and egg was energising. Mum made fry-ups for Dad most mornings after he'd milked the cows – and I usually joined him at weekends – but I hadn't had one since living in Italy. My mind wandered to Mum's letter, and I told myself to savour every minute of this time I was spending with Alessandro, so special, eating a meal together that he'd made especially for me. When I'd finished, I put down my knife and fork.

'That was delicious, thank you. I feel like such an idiot about last night.'

'You were fun company. And I guess it might have something to do with the antihistamine Isabella gave you.'

Isabella had really dropped me in it.

I undid the butterfly clip and my hair fell to my shoulders. His eyes drifted over my face as I twisted my hair and put it back up. A few tendrils escaped but I hoped it looked okay.

'I don't remember a lot after sitting on that step.'

'I feel kind of responsible for ordering the Vin Santo,' he said.

'Sorry you ended up having to look after me.'

'It was really no problem.'

The clock on the wall showed it was almost eleven.

'Don't you have a class to go to?'

'Thought I'd give it a miss today.' He smiled. 'Don't you have to get back to take over from Carla?'

'I should so I can shower before lunch.'

'Will Isabella be mad that you didn't go home last night?'

'She won't notice. My room is by the front door, miles away from everyone else. Sometimes I go out in the mornings without seeing anyone at all.'

'Do you have time for another coffee on the couch first?'

Glad he didn't want to get rid of me quite yet, I smiled and said, 'That would be good.'

Getting up, I went over to the couch, as he called it. The window was pushed up and I studied the lemon-yellow building opposite with a window box clipped to the balcony, stuffed with flowers. A woman was pegging sheets to a washing line.

Alessandro handed me an espresso and sat down next to me. I drank the coffee, wanting him to put an arm round my shoulder like the night before and pull me close to him. We'd certainly got to know each other better, but would all that be lost when I left?

After downing the coffee, I said, 'I should go,' reluctantly.

He ran a hand through his hair. 'Okay.'

'I need to put my dress back on.'

'You can keep my stuff for now, if you want.'

If I took his clothes, I could wear them round the flat and think of him, but the temperature outside would be approaching thirty degrees already. I'd be baking in his tracksuit bottoms and would need to roll them up as he was much taller than me.

'I'd be too hot walking back. Besides, your clothes would look silly with my shoes.' I nodded in the direction of my heels on the floor.

He shrugged. 'All right.'

I went into the bedroom, put the dress back on and picked up my bag. Back in the kitchen, he was standing at the sink, washing up.

'When will I see you next?' he asked over his shoulder. Oh good, he did want to see me again. This gave me a giddy feeling – thank goodness he hadn't gone off me after my drunken behaviour.

'We're going to the coast tomorrow for a few days, but maybe when I'm back?'

He turned to face me, his hands covered in soap suds, and wiped his hands on a tea towel. 'Well, I do hope I get to see you at the Palio at least.'

I still needed to speak to Isabella. I squeezed my feet into the heels, sucking air through my teeth. Walking back would take ages. I pulled my bag onto my shoulder.

'I'll let you know if Isabella changes her mind.'

He opened the door to the hall, gesturing for me to go first.

'You can always leave a note in my pigeonhole downstairs.'

I started hobbling down the hall, but the blisters hurt so much I had to step out of the shoes. The chemist round the corner should have plasters. When I reached the front door, I turned round to face him.

'Thanks for breakfast, and for looking after me last night.'

'I didn't have much choice.' He grinned. 'Are your feet okay?'

'Not really.'

'I'd give you Band-Aids, but I don't have any.'

I leant forward to kiss him on the cheek, but somehow instead his lips met mine. Surprised by this bold move, but also delighted, I relaxed into the kiss. His tongue explored my mouth, slow yet searching, and I wanted more. He put his hands on my waist, and we stumbled back against the door. The pit of my stomach ached with longing. How I wanted him to unzip my dress, to unhook my bra, to take me to his bed. I put my arms around his shoulders and caressed the smooth skin on the nape of his neck with a hand. He kissed me faster, the weight of him pressing against me, and I didn't want it to end. But I had to pull away. Not like this.

'I wish you didn't have to go,' he said.

'Same here.'

He kissed me once more on the mouth, then opened the door.

'I'll be looking out for that note.'

'I hope to be writing it.'

Picking up my shoes, I went down the stairs, almost skipping with joy. When I reached the floor below, I looked up to see he was still standing there, watching me.

'Goodbye, Jessica.' He went inside, closing the door behind him.

Now I absolutely *had* to find a way to go to the Palio.

CHAPTER 32

JESSICA

A few weeks later, I found myself lunching with Harriet.

'He kissed you?' she said.

I nodded, still unable to believe it had happened. The following day, I'd left Siena to stay at the Sabatinis' villa in Castiglione della Pescaia, a charming town on the Tuscan coast, with sandy beaches and marine pine trees. I'd played Sade on my Walkman while sunbathing on the beach, reliving the kiss: us falling back against the door, his lips on mine, his hands on my waist. I'd continued the scene from where it ended, picturing him carrying me to his bed in Gregory Peck style. While we were at the coast, Sofia kept asking why I was suddenly in such a good mood. I simply shrugged and claimed to like being by the sea.

Harriet refilled our glasses with chilled Vernaccia di San Gimignano, a local white wine, and put cold meats, tomatoes, cheese and a loaf of fresh bread onto the table on a wooden board. We were having lunch at her new boyfriend, Michele's, place. She'd dumped Fabrizio after touring Italy with him – she said he was overfriendly with his female fans. She already knew Michele, a fireman in his thirties, from Bar Atlantico. He liked to drive her to fancy restaurants in Tuscan hill towns and would buy her jewellery and handbags.

She sat down opposite me and rolled a slice of salami into a cigar shape. Harriet kept her trim figure by running daily, however tired or hungover she was. She'd dragged me along with her once, and I hadn't been able to last for more than ten minutes.

'I can tell you like him,' she said.

In two weeks I was due to leave Siena, as Isabella had told me the other au pair, Lisa Brown, was coming back. Alessandro would return to New York not long after that. What had I been thinking falling for an American man when there was no prospect of a future between us? Passing up the opportunity to experience being with him would be a mistake though, surely? I wouldn't want to look back in years to come, wishing I'd seized the moment.

I picked up my glass and sipped the Vernaccia. It was refreshingly cold, as well as perfectly dry and crisp.

'I've never met anyone like him,' I said.

'We have to get you to the Palio. Did you bring the number?'

I handed Harriet a scrap of paper with my predecessor's telephone number on. I'd copied it from Isabella's address book that morning while Carla was cleaning the bathroom. In Castiglione della Pescaia, I'd called Harriet from a payphone. She'd told me to get the phone number for the au pair returning in September and she'd deal with it. I didn't have a clue how Harriet would get me to the Palio with this information but after failing to persuade Isabella again at the villa, it was my last resort.

She lifted the handset off the telephone on the wall.

'Will Michele mind you calling England?'

'Michele would do anything for me. And anyway, by the time he gets the bill I'll be back in London.'

'What are you going to say to Lisa?'

'You'll see.'

She tapped out the phone number and lifted the receiver to her ear.

'Hello, can I speak to Lisa please? I'm Isabella Sabatini's secretary.'

She spoke in English with an Italian accent. Isabella didn't have a secretary. Wouldn't Lisa know that? I hoped Harriet wasn't about to make things worse, causing a problem with Isabella, and so I zoned out, doing my best not to listen. The tapping of drums to the dada dadada beat caught my attention and I got up and went over to the window. A group of young men in crimson tights and smocks from the Torre contrada marched past. Those not tapping drums swirled crimson flags, which displayed in yellow their coat of arms, an elephant carrying a tower. Tension for the Palio was building by the hour, each contrada trying to outdo the others. The men disappeared down a side street and I tuned in to Harriet's conversation.

'Isabella wondered if you could come back a week later than agreed.'

How would this help me?

'Thanks for being so understanding. Bye.'

Harriet hung up and sat back down. I joined her at the table.

'It's over to you now, J.'

'Isabella doesn't have a secretary. Did she believe you?'

Harriet sliced a tomato and sprinkled salt over it with the shaker. 'I told her that Isabella's been promoted. Lisa, who seemed very nice, asked me to pass on her congratulations.'

'How will that make a difference to anything?'

'Tell Isabella that Lisa phoned to say she's coming back a week late due to a family issue.'

The idea of bringing this up with Isabella filled me with dread. 'What will that do?'

'Oh J, you've got a lot to learn about this sort of thing. Isabella will ask if you can stay for an extra week, of course.' Harriet cut up the tomato with her knife and fork.

'And how will that get me to the Palio exactly?' I said.

'You'll say you need to check with your mother. It's your gran's birthday and she'll be upset if you're not there. After that you'll add, if only you could be in Siena for the Palio, then you'd be prepared to miss your gran's birthday to help Isabella with her situation.'

I sliced the bread, made a sandwich with salami, cheese and tomato and twisted the peppermill over the filling. We were going to Bar Atlantico later, and I needed to eat before going out with Harriet. Knowing her, there would be cocktails.

'Great idea, but what if Isabella doesn't take the bait?' I wasn't good at telling lies, not even white ones. I sliced the sandwich in half.

'Use a tone of voice that betrays no emotion, as if you're negotiating a business deal. And that's exactly what this is. Make it clear that, if you don't go to the Palio, she'll be without an au pair for a week.'

Isabella would never manage without an au pair, and it struck me that this put me in a stronger position than I'd previously thought. She really should be nicer to me. If I ever chose to walk out before Lisa returned, she'd be really stuck.

'I hope I can pull it off.'

I bit into the sandwich, and it was delicious, all the ingredients so fresh and full of flavour. When I got back to Yorkshire, I should find an Italian deli, and eat like this more often.

Harriet rinsed a couple of nectarines under the tap and put them on the table. She cut a slice off one and ate it.

'You just have to make this happen. Don't take no for an answer.'

I bit into my nectarine, the juice running down my chin.

Wiping my face with a napkin, I said, 'Alessandro's bringing his Australian flatmate, Matt, to the Palio. If I get to go, can you keep him company?'

'What's he like?'

'Just your type. Built like a rugby player.'

'Michele has no interest in going. So, that won't be a problem,' she said with a smile.

'Apparently, the winning contrada has a street party afterwards.'

Her eyes lit up and she clapped her hands. 'We have to go to that – it's going to be so much fun.'

She got up and cleared the table, then piled the plates into the sink and ran the tap over them.

'Let's go. Tomasso's working behind the bar tonight and you know what that means.'

Free cocktails. Life was certainly more interesting with Harriet in it.

My opportunity to speak to Isabella came the following lunchtime. She was in the kitchen, tasting the pasta sauce using a wooden spoon, and she studied the salad I'd prepared with lettuce, basil and tomatoes.

'I hope you haven't dressed the insalata yet?'

Sofia had taught me to not dress a salad too early, otherwise the leaves would go soggy.

'No, I was waiting until the rest of the meal was almost ready.'

'Va bene.'

I reached up to get the pasta bowls out of the cupboard. 'A girl called Lisa rang this morning,' I said, casually, lining the bowls up on the worktop.

'Did she leave a message?'

Draining the pasta in the sink, I gave the colander a shake. I then emptied the farfalle into the sauce and used a wooden spoon to stir it all together.

'Yes, she hopes you'll understand that she'll be a week later coming back.'

Isabella leant on the worktop and lit a cigarette.

'Mamma mia, what am I supposed to do?'

I shrugged.

'That is unacceptable. I'll call her back.' Isabella went into the hall and returned with the telephone handset and address book. Oh no, I couldn't have them speaking to each other. Racking my brains for an excuse, I tried to come up with a way to stall her.

She found a page in the address book and tapped out the number.

'I wouldn't bother calling back,' I said. 'She was about to leave for the airport to go on holiday.'

She drew on her cigarette. 'Did she say why she's coming back a week late?'

Harriet's plan had only said a family issue, but I needed to be more specific in order to convince Isabella, surely? Using a ladle, I scooped the farfalle into the bowls, trying to think of a valid reason.

'She's going to her aunt's wedding.' I got a piece of Parmesan out of the fridge and grated it over the pasta.

Flicking ash into an empty glass on the side, Isabella looked at me.

'Jessica—'

Here was my opportunity.

'As I said before, it would be so helpful if I could go to the Palio so I can finish the article I'm writing.'

She reached for her handbag and got out her Filofax. She flicked through the pages, the cigarette resting between her fingers.

'Let me think about this... Jessica, carina, if I ask my cousin

Roberta to look after Sofia on the night of the Palio, would you consider staying for an extra week?'

Phew. Harriet had been right after all. I dressed the salad with extra virgin olive oil, red wine vinegar, salt and pepper, and used the wooden servers to toss the leaves.

'I'd need to call my mum. It's my gran's birthday that week and she'll be upset if I miss it.'

Isabella handed me the telephone. I was getting an outgoing call too. Usually, I'd have to buy a phone card and make calls from the bar on the other side of the square.

'Call her now, please. I'll go and get Mamma so we can eat lunch.'

I tapped Michele's number into the phone. I couldn't wait to tell Harriet the good news. At last, I'd found a way to go to the Palio!

CHAPTER 33

JESSICA

On the night before the Palio, I decided to read the last page of Peter's diary in bed before going to sleep. It was another balmy evening, the air sticky and the sash window was pushed up as far as it would go. All was quiet outside, and I'd been listening to an Italian radio station on low volume as company, the bedside lamp providing my light. I'd been putting off reading the last page of Peter's diary just like I would when reaching the end of a good book – I didn't want to finish this story of my grandfather's wartime experiences because then it would be over, and what if it didn't give me the answers I so craved? The diary was the reason I was sitting here in Siena right now. I appreciated how it turning up had made me realise I was living a mundane life, having completely forgotten about following my dreams. But Alessandro coming to the farm that day had changed everything – I'd never go back to that life now, and when I got home the first thing on my list was to tell Tom I couldn't marry him. It was only fair to speak to him in person, and he wasn't expecting to hear from me sooner. Breathing in, I prepared myself for my grandfather's last words.

21 September 1943

From a distance Siena's a fine-looking place, its reddish-brown buildings situated on a hill like many medieval towns around these parts. Benedetto tells me Siena's piazza is the most beautiful in Italy. It's shaped like a shell and twice a year, in July and in August, except during wartime, there's a horse race they call the Palio. A crowd of people stand in the middle of the square whilst horses do laps around them, the jockeys dressed in medieval costumes. Siena is divided into seventeen contrade, meaning districts, and they all have their own animal as a symbol. There are flags and scarves and even fountains where babies are baptised. When the war is over, he said I can visit and watch from the balcony of his uncle's house, which overlooks the square. At the end of the war, Benedetto wants to marry a woman named Sofia. She is a schoolteacher and helps us by liaising with contacts in Siena to get fake travel documents. On occasion, she visits us, and when we met she said she was immensely grateful that I'd saved Benedetto's life on the day we first worked together. We'd set up some dynamite on a road in order to catch a fleet of German tanks, but one of the sticks was faulty and so the Jerries opened fire. When I saw what they were about to do, I pulled Benedetto to the ground, saving him from a stray bullet. Sofia brought me a handkerchief embroidered herself with the colours of the contrada where she and Benedetto live. It's called the Chiocciola, meaning snail, and the colours are red and yellow. This gift meant a great deal to me, and I shall treasure it.

To think that Peter had known all about Siena and the contrada system, and Benedetto had told him about the Palio. And here I was reading his words about it the night before I was due to see it with my own eyes all these years later. Peter had missed out, but I would get to go in his place, two generations later, and that was hugely satisfying, as if I was making up for his lost opportunity. However, if he'd survived perhaps he might have seen it? If he was alive, where on earth would he be living? I went on to read the last part, my eyes welling up.

A bell rings in the tower, which rises above Siena. The plane should be here in fifteen minutes. We're hiding at the edge of some chestnut woods, out of sight of the Germans. The drop will be in the wheat field next to us, and I can't wait to get it over with. We haven't eaten for at least twelve hours and I've only got one cigarette left. How I long for one of those Red Cross parcels that I used to take for granted. My mouth waters at the thought of a tin of stewed steak and a few squares of chocolate. I hope the drop will include the grenades we asked for so we're in with a chance when we ambush the Jerries tomorrow. I've become consumed with guilt because of the reprisals, where Italian civilians are shot because of what we're doing. I have to shut the thought out of my mind, otherwise we'll never win this damn war.

The sky's a burnt orange as the sun sinks beneath the yellow sea of fields. The cicadas are making one hell of a din, and a brook babbles a few feet away. I drink it all in and forget that we're living through a war for a moment.

My pocket watch says twenty past eight. Father's old watch is all I have from home except for this diary. Benedetto's snoring. He's been a reluctant leader since losing his cousin last week. I raised my fears about Luigi's loyalty again this morning. Benedetto said his only option is to trust Luigi as we need him to liaise between us and the partisans in Florence. I did tell Francesco about this, and he agrees we're taking a risk. It's almost dark and I must wake Benedetto. We need to light the small fire we've prepared when we hear the plane's engine. Then we'll hurry to bring the crates into the safety of the woods.

As I read those final words, tears ran down my face. He'd written them only moments before he was shot. But I still didn't know if he'd survived. Had the man called Francesco, who Alessandro had told me about, and who Peter had mentioned here, really taken him to the contessa's villa in the Tuscan countryside? And if this was true, had Peter survived? It was highly unlikely that he would survive a bullet wound, surely? The German soldiers would know what they were doing and were bound to aim for a place that would kill rather than wound him. But then as I closed the diary and ran my hand over the cover, over the hole left by the bullet, I remembered that me and Alessandro had talked about how the diary could have reduced the impact of the bullet. Perhaps it hadn't wounded him as deeply as it was destined to. Had the diary saved Peter's life? Imagine if this was true and here I was holding it in my hands. But then where was he right now? Even if he'd recovered from being shot that night, he might have died since then from something else. Should I try to find out if he was still alive?

Would Sofia be able to tell me anything about that fateful night? When I went back to the coast I'd ask her. And when I returned to Yorkshire, I'd need to have a big chat with Gran and suggest that, if Peter's mother was still alive, we should visit her in Leeds. We should also contact Auntie Mabel. I didn't want to bother Gran with all this while living in Siena. It was the kind of conversation that should happen face to face, just like the one I needed to have with Tom.

CHAPTER 34

MARIELLA

VILLA CAMPIGLIA, NEAR SIENA, SEPTEMBER 1943

It had been a long night, and I'd been to check on Peter a few times. My room was only next door, and whenever I heard him shouting I'd gone to hold a damp cloth to his forehead. He tossed and turned, and appeared to be having terrible dreams. I held his hand, and spoke to him softly in Italian, not knowing if he understood everything that I was saying. At least I hoped he appreciated the sentiment.

The next morning when I went to open the shutters, Peter was awake. As I entered the room, he mumbled, 'Buongiorno, Signora.'

I replied, 'Come va?'

'Così così,' he said. So-so was to be expected after all he'd been through in the past two days.

'Your shoulder hurts?'

'Yes, but I am lucky to be alive.'

'Certo, lei è fortunato.'

'How did I get here?

'Francesco brought you here last night and he told me your name is Peter and that you are a British soldier.'

'Indeed I am, or was. And you are?'

'You may call me Contessa.'

'All right, Contessa it is. Thank you for taking me in.'

'You are welcome.'

'I don't remember much about last night. It's all a blur.'

'Well, after Francesco left, I took care of you, talked to you and held your hand. You were shouting a great deal in your sleep.'

He turned his head on the pillow to look at me, and smiled. I took his hand once again. We seemed to have a unique bond, despite having only known each other for a short time.

'I can't remember what happened after Benedetto took the diary from my pocket.'

'What diary are you talking about?'

'I had a diary, and the woman who sold it to me, well, we were together before I left, and last night, in the heat of the moment, I asked Benedetto to make sure the diary is returned to her – when it's safe to do so, of course.'

'Do you trust that he will do that?'

Moving his head slowly from side to side, he said, 'I'm not sure. He is a good man, and we got to know each other well while I was living with the partisans. But I told him Luigi is a traitor, and so, when he informed us about a supply drop, I sensed it was a trap. Benedetto wouldn't listen, and it turns out I was right, after all.'

'Francesco feels that way about Luigi too.'

'I think that diary actually might have saved my life,' Peter said, looking up in wonder at the angels on the ceiling.

'How?'

'When Benedetto removed it from my pocket, there was a bullet hole in it. It probably slowed the speed of the bullet down before it lodged itself in my shoulder.'

'Yes, the physician couldn't understand why the bullet hadn't gone deeper. Perhaps that is why.'

'Thank you, Contessa, for all you have done for me.'

'It is nothing.'

'So, you are a real countess?'

'Yes, I am.'

'And the count?'

'He is dead, killed by firing squad in the village square for helping the partisans.'

'I am so sorry.'

'It is not long since this happened. I was devastated of course to lose my husband, and my time here in the villa has been lonely with the fear of German soldiers looting my house, and harassing me.'

'Well, you have me to protect you now.'

'You do not appear to be in any position to protect me, Signore.'

'May I ask that you call me Peter?'

'Va bene.'

'And what is your actual name?'

'Mariella, but still you call me Contessa.'

Pouring water from the jug into his glass, I sat down and once again held it to his lips while he drank.

'Grazie,' he said.

'Prego.'

I put the glass down on the bedside table and returned to the chair.

'So, are you bored, lying there in that bed?' I said.

'Indeed I am. If only I could read to pass the time and take my mind off the pain.'

'Well, I have a well-stocked library downstairs. Are you able to read in Italian?'

'Not much, but I'd like to learn.'

This was my chance, the perfect excuse to spend time with him.

'Would you like me to read to you in Italian?'

'You'd do that for me?'

Shrugging, I said, 'What else do I have to do? It would be my pleasure. These days, I get very little intellectual stimulation, so you would actually be doing me a favour. I did study Italian literature at university, after all.'

'I love books and have wanted to be a novelist for as long as I can remember. I studied English literature at university. So, if you read to me, I'd be delighted.'

'There we are. Domani, I shall bring a few books and tell you about them. You can choose the one I read to you.'

'That sounds like a splendid idea. Tomorrow it is. Grazie, Contessa.'

'Now, we need to clean that wound to prevent it from becoming infected. I shall go and ask the maid to bring up a bowl of water and a bottle of vinegar. Would you mind if she does this for you?'

Looking at me, he said, 'This is probably rather presumptuous, seeing as you are a contessa and all that, but I'd much prefer it if you cleaned my wound. I don't know your maid, and it's an intimate procedure, one imagines.'

'I can't say that we know each other well either. We've barely exchanged more than a few words since Francesco brought you here.'

'But I feel that I know you. You are so familiar to me, it is strange, but also wonderful at the same time. Ah, I do recall seeing you speak to the lieutenant when I was in the prisoner-of-war camp at Laterina, and I was quite mesmerised. How I hoped I might get the opportunity to speak to you one day.'

My face warmed, and I didn't know where to look. I'd had the very same feeling, but thought it was my imagination, that my emotions were heightened because of all I'd been living through. He was the first man I'd looked at in a romantic way since losing my husband. Guilt consumed me for being attracted to someone other than Giorgio, besides he was a few years younger than me, probably in his early twenties. But the way he looked at me with those blue-grey eyes as if he were reading my every thought... well, it was rather spellbinding, and sent a thrill right through me.

'I shall consider your suggestion, and in due course let you know my decision.'

'Va bene.'

'And now I need to go and pick green beans from the garden, and whatever else I can find, and then hide them in a safe place so the Tedeschi do not loot them from us. Ci vediamo, Peter.'

'A dopo, Contessa.'

As I put the chair back under the dressing table, I sensed his eyes on me, watching my every move, and I found myself smiling for the first time in quite a while. Francesco had changed my world by bringing this man to my house, and I had an inkling that my life was about to change for the better.

CHAPTER 35

JESSICA

On the day of the Palio, I spent the morning lazing in bed, making the most of the opportunity to have the flat to myself while Sofia and Isabella were at the coast. Then, after a light lunch of bread, tuna and tomatoes, I headed down to Bar Paolo, the one overlooking the Piazza del Campo, where Alessandro had taken me the day we bumped into each other in the bookshop. It was jam-packed and I took the last table in the corner. The barista frothed milk and lined up coffees on the counter and a waitress delivered them to tables. The day I'd been waiting for had arrived at last and I hoped it would be everything I wanted it to be. I'd buzzed the intercom, as promised en route, and when there had been no answer, I'd left a note in his pigeonhole.

Meet you in Bar Paolo at 2 o'clock.

Jessica x

PS The Chiocciola is competing.

Before leaving the Sabatinis' flat, I'd threaded the Chiocciola red-and-yellow scarf through the belt loops on my shorts. What if Alessandro missed my note, or he saw it and didn't turn up? And if he did, how would he act towards me after the kiss?

A middle-aged English couple sat at the next table, the woman completing the crossword in a newspaper. The man studied a map of Siena and wrote in a small notebook. Like other tourists around them, they drank cappuccinos, not the done thing in Italy after eleven o'clock in the morning. Barmen had teased me for doing this when I first came to Siena, so now I opted for espressos in the afternoons. The woman passed the crossword to the man, and they discussed the remaining clues. I thought about my parents, who were around the same age. They more or less lived separate lives, never really acting like a couple. I couldn't remember the last time they'd left the house together. Since receiving Mum's letter, I'd avoided calling home as I didn't want to get into an argument with her. I'd sent a postcard from the coast, and hoped regular letters would keep her happy until I returned home.

The door opened and Harriet breezed in. She wore a sundress and the blue-and-white Onda scarf round her neck, tied as if it was made by some fancy designer. The flat we'd shared was in the Onda contrada, meaning wave, and it had the dolphin as its symbol.

'J, I'm so glad you made it!' Harriet said.

We double-kissed.

'Thanks to you.'

Then Alessandro and Matt walked into the bar.

'Here they are,' I said.

Alessandro approached the table, and I stood up to greet him.

'How are you doing, Jessica?' he said.

'Good, thanks. You?' I leant forward and he kissed me on the mouth, quickly, perhaps because he didn't like public displays of affection. He and Harriet kissed each other on both cheeks.

He'd acquired more of a suntan since I'd last seen him and was looking really good. Was he really interested in me? He looked over, as if to say, 'I remember what happened,' and gave me a knowing smile. I reciprocated, glad all was okay between us. What a relief.

Matt moved to shake hands with Harriet.

'Hi, I'm Matt.'

Harriet ignored his proffered hand and went in for the double kiss.

'Hello, Matt.'

'I'll get some beers,' Alessandro said. He and Matt went to the bar, leaving me and Harriet to sit down.

'So, we're all set then,' she said.

'Yep.'

It was then that I saw a girl come through the door and go up to Matt and Alessandro standing at the bar. They did the whole double-kiss thing.

'Who is that?' Harriet said.

'I don't know,' I said, worry tugging at my stomach. Had Alessandro been seeing someone else while I was at the coast? But then why bring her here?

The girl approached our table. She was tall and exceptionally slim, and would have fitted in on a catwalk with her flawless skin and high cheekbones. She pulled out the chair opposite Harriet.

'Hi, I'm Natalie,' she said, in an Australian accent.

'What are you doing here?' Harriet said.

She could be so direct at times, and this could sometimes be embarrassing, but I wanted to know too. Natalie scrunched up her forehead as if offended by this question.

'I know Matt from back home.'

Oh, that was all right then – she must be the girl Matt had

stayed with that night in Florence. I exhaled, safe in the knowledge that she wasn't interested in Alessandro after all.

'Is he your boyfriend?' Harriet said.

Natalie shook her head and let out a laugh.

'He'd like to be, but he's not my type.' She ran a hand through her hair. 'His roommate is though,' she said, her eyes widening.

So Alessandro had invited her? After our kiss, and with me here? Who did he think he was?

'You're talking about Alessandro?' Harriet said.

'He's only got one roommate, hasn't he?' Natalie said.

The thought of her pursuing Alessandro, and him having any interest in her, made me feel sick. How could I have been such a fool? Of course he'd have other girls after him. Why would he only want to know me?

'Well, he's taken, so you'll have to find someone else,' Harriet said.

'Matt said he's on a break from his girlfriend in New York. Why would you care anyway?' Natalie said.

Harriet nodded in my direction, and I wanted the floor to swallow me up. How could I lay claim to Alessandro after one kiss?

Alessandro brought over beers for everyone. Matt sat next to Harriet, leaving a chair free for Alessandro, next to Natalie and opposite me.

'So, you've all met?' Alessandro said.

What a nerve. Had he got to know Natalie while I was at the coast? If he liked her, why had he kissed me on the lips when he arrived? And why bother to meet me here at all? I hadn't felt so irritated since Carla bumped into me at Sofia's party. Taking a deep breath, I couldn't meet Alessandro's eye. Looking straight past him, I feigned interest in the Grand Prix on a TV attached to the wall.

'We certainly have,' Harriet said.

'Natalie turned up at our apartment as we were leaving,' Matt explained.

'I heard about this horse race, and thought it might be a laugh,' Natalie said.

A laugh? The Palio was so much more than that, and Natalie was here on a whim.

'Thought I might stay with these guys, if that's all right with you, Al?'

She squeezed Alessandro's knee and looked across the table at me, a smile on her lips.

What a piece of work.

'Sure.' Alessandro nodded, then threw me a look as if to say he could hardly say no, could he? I needed to have a conflab with Harriet, and soon.

Looking at my watch, I said, 'Oh, look at the time. Harry, we need to go.'

'What do you mean?' she said.

I kicked her under the table. 'We planned to go and see a blessing of one of the horses, remember?'

We'd talked about doing this so I could gather information for my article and take photos.

'Oh yes.'

'Blessing of a horse. What are you talking about?' Natalie said.

'Every contrada competing takes its horse into a church to be blessed. The priest says to the horse, "Go and return a winner," Harriet said.

'Why waste your time going to see that?' Natalie said.

'I'm writing about the Palio for my dissertation, and Jessica is writing an article for a magazine,' Harriet said, proudly, adjusting the Onda scarf round her neck as she stood up. She'd made us out to be right nerds, but I didn't care as long as we had an excuse to leave the bar.

Standing up, I pushed my chair under the table. 'See you all later,' I said.

'What about your beers?' Alessandro said.

'You can have them.'

His brow furrowed. 'When are you coming back?'

'Four o'clock. Don't leave for the Piazza del Campo without us,' Harriet said.

We couldn't get into the church of the Onda contrada. Instead we stood outside with a small group of tourists and locals while the blessing of the horse took place. When they came out of the church, I photographed the horse and jockey, who was dressed in blue-and-white contrada colours. They headed off to join the historical procession, which was about to parade through Siena to the square. We followed and found the procession filling the breadth of Via Banchi di Sopra. With our backs pressed against shop windows, we stepped sideways until we reached an archway leading to a side street. And this was where we stood to take our photos.

Each contrada competing was represented by a group of men dressed in medieval garb, swirling flags. The racehorse and a parade horse, ridden by the jockey, followed the men, hooves clip-clopping as they went. Men played trumpets and bugles and tapped drums.

'They must be baking in those tights,' I shouted above the din. 'Some of them are our age. Can you imagine English lads dressed like that?'

'It's a huge honour to represent your contrada,' Harriet said. She looked at her watch. 'It's quarter past four. The others have probably left the bar without us.'

'Who cares?'

Twisting her camera lens, Harriet zoomed in on a chariot drawn by white oxen with horns. The chariot carried the Palio itself, which was a silk banner awarded to the winning contrada, and a few official-looking men. A bell rang from the chariot as it passed.

Harriet's camera whirred as it reached the end of a film. 'I thought you wanted to see the Palio with Alessandro?'

'With Natalie there? No, thanks.'

'You can't let her take him from you,' Harriet said.

I swigged my bottle of water. The air was thick with humidity, and I wiped a film of sweat from my forehead with the back of a hand. Hopefully soon it would cool down as we'd be stuck in the piazza for a while, possibly with no shade.

'If he really likes me, she won't be able to, will she?'

Harriet took a new roll of film out of her bag and swapped it with the one in her camera. 'After a few beers, he might not think twice.'

This was possible, but I wasn't prepared to fight Natalie for him.

By the time we got back to Bar Paolo, it was half past four. The radio played music to an empty room and the barman was cleaning the coffee machine.

'Great.' Harriet pursed her lips. 'We'll never find them in the crowd now.'

We stood outside the bookshop where Alessandro had surprised me that morning. I looked through the window and thought back to him tapping me on the shoulder, then inviting me for coffee. Everything had been so perfect that day, until I'd taken one of Isabella's antihistamines, so he'd been burdened with the task of trying to get me home safely. Perhaps we weren't meant to be. It was probably for the best seeing as we'd soon be returning to our respective countries anyway.

I sighed.

'Let's go to the square before they close the barriers,' I said, thinking it would be a huge shame to miss the Palio after all the effort we'd gone to, just because we couldn't get in.

'Wait.' Harriet clutched my arm, her eyes lighting up. 'They know we're going to the street party of the winning contrada.'

Scrunching up my face, I said, 'I don't know if I want to see him though.'

'Of course you do.' Harriet linked arms with me. 'We're going after the race and that's the end of it.'

CHAPTER 36

JESSICA

The bell rang in the Mangia Tower, and the historical procession entered the square and did a lap round it, the bell on the chariot ringing. Flags were thrown into the air and caught again, with drums, trumpets and bugles playing. The square was bursting with colour, each competing contrada represented by an abundance of scarves and flags. People sat in raised seats in front of the Palazzo Pubblico and stood on balconies from where swathes of red material hung. Children sat on the shoulders of their parents and a couple of television cameramen stood on scaffolding. The distance between us and the barriers bordering the square was a few people deep, and we were packed in like sardines. Although we were now in the shade, it was still baking hot, and I took a sip from my bottle of water. Eager to capture the moment as best I could, I took photos from different angles, and standing on tiptoes while raising my camera above heads in the crowd. At the same time, I wanted to soak up the atmosphere. Where could Alessandro be?

A group of teenage boys stood next to us, Chiocciola scarves round their necks. The boys shouted their anthem in the direction of a group of girls who wore yellow and blue Tartuca scarves across their shoulders. The girls sang their anthem back, even louder. I was glad we weren't with the others. Being trapped in a confined space with Natalie would certainly spoil the experience.

The bell in the Mangia Tower stopped ringing. Silence. Then people in the crowd shook scarves, waved their arms in the air, chanted and screeched, those around us shouting, 'Come on Chiocciola! Come on Tartuca! Come on Onda!'

Over the shouting, whips cracked, and the horses' hooves thundered around them. I could only see the top half of the jockeys. I knew they rode without saddles and that some of them might be thrown off onto the cobblestones, protected only by sawdust and their helmets. Mattresses safeguarded Via San Martino corner, where this was most likely to happen. Horses without jockeys would continue to gallop regardless and were still eligible to win. The noise produced by the crowd intensified with each lap, heads turning as it built to a roar. Then it was over. All the weeks of build-up had culminated in a race lasting no more than ninety seconds.

Cheering, booing, confusion. Which contrada had won?

A feeling of anticlimax swept over me. I'd been waiting to see the Palio for so long, and now it was all over and done just like that.

'So that's it?' I said.

Harriet nodded.

'Who won?'

'I've no idea. Who won?' Harriet asked the Chiocciola boys.

'The Tartuca,' one of them replied. 'I don't believe it.' He shook his head. The Tartuca girls were hugging each other, and jumping up and down.

Sofia had told me Tartuca was Chiocciola's enemy contrada. Each contrada had friends and enemies. If a contrada didn't win, the most its members could hope for was an enemy coming second, which was considered worse than coming last.

Harriet got a map of Siena out of her bag and unfolded it.

'Where's the street party for Tartuca?' she asked the Chioc-ciola boys. One of them pointed to a street on the map.

'There,' he said.

'Let's go,' Harriet said to me.

I unthreaded the Chiocciola scarf from the belt loops of my shorts and pushed it into my pocket. Turning up at the Tartuca party wearing the scarf of their enemy contrada might not be the best idea.

CHAPTER 37

JESSICA

A woman filled our plastic cups with red wine from a barrel. Yellow and blue flags with a tortoise as the symbol bedecked the street. People gathered round the jockey to take photos as he was lifted up into the air by two men. We were crammed into the street like sardines, and I followed Harriet as she pushed a path through the crowd. The air was so sticky that my t-shirt clung to my back. I sat on a windowsill and drank the wine, which was potent and I could feel its effect after only a few sips. Harriet went round taking photos and interviewing locals. I was about to do the same, even though I didn't feel like it, when I saw him. Alessandro was leaning against a wall, a bottle of beer in his hand. Natalie was speaking into his ear and his shoulders shook as he laughed. A huge pang of jealousy swept right through me. Matt stood on the other side of Natalie, staring ahead, playing gooseberry. If he was in love with Natalie, he'd be furious.

Harriet joined me on the windowsill.

'They're over there,' I said.

'So they are.' She put her notepad into her bag. 'And she's all over him.'

I stood by my decision that I wasn't going to fight Natalie for Alessandro.

'Oh, well.'

'Oh well? I won't let you give up like this.' Standing up, she said, 'You're coming with me.' She took hold of my hand and tried to pull me off the windowsill.

'No, I'm not.'

'How are you doing?' Alessandro was standing behind Harriet, flanked by Matt and Natalie.

The humidity, the wine, the situation was all too much.

'Okay,' I said.

'Thanks for waiting for us,' Harriet said, shaking her head.

'Sorry, mate, Natalie didn't want to miss the race,' Matt said.

'I didn't think she cared that much,' Harriet said.

'Course I did.' Natalie slurred her words. She was clearly drunk.

Alessandro sat down next to me and kissed me tenderly on the cheek. I couldn't bring myself to look at him.

'We missed you,' he said.

Getting up, I said, 'I need to go and get more wine.' I didn't want to drink any more, but headed for the woman with the barrel anyway. Maybe I'd just quietly disappear and wander back to the flat in Via San Marco. Someone tapped me on the shoulder and I turned round to see Giuseppe, the drummer from Azzurro, standing before me. It was good to see a friendly face.

Grinning, he said, 'Ciao, Jessica!' and then leant in for the double kiss.

'Ciao, Giuseppe. Come va?'

Shrugging, he said, 'Bene. You, on the other hand, look unhappy.'

'I'm fine.'

'Your beautiful green eyes are filled with sadness.'

'I have to get home.'

'I walk with you,' he said.

It would be good to have the company in case I got lost. Siena could be like a maze with all its tiny streets, and we were in a part I didn't know. Recalling Giuseppe's attempt at seduction while singing and strumming his guitar, it occurred to me that he might get the wrong idea. And I didn't need any of that.

'I don't need you trying to kiss me again though, Giuseppe.'

Raising his hands in the air, he said, 'Don't worry, we go as friends.'

'Well, all right... I'd appreciate you seeing me home then, thanks.'

'Hey Jessica, are you okay?' Alessandro had once again appeared from nowhere. Giuseppe looked up at him as if he was intimidated. It seemed he'd worked out that this was the man I'd been referring to when turning him down. The last thing I wanted was for him to retract his kind offer to walk me back.

'Where's Natalie?' I asked.

'Gone to get more beers. Who's this?'

Was he jealous?

'This is Giuseppe. Giuseppe, Alessandro.'

Giuseppe shook his hand with vigour, as if it was some kind of honour. Alessandro looked down at him, unsmiling.

'Let me know when you want to leave, Jessica,' Giuseppe said, and went off to speak to someone else.

'He's walking me back to the flat as I have no idea where I'm going,' I said to Alessandro.

He scrunched up his eyes. 'You know I can do that.'

How I wanted him to, but, after the way the day had gone, it would be better if he didn't.

Natalie appeared and leant into him. He edged away from her.

'I'll be all right with Giuseppe,' I said.

He scratched his chin and sighed. 'But when will I see you?'

How could we have a proper conversation with Natalie

standing there, listening in? The way she glared at me made me uncomfortable.

'I'm going back to the coast tomorrow,' I said.

'When do you get back?'

Why was he suddenly so interested?

'Saturday.'

'Can I see you then?'

I shrugged. 'I'm flying home not long after that.'

Natalie grabbed his hand. 'Al, are we going to that club?' she said.

He pulled his hand away. 'I'll be with you in a minute,' he said to her, curtly.

Natalie threw me a filthy look before flouncing off, and I was secretly pleased at his brusqueness.

'Jessica, I haven't seen you all day,' he said.

I looked at him and sighed.

Running a hand through his hair, he said, 'I guess it's goodbye then.'

He leant down and kissed me on the cheek, lingering longer than a friend would. The smell of him, that sandalwood scent on his neck, made me want to crumble, but I needed to accept there would be no Chianti-fuelled kiss under a streetlamp after all. I'd pictured us walking back together, hand in hand, and him pulling me through an arch into an alley, kissing me against the wall. Him leading me upstairs to the Sabatinis' flat, empty except for us.

'Bye, Alessandro.'

Turning round, I walked away from him, and went to find Giuseppe, blinking back tears. He was talking to a group of friends, and I tapped him on the shoulder.

'Do you mind if we go now?'

Glancing over my shoulder, I could see that Alessandro was watching me.

'Why don't you go and talk to him?' Giuseppe said.

'No.'

'But he looks at you with the eyes of love.'

How I wished Giuseppe was right, but I couldn't allow myself to believe it. I needed to say goodbye to Harriet.

'Wait there a minute,' I said.

Harriet was talking to Matt, and I told her Giuseppe was walking me back.

'Good.' She spoke into my ear. 'That will make Alessandro jealous.'

'I doubt I'll see him again anyway.'

'Matt said he thinks you don't like him,' she said.

How could he misinterpret my reaction to that kiss in his flat that morning? And I wouldn't have left the note suggesting we meet in Bar Paolo if that was true.

'Well, that's a load of rubbish.'

She gave me a hug, squeezing me tightly. 'I'll write – and don't forget, you're welcome to come and stay in London any time.'

Matt patted me on the shoulder. 'See you mate,' he said.

I went back to find Giuseppe. The day of the Palio had certainly not gone to plan, and I didn't expect to see Alessandro again.

CHAPTER 38

MARIELLA

Peter recovered slowly and, after a couple of weeks, started to move around the house. I found some of my husband's old clothes and gave them to him to wear. The trousers were too long as Giorgio had been a tall man, and so I took them up a couple of inches. Winter was hard, with snow covering the hills all around us. The maid couldn't reach the house from her small village nearby, and so we began to do everything ourselves in order to keep the house running. We made a good team, and this pleased me. I was thankful that he had come into my life that night – otherwise how would I have managed all alone?

We lived on the food supplies I'd built up over the summer and autumn months – thankfully I had a few hams and salamis and some prosciutto, and my maid had pickled vegetables from the garden including peppers, courgettes, cauliflower and onions. And she had made jars of jam with raspberries, strawberries and blackberries. I had a large sack of potatoes in the cellar, along with bags of flour and coffee, and plenty of dried pasta and tins of tomatoes and bulbs of garlic and onions. The maid had dried basil and oregano and rosemary that I could flavour our meals with. And then there were boxes of apples and pears collected from our fruit trees. The goat in the garden provided us with milk, and the chickens with eggs. I would make fresh bread and pasta once a week, being careful to ration the flour as we would not want to run out. When he was certain there were no Tedeschi nearby, Peter would go out into the garden and find snails for us to eat, and he would collect wood and chop it on an old tree stump outside the kitchen window. I would surreptitiously watch him while preparing meals in the kitchen, marvelling at how very masculine and capable he was. Oh, how I longed for him, and how difficult it was to hide my desire in his presence.

When the snow cleared in February, the maid didn't return, and she called to say that her husband had been shot by the Tedeschi for arranging to hide some partisans on a farm nearby. Of course, I understood that she must grieve. Peter and I had been managing just fine without her daily visits. In fact, we'd grown closer during those cold months, spending long evenings talking by the fire about the novels I had been reading to him, and our lives before the war.

In March, spring came, and it was a relief to see the garden come to life once more. The flowers blooming in bright colours were such a joy to see – blossom on the apple trees, geraniums in pink, daffodils and honeysuckle amongst others. The sun shone every day, and the temperature became warmer at last.

One morning, Peter came into the kitchen while I was whisking eggs for a frittata to have for our lunch.

'It's time to shave off this beard, Contessa,' he said. It had grown long and thick since his arrival at the villa, and it struck me that I had never seen him without it. 'Do you have a razor, a brush and some cream?'

I went upstairs and found everything he needed in the bathroom cupboard, and returned to the kitchen. He smiled and took them away, and half an hour or so later, came back. Well, I almost didn't recognise him! He was even more handsome now that I could see all of his face, and I gasped at the sight of him.

He smiled, as if knowing how good he looked.

'What do you think?'

And clearly he wanted me to tell him directly.

'You look very handsome,' I said, feeling we knew each other well enough now for me to say that to him.

'Grazie, Contessa.'

'The frittata is ready to eat now.'

We sat down at the table, and that lunchtime we didn't speak as we ate like we usually did. Instead, we exchanged glances across the table, the tension palpable, and it was then that I knew something would happen between us. Not quite yet, but when we were both ready, and it needed to be his suggestion, of course. But I realised I couldn't imagine my life without him in it. What would I do if he returned to England when the war ended? Did he have someone back home? I had never dared to ask this question. I couldn't bear to think about him leaving me, and was determined to make the most of our time together while he was still here.

One afternoon a few days later, there was a knock on the front door. Peter and I had been sitting in the kitchen drinking espressos and discussing a book, *Dante's Inferno*. I'd studied it at university and had enjoyed introducing him to one of my favourite pieces of literature. Peter went down to the cellar to hide, as he did whenever there was a knock at the door. No one was supposed to know I had a British soldier living with me.

When I opened the door, Herman, a German soldier who'd often come and ask for food supplies, stood there, alone, and my gut lurched. He'd usually be accompanied by another soldier, Klaus, and they were civil but I'd never liked the way Herman studied me for longer than was appropriate. We'd speak in a mixture of Italian and English – I didn't know any German and had no intention of learning it, and Peter had taught me a little English since his arrival.

'Good afternoon, Herman.'

'Good afternoon, Contessa.'

Leaving the door open, I went into the kitchen, and took a bag of food I'd put together for him out of the larder – it contained vegetables from the garden, a jar of home-made strawberry jam, a small salami and a precious ham that I really didn't want to give away.

I handed him the bag and he opened it and peered inside.

'Do you have any wine?'

'I can get you a bottle of wine, yes. It is in the cellar.'

'Very well, go and get it then.'

I opened the door to the cellar and went down the stairs, saying very loudly in order to make Peter aware, 'I'll be back in a minute, Herman.'

'Gut.' This was one German word I understood, meaning good.

I went down the steps, one by one, carefully as they were crumbling and in need of repair. Peter was hiding behind a barrel, and I could see his arm sticking out at the side.

I went to the shelf and took down a bottle of Chianti – we were running out and, being wartime, little wine had been produced that year. I didn't like giving it away, but I could hardly say no to a German soldier's request. But then I heard footsteps, and realised Herman had followed me. A rush of fear passed through me. What if he caught sight of Peter? I needed to get him to go back up to the kitchen. Why had he felt the need to follow me?

I passed him the bottle of Chianti.

'There you are, Herman, only the very best for you and your comrades. Shall we go back upstairs?'

'Ah, but, Contessa, I can see you have more bottles down here. Why don't you give me the rest of that box, make it a dozen?'

'You are asking me to give you all of my wine, Herman? How about one or two more bottles?'

'I want everything you have, and I shan't ask you so nicely a third time, Contessa. Give them to me.'

This would mean no more wine for me and Peter to share. Drinking together had made the long evenings bearable. I had some Vin Santo hidden away, but that would be the only alcohol left in the house. It wasn't fair of Herman to ask this of me, but I didn't have much of a choice. I lifted the box down from the shelf and gave it to him, but he placed it on the floor.

'Do you know, Contessa, you are rather beautiful. Those eyes of yours are mesmerising. Seeing as Klaus isn't with me today, and it's just us here alone together, how about we make the most of a wonderful opportunity?'

'I'm not sure what you mean, Herman,' I replied, trying to remain calm even as my heart began to race.

Leaning forward, he brushed my face with his hand, and this gesture filled me with horror. His beady eyes, filled with longing, betrayed his intentions – he wanted to kiss me, and I would have no choice in the matter. How was I going to stop him? Surely Peter would do something to protect me from this ogre?

'Herman, I am flattered that you find me bella, but I am still grieving for my late husband, murdered by you and your comrades in the village square only months ago. I do hope you understand.'

'Your husband, the count who squealed like a baby when he was waiting to be shot by the firing squad? You should not waste your time grieving for such a coward, Contessa.'

His words filled me with fury. How dare he speak like this about my husband, who had been a most courageous man.

'I will not allow you to speak about him like that, Herman.'

'Don't be so sensitive, Contessa. He is dead now and there is nothing you can do about it.'

I took a deep breath, quietly inhaling through my nose, in order to prevent myself from saying something I'd regret. I wasn't sure what else to say or do. Why wasn't Peter doing anything to help me?

Herman grabbed hold of my wrist, his grip unbearably firm, and led me up the stairs.

'I think you should show me your bedroom, Contessa. We could have a wonderful afternoon together, you and I.'

There was no way in the world he was taking me to bed. I would die stopping him from doing so if I had to. When we reached the kitchen, I discreetly picked up a frying pan off the hob and hid it behind my back. As he led me into the hall, I raised the pan in the air and smacked him on the side of the head with it, but it barely did anything apart from leave a mark. Blood trickled down his face, and he looked at me with eyes filled with fury.

'What do you think you're doing, Contessa?'

'You misunderstood me when I said no to you, Herman.'

He slapped me across the face.

'You do not have any choice in the matter, don't you understand? Being a contessa means nothing during this war. Your rights are no different from those of a mere peasant woman.'

'I shall not take you to my bedroom, Herman. Take out your gun and shoot me right here in my hallway, I implore you. I shall die for my country.'

'Don't be ridiculous, Contessa. You are making a fool of yourself.'

He moved forward to grab my wrist once again and, stepping backwards, I caught sight of Peter as he appeared at the top of the stairs leading to the cellar.

'Contessa, you are making me angry now.'

A gunshot came from nowhere, ringing loudly and making me jump out of my skin. Herman fell to the floor. Peter stood there, holding my husband's shotgun – the one he'd kept in the cellar for emergencies. Peter came over and bent down over Herman's body, feeling his wrist for a pulse.

'He's dead,' he said.

'Grazie, Peter, but what will we do with him?' I gasped, clutching my hand to my chest as tears pricked my eyes.

'Bury him in the garden.'

'But what if someone sees?'

'We'll do it later, after dark. For now, help me carry him down to the cellar.'

'But they'll come looking for him. Klaus will know he was due to come here today.'

'You'll have to say you gave him the supplies and he went off, and that was that.'

'I hope they don't get suspicious.'

'Let's get him down to the cellar, out of sight.'

Peter lifted Herman by the shoulders, and I took his feet, and we carried him down the stairs and hid him behind the barrel. I went to get a blanket from upstairs and we used it to cover his body.

'I need a stiff drink after that, do you mind, Contessa?'

Picking up a bottle of Chianti, I took a deep breath, reassuring myself that everything was all right now Herman was no longer a threat.

'Let's open this, and I'll make some pasta. And I think it's about time you called me Mariella.'

CHAPTER 39

JESSICA

At the villa in Castiglione della Pescaia on the Maremma coast, I started the days by sweeping the terrace, collecting sand, leaves and petals into a pile. It was strangely satisfying carrying out such a mundane task first thing in the morning. I breathed in the sea air and leant on the broom for a moment, taking in the view. A blue panorama lay before me, a canvas divided where the cloudless sky met the Tyrrhenian Sea, the blazing sun making it sparkle. A few yachts were dotted around, their sails billowing, and I could make out the black dots of early-morning surfers. Cicadas chirruped in the lush garden around the pool, and the sound of waves jostling against the shore came from below. The beach was a ten-minute walk downhill and I made the trip every afternoon when Sofia and Isabella were taking their siesta. Being an au pair at the coast wasn't too bad at all. Sofia slept or watched television most of the day, leaving me to sunbathe and swim in the pool. I was as tanned and toned as I'd ever been. Isabella spent some time at Tiziano's house in Follonica, a town nearby. Without Carla the maid, I had to do all the cleaning and cooking as well as keep an eye on Sofia, but the sun and the beautiful setting made it feel like more of a holiday than work.

The previous morning, I'd taken the bus from Siena, doing my best to forget the disastrous day of the Palio. I'd hoped that being at the coast would help me forget Alessandro. I couldn't help picturing him with Natalie though, and the thought of them in bed together tugged at my chest. I wasn't sure whether to contact him when returning to Siena for those few days before flying home. Would he want to see me? What if something had happened with Natalie and they were now an item?

On the bus, I'd tried to write a first draft of the article I planned to submit to *Italian Dreams* magazine, but had been unable to find an interesting hook. I bored myself with the words I wrote as they weren't really saying anything. This was probably because I wasn't in the best mood. Perhaps I needed a little time to pass before I could write about that day.

Sofia shuffled onto the terrace in her flip-flops.

'Are you ready, cara?'

She was waiting for me to do terrace laps – something we did together twice a day to help with the circulation in her legs. I propped up the broom by a terracotta pot filled with pink roses.

'Yes, of course.'

But first, Sofia put on the glasses hanging from a gold chain round her neck and set about searching for the bits I'd missed.

'It is good enough,' she said, finally taking hold of my arm. 'Andiamo.'

I started to walk to the other end of the terrace. We'd do twenty or so of these laps each morning and evening and this was when Sofia would talk to me about anything and everything. My Italian had improved since I'd started spending time with her, and, although she could be cantankerous sometimes, I enjoyed her company.

'So, when are you leaving?' she said.

'The week after next.'

'It will be good to see Lisa again but, between us, I much prefer you.'

It was unusual for her to give compliments, and her saying this gave me a warm feeling.

'That's nice of you to say, Sofia, grazie.'

'Did I tell you Liliana called yesterday to say she's sending the tickets?' she said.

'Which tickets are you referring to?'

'The ones for the opera of course. I'll give two to Alessandro so he can take a young lady.'

I couldn't imagine this was Alessandro's thing. And who'd want to go with him?

'Do you really think he'd want to go, Sofia?'

'Of course. It's an opportunity to see Puccini's *Tosca* at Massa Marittima, outside in the square, the stars shining from above. I wonder who he'll decide to take? My handsome grandson will have so much choice, I am sure. Liliana is hoping he'll choose her niece.'

Not Liliana's niece again. Hadn't he already said he didn't want to take her out? I expected he'd be too polite to turn down his grandmother's tickets, but doubted he'd invite this woman. What about Natalie? Sofia had made going to the opera sound so romantic that I found myself wanting him to take me.

'I'm sure he knows plenty of girls, as you say.'

Sofia shrugged. 'Mah. I'll also give two tickets to Carla for her mother's birthday. She loves opera and Carla has been loyal to me for many years.'

If only Sofia knew what Carla was really like. I had a strong suspicion that she took money out of the kitty.

'Don't you want to go?' I asked.

'Me?' Sofia laughed. 'I can't sit still for long, as you know, and operas go on for hours and hours.'

Maybe I wasn't so keen after all.

'Besides, I've seen *Tosca* with Benedetto many times. He took me to see it in Florence on our first night out together after the war. I remember him holding my hand during "E Lucevan Le Stelle", a song Mario sings when he writes a final letter to Tosca, remembering when they first met, how the stars were shining brightly. That song played its part in bringing us together. How I miss my Benedetto.'

'I can imagine you must miss him a great deal.'

'Indeed, but it won't be long before I follow and then we'll be reunited.'

The thought of Sofia dying was sad, and I didn't want to think about it.

I'd been thinking about Peter's diary since finishing it the previous week, and now was my chance to see if Sofia could remember anything.

'Sofia, you know that I've been reading my grandfather's diary?'

Nodding, she said, 'Yes.'

'Well, this may seem silly, but...' Would Alessandro mind me telling her what Benedetto had told him on his deathbed? Surely he would have told Sofia this anyway? 'I wonder if he might have survived that night he was shot?'

Stopping, she looked at me. 'Why would you think that?'

I told her what Alessandro had said.

'Hmmm. Benedetto did tell me about what Francesco said when he was drunk one night, but who knows if he was making it up?'

'But do you think it might be possible he survived that night?'

'Francesco said he took him to the contessa's villa, and maybe he did, but we didn't hear anything about him after that. She went to live in Lake Garda after the war and no one ever heard from her again.'

'Do you think he could still be alive today though?' This was a ridiculous suggestion, and as I said it I found myself doubting it could be true.

'Who knows?' she said. 'I did rather like him. I gave him a handkerchief embroidered with a snail and the Chiocciola colours because he saved Benedetto's life.'

As we walked, it seemed she was thinking, and then she looked at me.

'It's funny, I recall Enzo reading a novel last summer by P.J. Collina – a murder mystery set in Lake Garda – and we discussed Peter joking about staying in Italy after the war and changing his name to Pietro Collina, the Italian version of his name.'

What was Sofia saying? I knew Peter had wanted to be a novelist – he'd written this in his diary. And she'd just told me that the countess had gone to live in Lake Garda after the war.

'Really, do you think it could be him?'

'It's a coincidence, I'm sure, but we did all have a laugh about it one evening.' She stopped and wagged her finger at a piece of brioche under the table. 'Jessica, cara, you missed a bit.'

Rolling my eyes, I smiled.

'I always find something,' she said with a chuckle.

If I could make Sofia feel important for a few seconds because she'd located a few breadcrumbs, then so be it.

'Shall I clear it up now?'

'Yes, that's enough walking for this morning.'

She sat on the edge of a sunlounger in the shade created by the awning, and, slipping off her flip-flops, put up her feet and lay down. Time for her morning nap.

I went to get the dustpan and brush and swept up the piece of brioche she'd spotted. Once she was asleep, I'd do some lengths in the pool. What she'd said about Peter had got me thinking. I'd need to find one of those novels and see if there might be a photo inside the cover. Sometimes authors included biographies in their books, didn't they? And wouldn't Gran recognise him, even if he was older?

CHAPTER 40

JESSICA

That afternoon, I lay on the sunlounger with my eyes closed, the sun nicely tanning my skin. Car tyres crunched on the gravel at the front of the villa. I expected it was Enzo, who liked to drop in unannounced every now and again. Shuddering at the thought of him ogling me, I rushed to put on my bikini top and fastened the clasp. A car door slammed shut and there were footsteps on the path. Wrapping a towel round me, I reached for *Corriere della Sera*, and pretended to read an article about a tour the pope was doing. The footsteps edged closer, and then a familiar aftershave hung on the air, more discreet than Enzo would go for. The scent was sandalwood. Before looking up, I'd worked out who it was.

'Hey, Jessica.'

Alessandro stood above me, a holdall slung over his shoulder. He wore a white t-shirt and chino shorts. He was grinning at me, and seemed to think I should be expecting him.

Lost for words, I found myself grinning in return, but then remembered the day of the Palio and sighed.

'What are you doing here, Alessandro?'

He frowned. 'That's a nice welcome. Didn't Sofia tell you I was coming?'

Had she invited him? If I'd known, I could have mentally prepared myself. Shaking my head, I said, 'No, she didn't.'

He put the bag down. 'I called this morning and asked if it would be okay.'

He walked to the edge of the terrace and studied the sea. 'Mom was right, this place is something else.'

How was I going to cope with him being here after what had happened? I'd settled into my quiet routine, and didn't feel like dealing with him.

'What time did you ring?'

Alessandro stood with his back to me, studying the view. He didn't answer. Putting down the newspaper, I picked up Isabella's copy of *Ciao Bella*. I flicked through the magazine, scanning pictures of Italian celebrities on yachts, not knowing who any of them were. I didn't like him ignoring me and a wave of irritation stirred in my gut.

'Alessandro, when did you call?'

'I don't know. Around ten thirty.'

I would have been sweeping the terrace. Sofia had probably answered the telephone before she came out for her laps. Surely her memory could last the short distance from the telephone to the terrace?

He turned round to face me.

'You're the only English-speaking person who calls me Alessandro, apart from my mom.'

But I didn't want to call him Al. 'I'm sorry. Should I be calling you something else?'

He walked towards me. 'It's just an observation, that's all.'

'Why are you here?'

'Siena's so humid, I asked to spend a couple of days in this place. It's certainly a lot cooler. Seems I did the right thing.'

He looked at me as he said this. Did he mean that he wanted to see me too?

I lowered the magazine. 'Sofia's hardly renowned for her memory. You should have asked to speak to Isabella or me.'

Lifting his eyebrows, he said, 'You sound like a teacher.'

'Where did you get the car?'

'A guy in class lent it to me. Where are Sofia and Isabella, anyway?'

I wanted everything to be good between us, but how could I act as though nothing had changed since the Palio fiasco?

'Sofia's asleep, and Isabella's at Tiziano's.'

He sat sideways on the sunlounger next to mine, so he was facing me. I couldn't bring myself to look at him, so I flicked through the pages of *Ciao Bella* again from the beginning, feigning interest.

'Jessica, would you put down that damn magazine. I bet you can't even understand any of it.'

'What? I'm looking at the pictures.'

He leant forwards, gently retrieved *Ciao Bella* from my hands and cast it over his shoulder. Now I had no choice but to look at him.

'What on earth are you doing? I was reading that.'

'No, you weren't. Is me staying going to be a problem?'

He looked at me so intently, I wished things could go back to how they'd been. To that morning when we'd kissed at his flat and fallen against the door.

'You can have Enzo's room.'

He stared at me for a moment longer and then nodded. 'Could you show me where it is? I need to take a shower. Driving in this heat without air conditioning was a little sweat-inducing.'

Oh, what did I have to lose? He was here and, really, I should make the most of it. Deciding not to waste any more time, I stood up, allowing the towel to slip, revealing my bikini, knowing my body was the most toned and tanned it had ever been.

He looked me up and down, his mouth upturned at the corners, and I said, 'Follow me. I'll show you upstairs.'

CHAPTER 41

JESSICA

That evening, we all sat at the table on the veranda. Isabella had brought an octopus back from the market that morning, and it was slippery and slimy, reminding me of when we had to dissect disgusting things in biology at school. I had grappled with the thing to get it into the saucepan, its legs springing back when I pushed down the lid. Eventually I'd left it to boil with a couple of the legs partially hanging over the side. As I chewed the octopus it didn't get any smaller, and I spat it discreetly into my napkin while pretending to wipe my mouth. Taking a piece of bread from the basket to get rid of the taste, I saw that Alessandro was watching me, a slight look of amusement on his face as he appeared to be squashing a smile.

Nobody spoke during the meal, so I watched a cruise ship out at sea as the sun dropped towards the horizon, the sky a mix of pink, red and orange. Sofia hadn't told Isabella about Alessandro calling that morning either. Isabella wasn't happy about him staying in Enzo's room, as it meant Tiziano couldn't come over. Sofia didn't approve of him staying in Isabella's room, so she'd pretend they were sleeping separately but sneak in there to see him.

When everyone had finished, I got up to clear the table. Alessandro had polished off all of his octopus and I was grateful that he'd at least seemed to enjoy it.

'You cooked the octopus for too long Jessica,' Isabella said.

Piling the plates on top of each other, I said, 'This is the first time I've made it.'

'That was evident,' Sofia said. 'I don't like octopus anyway, cara. It's too chewy for an old woman like me. Why did you get it, Isabella?'

'It's a delicacy to be enjoyed, usually,' Isabella said.

'Well, I thought it was delicious,' Alessandro said.

Why was he standing up for me all of a sudden? I looked away, rolling my eyes.

'By the way, Jessica, I've been meaning to ask if you've seen my diamond earrings,' Isabella said.

She and Sofia glared at me, and I couldn't have felt more uncomfortable. Why would Isabella think I knew where they were? I didn't like what she was implying, and in front of Alessandro, too. He made a thing of folding up his napkin, and unfolding it again, as if he wanted to intervene but didn't know how to.

'What do you mean?' I said.

'You know, the gold dangly ones with diamonds.'

I recalled them catching the sunlight when we were discussing who should help Sofia get ready in the kitchen.

'Oh yes, you wore them at Sofia's party.'

'Are you quite certain you didn't borrow them?' Isabella said. 'If you return them now, we can forget all about it.'

Surely Isabella wasn't implying that I'd stolen them from her? Why wasn't Sofia defending me?

'I have no idea where they are.'

'Tiziano gave them to me on my birthday, and they're very special,' Isabella said.

The plates were weighing me down, and I started to head for the kitchen. 'I'm sorry, Isabella, but I don't have them.'

Inside, I scraped leftovers into the bin, unable to believe Isabella thought so little of me. I clenched my teeth. How could she falsely accuse me of stealing, and in front of Alessandro too? She'd made me feel so small and insignificant and I wanted to go to my room and curl up into a ball and cry. The earrings were probably in her bedroom in Siena. If not, Carla was the only other outsider who came to the flat.

When I'd finished loading the dishwasher, I shut the door and switched it on. At last, my work for the day was done. I went to the fridge and poured out a glass of Gavi di Gavi – a crisp white wine that Isabella kept stock of. I was glad that after dinner, she'd gone to stay at Tiziano's place. Sofia watched a beauty contest on television. Alessandro was on the phone to his mother, and I hoped he'd want to talk to me afterwards. I placed my glass of wine on the table outside and lit the mosquito burners around the edge of the terrace, and smoke swirled into the air. The burners didn't stop me from getting bitten, but Isabella liked me to light them every night before dark.

I sat down and sipped the wine, and instantly it took the edge off what had been an odd day. A mosquito buzzed round my ear, and I waved it away with my hand. A breeze rustled the leaves in the fig tree nearby, and cicadas called out to each other. I put on my cardigan and fastened up the buttons. The deep-purple and orange sky darkened, and I looked out to sea. A fishing boat moved through the water, its red and green lights glowing.

Alessandro stepped onto the terrace with a glass of what appeared to be whisky.

'Are you okay, Jessica?'

I assumed he was referring to Isabella accusing me of stealing, but didn't feel like talking about it.

'Yeah, I'm fine.'

He took a sip of his drink, the ice cubes clinking, then put the glass down on the table. 'That was the worst octopus I ever had.'

I laughed. 'Well, I appreciate you pretending you liked it. How's your mum?'

'Glad I'm here.' He slapped himself on the neck. 'Damn these bugs.'

I passed him a can of insect repellent. He nodded his thanks and set about spraying his legs.

'Mom's been saying I should spend more time with Nonna. And she wanted me to see this place. She used to talk about it fondly when I was growing up.'

So, he wasn't here to see me then.

'I didn't think we'd see each other again,' I said.

He sat beside me so we both had a view of the sea, propping up his bare feet on the chair opposite.

'That's another reason to be here, of course.' He sighed. 'The day of the Palio was a let-down, wasn't it?'

At last he'd broached the subject we'd been avoiding. I needed more to drink if we were going to talk about that dreadful day.

Standing up, I said, 'It certainly was. Can I get you another drink?'

He handed me his glass. 'More of Enzo's whisky, thanks, the expensive bottle on the left.'

When I brought back our drinks, we clinked glasses and said, 'Cin cin.'

The sky was now completely black apart from the full moon, which shone like a giant lamp, casting a white glow on the water.

'About Natalie...' he said.

I couldn't bear to hear her name. The candle on the table flickered in the breeze, which seemed stronger than usual.

Perhaps there would be a storm tomorrow – one had been brewing for a few days.

'I don't want to know,' I said.

'Okay, but can I just tell you—'

'Please don't.'

Shrugging, he said, 'Who was that guy you left with again?'

Was he jealous? 'Giuseppe?'

'Anything going on there?'

I shook my head with a laugh. 'Not at all. Although he'd like there to be.'

'Who is he?'

'He's in a band called Azzurro. Harriet used to go out with the lead singer, Fabrizio. He—'

'I mean, who is he to you?'

'Nobody.'

Standing up – was he going to bed already? – he said, 'An ex?'

'No. He just tried to kiss me once, that's all.'

He stretched his arms above his head, put a hand over his mouth and yawned loudly.

'Okay. Well, I'm exhausted.' He leant down and kissed me gently on the cheek. 'See you in the morning, Jessica.'

He went inside and, glancing over my shoulder, I watched him climb the stairs. He gave me a nod, and I smiled slightly in return. Once again, Alessandro had left me feeling so confused. I just wanted to go to bed and sleep and hope for a better day tomorrow. But I needed to keep Sofia company until she'd finished watching the beauty contest. Blowing out the candle, I decided nothing was ever going to happen with Alessandro. If he was that interested, he would have stayed and talked for longer. Maybe it was time to move on...

CHAPTER 42

JESSICA

The following morning, I dragged the net over the surface of the pool, collecting leaves and insects. There was no sign of Alessandro. Clouds scudded across the sky and waves crashed rather than jostled against the shore below, the size of the crests hinting that the weather was about to turn. According to the weather forecast, a storm would come this afternoon or evening.

'Good morning, Jessica.'

Alessandro was standing on the terrace in swimming shorts. When I saw his bare torso and remembered that my bikini left little to the imagination, I felt my cheeks flush. I tipped the contents of the net onto the roses so I could turn away from him.

'Hi,' I said over my shoulder.

He ran across the lawn and dived into the pool from the deep end, barely making a splash. He stayed underwater for a few seconds, then surfaced and broke into a crawl. He swam length after length, and I couldn't take my eyes off his broad shoulders and muscular thighs. After a few minutes he swam to the edge, next to where I was standing, and I carried on collecting stuff with the net, despite the distraction of him being right there. He rested his elbows on the side and ran a hand through his hair as he squinted in the sun. His hair looked even better wet.

'Are you coming in?'

'I can't.'

'Why not?'

As I moved around the pool with the net, he followed me.

'I've got things to do.'

'I'm sorry about the Palio, about yesterday. Can't we start again?'

'Yeah, why not.'

'That's great. You have a bug in your hair,' he said.

Shaking my head vigorously, I accidentally dropped the net into the pool.

'What is it?'

'Could be a wasp. Come here, let me see.'

I squatted on the tiles next to him, but he got hold of my hands and pulled me into the pool.

'Aaaahhhh!'

Splasssh. My head went underwater, and I pushed my feet against the bottom of the pool and bounced to the surface. He laughed, letting go of my hands. As I squeezed the water out of my hair, I couldn't help smiling, and appreciated his attempt at flirtation.

'So, there's no bug, as you call it, in my hair?'

'I couldn't help myself.'

How I wanted him to kiss me. He moved towards me, those dark-brown eyes locking with mine.

'Jessica!' Sofia shouted from the terrace.

Damn, another missed opportunity.

'I have to go.'

Swimming to the steps, I grabbed the railings and climbed the ladder. The bikini, now wet, clung to my body even more, and I could tell out of the corner of my eye that he was watching my every move.

'Trust Nonna to spoil everything. Do you ever get any time off?' he said.

I turned to face him, and he handed me the net out of the pool.

'I go to the beach during siesta.'

'Can you show me where it is?' he said.

That afternoon, we walked down the hill without speaking, tension hanging between us. I couldn't wait for something to happen. Would something happen? The butterflies in the base of my stomach told me it might.

When we got to the beach, we placed our towels side by side on the golden sand. Alessandro lay on his stomach and opened the *New York Times* in front of him. I kicked off my flip-flops and sat down, wrapping my arms round my knees. The breeze was stronger than usual, and sand blew into my eyes. Reaching inside my bag, I got out my sunglasses. Grey clouds loomed overhead, and surfers messed about on the big waves.

Leaning on one elbow, Alessandro looked over at me.

'So, Jessica?'

Smiling, I said, 'Yes?'

'Can we go back to how we were?'

Was he suggesting we kiss again?

'What do you mean?'

'You know, that morning when I made you breakfast, and it was so cool. And then, as you were leaving...'

I shrugged. 'Everything changed on the day of the Palio.'

'We need to get past the Palio,' he said.

A mother with a baby packed up her things, the baby crying. A gust of wind knocked over an umbrella, and a woman fought to push it back into the sand, shouting in Italian. She started to pack her things into a beach bag. Should we be leaving too?

'Why didn't you wait for us in the bar?' I asked.

'We did, for twenty minutes.'

'You did?'

'Yeah. I should have made Matt and Natalie wait for longer, or I could have stayed in the bar on my own,' he said.

I studied my toenails. The varnish was chipped, and I needed to repaint them.

'It's a shame the day played out that way,' I said.

'Can I tell you about Natalie?'

Although deep down I was curious to know the truth, I'd be devastated to find out that something had happened between them.

'Let's get it over with then.'

'Nothing happened, I promise. She did try, though.'

'Well, she was all over you at the street party.'

'I was fighting her off while waiting for you to show up.'

Was he telling the truth? Natalie had been drunk, and I knew from our dinner that he wouldn't take advantage of a woman in that situation.

'You didn't seem to mind her attention.'

'She's Matt's friend from home and I was there with him. I considered kissing her when I saw you leave with that guy, what's his name?'

'Giuseppe.'

'Giuseppe. I was real mad when you left with him.'

It started to drizzle. We were the only people left on the beach, apart from surfers and a group of teenage boys playing football, with t-shirts as goalposts.

'I asked him to walk me home because I didn't want to get lost. Those narrow streets in Siena are like a maze, especially if you don't know the area.'

'I have a confession, Jessica. I did actually come here to see you.'

Lightning flashed across the sky, which had turned a blue-black colour. Rain started to pour down on us, and a crack of thunder made me jump out of my skin. But he was here to see me and that was all that mattered.

'We'd better make a move,' he said.

Getting up, I rolled up my towel, and pushed it into my duffel bag. I started heading for the footpath that ran in front of the beach huts, not realising Alessandro wasn't right behind me.

'Jessica, wait.'

He caught up with me and got hold of my hand, and wrapped his fingers tightly round mine. We ran up the path together and I didn't care about my hair getting wet or the water running down my face. The sky flashed, then came another crack of thunder.

'We need to find shelter,' he shouted.

He pulled me into a beach hut and closed the door. The door blew open, the rain coming in, and he slammed it shut, then pushed the bolt across. He pressed the light switch, but nothing happened.

'We'll have to get by without electricity,' he said.

I didn't know what to say. Here we were in a confined space in the dark with a thunderstorm raging outside. There was nowhere else to go. The only light came from the gap between the door and its frame. If he didn't make his move now, he never would. He spread out his towel on the floor and we sat beside each other on it, our clothes all wet from the rain. I was shivering, and my teeth chattered. He put an arm round me and pulled me close to him.

'When you didn't show up at Bar Paolo, I thought you'd changed your mind about me.'

Had he misread my feelings for him, or was he feeding me a line? I tried to shake the question from my head. I needed to trust what he was saying. If I turned him down now, I'd always wonder what might have been.

'Well, I hadn't.'

Then he leant in and kissed me, pushing his tongue into my mouth, at first gently then harder, and we fell to the floor. Rain hammered on the roof. He untied my bikini top and cupped my breasts, his hands somehow still warm from the sun. Grains of sand crunched beneath me as we rolled around on the floor, but I didn't care. A crack of thunder. He lay on top of me, his torso pressing against my breasts, the weight of him on me. At last we seemed to be getting somewhere...

CHAPTER 43

JESSICA

We walked uphill, the sun forming dappled light on the road through the trees. Usually, intense heat made walking back to the villa a struggle, but the storm had cleared the air and the temperature was much cooler. Alessandro held my hand and I breathed in the scent from the marine pine trees, their pungency drawn out by the rain. Scraps of brown fern lined the edge of the road like a carpet, and I bent down to pick up a pine cone. The pattern on the outside looked like fish scales and I slipped it into my pocket to keep as a memento.

The villa's terracotta roof came into view through a gap in the trees, and I wished we had the place to ourselves. When we got back, I'd start preparing dinner and later we'd eat with Isabella and Sofia. Then I'd clear up, and Sofia would watch game shows or old black-and-white films until her bedtime. Only then could me and Alessandro carry on where we'd left off in the beach hut, and butterflies fluttered in my belly at the thought. We reached the brow of the hill and Alessandro stopped at the foot of the crumbling steps leading to the villa. Water dripped from the trees, making a pattering sound, and cicadas chirruped from clumps of grass lining the edge of the road.

'I'm glad you came out here,' I said.

Wrapping his arms round my waist, he pulled me to him and kissed me with such intensity, I was swept away. Tomorrow he'd drive back to Siena, and I shut this thought out of my mind. He brushed my face with his hand and looked down at me.

'So am I,' he said, 'Will you come to my room tonight?'

Who wanted to play more games when there was so little time?

'Yes.' Glancing at my watch, I saw it was ten past four. Isabella liked me to be back at four o'clock sharp and I was being rebellious breaking one of her rules. 'We're late and Isabella will no doubt give me a good telling-off. Come on then. And we'd better let go of each other.'

He allowed my hand to slip out of his and led the way up the steps while I admired his taut backside. When we reached the top, Isabella was putting a designer holdall – the one containing Sofia's blood pressure monitor and pills – into the back of her car. No doubt I'd be expected to accompany them wherever they were going.

'Jessica, you're late,' she said.

'I'm sorry.'

Slamming the boot shut, she clicked in her heels along the path towards the back of the villa. Sofia was sitting on the terrace in her blue floral dress, the one she wore when visiting other people's houses. I hoped they weren't going to Enzo's as I didn't have a valid excuse ready.

'Buonasera,' Sofia said.

'Where have you both been all this time?' Isabella said.

'We got caught in the storm and had to find shelter,' Alessandro said. 'It's my fault. Jessica wanted to come back up the hill in the lightning, but I thought it would be dangerous with all the trees.'

He was standing up for me, and this gave me a warm feeling.

'Va bene. Tiziano's mother, Lucia, has invited us for dinner, as she wanted to meet Mamma.'

I didn't relish the thought of yet another evening at a stranger's house. Usually, I'd sit quietly at the table counting down the minutes until it was time to leave. Good wine and Italian home cooking weren't enough to compensate for me feeling like a spare part.

'Do I need to come with you?' I said, emboldened by Alessandro's presence.

'Lucia has a maid who'll look after Sofia, so you can stay here if you like,' Isabella said.

What a stroke of luck. Alessandro caught my eye, and gave me a slight smile.

'I'll be going to bed early as I have to leave first thing to get back for class. Shall I say goodbye to you both now?' Alessandro said.

'Perfetto. Tiziano wanted to stay tomorrow night, and we'll need Enzo's room,' Isabella said.

He double-kissed them both. 'Thanks for having me to stay,' he said.

'When shall I see you next, caro?' Sofia said.

'I'll visit when you're back in Siena.'

'Jessica, please cook something delicious for Alessandro,' Sofia said.

'Don't worry, Nonna, I can fix myself a sandwich,' he said.

'A sandwich, what nonsense! Alessandro, a man needs to eat. Jessica will make you a pasta starter, and there's a steak in the fridge that I asked Isabella to buy especially. Did Jessica show you the beach?'

'Yes, she showed me everything.'

He threw me a look, his lips upturned, and I did my best not to burst out laughing.

Isabella helped Sofia out of the chair, and they walked slowly to the car.

'What time will you be back?' I called after them.

'Around eleven,' Isabella replied.

That would give me and Alessandro plenty of time together. I couldn't believe my luck.

I cleared the empty glasses from around the terrace, and slotted them into the dishwasher. Alessandro went upstairs and came back holding a bottle of prosecco, the white towel wrapped round his waist accentuating his tanned skin. He looked so good, and I still couldn't believe he was interested in me.

'Where did you get that?'

'Enzo's got a fridge up there.'

'What if he notices?'

'I'm sure he won't – there are a few bottles.'

I opened the glasses cupboard and handed him two flutes.

Taking my hand, he led me upstairs. 'Let's go and get this opened.'

Later, we lay in bed, and Alessandro held me in his arms. Nothing else mattered except being there in that moment with him. I looked up at the cherubs floating in a circle on the ceiling and couldn't remember the last time I'd felt so happy. I'd never felt like this after a night spent with Tom.

'I've wanted to do that since I first saw you standing at your door that day,' he said. 'I saw these incredible legs' – he ran his hand along the inside of my thigh, his touch making me quiver – 'and couldn't get you off my mind.'

'I wasn't sure if you liked me.'

'Are you kidding? Whenever you walked out of a room, my eyes were glued to your ass.'

I laughed and he leant in to kiss me.

Saying goodbye in a few days was going to tear me apart. For now I needed to enjoy every second of our time together.

CHAPTER 44

JESSICA

The light woke me up because we'd forgotten to close the shutters. The radio alarm glowed five o'clock in red numbers. I studied the man who I was madly in love with. His breathing was soft, and he looked about as content as a man could be. He'd set the alarm for six because he'd fail the course if he missed two more classes. I got out of bed and picked up my bikini from where it had dropped to the floor when he peeled it off. Putting it back on, I saw a notepad and pen on the desk. I wrote a message:

I'm so glad you came to Castiglione. See you back in Siena. J xx

I tore off the page and left it on the bedside table, under his watch so he'd see it. As I put the notebook back on the desk, a row of novels on the desk above with blue and yellow spines caught my eye. They were all written by P.J. Collina. Sofia had mentioned seeing Enzo reading one of these novels. I ran a hand along them – were these written by my grandfather? My breath shortened as the reality of this discovery struck me, but I mustn't get too excited in case it wasn't him. Taking one down from the shelf – *Sporchi Trucchi a Lago di Garda*, meaning Dirty Tricks in Lake Garda – I opened it and flicked through the pages. It was written in Italian, of course it was, and my knowledge wasn't up to reading and understanding it all. Perhaps I could get an English version back at home. I'd love to see what kind of writer he was, if indeed it was him. I turned to the inside of the back cover and there it was – a photo of a distinguished-looking man with white hair, and eyes of a blue-grey colour. Clearly he'd been handsome in his youth. There was a biography. I'd learnt just enough Italian from my course and living with the Sabatinis to be able to translate it into English:

> Bestselling author P.J. Collina lives in a villa on Lake Garda, the setting for all his books, with his wife, Mariella. He likes to go out on his boat and is fond of gardening, and especially enjoys spending time with his family. He is proud to have two sons who are happily married, and five grandchildren.

Envy stirred in my gut. If this was him, how dare he be proud of grandchildren who weren't me? And who did he think he was, boasting about his two sons when he'd never wanted to know his daughter, Mum? And was this Mariella the countess? How could he choose her over Gran, the mother of his child? Sofia had said she went to live in Lake Garda after the war, and so it all fitted together. Mariella had to be her and P.J. Collina just had to be him. Would Gran recognise him from this photo?

Taking the book, I left the room, stealing one last glance at Alessandro. It would be a very long day with him gone. I needed to squeeze in an hour or two of sleep before starting work, and so I headed back to my room, where I could close the shutters without waking him up. This was a cop-out, I knew that, but I just couldn't face what was bound to be a sad goodbye.

· · ·

A few hours later, on the terrace, after managing to get some sleep, I turned the handle on the awning to make shade for breakfast. Now the storm had passed, the sky was once again a deep-blue colour and the sea shimmered in the sun. For once the view did nothing to lift my mood.

Alessandro would be back in Siena by now, and I could have kicked myself for sneaking back to my room without saying goodbye. What had I been thinking? Sleep deprivation didn't always lead to the best decisions. Would he contact me when I returned to Siena? Picking up the broom, I swept up leaves and petals blown onto the terrace by the previous day's storm.

At breakfast, Isabella and Sofia sat at the table on the veranda and I poured coffee into their espresso cups.

'How was Tiziano's?' I said to Isabella.

'Lucia and Sofia got on well didn't you, Mamma?' Isabella said.

'Yes, we did,' Sofia said.

I pulled up a chair and took a brioche out of the basket. Isabella downed her coffee and lit a cigarette. Sofia did her best to chew a slice of bread. How would I get through the next few days? All I wanted to do was see Alessandro again and spend those last precious moments with him before we parted ways. I stirred an extra spoonful of sugar into my espresso. It didn't help that I was oh so tired.

'Good morning, Alessandro,' Isabella said.

What?

I knocked over my espresso cup, coffee spilling onto the table. Turning round, I saw him standing in the doorway, wearing swimming shorts and a t-shirt. He ran a hand through his hair, which stuck up at the front from where his head had been on the pillow. He didn't look at me, and I guessed he didn't want to make it obvious we'd spent the night together. As I blotted the coffee with a napkin, thoughts raced through my mind. I was so happy to see him, but what was he still doing here?

'Alessandro, come and join us,' Sofia said.

'Sorry I'm still here, I slept through my alarm,' he said.

He probably wouldn't need to go back to Siena until the following morning now he'd missed his class. Would I get to spend another night with him? I couldn't help beaming at the thought.

'Jessica, go and get a cup for Alessandro's coffee,' Isabella said.

'I can do that myself, Zia.'

He went into the kitchen, returned with a cup, and pulled up a chair, winking discreetly at me. I smiled at him, happy to have his company for another day and night. He ran his foot up my calf under the table, and I did my best not to show any reaction on my face.

'When are you leaving, Alessandro?' Isabella said.

He poured coffee from the pot, reached over to take my knife and plate and spread jam on a slice of bread.

'Well, I was hoping I could stay another night now I've missed my class.'

'Don't forget that Tiziano's coming tonight, and he'll need Enzo's room. Jessica, can you strip the bed after breakfast and wash the sheets?'

I nodded, my heart sinking.

'I can do that,' Alessandro said. 'I'll leave at four o'clock then, when it's cooler.'

'Alessandro can stay another night if he wants to,' Sofia said.

Isabella sighed and stubbed out her cigarette in the ashtray.

'If he must stay for longer, I can go to Tiziano's, again.'

'I should probably get back to Siena,' he said. 'If I oversleep tomorrow, I'll fail my class.'

His reply left me with a sinking feeling, but I did my best

not to show this on my face. I looked across the table at him, gently lifting my eyebrows and he gave me a slight nod. What a shame he couldn't stay another night. Oh well, at least we could go to the beach during siesta.

CHAPTER 45

JESSICA

'Jessica, wake up.'

Alessandro lay on his side, propped up by an elbow, his chin resting in his hand. We'd come to the beach after lunch, put our towels together, then I must have fallen asleep. Visions from a dream flashed through my mind and I tried to piece them together.

'What time is it?'

'Three o'clock. Thought I should wake you.'

The dream came back to me, and I hoped it wasn't an omen. Me and Alessandro had been running through a field on Birch Farm, holding hands as we tried to get away from a herd of cows. We ran towards an aeroplane in a field, got in, and he sat in the pilot seat. He started the engine and the aeroplane taxied, knocking down a drystone wall. The plane took off and I saw through the window that Mum, Gran and Dad were chasing the aeroplane, with a herd of cows following them. Tom sat in the back dressed in a morning suit, a carnation in his lapel. He jumped out of the aeroplane and a parachute opened with words printed on it saying, 'You're making a big mistake.' We flew past the Statue of Liberty and landed in a garden. Alessandro's family held glasses of prosecco, their arms outstretched. They said, 'Welcome to America, Jessica!' A beautiful woman with dark hair appeared, wearing a wedding dress. She said, 'He's mine, you need to leave.' Alessandro shrugged and said, 'I have to marry Gabriella.' His whole family chased me down the garden and, when I got back on the aeroplane, the engine wouldn't start. A policeman appeared to tell me that I was in America illegally and he was going to arrest me. He was about to clip handcuffs on my wrists, and that's when I woke up.

'Are you okay?' Alessandro asked, a look of concern on his face.

I sat up, slowly, feeling slightly dazed, as you do when sleeping during the day.

'I had a weird dream.' I put on my sunglasses. A couple were playing with wooden bats and a ball, the ball making a tick-tock sound as they hit it to each other. A group of teenagers messed about on a pedalo, shrieking as they jumped off it into the sea.

'I was just thinking about that time when we went for dinner. I asked if you had someone back home and you disappeared to the restroom,' he said.

Now, he'd caught me at a weak moment when I hadn't properly woken up, and my guard would be down. I needed coffee. He deserved an answer, but I didn't know what his reaction would be.

I pushed my toes into the sand. 'He's called Tom.'

'I knew there had to be someone.'

'We've been going out for a few years, since school.' I thought back to Valentine's Day. 'He proposed before I came to Italy.'

Inhaling, Alessandro said, 'You're engaged, but chose not to wear the ring?'

'No, not at all. We agreed that I'd tell him my answer after Siena and we wouldn't be in contact until I got back.'

'Do you love him?'

'No, but I don't think he loves me either. He's a farmer and needs a wife. I fit the bill because he wants to get his hands on my mum and dad's land. It will be like that with whoever I marry.'

'Why?'

'Because that's my future. It's been mapped out for me since the day I was born.'

'Your parents want you to marry someone who can take over the farm?'

'My mum is keen, yes.'

'Tell her you won't do it,' he said.

'I know, but she'll be so upset.'

'You can do whatever you like.'

'Did your parents put pressure on you to follow their agenda?' I said.

'I'm lucky. It was tough for my oldest brother, Marco, who Dad expected to take over the delicatessen. My other brother, Paolo, always had a thing for cars, so he runs his own garage.'

'What about you?'

'I got to do what I wanted. My mom wrote to Sofia when I was at high school, asking if she'd fund a university education. She obliged, and I studied art history and economics. After university, I got some work experience at an art gallery. Then I got the job at Pimsy's.'

Standing up, he shook the sand from his towel. 'Anyway, do you want to come to the opera with me?'

'Doesn't Sofia want you to take Liliana's niece?'

He laughed as he rolled up his towel and pushed it into his rucksack. 'I said I wanted to take a girl from class.'

'Who?'

'Well, I meant you, but I couldn't say that, could I?'

'I guess not.'

'Will you come with me?'

I nodded and smiled, and then remembered about finding the P.J. Collina book in Enzo's room. I hadn't got round to updating Alessandro on my discovery and so I told him all about it, and the photo.

'I just need to find the English version so I can actually read it,' I said.

'What's it called?' he said.

'*Sporchi Trucchi a Lago di Garda.*'

'*Dirty Tricks in Lake Garda.* I'll look out for it. They might have it in that bookshop you like back in Siena. They have a lot of English novels there set in Italy for the tourists.'

'Oh thank you, that would be kind. If not, I'm sure I can find it at home.'

He looked at his watch and said, 'Let's go, we still have twenty minutes.'

'For what?'

Standing up, he held out his hand. 'I thought we could stop by that beach hut before I leave.'

It would be a long night after he'd gone.

CHAPTER 46

JESSICA

The next morning, after a night lying awake, thinking about Alessandro, I Velcroed the cuff of the blood pressure monitor round Sofia's arm.

'I miss Alessandro,' Sofia said.

I couldn't admit that I did too. Since he'd left, I hadn't stopped replaying our time together in my head. After the beach, he'd got his holdall from upstairs, and we kissed goodbye in Enzo's room. I watched him drive down the hill from my bedroom window. The night at the opera couldn't come soon enough.

I pumped air into the cuff, inflating it like a balloon around Sofia's arm, then released the air and read the gauge. A high reading. I pushed two pills out of the foil and gave them to her. She swallowed them and washed them down with her glass of water. When Isabella had shown me how to do this, I'd worried about having so much responsibility. What if I accidentally killed Sofia? Now I thought nothing of it. I pushed the monitor with its wires, the pump, the gauge, the stethoscope into the bag and put it on the sideboard.

Sitting down, I said, 'I'm sure you do.'

It had been raining for the past couple of days, and we were in the kitchen-diner, the sliding doors pushed open, the cooler temperature a respite from the heat, at least. It would be back soon enough. Puddles formed on the terrace and rain pitter-pattered onto the tarpaulin covering the pool. There were no yachts out at sea that day, but in the distance I could see sun on the horizon.

'His mother, Beatrice, called to ask if he could stay with us for a few months. Isabella said there wasn't enough room, so I suggested he enrol for a course at the language school. The school helped him find somewhere to rent. I asked Beatrice why she didn't want him to wait until the autumn and work on his uncle's olive grove in Sicily like his brothers. Beatrice said a girl was pressuring him to get married and she worried he'd get caught up in something he didn't want. I laughed and reminded her of what happened when we sent her there to get away from a boy. She said, "Mamma, if he falls in love there, nobody can do anything about it." She was right, of course.'

Oh the irony. Although I wasn't sure if he loved me. Did he? I was certain that I had strong feelings for him, especially now we'd slept together, and couldn't bear to think about the little time we had left together. I refilled Sofia's glass of water with a bottle from the fridge, and poured one for myself. I hoped at least that Alessandro would ask to stay in touch. Would we spend more time together after the opera? I hoped so.

'Will you paint my toenails, dear? The polish chips easily here by the sea when I wear flip-flops all day,' Sofia said.

'Certo.' Placing a chair by Sofia's feet, I went to get the manicure bag from a drawer in her room. I removed the polish from the previous week. It had become part of our routine at the coast. A way to pass the time, and to make Sofia feel glamorous.

'That's why I'm grateful to have met Alessandro. What shall I do when he goes?'

I had no idea what I'd do either. 'Maybe he'll visit next summer.'

'He said he will with his mother,' Sofia said.

'That would be nice,' I said.

'I wonder if he'll find love in Siena, or if he has already?' Sofia looked up, her eyes twinkling, and I wondered if she knew what we'd been up to right under this very roof.

'I wouldn't know.'

'He's taking a girl from class to see *Tosca* tomorrow. Liliana's disappointed he isn't taking her niece. I wonder who the girl is.'

I painted the last toenail and put the polish back in the bag. I'd asked Isabella if I could meet a friend so I could go to the opera with Alessandro. Did Sofia suspect he was going with me?

'Is that all right?'

Sofia sat up and wriggled her toes. 'Perfetto, cara. Grazie. And what about you? Are you glad the diary brought you to Italy?'

Nodding, I said, 'Yes, I am. That diary has changed my life.'

'Just think, it's all because Benedetto was dying that he asked Alessandro to bring it to your grandmother when he was working in London. At least one good thing has come from my husband's terrible illness.'

The diary had made me rethink my whole life, but also it had brought Alessandro to me. And even if we had no future, I would never forget him – he'd always live in my heart, whatever happened.

'Why don't you tell me the story of *Tosca*?' I said.

CHAPTER 47

MARIELLA

VILLA CAMPIGLIA, NEAR SIENA, 3 JULY 1944

'The war is over. Siena has been liberated by French troops,' I said.

Peter was sitting at the kitchen table, his shirt-sleeves rolled up. He cut thick slices off a peach and put them into his mouth, one by one. The juice ran down his chin, and he wiped it with a napkin.

'What, how do you know this?' he said.

'Francesco just put a note through the door.'

I placed the note in front of him and he read it, then looked up at me, a smile filling his whole face. He pushed back his chair and stood up, put his arms around my neck and held me to him tightly.

'Thank goodness, cara Mariella. At last, we are free.'

'When they liberate the north of Italy, we shall go to Villa Selva on Lake Garda, and you can write your books like you always dreamt.'

'Bellissima Mariella, I cannot think of anything I'd like to do more.'

After Peter had shot Herman dead that night in the spring, we buried him in the back garden. We did not place a cross there as he did not deserve one, for not only had he attempted to take advantage of me as a woman living on my own – as far as he was aware – but he'd been part of the firing squad that murdered my husband. And he was allied with the men who shot Peter that night in the chestnut woods. Besides, we could not allow anyone to know he was there. Committing murder was a sin, and I knew this, but Peter had no choice in the matter – he did it to protect me and himself. Otherwise, we would have been the ones being buried under the ground. It was Herman or us, and surely we deserved the right to live? All I could do was spend more time at Santa Lucia, the church in the village. I had been to confession and spoken to Padre Nico, who I trusted implicitly – for he had helped many Jews – and I prayed to the Lord every day, asking for forgiveness. In time, I hoped to forget all that had happened and live a happy and fulfilled life.

Klaus did indeed visit the villa to ask if I knew of Herman's whereabouts, and I was grateful when he believed my story – that Herman had been to collect supplies and left again. I gave Klaus the bag of food intended for Herman and he was delighted with the ham. Although he was an enemy soldier, I sensed that Klaus was a better man than Herman, that he hated every moment of this horrific war. He told me that he had a beautiful wife and two children at home, and hoped to see them again one day.

After the Herman incident, Peter and I grew closer, for it was only natural after what we'd been through. We spent more and more time together and I never tired of his company. There were moments when I caught him looking at me with lust in his eyes. This pleased me, for I found him very attractive. One afternoon in the kitchen, when I was making pasta, mixing the flour and water together on the marble worktop, Peter came in from the garden. He'd been chopping wood and his clothes and hair were all wet from a rain shower. When I looked up and saw him, our eyes met, and he came over to me and put his hands on my waist, and I threw mine round his neck, and he leant in and kissed me, and it was the most stupendous kiss I had ever experienced in all my life. Then he picked me up in his arms, and carried me upstairs to my bedroom, and there, on the bed, we undressed each other and he made love to me for the first time, slowly, and releasing the passion built up over all those months of living together. After that, he came to my bed every single night, and I thanked the Lord for sending him to me. How would I have survived those long months without him?

On Easter Sunday, after I returned from Mass, Peter and I had a special lunch together. He'd seen a rabbit cross the garden that very morning while picking tomatoes – what a stroke of luck for us – and so I made a delicious rabbit stew with tomatoes and onions, cooked slowly on the hob, the wonderful smell filling the villa. When it was ready, we devoured the stew together along with a bottle of Chianti. We enjoyed ourselves so much that Peter went down to the cellar to get another bottle. We would allow ourselves that indulgence for just one day. As he removed the cork with a pop, he said,

'Mariella, I have consumed a great deal of wine, but I feel I must tell you something. Will you indulge me?'

'Yes, what is it, Peter? Tell me.'

'I must confess that I have fallen madly in love with you, Mariella, over these past few months, and hope that, after the war, you might consider marrying a man like me?'

'A man like you? You may not be a count, but you are so brave, and intelligent and a wonderful writer.' Peter had started to write in Italian in recent months as we had spent many hours reading together. I'd even taught him how to conjugate Italian verbs. He'd shown some of his stories to me and I thought him to be very talented. One day, I hoped, he would fulfil his dream of being a novelist. 'I am glad that at last you are telling me this, for I love you more than any man I've ever known.' It was true that I loved him more than the count – that marriage had been arranged by our parents, and we had loved each other, certainly, but not in the way Peter and I did. He smiled.

'So, Mariella, you are agreeing to marry me?'

'Yes, I shall be your wife, and we shall go to live at Villa Selva in Lake Garda. It is very beautiful there on the lake and the garden is filled with bougainvillea and olive trees. We shall be sure to live a good life. There is a boat and we can go sailing and take a picnic, and you can write with the most majestic view in front of your eyes. We can forget all that we have lived through here in Tuscany, leave it behind, and start a new life together.'

Peter's eyes lit up and I expected he was picturing the villa on the lake. But then he looked down and fiddled nervously with the tablecloth. 'Mariella, before you agree to spend your life with me, I must tell you about a woman named Eleanor, who I bought the diary from, you know the one I gave to Benedetto?'

'Yes?' I prompted, an uneasy feeling sweeping over me. 'She is your wife, perhaps? In England?'

'Not quite, no, but still, I think you need to be aware of this—'

CHAPTER 48

JESSICA

The architecture in Massa Marittima was similar to Siena's, with red-brown buildings dating back to medieval times. While Alessandro parked the car, I went to join the queue for ice cream. The air was much stickier than at the coast, and I wore a strappy sundress, showing off my newly acquired tan. The stage for the opera was in the square, next to a small church, with rows of seats in front of it. The surrounding bars and restaurants were all open, with tables outside, the hum of operagoers talking filling the air.

And then there she was. Carla, at the front of the queue, her mother standing beside her. I'd dreaded bumping into them – Carla would then tell Sofia that I was there with Alessandro.

Carla turned round, holding two ice creams. I did my best to hide behind the man in front of me – he was wearing a panama hat, but it was no use.

'Jessica, what are you doing here?' Carla said.

'I like opera. How about you?'

'Sofia gave me tickets because she values me as her favourite employee. Presumably you're here with Alessandro?'

Her mother looked like an older version of Carla. They had

the same cropped hairstyle, but hers was peppered with grey flecks rather than blond highlights. My eyes were drawn to her earrings, the tiny diamonds twinkling as they caught the light from a nearby streetlamp.

'Alessandro's here?' I asked, deciding to take the pleading-ignorance route.

'How did you get here without a car?' Carla said.

Looking again at the earrings, I recalled seeing the same ones dangling from someone else's ears.

'That's none of your business.'

She glared at me, and opened her mouth as if about to say something else just as Alessandro appeared, pushing the car key into the pocket of his jeans. Carla lifted her thick eyebrows and all I could do was look at her blankly.

'Oh, it's you,' he said to Carla.

'Sofia thinks you're bringing a girl from class.' Carla's ice cream dripped down the side of the cone and she raised it to her lips and licked it. 'She was upset when you turned down Liliana's niece.'

Ignoring her attempt to get a rise out of him, Alessandro offered his hand to Carla's mother. 'Alessandro, piacere.'

Shaking it, she smiled. 'Mi chiamo Veronica, piacere, Alessandro.' Turning to Carla, she said, 'What a charming young man.'

Carla tutted, and took hold of her mother's arm. 'Let's sit down, Mamma.'

'Enjoy the opera,' Veronica said.

As they walked away from us, tottering over the cobble-stones in their heeled sandals, it dawned on me where I'd seen the earrings before.

'I don't believe it,' I said.

'What?' Alessandro said.

'Veronica was wearing Isabella's earrings.'

'Are you sure?'

'Yes. Isabella wore them at Sofia's party. Do you remember when she accused me of stealing them at that awful octopus meal?'

'Yes, that was a tad awkward – I was taken by surprise and didn't know what to say.'

'I *thought* Carla might have taken them.'

'That's a serious accusation to make,' he said. 'She could just be borrowing them?'

'It's a possibility, but...' I told him about Carla stitching me up with the change during my first few days working for Isabella, and that I suspected she took money from the kitty. 'Just wait until I tell Sofia.'

'Carla's had it in for you from the beginning, but I guess she'll get her comeuppance now,' he said.

'She'll tell Sofia about seeing us here together, though.'

'It'll be okay.'

He didn't mind Sofia knowing about us?

'Are you sure?'

'Nonna thinks you're great.'

'Really?'

'She likes it that you talk to her. Apparently her other au pairs aren't as interested in listening to her stories as you are.'

This pleased me. I'd become fond of Sofia in the short time we'd known each other.

'We'd better get our ice creams and take our seats,' he said.

The opera opened with a woman, Tosca, arguing with her boyfriend Mario over the identity of the woman in a painting he'd recently finished. He claimed she was Mary Magdalene, but Tosca suspected the woman was his lover. The intensity of the music reflected the passion Tosca felt. The words were stretched out and I couldn't understand much. The same words kept coming up, like in modern Italian songs: la luna meaning moon; stelle, stars; amore, love; occhi, eyes, and I just about understood those words from my short time in Italy. Luckily, I remembered the plot from when Sofia had explained it to me. I finished the last of my ice cream and rested my head on Alessandro's shoulder. Stroking my hair and smiling, he drew me closer to him and I inhaled the scent of his neck.

A policeman showed Tosca a fan belonging to the woman in the painting. It had been found in the church and the policeman said it proved she was Mario's lover. But she wasn't. While painting in the church, Mario had seen her praying for her brother, an escaped political prisoner who Mario helped to find refuge there.

The argument over another woman reminded me of Gabriella. When Alessandro had been in the shower earlier, I'd spotted a mix-tape of love songs on top of his chest of drawers, made by Gabriella and dated the previous week. Clearly she still expected to be with him when he got back to New York.

Mario sang 'E Lucevan Le Stelle', meaning when the stars were shining brightly. It was the song that had made Sofia cry when she held Benedetto's hand on their first date. Mario wrote a final letter to Tosca because he was due to be executed for helping the woman's brother hide from the police. Sofia had told me that during the song Mario is overcome with memories of the shining stars from the night he met Tosca.

The music tugged at my heartstrings and tears ran down my face as I thought about my situation with Alessandro. We only had two more nights. I didn't want to say goodbye to him or Siena. He passed me a crumpled handkerchief from his pocket and spoke into my ear.

'I've no idea what's going on.'

I wiped my face, laughing through the tears, and he took my hand and squeezed it tightly. At least Matt had offered to stay at a friend's house so we could use the flat. Alessandro hadn't said whether he wanted to see me after Siena, and I wondered when or if we'd have that conversation.

Tosca believed Mario's execution would be fake because she'd done a deal with the policeman who found the fan in the church. But the policeman had lied. On discovering Mario's death, Tosca threw herself off the stage, which represented a castle, ending her life. The ending didn't surprise me as Sofia had told me what happened, but the tragedy was very sad.

I was proud to have seen my first opera but, although I'd been moved, it had also gone on for quite a long time. My back ached from the plastic chair, and I couldn't wait to get back to Alessandro's place in Siena.

CHAPTER 49

JESSICA

FLORENCE

We stood under the beautiful yellow arches on the Ponte Vecchio, looking down the River Arno. It was bustling with tourists, going in and out of the jewellery shops and taking photographs all around us.

'This is the only bridge in Florence that wasn't bombed during the Second World War,' I read from my guidebook.

'Really?' Alessandro said.

'The Germans destroyed access to it when retreating north in 1944, but Hitler spared the bridge because he'd visited at the beginning of the war.'

'That's interesting.' Alessandro grinned. He'd been teasing me all day about reading out random facts from my guidebook.

I squeezed his arm affectionately. I'd persuaded Isabella to give me the afternoon off to research an article about the Botticelli paintings at the Uffizi art gallery. Alessandro had driven us to Florence after his class. We'd bought brioches, filled with custard, and coffee at a lovely bakery called Pasticceria Mancini that he'd visited before with Matt. After exploring the pretty streets at a leisurely pace, we'd stopped for pizza at an osteria with outside tables in a side street off the Piazza della Signoria, where the replica of Michelangelo's statue of David stood. Then we'd bought ice creams – pistachio for Alessandro and stracciatella for me. We ate them on a bench in the shade under the small area with pillars outside the Uffizi before going inside. I'd been blown away by seeing *The Birth of Venus* and *Primavera* by Botticelli and stood there for quite a long time studying them while Alessandro went and looked at the paintings in the room next door. I took photographs, and thought about what I could say in my article. *Primavera* was about love, peace and prosperity; *The Birth of Venus* was about the birth of love and spiritual beauty as a driving force in life. Both paintings inspired me, and I'd mull over how to find the hook for my article and relate them to my experience of living in Italy.

A rowing boat glided up the river, a man shouting instructions through a megaphone from the motorboat alongside it. Cars passed over the next bridge along and flats with balconies lined the river. Graffiti on the crumbling wall said, 'Stefano loves Serena'. There were many declarations of love on that wall. Many lovers had stood there before us.

'Let's get out of here,' Alessandro said.

He took my hand and made a path through all the people, leading me off the bridge and along the pavement. He stopped and we stood by the wall running alongside the river.

Alessandro leant forward and kissed me.

'I like being with you,' he said.

He hadn't said anything like this before. We stood there kissing with people moving around us, the breeze from the river brushing my face.

'I'll miss you,' he said.

And how I would miss him. We'd started something that

was bound to leave me broken and dealing with it would be a challenge. All we could do was make the most of our remaining time together.

'Me too,' I said.

'Shall we head back to my place?'

I nodded and smiled.

Back at his flat, we lay together skin to skin like spoons, his body enveloping mine.

'What are your plans when you get home?' Alessandro said.

'I don't want to think about home.'

'There are conversations you need to have when you get back.'

'Do we have to talk about this now?'

'We could do it later, but it will be our last night together.'

It was nice of him to try to help, but really I wanted him to bring up the subject of us – that mattered to me the most in this moment.

'I need coffee.'

Climbing out of bed, he put on his shorts and t-shirt.

'Where are you off to?'

'To get breakfast,' he said, picking up his wallet from the chest of drawers.

He kissed me on the cheek before leaving the flat. I propped up the pillows, and swigged some water from the bottle on the bedside table. A moped buzzed down the street below. Wrapping the sheet around me, I leant out of the window to watch life go by. The owner of the fruit and vegetable shop was putting out crates of tomatoes, onions, oranges, peaches and I could hear a woman asking him how ripe they were. The baker hosed the road outside his shopfront, brushing the excess water with a broom. Then I saw Alessandro come out of the bar on the corner, a brown paper bag tucked under his arm. Watching him walk up the street, I wished I could freeze that moment when everything seemed so perfect. After breakfast he'd go off to his class, but at least we'd have one last night together.

He came back and put two coffees on the bedside table, then swiftly undressed and climbed into bed, taking one of the pillows and sitting up beside me. I took a sip of my coffee and waited for the caffeine to work its magic. He reached inside the paper bag and handed me a warm brioche covered in icing sugar. I bit into it and tasted custard – delicious. He unwrapped the paper on a focaccia sandwich.

'You need to tell Tom, and your mom, you're not getting married.'

'I know.'

'And you need to find somewhere else to live.'

He was right, living on Birch Farm after Siena would be difficult.

'How will I do that?'

'What's stopping you?'

'I don't have enough money.'

'Get a better-paid job, or maybe a loan.'

I finished the brioche and wiped the icing sugar from round my mouth with a napkin.

'I wish it was that easy, but yes, something to think about.'

He finished the focaccia and started on his brioche. 'You'll find it tough living with your folks after being here.'

'Don't you live with your parents?'

'I was, but I'll be renting a studio in Manhattan when I get back.'

I couldn't bring myself to ask what he planned to do about Gabriella. The bells rang in the Duomo, and I counted the number of chimes. Nine o'clock.

'Oh no,' he said.

'Your class.'

'It's too bad.'

He'd fail the course if he didn't go. 'You'll only be ten minutes or so late if you leave now.'

'I'm not going.'

'What about your certificate?'

'Forget the certificate.'

'Didn't your mother buy a frame for it?'

'I'll say it got lost in the post or something.'

He polished off the brioche and drank his coffee, then reached over me to put the cup on the bedside table.

'You could still make it, though,' I said, not wanting to be responsible for him failing his course.

'Jessica.' He kissed my neck. 'It means a lot that you're trying to help, but I want to spend the next three hours with you. We only have now, and tonight.'

He was giving up the certificate for me. Surely that had to mean something. He ran a hand over my breast and the last thing I was going to do was stop him.

'Are you sure?' I said, not meaning it one bit.

'You know this means I can drive you to the airport tomorrow?'

I pictured detaching myself from him to go through customs, the final call for my flight flashing on the screen. I'd look over my shoulder to see him standing there, my eyes brimming with tears. It was bound to be emotional.

I put my head on his chest. 'You know I'm flying from Pisa?'

'So, we leave first thing, visit the Leaning Tower, and grab an early lunch. Then I'll take you to the airport.'

This was a lovely thought, spending those last few hours together doing nice things.

'That would be great, if you don't mind.'

'It will be my pleasure.'

Any opportunity to defer the big farewell was too good to miss. He put his arm round me and squeezed me to him.

'Will you write to me?' he asked.

'Of course. Will you write back?'

'Sure. I have a business trip to London scheduled for November.'

'You do?'

He cupped my face, and I looked up at him.

'Can I visit you?'

Mum might not make him very welcome – not just after the news he'd brought to her door, but also because of Tom. I guessed we could always stay in a hotel if we had to, maybe at the Old Hare. Or I could go and visit him in London.

'I'd like to see you.'

'I was hoping that at some stage we could find a way to – well, I don't know, what do you want?'

Everything.

'Go on.'

'I was hoping we could find a way to be together.'

I hadn't expected this but had daydreamed about the two of us sharing a flat in London. We'd eat breakfast together before work, and I'd have him on tap after work. I'd introduce him to everyone as my boyfriend.

'How?'

'I could maybe get a transfer to London – they're always saying I should when I visit.'

He'd move to London for me?

'And Gabriella?'

'I told you already, I'll end it when I get back.'

'What will she say?'

'She'll understand.'

'What if the transfer takes a long time? How would we get to see each other?'

'We'd make it work. I couldn't live without seeing you again, Jessica.'

He seemed to mean what he was saying, but his suggestion

was so huge that, if it didn't happen, I'd be absolutely devastated.

'We can try,' I said.

He pulled out the pillow from behind my neck and threw it onto the floor, then he leant down to kiss me.

'Let's make the most of the precious few hours we have left.'

CHAPTER 50

JESSICA

'What are you doing tonight, cara?' Sofia said.

She had her arm linked through mine, her cotton dress billowing in the breeze as we walked around the little square near Via San Marco. I always worried about taking Sofia out in public in case she tripped over an uneven cobblestone and fell over. Looking after her felt like such a responsibility and it was impossible to relax when leaving the flat together.

Alessandro had booked a table at L'Osteria Giancarlo for us that evening, but I thought it best not to tell her. Had Carla said anything about seeing us at the opera?

'I'm going out with a friend.'

'That's a nice way to spend your last night in Siena. Will you be sad to leave?'

Tears pricked my eyes, and I swallowed, the reality of going home suddenly hitting me hard.

'I'm not quite ready yet,' I said, my voice wavering.

'You'd rather look after an old battleaxe like me?'

'You're not a battleaxe. We've had some good times.'

I wasn't just leaving Alessandro. Siena had brought me independence, enabling me to have a different outlook on my life. And looking after Sofia had taught me a great deal. I now knew how to cook and take care of a house. Mum had never encouraged me to do any of that, perhaps to keep me close to home as then I'd need her.

'I'll be sad to see you go,' she said.

Sofia was a woman who didn't dish out compliments often and now tears were running down my face freely, emotions consuming me. I used my free hand to wipe them away, hoping she wouldn't notice. I had to find a way to leave Little Vale and continue the journey I'd started. But now it was time to bring up the matter of Isabella's earrings. Sofia might accuse me of lying, and that would spoil the special moment we'd just shared. But I couldn't chicken out of this – who knew what else Carla had taken or what she might take in the future?

'I have to tell you something, Sofia,' I said.

'What is it?'

'Alessandro took me to see *Tosca*.'

Sofia stopped walking and looked at me. 'Oh, really? Why didn't you tell me before?'

She gestured for us to sit on a bench outside the church, shaded by trees. An old man with a walking stick passed us and went inside the church. This part of Siena was quiet, away from the tourists, almost like a different city.

'That's not all.'

Wiping the tears from under my eyes, I hoped this revelation wouldn't mean leaving Sofia on a bad note.

'I saw Carla and her mother at the opera. Her mother was wearing Isabella's earrings.'

Sofia's hands started to tremble.

'You know the gold ones with the diamonds, that dangle?'

There was no going back now.

'Why are you crying?'

'Because of everything. I'm sad about going home. And I was nervous to tell you about the earrings.'

She took a handkerchief out of the pocket of her dress and handed it to me – it was embroidered with a snail and the red and yellow colours of the Chiocciola contrada.

'Grazie.'

I dabbed my face. Then I studied it. Was it the same as the one she'd given to Peter all those years ago?

'Didn't you give one of these to Peter?'

She nodded. 'Yes I did, and you may keep it, a memento of our time together.'

'Really?'

She nodded. Not only had she given one of her special embroidered handkerchiefs to my grandfather, but now she'd given one to me, all these years later. I was quite touched by this gesture. It seemed significant, linking my visit to Siena with Peter's.

'Grazie, Sofia.'

'Prego, cara. And will you be sad to leave Alessandro?'

Sniffling, I smiled and nodded. She took my hand and gave it a gentle squeeze. This gesture surprised me, as she didn't often show affection.

'I'm not surprised about Carla,' she said.

I exhaled, so relieved that she believed me.

'What will you do, get another maid?'

'Carla has worked for me for ten years. My au pairs change all the time and Isabella is always at the hospital, or with Tiziano. I've spent years teaching Carla how to do everything the way I like it. She takes me for a fool, but when I meet my solicitor next week I'll take her out of my will. Isabella will be instructed to dismiss her on the day that I die.'

It struck me that I wouldn't see Sofia again after this afternoon, unless I happened to return to Siena. Would I return? This octogenarian had touched my life more than I could have imagined.

'Did I do the right thing telling you?' I said.

'Of course you did. And do you think I wasn't aware of what was going on between you and Alessandro? I've seen the way you look at each other. I'm sure you'll meet again.'

So, she had known, all along. How I hoped she was right...

The bell in the church nearby chimed and the clock struck a quarter past eight. Where had Alessandro got to? Maybe our conversation that morning had been too much, and he'd changed his mind about us being together after Siena. My room was as hot as an airing cupboard and, looking in the mirror, I dabbed my face with powder, then put the compact in my bag for later. Perhaps I should go and stand outside the front door where it would be cooler. Sitting on the bed, I looked down at the square below – I'd miss it. Tomorrow, my view would be of the muddy farmyard again. If Alessandro didn't turn up by half past, I'd put my shorts and top back on – the dress was already clinging to me. What if he didn't turn up? I couldn't bear to think about how that would make me feel.

Picking up the P.J. Collina novel, I turned to the inside of the back cover once again – I'd studied the photo a few times since getting back to Siena. Was this really my grandfather? I needed to find an English version of this novel so I could read it. I thought about the journey the diary had brought me on, and glanced at it, the beautiful tan-brown notebook sitting there on my bedside table, where I kept it as if to bring me some kind of luck. It was interesting how this diary had travelled back to England from Tuscany and then back again – to the very same house it had been brought from, where it had been sitting in a drawer for all those years since the war. I'd finished writing my article about the Palio that afternoon, and was pleased with it. I'd eventually found my angle, making it about how the diary had turned up in Yorkshire and brought me to Siena to see the Palio that my grandfather, a British prisoner of war, never got to

see. I'd type the article up on Mum's computer and submit it to
Italian Dreams when returning home. I still needed to write one
about the Botticelli paintings, but had to think about them some
more first.

A woman next door clanked pots and pans in her kitchen
and the smell of tomato sauce wafted through the window. I
looked up the street, but Alessandro was nowhere to be seen. I
sat sideways on the windowsill and put up my feet, willing him
to appear. Then there he was, dressed in jeans and a white shirt,
walking just about as slowly as was possible. Why was he doing
that when running late? A bad feeling tugged at my gut. Something was wrong.

I called out, 'Hello, there, handsome.'

Looking up, he said, 'Hi,' throwing me a smile without
displaying teeth or creases around the eyes. It was one of those
smiles someone gives when they're pretending everything's all
right.

'I'll come down.' I pulled the shutters closed as it would be
dark when I got back, and picked up my bag and cardigan, reassuring myself that he'd probably had a row with his mother on
the phone or something.

I went downstairs and stepped outside, tying the arms of my
cardigan round my shoulders.

'What's the matter?' I asked.

'Nothing.' He kissed me on the lips, but the kiss felt different, as if we'd lost some of our connection. I breathed in the
scent of his cologne, and tried to meet his gaze, but he looked
down at his shoes.

'Are you sure?'

He smiled, a forced smile like before. 'Sorry I'm late, Jessica.
I got held up.'

He sounded so formal, like when we first met.

'What is going on?'

'Nothing. Here, I brought you something.'

He produced a book from behind his back and handed it to me. Looking at the cover, I realised it was Peter's novel, in English! *Dirty Tricks on Lake Garda*.

'I don't believe it. Where did you find this?'

'In the bookshop – I went down there this afternoon and they found me a copy.'

'Oh, Alessandro, this is so thoughtful of you. Thank you.'

I kissed him on the lips but the smile he gave me once again didn't reach his eyes.

'Do you want to leave it upstairs so you don't have to carry it around all night?'

'Okay, that's a good idea.'

I went back inside and left the novel on the bedside table next to its Italian version and the diary, as if I was forming some kind of collection of Peter-related items. I couldn't believe Alessandro had done such a kind thing for me. I put his lateness and forced smiles down to being flustered from the humidity. I went back downstairs to where he waited outside the front door. He was staring into space and I tapped him on the shoulder.

Alessandro took my hand, and started walking. 'Let's go, shall we? I need a drink.'

Something really did seem to be wrong, but I was sure he'd tell me en route to the restaurant. Hopefully it wasn't a big deal and wouldn't spoil our last evening together.

I raised my glass, doing my best to act as though the evening was going perfectly.

'Cheers, this Brunello is wonderful,' I said.

Brunello di Montalcino, made locally, was pricey, but so good – rich and warm and just about the best red wine I'd ever tried.

'It should be. It's twice the price of the wine we wanted,' he said.

The group of American students next to us had ordered all the Chianti and uncorked bottles cluttered their table, along with glasses filled to the brim and red splashes marking the white tablecloth. They shouted over each other, sucking the romance out of the atmosphere that had made L'Osteria Giancarlo so special last time. I thought back to that night, when he'd put his hand on mine, when he'd pushed his leg against mine under the table. Tonight he hadn't touched me since we'd arrived at the restaurant. He hadn't fixed those dark eyes on me across the table like he usually would. Whatever he needed to say was not going to be good for me.

'It's not about the wine, is it?' I said.

Biting his lip, he said, 'I have to tell you something.'

I didn't speak, and just waited for him to go on.

'I've received a letter from Gabriella.'

I felt a gnawing inside of me, like when I'd pictured him in bed with Natalie. There was silly old me mapping out our future in my little head since our conversation that morning. Now he'd changed his mind after only a few hours, and had decided to choose Gabriella. How could I have been so naive?

'What did this letter say?'

'She's—'

'Still pressuring you to get married?'

'Pregnant.'

'What?' I shook my head. This, I hadn't expected. 'No, she can't be. It's not possible. You've been here, how long – six months?' My hand shaking, I lifted my wine glass and glugged down what was left in it. Then I picked up the bottle and refilled it. 'You haven't been near her since when, March? Are you sure it's yours?'

'She's six months gone. The night before I came to Siena, I went to her papa's sixtieth birthday party. We drank a lot of prosecco and, well, one thing led to another. It was my last night and it was kind of a goodbye...'

A farewell shag, like with Gran and Peter. What were the chances?

'You didn't use contraception with a girl you were leaving the country to get away from?'

'She says she must have missed a pill.'

'Is she ready to have a baby?'

'You know we're both Catholic. Our parents will expect us to get married. She expects us to get married. I... Jessica, I have to marry her.'

It was just like Gran and Peter, except Alessandro was ready to do the right thing. Although I appreciated that Peter hadn't been given the opportunity. If he hadn't been shot, would he have changed his mind and returned to Gran when the war ended? Who knew the answer? Only him. Maybe if he was alive and we ever did meet in person I'd ask.

It seemed a shame to let such good wine go to waste. I took one last, deep glug, doing my best to savour it. A little ran down my chin, and I wiped it away with a hand. What on earth? I stood up, pulling my bag onto my shoulder, fury filling every part of me. How could he bring me here to our special restaurant to do this? He could have just told me at the flat, and saved himself some money too.

'Well, it's been nice knowing you, Alessandro,' I said.

'Jessica, you know I wanted us to be together after Siena, but how can I not be there for her?'

He was right of course, and I knew it. But still, I was livid. And completely broken. How would my heart heal from this? I got up from the table and made for the door to leave the restaurant, knowing he wasn't going to try to stop me. He belonged to Gabriella now. The American students watched me, laughing, as I left – it was so obvious to everyone that we'd just had a huge row and I was storming out. One of them said, 'What's her problem?' This triggered the emotions I'd been saving to release later when home alone, and my eyes brimmed with tears. Opening the door, I turned my head away from them all, sniffling – there was no way I could allow any of them, or Alessandro, to see that I was crying.

A light glowed in the window of the tabacchi opposite, where we'd sat on the step that night, when he wrapped his jumper around my shoulders and pulled me to him. The temperature had dropped, and my arms were cold – damn, I'd left my cardigan on the back of my chair. There was no way I would humiliate myself and go back inside to get it. I ran up the steps, through the arch onto Via Banchi di Sopra, shivering and full-on sobbing, desperate to get back to the flat and do my best to forget the whole miserable evening.

CHAPTER 51

JESSICA

LITTLE VALE, SEPTEMBER 1994

Light coming through the floral-patterned curtains woke me up. Glancing at the red numbers on my radio alarm clock, I saw it was only half past six. I'd got used to having shutters in Siena and would have to put a blanket over the curtains or something. Posters torn from magazines were Blu-tacked to the floral-wall-papered walls, and they seemed so dated, just like Mum's chintzy decor from the 1980s. Jon Bon Jovi, Tom Cruise and Patrick Swayze took me back to a life before Siena, before Alessandro.

Since returning to Little Vale, I'd been living in my room, shutting myself off from the world. How would I ever get past what had happened? Alessandro had offered me everything and swiftly taken it away again. It wasn't his fault, but still, the whole situation was unbearable. I rolled onto my side and pulled the duvet over my head, tucking it round myself to make a cocoon. I pictured the day Alessandro came to the farm with the diary, him studying my legs at the door, him saving me when claiming responsibility for the broken glasses at Sofia's party, our time in the beach hut during the thunderstorm – I relived it all, pretending the last night hadn't happened, and drifted back to sleep.

A knock on my bedroom door woke me a few hours later.

'Are you up, love? It's ten o'clock,' Mum said.

I didn't answer and hoped she'd just go away. But she came in, shutting the door behind her. Keeping my eyes closed, I hoped to fool her that I was still asleep. She sat on the end of the bed, making it creak, and switched on my lamp.

'Tom's downstairs,' she said.

That was all I needed.

'Jessica?'

'I don't want to see him now,' I said, my voice muffled by the duvet.

'When will you see him?' She lifted the duvet off my head, and looked down at me.

'What are you doing?' I asked.

'It's about time you sorted this out.'

'I can't face it, Mum.'

She brushed a stray hair out of my face, as if I was a small child. 'Well, this might cheer you up, at least – your new friend Harriet rang last night, inviting you to stay in London.'

If anyone could bring me back to life, it would be Harriet. And any opportunity to get out of Little Vale again wasn't to be missed.

'I'll leave tomorrow.'

'You're not going anywhere until you've spoken to Tom,' Mum said.

'Can I at least have a shower first?'

She put the box containing the engagement ring on my bedside table.

'He asked me to give you this.'

Opening the lid, she showed it to me, the diamond catching the light.

'That's quite a ring, isn't it?' she said.

It certainly was, far too over the top for me – if Tom really knew me, he would have chosen something more understated. But he had gone to a lot of effort, and I appreciated that. It was so Tom though – he was all about the grand gestures with little substance underneath.

'I'll go round there and give it back later.'

'You're out of your mind if you turn that boy down, but I'm done with arguing,' Mum said.

Had she finally given up? What a relief if she had.

'Thank goodness for that.'

'Promise me you'll drop in this afternoon, and I'll get rid of him now.'

I really couldn't bear the thought of having that conversation with Tom, but it was time to face the music. Afterwards, I'd call Harry about going to London the next morning.

'Tell him I'll go at four o'clock when he breaks for tea.'

'Good lass.' She opened the curtains and pushed up the window. 'It's very stuffy in here. You need to get some fresh air.'

Smells from the farm came in – manure mostly. It was hardly fresh. A tractor, probably Dad, chugged in the distance. 'I'm not bringing any more meals upstairs. And your gran wants to spend some time with you. Why don't you come down for lunch at one o'clock? I'm trying a new chicken curry recipe from the WI with leftovers from Sunday's roast.'

'I don't feel like talking to anyone though, Mum.'

It struck me that I still needed to tell Gran about the possibility of Peter still being alive – well, that would have to wait for another day. I had enough on my plate for now.

'Just get dressed and turn up. You can sit there and say nothing for all I care. Please don't wear your pyjamas though.' She picked up all the empty mugs I'd collected from around the room. 'I know you miss Italy, love, but you need to move on.'

'It's not that easy.' Then, surprising myself, I burst into tears.

Putting the mugs down on the chest of drawers, she said, 'Budge up.'

I shuffled sideways and she sat on the bed next to me.

'I know it takes a lot to make you cry. What really happened with that Alessandro in the end?'

Putting the pillow behind me, I sat up. Mum passed me a floral-patterned tissue from the box on my bedside table.

I dabbed my eyes. 'It's over.'

'Didn't he want to see you again?'

Then I full-on sobbed, shoulders shaking. She put an arm around my shoulders and pulled me to her. I inhaled the familiar scent of the rose perfume she liked to wear.

'Come here.'

He'd gone and broken my heart, that's what. I'd never known you could feel like that about anyone. It had been exhilarating at the time, but now I couldn't feel more of a mess. Mum put the box of tissues on the duvet in front of me. I pulled out a couple and blew my nose, then scrunched them into balls. A wood pigeon cooed from on top of the chimney pot, down into the fireplace. It would do me good to get everything off my chest, although Mum would no doubt tell me what I didn't want to hear.

'I get the feeling something happened between you and Alessandro in Siena. And now he doesn't want to stay in touch?'

'He did, but...' I told Mum about our romance and how it had ended with the letter from Gabriella on my last night.

Mum shook her head and let out a big sigh. 'You're well rid of him. Don't give the man another thought.'

Confiding in her had just made me feel a whole lot worse, as predicted. This whole situation was bound to resonate, seeing as she'd been in the position of Gabriella's baby, but instead was abandoned by her father – although I still didn't know if this was because he'd died or just didn't want to come back. If he was still alive, she'd have all that to deal with too.

'But I loved him.'

'All you can do is get back to your life here.'

But I didn't want to be in Little Vale.

'I can't believe it ended because of something that happened before we met.'

'Life isn't fair. You'll find that out as you get older.'

'We'd talked about him getting a transfer to Pimsy's in London.'

'He might not have gone through with it. Anyway, making a marriage work with an American would have been tough.'

'Why are you so cynical?'

'What's the point in being romantic? Your gran's lived with a broken heart for most of her life because she got involved with a man when he was about to leave for war.'

'We wouldn't be here now if Gran hadn't spent that night with Peter.'

'But your grandpa looked after her well, and took on another man's child, and that was courageous of him. Marriage is about being practical. As long as you get along with your other half that's good enough.'

'You married Dad so he could take care of the farm, but is it good enough for you, Mum?'

'That's beside the point.'

'If you play it safe all of the time, how can you expect any excitement from life?'

'Real life isn't exciting. At your age you can have fun, but getting married and having children is hard work. This Alessandro shouldn't have slept with that girl the night before he left for Italy.'

'She told him she was on the pill.'

'It's an absolute mess and you're best off out of it.' Mum kissed me on the head, and picked up the mugs. 'I'd better go downstairs – Gran's no doubt giving Tom the Spanish Inquisition. You might at least consider accepting that ring before making any rash decisions.'

She opened the door.

'I've already told you I'm not doing it. Anyway, I want to have a go at being a travel writer,' I said.

'How on earth are you going to do that?'

I shrugged. 'Maybe go to London and try to get a job at a magazine. I need to work it all out.'

'London's a hectic city for someone like you, and so expensive. It's not what we're used to.'

'I can handle it. Living in the countryside feels so boring after Siena.'

Mum just shook her head, but I could tell I'd hurt her.

'I don't know what to say any more.'

She left the room, closing the door firmly behind her, and I could hear her footsteps on the stairs as she returned to the kitchen.

Climbing out of bed, I took my holdall off the top shelf of the wardrobe. The thought of staying with Harriet lifted my mood, despite the guilt tugging at me after all I'd said to Mum. After visiting Tom, I'd call Harriet and work out which train to get the next morning. I couldn't deal with telling Gran that Peter might be alive – that would need to wait until I got back from London. After all that had happened with Alessandro, facing Tom was quite enough for the moment. My emotions could only handle so much.

CHAPTER 52

JESSICA

'Hello, Jessica, how lovely to see you.'

Tom's mother, Patsy, opened the door, immaculate as always in an A-line skirt and a shirt with a crisp white collar, not the kind of clothes my mum would wear unless she was dressing up for something. Patsy liked to take care of her appearance, and spent a lot of time watching what she ate and doing aerobics in figure-hugging outfits.

We kissed on both cheeks, something Patsy had always done. After being in Siena, I did it without thinking. Did Patsy know what I'd come to say to her son?

'Hello, Patsy.'

'Do come in. Tom will be back in a few minutes.'

The aroma of baking filled the kitchen and I stood awkwardly next to the table, which was covered in magazines, all open at the society pages. Patsy's housekeeper, who wore an apron, was using a feather duster to clean the corners where the walls met the ceiling – corners that at Birch Farm hadn't been touched for years, if ever.

I took a moment to consider what my life would be like if I married Tom – very different from Mum's. I'd probably have a

housekeeper too, and someone to help with the accounts – a task
that Mum hated, and I didn't blame her. If we had children, I'd
hire a nanny like Patsy had. Money would be no object. My
days would be spent exercising and organising local coffee
mornings like Patsy. Was that a life I could get used to? Would
it be worth giving up on my dream of being a travel writer and
living in London? Gran and Mum had given up on dreams for
the men they married, but I didn't have to.

'Do sit down.'

Patsy put on a pair of oven gloves and opened the door to
the Aga. She took out a loaf tin and placed it on a cooling rack.
Whatever it was smelt amazing, and I hoped she was going to
offer me a slice.

I pulled out a chair, hoping Patsy would make herself scarce
when Tom came into the house.

'I'm trying a recipe that a friend from the WI gave me for
banana cake. Handy if you have bananas going brown in the
fruit bowl. I don't eat cake myself, but the boys need it with all
that physical work they do. Would you like a slice?'

'Yes, please.'

'I'll make a pot of tea.'

She put the kettle on, and spooned fresh leaves into a
teapot. 'You've got a lovely tan and are looking very svelte. Italy
has been good for you.'

I had indeed toned up from all the walking in Siena, as well
as swimming in Castiglione della Pescaia. But also, I hadn't
snacked or eaten any processed food. All of my meals had been
made from scratch and I'd consumed so many lovely salads and
so much fresh fruit and vegetables. I couldn't remember the last
time I'd eaten a bag of crisps.

Patsy was nice enough, but that was no reason to marry her
son. Remembering Tom's father had a bad back, I asked, 'How's
John?'

'Much better, but he can't wait to hand over to Tom in the

new year. He wants to have the riding school rebuilt – the roof's caving in – and he plans to expand the holiday cottage business.'

A tractor pulled into the yard and my stomach churned.

'Here he is.' She poured out three cups of tea through a strainer. 'Help yourself to milk and sugar while I sort out the cake.'

She ran a palette knife round the edge of the tin, and tipped the cake onto a blue-and-white plate. She cut thick slices, put them onto side plates for me and Tom and placed one in front of me. He was probably going to appear any second.

Tom opened the back door and took off his wellies, banging them together in the porch. I'd forgotten how big and burly he was, with a body taut from physical work.

'How do, Jessica,' he said in his thick Yorkshire accent.

'Hello, Tom.'

'Well, isn't this nice,' Patsy said.

He came into the kitchen and leant down to kiss me on the cheek. He smelt of horses and manure, as always.

Studying me, he said, 'You're not looking bad.'

Patsy picked up the telephone handset. 'I must ring Mummy and ask about her hip,' she said, before moving swiftly into the living room, and closing the door behind her.

Tom pulled out a chair at the table and sat down to face me.

'So, how was Italy?'

'It was really good, thank you.'

'No doubt you had plenty of Italian men chasing after you?'

I looked at the floor, imagining my face was going the colour of beetroot. There was no answer to that question. I opened my handbag, took out the box with the ring inside and handed it to him.

'I'm sorry, Tom, I can't do it.'

He put the box on the table, not quite meeting my eye. Crossing his arms, he sat back in his chair.

'I thought as much.'

I hesitated, feeling like there was more to say, but couldn't find the words. Pushing back my chair from the table, I said, 'I should go.'

'Jess.'

He got up and held me by the tops of my arms, his blue eyes pleading.

'Imagine if we put our land together. There would be more holiday cottages, a spa, Mum talked about exercise classes and a restaurant with a French chef.'

I pulled away from him. 'It's all about the land for you, isn't it?'

'Of course not, you know I love you as well.'

I headed for the door. 'You don't love me, Tom.' I sighed, 'I'm just part of your family's business plan.'

For a minute, I wondered if he'd had an agenda from the beginning, from when we first had that slow dance at an eighteenth birthday party. Maybe Patsy had put him up to it – she could be manipulative, and Mum had never been a fan, even though Dad was friends with John. I went into the yard and got in the car. Tom followed and knocked on the window and I wound it down.

'It's not just about your land, Jess, I promise.'

'Goodbye, Tom.' I turned the key in the ignition and pushed the gearstick into first. 'You'll find someone better than me, someone who wants what you have in mind for them. I'm just sorry it's not me.'

Glancing in the rear-view mirror as I sped off down the drive, I saw him walk back inside, shoulders slumped. It hadn't been the best exchange, and I felt slightly breathless. Inhaling deeply, I switched on the radio, and a Phil Collins song came on, 'In the Air Tonight', and then a sudden liberating feeling swept over me. Now I could do what I wanted with my life. I'd just have to find a way to get over Alessandro. But how hard could it be when there was no possibility of a future with him?

Now he had to think about Gabriella and his baby, and I would do my best to be happy for him. That would take some time, but it was my only option. Perhaps he'd come into my life in order to bring me the diary and get me to Italy. To set me on the right path, away from Little Vale and Tom, so I could follow my dream of being a travel writer, and that was all.

CHAPTER 53

JESSICA

Harriet raised her pina colada in a toast and we clinked glasses and said, 'Cin cin.' We were sitting on barstools at the Crocodile Lounge, a nightclub on the King's Road.

'Thanks for what you did today,' I said. Harriet had put me in touch with an agency and I was grateful. 'And if I do get a job, are you sure you don't mind me living at yours for a bit?'

Harriet sipped her drink through the straw. 'Absolutely, of course. I want to help you get to London. It isn't easy finding money to rent somewhere, and you'd need a deposit too. But once you're earning a salary, you'll be able to get a flatshare or something.'

Earlier that day, while Harriet was at a lecture, I'd borrowed her laptop to write up my article for *Italian Dreams* magazine. I'd used the angle I came up with during those last days in Siena – it was my story: Peter's diary turning up and how it had taken me to Siena to live my dream for six months. Of course, I didn't mention Alessandro or the fact that Peter could still be alive. Now all I could do was wait. After printing the article off and reading it through, I went to post it straight away, so I could daydream about having it published. That would be an exciting prospect, but Mum wouldn't take it well. For now, though, I was on a quest to forget about what she'd think, along with everything else.

Two blokes were standing nearby, one in jeans, the other in red chinos, and one of them was staring directly at us. Harriet attracted attention from men everywhere she went – they were drawn to her like a magnet.

'You seem to have a new fan,' I said.

'Oh, that's Tarquin, and he's brought Sebastian, as requested. I asked him to meet us here,' she said.

Typical Harriet, making a plan without telling me. It would have been nice to know in advance. I wasn't in the mood for socialising with anyone I didn't know.

'I'm not really in the mood to talk to them,' I said.

'Well, they're here now and I can hardly tell them to go away.'

She went over and kissed them both, one after the other, then waved me over. I forced a smile. 'Forget Me Nots' blared through the speakers, and Harriet playfully pushed them onto the dancefloor, then took my hand and dragged me over there too. She danced close to Tarquin, tipping her head to one side, in full seduction mode. Sebastian stepped away from them, throwing me a look, and I rolled my eyes. He was quite nice-looking, but I wasn't ready to meet anyone new. I danced, half-closing my eyes, allowing the music to wash over me, doing my best to forget everything.

Next came 'Lost in Music' and 'Good Times', then 'The Most Beautiful Girl in the World' by Prince. '*Could you be...*' Tarquin grabbed Harriet by the waist '*... the most beautiful girl in the world...*' and she wrapped her arms round his neck, winking at me over his shoulder. Dry ice hissed and snaked its way around couples with their arms round each other. It made my throat scratchy and I coughed, feeling the need for a drink. Sebastian moved in my direction, his arms outstretched, but I certainly wouldn't be slow-dancing with him. I left the dance-floor, sank into a purple velvet sofa and ordered a vodka and tonic from a passing waiter. And there I would wait until Harriet was ready to go home.

I thought back to all the times in Italy when I'd been relegated to the sidelines while Harriet was snogging some bloke. This time, I couldn't object as she had done me a big favour by inviting me to stay at a time when I needed to escape Little Vale. And she'd put me in touch with the agency too.

'Harry told me about the American arsehat.'

I looked up to see Sebastian was standing over me, a waiter beside him, holding an ice bucket, a bottle of champagne and two flutes. 'This should help you forget about him.'

Allowing Sebastian to speak about Alessandro like that seemed disloyal, despite how things had ended.

'That was good of her. But what happened wasn't really his fault.'

'Nah, what was he thinking?'

'It's complicated.'

The same words Alessandro had used the day we went for coffee at Bar Paolo. Gabriella had been a threat from the beginning, and I'd been in denial. I should have abandoned any idea of us being together right then. But how could a girl say no to him? Who knew if I'd ever meet anyone like him ever again?

Sebastian sat beside me, and clearly wasn't going anywhere. The waiter uncorked the champagne with a pop and filled the flutes, holding the bottle at the base like Carla had shown me at Sofia's party. The evening when Alessandro had taken the blame for the broken glasses. Now here I was in a posh London nightclub, feeling out of place, being the only girl in jeans, stuck with the friend of Harriet's latest catch. Sebastian passed me a flute and I thanked him.

I would have to talk to him in exchange, but it was quite difficult to turn down a glass of champagne on a night when I was feeling down. We clinked glasses and locked eyes, and said, 'Cheers.' I took a sip, the bubbles fizzing in my mouth, then hiccupped.

'Charming,' he said.

I laughed. Making small talk with him couldn't be that difficult, could it? 'How do you know Harriet?' I asked.

'She went to school with Tarquin's sister, Tabby. We used to stay at their house in the Cotswolds during the holidays. We swam in the pool, played tennis, emptied the drinks cabinet.'

Were he and Tabby as close as Harriet and Tarquin?

'Oh yes, now I remember, Harry mentioned Tarquin when we lived in Siena, but I didn't realise they—'

'Shag now and again?'

'If you want to put it like that, yes.'

'They've been at it for years. Both of them are too damn promiscuous to be an item.'

Was Sebastian like that too? Of course – the champagne was part of a grand seduction plan. Why would he spend so much money on a girl he wasn't trying to get into bed?

'You seem like a girl who knows how to have fun?'

And there it was.

'I'm not like Harriet, if that's what you're really asking.'

He tucked one of his curtains behind an ear and studied me. 'I recently ended it with my girlfriend, Emily. We argued all of the time, and I found it utterly exhausting.'

Why was he telling me this?

'I'm sorry to hear that.'

'Did you know you're rather pretty?' he said.

He grinned, displaying perfect teeth, and then edged closer, cupping my chin with his hand, but I pulled away. I wasn't kissing anyone so soon after being with Alessandro. The dull ache inside me would remain for weeks, months, probably years, but even though it wouldn't happen tonight, Mum and Harriet were right: I needed to move on.

Later, when we were all outside, Sebastian said, 'You should come and stay one weekend. I'm living in my father's pied-à-terre on the Fulham Road.'

I couldn't see that happening and lifted my eyebrows.

'Maybe.'

'You don't want to?' he said.

I shook my champagne-filled head. We'd talked for the past two hours non-stop, telling each other all our problems. I'd told him about my quest to get out of Little Vale. He'd confessed he still loved Emily and had tried to get her back, but she'd found someone else, a derivatives trader in the City. His mother wasn't happy about him letting Emily get away, seeing as her father was a QC, and therefore she was suitable marriage material.

'I'd really like to show you London,' he said.

We were both still in love with exes, but perhaps getting to know him would be a way to pass the time.

'Let's see.'

'I'll take that as a yes. Harry can give me your details, if you don't mind?'

Nodding, I said, 'Okay,' expecting he'd forget to ask her for them.

'Come on, J,' Harriet called from the back seat of a black cab. Waving goodbye, I got in, but then clocked Tarquin sitting on the other side of her. That would be the end of us spending any more time together. Harriet couldn't be without a man for one second. Never mind – I needed to get back to Little Vale anyway, I guessed, and tackle the next thing on my list: talk to Gran about Peter possibly being alive. The night out had done me the world of good, enabling me to forget all my troubles, and I'd go back home feeling recharged.

Sebastian closed the cab door after I got in, and leant down to speak through the open window, 'I'll be in touch, Jessica,' he said with a big grin.

Perhaps he would remember to ask Harriet for my details after all. Unsure whether this was what I wanted, I waved again as we drove off, thinking that seeing him again couldn't do any harm – he had been fun to hang out with and that could only be a good thing.

CHAPTER 54

MARIELLA

When Peter told me about Eleanor and their baby that day the war ended in Siena, I didn't know what to say. Giorgio and I had tried to have children and failed, and I wasn't sure whether he'd been the reason for this or me. I longed to be a mother and hoped Peter would be able to give me what Giorgio couldn't. I told Peter that he should consider carefully whether he would want to know this child of his back in England. Did he want to return, now the war was over, and ask this Eleanor woman to marry him? But he said she'd written to him to say she would go into a special home for unmarried mothers, that the child would have been adopted by now and he'd have no way of finding him or her. He confessed that he did not love Eleanor in the same way he loved me. When he left for war, he'd thought he might grow to love her, and had good intentions. He had planned to propose if and when he returned to England. While lying in bed, recovering from the bullet wound, he'd done a great deal of thinking about Eleanor. If he did make it back to England, what would their life be like together, if she'd already given up their child? Wouldn't it be better to allow her to think he was dead? She could then move on with her life and forget all about him. He felt it would be kinder to do this. Besides, he loved me and wanted to spend the rest of his life with me in Italy. He wanted to try to give me children and have a family. He'd grown up without a father, and wanted to give his own offspring everything he'd missed out on.

I hadn't been to Villa Selva for many years. Giorgio had inherited it from his family and during the war it had been taken over by German soldiers – my neighbours there had written to inform me. And so, when we arrived, the place was in such a dreadful mess that we had to stay at a pensione nearby while it was cleaned up. I hired a maid, a cook and a gardener, for the villa was vast, with beautiful gardens on the edge of the lake. Before long the place felt like home, and the two of us couldn't have been happier together.

Peter claimed the library as his place to write, and rightly so. He deserved it after all he'd lived through. It overlooked the lake and mountains beyond, and, as he tapped away on his type-writer, he'd watch the boats go by and look down at the vast gardens filled with roses and rhododendrons and hydrangeas and bougainvillea. To one side was a thriving walled kitchen garden, with every fruit and vegetable and herb one could wish for when preparing a meal.

Once we'd settled into the villa, we established a daily routine. Peter would write most mornings at his desk over-looking the lake, and I would tend to the garden – an activity I enjoyed. Sometimes, I would sit at my easel on the terrazza and paint the beautiful scene before me, or work on a tapestry, or read a novel. At eleven o'clock every morning, I took him a fresh cup of coffee and I'd sit in an armchair while we talked during his break. Every now and again, he showed me what he'd written that morning, and I would tell him what I thought. He would often ask for my advice, and it meant a great deal that he trusted me to help him improve his writing.

One morning, Peter told me that he'd made a decision: it was time to write to his mother and tell her he was alive. Now the war was over, perhaps she and his sister, Mabel, could visit? Would that be all right with me? Of course they would be most welcome, for they were his family. And so that day he wrote a heartfelt letter to his mother, asking her to pass on the news to Mabel as he didn't have her current address. He was so worried about his mother's reaction. Would she be angry with him? With the Tedeschi occupying Italy, it hadn't been possible to write to her before, he explained. He hoped she'd be relieved to hear he was alive, and that she would reply in haste. We'd discussed Eleanor and her situation over and over, since he first told me about her, and he did feel so very guilty about the baby. I did urge him to consider getting in touch, but he was adamant that he didn't want to. In the end, he asked his mother not to pass on the information about him being alive to Eleanor, and to request Mabel didn't either. He knew this was putting his dear sister in a difficult position, seeing as she was Eleanor's oldest friend, and he so hated to come between them, but, after a great deal of soul-searching, he decided it was for the best.

CHAPTER 55

JESSICA

When I returned from London, I felt able to go and see Gran and tell her about the possibility of Peter still being alive. After unpacking, I went over to Camellia Cottage and we had a cup of tea by the fire. After telling her about my time with Harriet, and how much fun we'd had, I set about breaking the news.

'Gran, I have something to tell you.'

'What is it, Jess?'

'Well, when I was in Italy, Alessandro said that Benedetto told him something on his deathbed about Peter.' I went on to tell her the whole story, and she shook her head.

'I don't understand, what are you saying?'

'That he might have survived that night in the chestnut woods.'

'What, Benedetto showed us a grave that didn't exist? He made it all up? Why would he do that?'

'I don't know. Perhaps he didn't believe Francesco's story, and felt that he was doing the right thing. Maybe he believed that Peter was there.'

'Well, this is all quite ridiculous. If he was taken to the countess's villa, how do we know he survived? And if he did, who knows if he's alive now? I think we should just forget about the whole thing.'

'Well, Gran, I have a hunch that he could still be alive.' Taking the novel, *Sporchi Trucchi a Lago di Garda*, out of my bag, I opened the back cover and passed it to her.

'What is this?'

I explained that Peter had joked about changing his name to Pietro Collina, that the countess had a villa in Lake Garda.

'Do you think that photo could be him, Gran?'

Her hand trembling, she studied the photo, then reached for her reading glasses on the trestle table and put them on.

'Well I never, Peter Hill. You continue to shock the life out of me.'

'So, it is him?'

'He's much older, obviously, but the eyes, they're that blue-grey colour, and, after everything you've said, well it does kind of add up, doesn't it?'

'It does.'

She handed the book back to me.

'Will you come with me to see his mother in Leeds?' I said.

'What? Don't be silly.'

'Do you know if she's still alive?'

'She is, Mabel would have informed me otherwise. But hold on, Mabel... would she have known and kept this from me? Would he have asked her to, surely not?'

'There's only one way to find out. I think we need to go and see Peter's mother.'

Gran sighed, and looked at me.

'I'll do it for you, Jessica. You seem so determined to know the truth, but it might be an ordeal for me, you understand?'

'Yes, and I'm sorry to ask, but I do think, even though it might be painful, you should know the truth.'

'You are right, of course. But let's hold off telling your mother for now, until we're sure. I wouldn't want to upset her again – she's been doing so well since she started seeing that counsellor, going to her yoga classes and helping out with WI coffee mornings and talks.'

Putting my hand on hers, I said, 'I agree, that's a good idea. Thank you, Gran.'

'Goodness me, that diary turning up has changed everything for me, you and your mother, hasn't it?'

I placed the bowls of spaghetti with tomato sauce, made using Sofia's recipe, on the table, then filled the wine glasses with Chianti – I'd managed to find a bottle in the village off-licence, and was pleased with myself. I wanted to give Mum and Gran an authentic experience of my time in Italy.

'This looks wonderful, love,' Gran said.

'It does,' Mum said.

'You need to grate cheese on top,' I said.

Gran struggled with the grater because of her arthritis, and I got up to do it for her. She passed the Parmesan to Mum, who held it under her nose.

'This cheese smells like feet.'

I laughed. 'It tastes better than it smells.'

'All right, I'll give it a go,' Mum said.

She grated it cautiously over her spaghetti.

Dad was down at the Old Hare with friends. That afternoon, I'd asked Mum if I could make dinner for once. She put the chicken fillets she'd planned to cook in the freezer, and I bought what I needed at the village store.

Mum and Gran picked up their knives as well as forks, like I had done before learning how to eat spaghetti like Italians did. Living with Sofia and Isabella had given me plenty of practice, and I twirled the spaghetti around my fork in an expert way.

'This is delicious,' Gran said.

'I'm glad you like it,' I said.

'Look at you eating like an Italian. You'll have to show me how to make it,' Mum said.

'I have something to tell you both,' I said, putting down my fork for a moment. Picking up the napkin on my lap, I wiped round my mouth, stalling, as I was so worried about Mum's reaction. I really didn't feel like arguing with her again, especially now she'd accepted my decision about Tom.

Mum rolled her eyes. 'What is it, Jess? You've got us on tenterhooks.'

'I want to move to London.'

'What? I've only just got you back home,' Mum said.

'I know, but I am almost twenty-five.'

She sighed, and pressed her lips together as if trying to stop herself from saying something she might regret. Pushing her fork into the spaghetti, she twisted it round and round. Gran carried on eating, clearly thinking it best not to get involved. Eventually, Mum spoke. 'Where will you go, Jess?'

'Harriet put me in touch with an agency that will hopefully help me get a job on a magazine.'

'That Harriet's got all the answers, hasn't she?' Mum cut her spaghetti in a criss-cross pattern as if she were about to give it to a child. She pushed a forkful into her mouth, almost as if she was trying to mute herself. I knew how strongly she felt about me leaving – she'd made it clear before. I was her whole life – well, I had been before Siena. And all those new activities she'd been involved in while I was away, I was impressed that she'd somehow pulled herself out of the slump she'd been in for years. She'd be okay without me around, I was sure of it.

Gran reached across the table and gave Mum's hand a squeeze. 'It's time to let Jessica go, Mary.'

'Where would you live?' Mum said.

'Harriet said I can stay at hers until I can afford to get a flat-share or something.'

'Let's encourage Jessica to spread her wings,' Gran said.

Mum put down her knife and fork and took a sip of Chianti. I had a feeling she didn't think much of the spaghetti, but at least she seemed to like the wine.

'This is all such a shock, out of the blue like this. I just don't know what to think or say.'

'When will you go?' Gran said to me.

'Next week,' I said. 'Then I'll be there for interviews.'

'Will you come back sometimes at the weekends, at least, and join us for Sunday lunch?' Mum said.

'Of course, I will, Mum!'

A smile of relief crossed her face, and I got up and put my arms round her neck and gave her a big hug. It must be hard with me being the most important thing in her life, but Gran was right – she needed to let me go.

'Oh, I forgot, a letter came for you today,' Mum said.

She took an envelope from the pile of paperwork on the dresser and handed it to me. I opened it. The letter was from *Italian Dreams* to say they were going to publish my article about the Palio in the next issue. And they wanted me to send the article about the Botticelli paintings when I was ready. That had been quick. I couldn't believe my luck. I was actually going to be a published travel writer. I told them both.

'That's just wonderful, love,' Gran said.

'Well done, Jess, darling,' Mum said. She was smiling, and I knew she was pleased for me. But at the same time, I expected she was still worried this article was the beginning of me breaking away.

The next morning, me and Gran got up early, and drove along country roads to Leeds – through Settle, Skipton, Ilkley and Otley, until we reached the Leeds suburbs where Gran had grown up. She directed me until we got to a pretty street with

Edwardian houses, lined with trees in autumn colours. We parked outside the house and knocked on the door.

A young woman came and opened it.

'Hello, can I help you?' she said.

'We're here to see Mrs Hill.'

'Who shall I say is calling?'

'It's Eleanor, but she might not remember me. Tell her I'm Mabel's old schoolfriend. Perhaps that might jog her memory.'

'All right. Wait there for a minute.'

The young woman went away, then came back a minute later and gestured for us to go into a living room at the front of the house with a large bay window. An elderly lady, very frail and thin with white hair, sat in an armchair, facing the window.

'Hello, Mrs Hill. I'm not sure if you remember me?'

'Yes, of course I do. Lottie, will you go and make a pot of tea. And there should be a packet of custard creams in the cupboard. Do sit down, both of you. That is my home help, Lottie. She comes every day to look after me – cleans and makes my meals and keeps me company when I need it.'

'And this is my granddaughter, Jessica,' Gran said.

I looked at Mrs Hill – so this was my other grandmother? It was hard to believe. And then I saw them – photo frames on the mantelpiece, so many of them. I could make out wedding photos and groups of beaming parents and children. Was Peter in these photos?

'So, Mrs Hill, we are here about a rather sensitive matter,' Gran said.

'I think I know why you're here,' she said.

Nobody spoke, and you could have cut the atmosphere with a knife. Gran should be furious really, if Peter was alive and no one had thought to tell her this information.

'I have your son, Peter's, diary,' I said. And then I went on to explain about Alessandro bringing it to the farm because Benedetto was dying. I got it out of my bag and passed it to her.

Her hands were shaky as she took it and ran her hand over the cover with the bullet hole in it.

'This is the diary that saved his life?'

'Well, we don't actually know if he's still alive,' Gran said, sharply, 'Is he?'

Mrs Hill sighed, looking uncomfortable, and then, nodding towards the photographs on the side, said, 'That wedding photo in black and white, that's him and his wife, Mariella.'

'The countess?' I asked.

She nodded.

'She is mentioned in his diary, and apparently Francesco took Peter to her house after he was shot,' I said.

'I have a letter that will explain everything,' Mrs Hill said.

She picked up a bell from the trestle table beside her and rang it. Lottie came into the room. 'Lottie, dear, will you go and get the green shoebox from the top of my wardrobe?'

'Of course, Mrs Hill.'

She disappeared and I heard her footsteps on the stairs. A few minutes later, she came back with the shoebox, and handed it to Mrs Hill, who carefully lifted the lid. Inside were letters and postcards piled right to the top. She sifted through them all, selected a blue airmail envelope and passed it to me.

'I think you should read this,' I said, holding it out to Gran.

'You read it first, Jess. I can't bear to,' she said.

I removed the letter from the envelope.

Villa Selva
27, Via delle Fiore
Gardone
Lago di Garda
Italia
15 November 1945

Dear Mother,

I have a confession to make. I'm still alive and well! You will no doubt have received a telegram about me being missing in action in around 1942/43. But now I must explain what happened.

I fell in love while working with the partisans in Tuscany – she is a countess, and her name is Mariella. I can't wait for you to meet her. We are living in a house in Lake Garda and it is so beautiful here. Villa Selva is on the lake, and we have a wonderful garden, and a boat. The house belonged to her late husband, and I've somewhat landed on my feet.

I was shot by the Germans while working with the partisans in Tuscany in September 1943. A man named Francesco saved my life. He carried me to the countess's house and found a trustworthy physician to remove the bullet and treat the wound. I was lucky because my diary was in my breast pocket, and this lessened the impact of the bullet. The physician said I would certainly have died if it wasn't for the diary. I gave it to a man named Benedetto as I thought I was dying, and asked him to take it back to Eleanor at Birch Farm in Little Vale. I'm not sure if you're still in touch with her, but please may I ask you not to tell her that I'm alive. I would rather she thought I was dead than with a woman I'd chosen over her. The countess, Mariella, nursed me back to full health – well, she had to hide me in the cellar whenever the Germans visited, which they often did, taking her supplies and harassing her.

When the time is right, I intend to bring you here to see this place. I am sorry if you thought I was dead all of this time. I could not bring myself to leave this woman who is a goddess, and this country which quite frankly has stolen my heart. We intend to get married soon, and for now I'm teaching English at the village school. And I am writing a novel. Do you remember that was always my dream? And what a place to do it in with a room of my own, a library filled with books no less, overlooking the lake and surrounding hills, watching the boats go up and down through a vast window. I couldn't be writing in a more perfect setting. I am more or less fluent in Italian now, and have changed my name to Pietro Collina, the Italian version of my name. When you reply, address the letter to Signor P.J. Collina.

Please may I ask you to tell Mabel? I do not have her current address and would very much like to re-establish contact with her. Again, it is imperative that Mabel does not tell Eleanor I am alive. I realise this is an unreasonable request, seeing as they are such old friends, but really, I think it's best for all involved. Please do reply in haste, dear Mother, and I hope you are keeping well.

All my love,

Peter

When I'd finished reading the letter, there were no words. Poor Gran.

'I think it's important for you to read this, Gran,' I said.

She took her glasses out of her handbag. 'All right.'

While she read the letter, I couldn't look. I knew she'd find it painful to discover Peter had chosen to remain in Italy with another woman over being with her and Mum. But also seeing him ask for his news to be kept from her must be devastating to read. What a dreadful situation to be in. Would she have been better off if Alessandro hadn't turned up with the diary that day? Then Mum would still think Grandpa was her real father, and I wouldn't have gone to Siena. And I wouldn't be about to move to London. I'd probably still be stuck in a dead-end job at the *Dales Echo* with no prospect of promotion ever, and would I even be engaged to Tom? The diary had set me on a different path, and for that I was grateful, although I couldn't help feeling immensely sad for Gran.

When Gran had finished reading the letter, she looked at me, her eyes filled with sadness.

Squeezing her arm, I said, 'Shall we go home?'

'Yes, love, that's a good idea.'

'I'm so sorry, Eleanor,' Mrs Hill said, 'I know this must be a terrible shock. I had to keep it a secret like he asked – he is my son. I hope now perhaps you can finally have some closure.'

'Thank you for the tea, Mrs Hill,' Gran said, standing up, although she had left her cup untouched. We left the house, and got into the car, and drove in silence all the way home. When we pulled into the farmyard, Gran went straight to Camellia Cottage, saying she wanted to spend the evening alone, and asked me to tell Mum she wouldn't be eating with us that night. I guessed she needed to process it all. It was certainly a lot for her to take in. When she was ready, we'd tell Mum, and then we'd have her reaction to deal with too. The dust needed to settle, but then I'd think about asking Gran to contact Mabel, to see if she might know whether Peter was still living at the same address. Gran was no doubt furious with Mabel too for keeping the secret from us all these years, but it wasn't her fault if her brother had asked her to do that, was it? Besides, Mabel didn't know that Mum was Peter's daughter, so she had a right to be furious with Gran too for keeping that from her. Perhaps, if I was brave enough, I could go and see Peter in Lake Garda. How I'd like to give him a piece of my mind! I would give it some serious thought.

CHAPTER 56

JESSICA

'My father wants me to work for him,' Sebastian said.

'Doing what?' I asked.

'He owns an estate agency in Manchester.'

We were sitting on a bench in St James's Park, opposite the lake. A duck waddled near to us and pecked at a left-over sandwich on the ground. The trees had put on a show for autumn and the ground was a carpet of leaves in red and yellow mixed with acorns and horse chestnuts. A young boy ran ahead of his parents and crouched down to collect the shiny brown conkers, slipping them into his coat pocket.

'Will you?'

'I don't know.'

'It sounds like you're happy in London though.'

Sebastian worked for a law firm, Tobias Smith, and dealt with complicated legal contracts.

'I suppose I am. My job pays well, but sometimes I have to work until the early hours of the morning. Working for my father would mean an easier life, but I'd be answering to him.'

'That's a difficult decision to make.'

'Anyway, tonight I'm taking you to La Vie, in Mayfair, my favourite restaurant in London,' he said.

Earlier that week, I'd received a note on headed paper:

Fancy visiting me this weekend? - call me, Sebastian x

I'd dithered for a day before deciding to go. The thought of seeing him sober, in the daylight, was daunting. Would conversation be awkward? He'd met me at King's Cross station that Friday afternoon. We made small talk on the tube journey until reaching his flat on the Fulham Road. There he opened a bottle of champagne that had been chilling in his fridge. Later, he went over the road to collect a Chinese takeaway. That night we slept in his bed but didn't sleep together. This morning, he'd offered to show me the sights, so we'd watched the changing of the guard at Buckingham Palace, then walked to St James's Park nearby.

I was wearing jeans and a chunky red jumper under my denim jacket, and had a brown scarf knitted by Gran wrapped round my neck. After days of rain, the temperature had dropped, bringing a blue sky and a chill to the air. The sun shone so brightly that I wished I'd brought sunglasses. Sebastian wore a pair with the name of some designer on the side.

He turned to look at me. 'Hope you've got something nice to wear tonight?'

I hadn't expected to be dining at a fancy restaurant. 'Only this, I'm afraid.'

'Really? That's what I like about you, Thomson.'

Sebastian seemed to like calling me by my surname.

'What do you mean?'

'You really don't care, do you?'

No, I wasn't like the girls he'd been out with, most of whom wore designer clothes all of the time, like Harriet.

'I wasn't expecting to need anything special,' I said.

'Let's go to Bond Street and find you something to wear.'

'I can't afford to do that.'

'It would be my treat.'

'Don't be daft. Can't we go to a restaurant where I can wear jeans?'

'The oysters at La Vie are out of this world and I'd love you to try them. Besides, I'd like to get you a gift.'

If Sebastian spent money on me, I'd feel that I owed him something. And how was I going to deal with oysters? I had no idea how to go about eating such highbrow cuisine, and not being a fan of seafood, the thought of consuming raw slippery shellfish didn't appeal much.

'That's generous of you, but—'

He put a hand on my knee.

'I insist.'

There was no point in arguing about it. 'Okay then, thanks.'

Standing up, he took my hand. 'Right, let's go and buy you a dress.'

I stood up and he kissed me on the lips. When we kissed, there was no fluttering in my stomach, although I did find him attractive. We walked up the path, my arm linked through his, and I wondered if getting to know him was all it would take to feel something. He'd made an effort, bringing me to a beautiful park, and he wanted to take me to his favourite restaurant. And he was about to buy me a new frock. I couldn't help enjoying his attention.

I often thought 'what if?' about Alessandro. What if Gabriella hadn't got pregnant, what if she'd decided not to have the baby, what if he hadn't felt obliged to marry her? They'd no doubt be married by now, but there was little point in torturing myself. We could never reconcile with a baby involved, so I needed to forget him. And here was Sebastian offering the chance for me to move on. Perhaps there was no harm in taking it.

CHAPTER 57

JESSICA

A couple of weeks later, I waited in the foyer at *Go You Travel* magazine for an interview with one of the editors, Teresa Cox. Nerves engulfed me. The office was located on the Strand in a building that apparently housed a few magazines, newspapers and a couple of book publishers. Huge plants flanked the leather sofa, modern art with shapes formed from splattered paint hung on the walls and a sculpture between reception and the lifts looked like car parts super-glued together. People pushed their way through revolving doors, faces taut as they beeped passes at the turnstiles, heels tapping the marble floor, echoes rising to the ceiling. Some carried brown paper bags with handles and clutched cardboard cups with lids.

I wore a suit – the only one I owned – mustard-coloured because I'd bought it in the sale. I smoothed down my skirt, creased already from the tube journey. Since arriving in London I'd attended three other interviews. In each case, the agency had told me the employer decided they preferred someone with more experience, so I was feeling demotivated by it all. Sebastian had run through some questions the night before: 'What are your strengths and weaknesses? Are you good at working as part of a team?' etcetera. I picked up an old copy of *Go You Travel* from the glass coffee table. I had a few copies at Harriet's flat, and had flicked through them the night before, trying to come up with ideas about articles I would write if I got the job.

'I'll get to the point, Jessica, as I've got a meeting in fifteen minutes,' Teresa Cox said.

I smiled and sipped my coffee.

'I'd normally get my deputy to do an initial interview, but we need a temp to start Monday.'

Today was Thursday. That would be convenient money-wise, and perhaps Teresa would be more prepared to take a chance on me for a temping role.

She looked down at my CV on the table. 'So, you've spent some time in Tuscany, I see?'

'Yes. I lived in Siena.'

'We need someone to cover maternity leave, and write articles for our popular feature, "You Culture Vulture". I read a copy of your piece about the Siena Palio in *Italian Dreams* – that was really interesting about your grandfather's diary turning up like that and how it took you to Siena. We're looking for more articles along those lines. Personal stories are always good – a twenty-something woman's point of view always goes down well with our readers.'

'Sounds perfect.'

'Yes. I see you looked after an eighty-year-old woman. That can't have been easy?'

Working on a magazine would be so different from spending all day with Sofia.

'I had to mostly keep her company and make sure she took her pills. We got on well and she was nice to talk to. I've always wanted to be a travel writer, and the journey that my grandfather's diary took me on has made me realise it's about time I tried to make it happen, hence why I'm here.'

Teresa looked at me and smiled.

'Yes, that really came across in your Siena Palio piece, how the diary has changed your life. And I can see the inspiration in your eyes. The job is yours, if you want it, starting Monday. Are you interested?'

'Definitely, thank you! I promise I'll work really hard.'

'I'm sure you will.'

She stood up and led me out of the room, back to the lift, and we shook hands. I couldn't believe my luck. Yes, I'd be covering someone who was likely to come back in a few months, but having *Go You Travel* on my CV would be a real boost. Outside, as I made my way along the pavement towards Charing Cross station, people coming from the opposite direction threw me odd looks, and I realised that I had the biggest grin on my face. But I didn't care – I'd got my first proper job in London, working for a travel magazine. This was the beginning of an exciting new era for me. I'd done it!

Before long, I found myself living at Sebastian's father's flat on the Fulham Road. Somehow it just happened naturally. Tarquin was at Harriet's place most of the time, and Sebastian liked having me around. His flat was really plush with thick carpets and stylish furniture, a nice place to be. We slipped into an easy relationship, and I began to put Alessandro out of my mind. I gave Teresa a list of articles that I could write about Italy to keep me going for the next few issues, which came out monthly. After that, I'd need to travel somewhere, and she said that could be arranged on expenses. The magazine was bought by airlines to put in the pockets of the back of seats, so discounts could be arranged.

A couple of weeks after I'd moved in with Sebastian, I went home to Birch Farm. Now Mum had come to terms with me working in London, I was ready to talk to her about the possibility of Peter being alive. Gran had asked me to speak to Mum without her there as she couldn't handle her initial reaction. Gran herself was still struggling with the whole idea of Peter still living in Italy with this other woman, Mariella, and she'd written to Mabel to tell her she knew everything.

Me and Mum sat at the kitchen table with a pot of tea.

'Mum, I need to tell you something.'

'What is it, Jess?'

'Well...' And so I told her the story from beginning to end, from Alessandro first telling me about what Benedetto said on his deathbed, to me and Gran visiting Mrs Hill in Leeds a few weeks previously.

She put her head in her hands.

'I was only just beginning to get over finding out about him being my real father, and now this?'

'I know. I'm sorry, Mum. I wanted to give it a few weeks before telling you. Gran has been finding it difficult, obviously.'

'Of course she has.'

I explained that Gran had written to Mabel to say she was furious with her for keeping the secret all these years, especially after being made Mum's godmother.

'Yes, but your gran also kept me a secret from Mabel too, so—'

'Yes, everyone has been keeping secrets from each other, and perhaps now it's good for it all to be out in the open.'

'So, what next. Are you planning to go and see him?' Mum asked.

Looking across the table at her, I said, 'How did you know?'

'I know you, Jess, and how you won't rest until you've tracked him down and given him a piece of your mind on all our behalves.'

I laughed. 'Would you mind if I did that?'

'Not at all.'

'Do you want to come with me, if I do go and see him?'

She shook her head. 'Oh no, I couldn't possibly do that. You go ahead though, and maybe, in time, I might change my mind. That's if he wanted to see me. When will you go?'

'I'm sure he would. Not at the moment. I need to settle into my new job. Maybe in a few months.'

Remembering that I'd brought my copy of *Sporchi Trucchi a Lago di Garda*, I got it out of my bag and turned to the photo inside the back cover. For a moment, I was reminded of the English translation that Alessandro had given to me. I'd put it in the drawer of my bedside table, not wanting to think about that miserable last night in Siena. Some time would need to pass before I could look at it.

'This is him. He's a novelist.'

'What?' Mum studied the photo, ran her finger over it. 'Your gran mentioned those blue-grey eyes of his. And that must be where you get your love of writing from.'

'Yes, who would have known how much our lives would change when Alessandro turned up that day with his diary?'

'Who would have known?' Mum said, looking away, her eyes glazed over. She placed her hand on mine. 'Don't worry about me, Jess, I'll be all right. What with my yoga classes and all I've got going on in my life now, I can get past this.'

'That's so good to hear, Mum.'

'And, of course, it will give me something to talk about at my next counselling session,' she said, winking at me.

She had taken it rather well, and I breathed a sigh of relief. I guessed it wasn't as big a deal as her finding out he was her father. Now she had all the tools at her disposal in order to cope, hopefully she'd find a way to work through it all.

CHAPTER 58

ELEANOR

Everything began to settle down after Jessica returned from
Siena. She enjoyed working for the travel magazine, and the
woman she'd been covering while on maternity leave didn't
come back, and so Jessica stayed on. She moved in with her new
boyfriend, Sebastian, a lawyer from a wealthy family in
Manchester. Mary was hoping that he'd move there so Jessica
could be closer, but I'd told her to give it a rest. Jessica was free
to do what she wanted now and Mary needed to be happy with
her weekend visits every now and again. Jessica had brought
Sebastian to the house once for Sunday lunch, and he seemed
like a nice enough lad, with good manners. I wasn't sure if she
loved him as much as Alessandro. But I was impressed by how
well she'd dealt with losing him – it was a little like me losing
Peter, but not quite the same. She wasn't the one carrying his
child, and he'd done the right thing going back to the girl he'd
knocked up in New York. Still, I couldn't help feeling angry
with him for treating our Jessica like that. He had made a
mistake sleeping with that girl before leaving, but then how

could I talk? I'd done the very same thing with Peter before he left for war. If anyone knew how adrenaline pumped through your veins when you knew it was your one last chance to be with someone for a while, if ever, it was me. And I empathised with him a little – but still Jessica was my granddaughter and, so far as I was concerned, he'd let her down after promising her a future with him.

I was glad as always when spring came and the long cold winter was finally over. Daffodils and snowdrops popped up around the farm and bluebells came out in the woods, and me and Mary spent more time outdoors, going for walks in the orchard and across the fields. Sometimes I'd help her out in the kitchen garden and we'd set up chairs by the shed and have a flask of tea together. And as spring progressed into summer, we continued to make the most of the good weather and longer days. August was a time for picking wild blackberries on the land and taking apples off the trees in the orchard, storing them for winter and making pies and crumbles with some of them.

One lunchtime in August, me and Mary were sitting in the kitchen. It was a bright sunny day with light coming through the window.

I cut into the quiche Lorraine Mary had made that morning. She was a good cook, and had taught herself all of the recipes I'd written down over the years, many of them used by my own mother. 'This pastry's nice and crumbly,' I said, taking a bite. It was delicious.

'I had to use up some eggs before they went off, and quiche goes well with salad. There are so many lettuces in the garden, and I've been looking for ways to use them up,' she said.

While eating the quiche, I flicked through the pages of the latest *Sunday Times* magazine from the weekend. That newspaper kept us all going for a few days, there were so many sections. I came across an interview with someone who'd set up a farm shop in the Cotswolds. Since the diary had turned up, and seeing the journey it had taken Jessica on, inspiring her to follow her dream of being a travel writer, I'd been thinking about my own unfulfilled dream. I thought back to that meal at Raymond's when I'd told Peter about maybe having my own tea shop one day. Discovering he'd achieved his dream of being a novelist had made me think. Why shouldn't I achieve my dream too? My seventieth birthday was coming up, but I was in good health – there was still time.

'Have you ever thought about opening a farm shop, Mary?' I held up the newspaper and she looked at me blankly. 'This article is about one in the Cotswolds and the owner explains how he went about setting it up. You could sell your lettuces, and apples from the orchard, along with other fruit and veg. People would pay a small fortune for your home-made chutneys and jams.'

'Wouldn't it be a lot of work?'

Mary was a glass-half-empty kind of person. I expected this came from Peter's side of the family, as I was more of an optimist, like Jessica. Although, admittedly, over the past year Mary had begun to make more effort when it came to enjoying life, and I was proud of her. Sometimes she just needed a bit of persuasion, and I was rather good at that.

'This quiche would sell for a good price, and you could make cakes, open a small café even. We could get one of those coffee machines. I've always dreamt about having a tea shop. It would give you something to do, with Jessica not being around so much. And I'd like it too. It might give us both something to get excited about. And do you know, it might be nice to make the most of my final years.'

Looking at me, she smiled, and I was sure I spotted a tear in the corner of her eye. That had been a little mean, using the impending-death card. But it seemed to have worked.

I finished eating, and put down my knife and fork. Mary cleared the table.

'It's a possibility. Why don't you give me some time to think about it?'

This was a good start. 'All right, thank you, Mary. I appreciate that. I'll remind you in a week or so, just in case you forget.' I threw her a wink and she laughed.

She washed the plates and slotted them into the drying rack. 'Oh, who's that?' She paused at the sound of a car coming into the yard, and looked through the kitchen window. 'Well I never! It's that American lad who brought the diary here.'

'What? You're having me on! It can't be. Alessandro? Didn't he get another girl pregnant, and break our Jessica's heart?'

'He's got a nerve showing up like this,' she said. 'What on earth does he want? If he thinks he's getting our Jessica back, he's got another think coming.'

Shaking my head, I said, 'Perhaps he's found out more about Peter, although I'm not sure I can face hearing any more about the man.'

Mary went through the porch to open the door, and came back into the kitchen with the American lad behind her. He threw me the biggest smile, and I had to admit it was difficult not to warm to him.

'Good afternoon, Eleanor.'

'Good afternoon, Al. What have you brought with you this time?' I said.

He laughed. 'Nothing, as it happens.'

Mary went to the sink and filled the kettle, her shoulders all hunched. She seemed uncomfortable about him turning up. It was understandable if she didn't want Jessica having anything to do with him.

'Want a cuppa, Al?' she asked, reluctantly.

'Sure, thanks.'

'Why don't you sit down and tell us why you're here?' I said.

He pulled out a chair and joined me at the table.

Mary started to dry the plates in the rack with a tea towel.

Usually she'd leave them, but it seemed she couldn't bring herself to sit at the table. The kettle whistled on the stove, and she filled a teapot and put it on the table with a cup and saucer for the lad.

'Thank you, Mary,' he said, pouring himself a cup and adding a lump of sugar from the bowl on the table. He gave his tea a stir.

'I'm looking for Jessica. Is she here?'

'No, she isn't, I'm afraid,' I said.

'Do you know if she received my letter?'

Mary leant on the kitchen counter, facing us, and folded her arms.

'What letter are you talking about?' she said.

And there it was. I knew my daughter and what her body language said about the thoughts going through her head. She'd started to fiddle with her earlobe and had to be hiding something. It was more than likely that she knew what letter he was talking about. What could she have done with it? Had she thrown it away?

'I wrote to Jessica six months ago, and was hoping she might get in touch.'

Neither me nor Mary said a word.

Sitting back in his chair, he held up his hands. 'I understand you don't want me here. If you could just tell me how to reach Jessica, I'll leave.'

'Did you split up with the mother of your child then?' I blurted out.

'Well, there's more to it than that, but I'd rather tell Jessica myself, if that's all right with you.'

'You're too late. She's living in London and has a nice young man as a matter of fact. They make a lovely couple,' Mary said.

Alessandro frowned, his eyes filled with sadness. 'Oh really, she's found someone?' He picked up his cup of tea and put it down again.

'Yes, she has,' Mary said.

'Well, I'd like to talk to her anyway. I need to tell her what I wrote in the letter.'

Mary rinsed a cloth under the tap and wiped the worktop. 'Jessica's got a fantastic job, by the way, working for a magazine.'

'Sounds like she's doing great. I know that's what she wanted. So, is she living with the guy you mentioned?'

'Yes. Maybe her phone number will do?' Mary said.

He shook his head.

'No, I'm sorry. I must see her face to face.'

It was clear he wasn't going anywhere until he had her details. The poor lad at least deserved a chance to explain himself. It did seem that he was no longer with the woman he'd had the child with.

'We should give him Jessica's address so she can make up her own mind, don't you think, love?' I said.

Mary opened the microwave door and wiped drips off the revolving plate, something she rarely did.

'I don't know, Mother.'

'Mrs Thomson,' he said.

'You can call me Mary.'

'Mary, I just drove all the way from London, in a car with a stick shift, to see your daughter. I'd be real grateful if you could tell me where she lives.'

'What's a stick shift?' Mary said.

'I think you say gearstick? I usually drive an automatic.'

'What's that got to do with anything?' Mary said.

'Well, I've only driven a stick shift once before and it wasn't easy, I can tell you.'

'Let's write down the address, love,' I said.

Mary went over to the dresser and tore a sheet of paper off her notepad. She copied Jessica's details out of the address book, then handed Al the note.

'I doubt her other half will make you welcome,' she said.

'I'll just have to take that risk.'

Standing up, he read the note as if checking that the address looked like a real one, and folded it up. 'Thanks, I appreciate it.' He pushed the note carefully into the front pocket of his jeans, as if Jessica's whereabouts meant everything to him. 'I'd better get back to London. Thanks for the tea.'

He made for the porch and I heard the door closing, followed shortly afterwards by the sound of a car engine. Mary threw the cloth into the sink and sighed.

'I can see why Jessica likes him,' I said.

She shook her head and pressed her lips together.

'I know, Mother. So can I.'

CHAPTER 59

JESSICA

AUGUST 1995

The beef joint and potatoes were roasting in the oven, the carrots were peeled and chopped, waiting in the steamer, and the Yorkshire pudding batter rested in a jug on the side. It was a baking hot day and I was wearing shorts and a vest top, but would change into a dress before Sebastian's parents arrived for lunch.

The flat got hot and claustrophobic in the summer, especially when the oven was on, but we made the most of the roof terrace, reached through a hatch by pulling down a ladder above the living area. I'd taken pride in making the terrace look pretty, filling terracotta pots and window boxes with geraniums and pansies, which continued to flower despite me forgetting to water them most of the time.

Sebastian hadn't offered to roll up his sleeves and pitch in with the cooking, which didn't bother me because I preferred to be in control in the kitchen when making a special meal. Instead, he'd set up camp on the terrace to read the Sunday newspapers and tuck into pastries from the café downstairs. I'd

told him that I hoped he wasn't ruining his appetite but he'd
gone ahead and eaten them anyway.

Mum had been overjoyed when I told her we were going to
live together, especially as she still thought Sebastian would go
and work for his father in Manchester. I'd allowed her to think
this after first mentioning it at Christmas, despite Sebastian
having told me on New Year's Eve that he'd declined his
father's offer. I would break the news to her at a later date.

I needed to get the Yorkshire puddings in the oven so everything would be ready when his parents arrived. Then Sebastian's plan was to open a bottle of fizz and make a toast to us
living together. I got the tin out of the oven and poured batter
into each mould, the fat spitting. But then the intercom buzzed,
making me start, and I spilled batter onto the marble worktop.

'Damn,' I said. It was likely to be Tarquin, who often
showed up unannounced at the most inconvenient moments.
Sebastian would have to get off his backside and tell him to go
away.

'Seb,' I called up through the hatch.

'Yes, darling.'

'Can you get the door? It's probably Tarquin here to see
you.'

The fat would be cooling down, and I had to get the Yorkshire puddings in the oven before it did. The buzzer went again,
but there was no sound of movement on the roof. Sometimes
Sebastian's laid-back attitude could be irritating. I sucked air
through my teeth in order to stop myself from saying something
I shouldn't.

'Seb?' I shouted.

'Yesss, I'm coming.'

His bronzed legs appeared on the top rung of the ladder,
and he climbed down – could he have moved any more slowly?
He went to pick up the intercom and I poured the remainder of
the batter into the moulds, hoping the Yorkshire puddings

would still rise. Using oven gloves, I put the tin in the oven, then closed the door, checked the clock and told myself to remain calm. It was only Sebastian's parents. How bad could they be? Surely they'd be happy their son had found a girlfriend? But what if they wanted him to be with someone like Harriet, who'd grown up in the same world? I still needed to have a shower before they arrived, and make myself look half-decent.

When I turned round, Sebastian was standing behind me, his hands on his hips.

'We've got a bit of a problem,' he said.

It was then that I realised I should have turned the potatoes and checked the beef joint before putting the Yorkshire puddings in the oven. Now I wouldn't be able to open the oven door for at least fifteen minutes, otherwise they wouldn't rise. Tarquin's interruption had made me lose focus.

I sighed.

'What does Tarquin want?'

'It isn't him,' Sebastian said, scratching his head.

'Are your parents early? I'm not ready for them yet.'

'Nope, it's not them either.'

'Who is it then?'

'It's—'

The telephone rang and went straight to answerphone. Sebastian liked to screen his calls.

'Jessica, it's Mum,' came her voice.

Just what I needed.

'I've tried ringing a few times since yesterday, but you never answer the phone.'

And I certainly wasn't about to. There wasn't time to get drawn into a long conversation.

'As you know, I don't like answerphones, which is why I didn't leave a message sooner. I'm calling to say the American lad's on his way to see you. Gran made me give him Sebastian's address. I didn't want to, but...'

A pause, then rustling.

'Goodbye.'

The closing beep sounded.

Mum couldn't be referring to Alessandro, surely? The buzzer went again. How did she know this information and why would he bother coming to see me? He must have been up to Birch Farm. The thought caused a warm feeling to unfurl in my stomach, but it shouldn't. He had a child with someone else. And he was married, for goodness' sake. And I was happy. Wasn't I...?

'There's your answer,' Sebastian said.

'Is it really him downstairs?'

He nodded.

'How can it be?'

'You'd better ask him yourself. He said he's not going anywhere until he's seen you.'

How crazy to have Alessandro turn up almost a year after I'd walked out of L'Osteria Giancarlo. Perhaps he'd split up with Gabriella – but they still had a child together. Could I live with that? Was it too late after all that had happened? I didn't want to upset Sebastian, especially just before his parents turned up. If his ex, Emily, turned up making such demands, I wouldn't be happy.

'He's not coming up here, so I suggest you get rid of him before Mother and Father arrive.'

I took off the oven gloves and put them on the side, wishing I had time to change and put on some make-up. I probably looked like a right mess.

'You'd better keep an eye on those Yorkshire puddings,' I said, doubting he would.

When I got downstairs, Alessandro was standing on the pavement, and, when I came out of the door, he studied me with those dark-brown eyes. He wore shorts and a t-shirt. Seeing him again took me to Siena, but the empty beer cans, cigarette butts and takeaway cartons brought me right back to the Fulham Road. Not the best way to be reunited.

'Hi, Jessica.'

I stepped round a half-eaten burger and leant in to double-kiss him, breathing in the familiar cologne. Despite the way we'd parted, it was so good to see him, but I fought the grin trying to escape. Our eyes met, and none of it seemed real. How was this happening?

'What are you doing here?'

He ran a hand through his hair in that way he did.

'I have something to tell you.'

'I have guests coming for lunch, and can't talk for long.'

'Sorry, Jessica. I've showed up at a really bad time.'

'I just can't believe you're actually here,' I said with a laugh.

'Should I go?'

I hesitated for a second. 'No.'

'You look great,' he said.

I wouldn't normally venture onto the Fulham Road in tiny shorts and a vest top with no bra, and had forgotten what I was wearing.

He kicked the half-eaten burger to one side and sat down on the step, patting the space next to him. I remained standing.

'I came to London for work, and stayed for the weekend to look for you,' he said.

'Did you go to Birch Farm?'

'I drove up there in a rental car with a stick shift,' he said. 'Your mom and gran weren't exactly pleased to see me.'

Mum and Gran could be unfriendly when they wanted to be, and they wouldn't want me to have anything to do with him. He must have been persistent for them to give away my where-abouts. Customers gathered at tables outside the café opposite, the awning providing shade from the sun, and I wished there was time for us to get a coffee and sit face to face like that morning in Bar Paolo. Instead, I joined him on the step.

'Why are you here, Alessandro?'

'I wrote you a letter, but I get the feeling you didn't receive it.'

'What did it say?'

'That Gabriella's baby wasn't mine.'

I blinked, thinking back to that night when I'd stormed out of L'Osteria Giancarlo. My anger had lessened with time, but now it returned with full force. How could Gabriella do that to him – to us? And here I was, about to host lunch for the parents of my new boyfriend. Putting my head in my hands, I took a deep breath and tried to pull myself together. I needed to stay cool.

'I don't know what to say. Who was the father?'

'A guy called Frank, who worked at my brother's garage. He'd always liked Gabriella, and he seized his chance to ask her on a date one afternoon when she went to get her car fixed.'

Tracking me down and revealing all this news was a bold move, especially as he had no idea what my situation was.

'Did Gabriella know you weren't the father when she wrote that letter?'

'Yes.'

'What did you say when you found out?'

'I was real mad, obviously, but now I'm kind of relieved. Would you have replied to my letter if you'd received it?'

'When did you send it?'

'Six months ago.'

Around the time when Sebastian asked me to move in with him. I glanced at my watch, and saw that it was almost midday. Perhaps the letter had got lost in the post or in the pile of paper-work Mum constantly moved between the dresser and kitchen table.

'Probably. I wonder what happened to it.'

He stroked his chin, and I noticed it was covered in a day's worth of stubble. I liked him best like this.

'I'm here to ask if we still have a chance.'

Why couldn't he have visited before I moved in with Sebastian?

'It's difficult. I'm kind of with someone now.'

'Are you happy?'

I'd decided to embrace a future with Sebastian, relegating Alessandro to the past. I couldn't break it off with Sebastian just because Alessandro had suddenly become available. What if he found a way to let me down again?

'Yes, I think so.'

'You think so. Hmm. Would you consider visiting me in New York one weekend? I could mail you tickets for the flights.'

I hadn't been to New York, but had always wanted to go. I'd even thought about asking Teresa if I could visit and write a few articles.

'I don't think so.'

Getting a pen out of his pocket, he wrote on the back of a business card. He handed it to me.

'Here's my home address in case you want to write.'

'Okay.'

'Jessica...' He took a deep breath, 'I love you.'

The words hung in the air. I still loved him too, but it wouldn't be right to tell him.

'Where are you staying?' I asked instead.

'At the Vacation Hotel, Regent Street, until 6 a.m. tomorrow. Why don't you come over later and we can talk?'

I shook my head. 'We're expecting my boyfriend's parents for lunch. I need to go and get ready – they'll be here soon.'

'Right.'

I'd lain in bed so many times, playing out this conversation, never actually expecting it to take place.

'You told me we had no future, and I met someone else,' I said.

'I get it.'

'Do you just expect me to drop everything now?'

'I shouldn't expect anything, but I do wonder what might have been.'

I sighed. 'Me too, but you're too late.'

'I have a hunch you're not sure about this guy.'

'How would you know?'

'I know you.'

'How could you know me after the little time we spent together?'

'I knew you from the moment I first saw you.'

A moment I'd never forget.

'So, you probably would have replied to my letter?' he said.

'Yes, of course, if I'd seen it.'

'Damn, what a mess.'

He took my hand in his and squeezed it and I let him.

'I wish we could have met somewhere nicer, without the prospect of my boyfriend's parents interrupting us.' Imagine if they turned up now and saw me holding hands with another man on the step.

'Come to the hotel after lunch?'

I pulled my hand away and shook my head.

'Can't you make some excuse?'

Standing up, I brushed the dust off the back of my shorts with my hands. 'You know that's not the reason.'

He got up and locked eyes with me, and grinned. He knew the reason. We'd end up in bed together, and then there would be no going back. I couldn't help smiling. He wrapped his arms around me, and I inhaled the scent of him, wishing things could be different. We stood there for a few minutes, me no longer caring that Sebastian's parents might turn up, and that Sebastian himself might be watching out of a window.

'I should have tried to find you sooner,' he said into my ear.

He kissed me tenderly on the cheek, and I slowly untangled myself from his embrace.

He flagged down a black cab and the driver pulled over.

Alessandro got into the back seat and wound down the window.

'Call me if you change your mind, Jessica,' he said.

I rolled my eyes, but found myself smiling again and waving as the driver pulled out and sped off up the road. What if I grabbed my bag from upstairs and followed him in another cab to his hotel? I could go over there later? No, I really shouldn't. I went up to the overflowing bin, turning the card over in my hand, and almost threw it away. But I couldn't part with it just yet. I'd hold on to Alessandro's details for a little while, add the card to my Siena mementoes box. Just in case I changed my mind.

CHAPTER 60

JESSICA

NOVEMBER 1995

A few months passed, with summer turning to autumn, and me and Sebastian carried on as if Alessandro had never turned up that day. One evening when getting home from work, I hung up my coat and slipped off my shoes, ready to unwind after a tube journey blighted by signal problems. It had taken twice as long as usual, and I really needed to relax. I'd sat in the tube carriage as we didn't move, thinking about Alessandro. After he'd left that day in the summer, I'd showered and dressed, psyching myself up to adopt a brave face. Sebastian's parents had seemed happy for me to be in his life, but my relief was overshadowed by what Alessandro had told me. After Sebastian had seen his parents to a cab, he came to find me at the sink as I was scrubbing beef fat off the baking tray. He'd asked if I wanted to see Alessandro again and I said, 'No, of course not.' But since then, Alessandro had consumed my thoughts a great deal. I couldn't help remembering the way he'd held my hand, our embrace, and those three words: 'I love you'. His business card was safely tucked into the zip pocket of my handbag, next to my keys. I'd even copied the details into my diary, just in case the card went missing.

Crossing the room, I could feel the carpet was wet under my bare feet. I looked up and saw that water was dripping from the ceiling. Not another leak. Six months earlier, water had started pouring into our living room when a man called Ross showered in the flat above. That time, the sofa had been soaked through and the cushions had taken days to dry out. Ross had reapplied sealant around his bath, and there hadn't been a problem since.

I went to get a bucket from under the kitchen sink and placed it underneath where the water was dripping from, then pressed a towel over the wet patch. When I went upstairs to knock on Ross's door, no one answered. He'd probably showered before going out for the evening – great. I called Sebastian's mobile to get Ross's phone number, but it went straight to voicemail. I left a message and tried his work number. A colleague of his, Sheila, told me Sebastian had left the office half an hour previously.

For three hours I watched television, waiting for Sebastian to call me back. Where on earth was he? Was he stuck on a tube in a tunnel because of the signal problems? The water had stopped dripping, but still I wanted to contact Ross so it didn't start again when he had his morning shower. Eventually, Sebastian called from a black cab on his way home to give me Ross's number, apologising profusely in that way he did. He'd been stuck in late-night meetings at work, apparently. So, where exactly had he been since leaving the office? I didn't say anything until he got home, but could smell beer on his breath when he greeted me with a kiss. I didn't care if he went out for a drink but, if he wasn't telling me about it, who'd been with him?

'Have you really been at work all that time?' I asked.

'Why would I lie about it?'

'I called your office, and your colleague said you left hours ago.'

He pointed the remote at the television and put on a sports channel. A football match came on, with a lot of crowd noise.

'Which colleague?'

'Can you turn that down – I can't hear you.'

Sighing, he pressed the volume button on the remote.

'Sheila.'

'Well, she must have been mistaken.'

'You stink of beer.'

'I went to the pub for one with a couple of clients – what's the big deal? Then I got a cab home, that's all.'

Something wasn't adding up. Had he been with a woman?

I kissed him on the cheek and said, 'Goodnight,' before going to get ready for bed.

He turned the volume back up and said, 'See you in the morning,' his eyes glued to the television.

Could Sebastian be seeing someone else? He had so many opportunities to meet other women. He worked long hours at Tobias Smith, and travelled to Paris every other week for a contract. At weekends he'd go cycling in the Surrey Hills or play tennis or golf with friends. His schoolfriends were a tight-knit group, and they seemed to spend a lot of time together. But had he been lying about these activities too? On Saturday nights, he always wanted to stay in with me and get a takeaway and watch a film – we hadn't eaten out for ages. After taking off my make-up, I put on my pyjamas and got into bed. Switching off the lamp, I closed my eyes, hoping my paranoia would subside by the morning.

CHAPTER 61

JESSICA

'Do you know what happened to that letter, Mum?' I asked. 'The one from Alessandro?'

I'd got the train up from King's Cross that afternoon. The past few weeks had been hectic, and it was good to be home for Christmas, where I could relax and enjoy Mum's cooking. I finished peeling the last potato and dropped it into the saucepan of water. Mum let me help out at home these days, and this meant we would talk while preparing meals or baking cakes. She reached inside the turkey for the giblets, then dropped them into a saucepan.

'You think I did something with it?' she said, suddenly in deep concentration as she bent down and searched for something in a cupboard.

'No, I can't work out where it went, that's all.'

I could tell by the way she wasn't meeting my eye that she'd probably seen the postmark from New York and thrown it in the bin. But I found it hard to be angry if she had – she was probably doing her best to protect me. I doubted very much she'd have opened it and read Alessandro's words. I made a start on peeling the carrots.

Mum produced a saucepan lid from the cupboard, and said, 'Ah, there it is!' a little too enthusiastically, but I let it go.

She dropped a carrot, celery, garlic, a bay leaf, a sprig of rosemary and peppercorns into the saucepan with the giblets, covered them with water and put the saucepan on the hob. She liked to get ahead and make the gravy on Christmas Eve.

'You know I'm not a big fan of the American lad, but I certainly wouldn't meddle with a letter that had your name on it.'

I couldn't find a way to believe her.

Standing over the hob, she stirred the gravy with a wooden spoon, blinking in that way she did when on the brink of bursting into tears. I wasn't sure what to do – she didn't like any vulnerability to be acknowledged.

'Where shall I put these carrots?' I said, brightly.

'Chuck them in with the parsnips. Is everything all right with Sebastian?'

I couldn't bring myself to tell her about the evening of the leak.

'Why shouldn't it be?'

Gathering the mountain of peelings off the worktop, I chucked them into the crate for the compost heap.

'Why did you change your mind about spending Christmas with his family in Manchester?'

More recently, me and Sebastian had clashed daily – the evening of the leak making things worse.

'We just need a break from each other. And I missed you all.'

'Why would a couple who are in the honeymoon stage of their relationship need a break from each other?'

I sighed. 'I don't know, Mum.'

She wrapped tin foil round the turkey and put it in the fridge.

'Were you and Dad happy at the beginning?'

Realising I'd implied they weren't happy now, I instantly regretted my words.

Mum looked as though she were really about to burst into tears, and her hands shook as she lathered them in soap. I put an arm round her shoulders, wishing I could retract what I'd said. It had somehow just slipped out.

'I'm sorry, I don't know what I'm talking about,' I said.

Mum rinsed her hands under the tap, leaving the water running for longer than it needed to.

'My greatest achievement is having you, Jessica. I love you so much, and want you to be happy,' she said, her voice all shaky.

She didn't say, 'I love you' often. I couldn't remember the last time she'd said it.

'I love you too, Mum.'

She gave my shoulder a squeeze. 'Let's have a sherry, shall we? It is Christmas Eve, after all.'

'Good idea.'

We went into the sitting room, lit by the glow of the fire that crackled and popped in the hearth. Mum switched on the lamps and poured us a generous measure of sherry in the posh crystal glasses usually saved for special occasions and Christmas. I picked up a box of chocolates from the coffee table and sat down by the fire, the heat a comfort. I studied the chocolate menu and picked out a caramel. Sometimes being mothered wasn't so bad.

Mum sat opposite and propped up her feet on the pouffe. 'So, what do you think about the farm shop and café idea?'

In Mum's last letter, I'd been pleased to learn that Dad's friend would be converting Manor Barn into a shop and café in the new year. It would be called Eleanor's, after Gran – it had always been her dream to have a tea shop. I was pleased for them both – it would be a project for Mum to get her teeth into, and Gran would be happy sitting there all day instead of the kitchen. I raised my glass of sherry.

'It's such a fantastic idea. Cheers to your and Gran's new venture.'

CHAPTER 62

JESSICA

Back in London after Christmas, I sat at my desk. The office was still fairly quiet as many colleagues had booked extra time off to spend with their families. The computer monitors were still draped with tinsel and there was a dancing reindeer next to the printer, the battery long since depleted. Reminders of the run-up to Christmas irritated me – the month-long anticipation with work do after work do and lunch after lunch. And now it was all over for another year. Sipping my coffee, I looked out of the window at life going by – double-decker buses and black cabs moving along the Strand. People walking along the pavement.

Sebastian had left an answerphone message the night before, announcing he was going to stay in Manchester for New Year's Eve. He suggested I join him. Seeing the new year in with people I didn't know wasn't appealing and I called him back to say no. The telephone call left me with a knot in my stomach, like many of our conversations of recent weeks. I'd planned to make us a romantic dinner, but now I'd spend the night alone on the sofa with wine, a ready meal and Jools Holland on TV. He was due to come back early in the new year for a few days before skiing with Tarquin and other friends. Then I'd be left on my own again.

Being back at Birch Farm had given me time to realise that being with Sebastian wasn't working out. At night, I'd lain awake thinking about Alessandro, and had sometimes gone downstairs to watch television with a glass of milk. I reached into the zip pocket of my handbag and took out his business card. It was tempting to call him right now. I wasn't sure exactly what time it would be in New York, but recalled they were a few hours behind us. Calling would put him on the spot, and I might get it all wrong over the phone, wasting my chance. I could write a letter, but it might go missing like the one he'd sent to me. An email would drop into his inbox immediately, but what would I write? If he wasn't seeing anyone else, would he invite me to visit him in New York? How would I explain that trip to Sebastian?

The only way to get to New York would be through work. Perhaps I could come up with a few articles to write and propose that Teresa send me there for a few days on expenses. Boldly, I sent her an email hoping she'd agree.

It was a few days later. I sipped my champagne and hiccupped.

'Teresa said I can go to New York.'

Harriet was perched on the stool next to me at some new bar she wanted to try on the King's Road. Tarquin had proposed in the Maldives, and we'd come out to celebrate. Sebastian and Tarquin were away skiing. On a Tuesday in January, a month when a lot of people took a break from drinking, the bar was virtually empty.

'Will you go and see Alessandro?' Harriet said.

I'd somehow convinced Teresa that I could write a double-page spread about spending a weekend in New York. I could then go and see Alessandro – if I still wanted to, and if I was brave enough. Perhaps I'd chicken out once I got there.

'I can't do it to Sebastian. Can I?'

'Alessandro came to find you. Why not see what happens? You and Seb are like chalk and cheese. When I set you up that night in the Crocodile Lounge, I thought you'd have a rebound fling, not shack up with him.'

I told Harriet about the night of the leak, when I couldn't get hold of him.

'Would he cheat on me?'

Harriet shrugged, and looked away. I could sense she wasn't telling me something.

'What do you know?' I asked, half dreading the answer.

She lifted the champagne bottle out of the ice bucket. The barman rushed to whisk it from her and refilled our flutes.

'He meets Emily for lunch, at that place on Moorgate where they do curly chips.'

It made sense, as Emily recruited staff for law firms and her office was round the corner from Sebastian's. Had he been with her that night?

'Do you think that's all they do?'

Harriet squeezed my arm. 'Tarquin swore me to secrecy, but my loyalties lie with you.'

I took a deep breath. 'What is it?'

Leaning forward, she said, 'Emily's at the same ski resort as Seb and Tarquin with a group of girlfriends.'

I shook my head in disbelief. And I'd been feeling bad about contacting Alessandro.

'Are they seeing each other?'

'Tarquin said they aren't, but I don't believe him. They were very much in love before, you know.'

The drawer in Sebastian's bedside table was stuffed with Emily's old letters. *I love you darling Seb, you're always in my heart* – her cheesy words flowed across headed paper in fountain pen. I'd read them one Sunday afternoon when he and Tarquin were supposedly playing golf. Underneath the letters, I'd found photographs of them backpacking across New Zealand. Emily was a beautiful redhead and had legs that went on forever. She'd done some modelling as a teenager. The thought of Sebastian cheating with her didn't gnaw at my gut as much as it should.

'Can you find out more?'

Harriet nodded. 'Sure, I'll give Tarquin a call, but you must go to New York anyway. And don't forget it's our engagement party when you get back.'

I couldn't believe my maneater friend was settling down, but if it was with anybody I supposed it would have been with Tarquin – they couldn't be more suited to each other.

CHAPTER 63

JESSICA

I sat on the bed in pyjamas eating a Chinese delivery. The sesame chicken was delicious, but the portion was far too big. The television in a walnut cabinet was showing the film *Superman*, and I'd muted the volume. Alessandro's business card with the Pimsy's logo lay on the bed in front of me and I tapped his number into the telephone, then replaced the receiver. Now that I was in New York, the idea of calling him seemed ridiculous. What had I been thinking, coming here? Almost six months had passed since his visit – for all I knew, he could have a girlfriend by now.

I tapped in Alessandro's number again.

Hi, you've reached Al. I'm not home right now. Please leave a message and I'll get back to you.

The beep sounded and I hung up – I had no idea what I would say in an answerphone message. Besides, it could be deleted by mistake, just like letters could go missing.

Tomorrow, I'd try calling Alessandro again.

. . .

The next day I was in the office, writing up my article about what to do in New York on a mini-break, when an email from Harriet dropped into my inbox. I clicked it open.

J,

Haven't got time to call today as I've got an essay deadline. Tarquin thinks Seb and Emily shared a room on the last night of the ski trip but can't be sure. You should call Seb and find out what's going on. Hope you've managed to contact Alessandro. Give him a kiss from me.

Harry x

I'd tried to shut the Sebastian situation out of my mind, but Harriet's email had brought it all back. Sipping my tall cappuccino from the canteen, I watched the blizzard out of the window. It hadn't stopped snowing since I'd arrived in New York, and the roads were lined with heaps of the stuff, cleared by ploughs that hummed all day long. As I looked back at my screen, my eyes met those of Kelly, who was standing up at the cubicle opposite, holding a takeaway coffee, just back from the canteen. We'd chatted a bit since my arrival, and she'd shown me where everything was and introduced me to other members of staff.

'Hey Jessica, do you need to talk?' she said.

I squeezed hand cream onto my palms and rubbed it into the cracks between my fingers. The cold weather had made them extra dry. Tears pricked my eyes. Trusting a person I didn't know wasn't my thing, but I needed to confide in someone. I explained about Harriet's email and how I'd planned to get in touch with Alessandro.

'Sebastian doesn't sound right for you. You have to call Alessandro,' Kelly said.

'I tried last night, but he wasn't there.'

'So, call him now.'

'Okay,' I said. She sat down, disappearing from view behind the wall that divided our cubicles.

I took the business card from my handbag and keyed his number into the telephone.

'Good afternoon, Pimsy's.'

It was a woman's voice, presumably a PA or similar.

'Hello, I'm looking for Alessandro?'

'He's on vacation. In Italy, I believe.'

Another setback. He was in Italy?

'When's he back in New York?'

'Hold on... his flight is booked for Friday.'

Alessandro would return to New York on the day I was due to leave.

'Do you know what time?'

'He'll be back in the afternoon.'

The woman hung up, and my grand plan was shattered.

'I don't believe it,' I said, standing up in order to talk to Kelly.

'What did he say?' she said.

'Alessandro's away until Friday, the day I fly home.'

Kelly rested her head in her hands. 'I'm so sorry.'

On Friday, the taxi pulled up outside the brownstone, skidding a little as it stopped. A fire escape criss-crossed the façade and steps led to the front door, like the building in *Breakfast at Tiffany's*. I hoped he'd be back and pleased to see me. What if he'd met someone else over the past few months?

On the day I'd received Harriet's email, I'd called Sebastian, wanting to give him a chance to confess all. We made small talk about work, then he made an excuse about a call on the other line. A few days later, Harriet had emailed to say Tarquin's sister Tabby had seen Sebastian snogging Emily outside a pub in Covent Garden. Whatever happened with Alessandro, it was over between me and Sebastian, and I felt a sense of relief. We weren't meant to be together, and I'd be better off on my own than with the wrong man.

I got out of the car, struggling not to slip as I stepped onto a pavement covered in fresh snow. Trees lined the street and the smell of roasted chestnuts wafted from the stall of a nearby street vendor. It was all so New York. I pressed the intercom button for his flat.

'Hello.'

It was him. Thank goodness he was there. My breath shortened.

'Hi, it's Jessica.'

'What?'

'It's Jessica, you know, from Siena.'

'You're kidding! Come on up.'

The door clicked and I went inside. I walked up the stairs and saw him holding the door to his flat open with one hand, a bottle of beer in the other. He wore suit trousers and a shirt, undone at the collar, and he looked especially hot. It was so good to see him.

He grinned.

'What are you doing here?'

'I've been working in New York.'

Leaning forward, he kissed me on both cheeks. He smelt of beer and a hint of that cologne that I loved.

'No way. I've been in Florence.'

I took off my gloves and pushed them into my coat pockets. 'Your colleague said you were on vacation.'

'It was a kind of business trip, but nobody knew that. I'll explain later.'

I bit my lip. 'I'm on the way to the airport, and only have ten minutes.'

'Oh Jessica, really? Did you leave a taxi waiting downstairs?'
I nodded.

'Ten minutes isn't long enough.'

'I know.'

'This is like when I came to London. Are you still with that guy?'

'I'll be ending it when I get back.'

He groaned, 'Jessica, how can you do this to me?'

'I wanted to see you so that...' I hesitated. What should I say?

'Why don't you come in for a few minutes, at least?'

I entered the flat and he closed the door behind me. Hot from climbing all the stairs, I took off my coat and put it over the back of a chair. You certainly didn't get much for your money in Manhattan. The living area was open plan with a kitchen, table and chairs, sofa and television. There was a bookcase in the corner, crammed with books about art, antiques and Italy. The walls were painted cream, and the floor was made from wood, but there were no paintings on the walls or framed photos or vases of flowers. No sign of a woman's touch.

'If you only have ten minutes, which is kind of crazy, you should follow me,' he said.

He led me into the bedroom, where he opened the wardrobe and slid some clothes along the rail. What was he doing? He passed me a cardigan, and it was mine – the one from Siena.

'This is the sweater you left behind the night I told you about Gabriella's letter. I kept it because it smells of that perfume you wear.'

I removed the cardigan from the hanger and held it to my nose, inhaling the scent, Eau de Vivre, that I'd worn in Siena. I'd stopped wearing it because Sebastian didn't like it – how could I allow his opinion to influence me like that?

'I can't believe you kept it.'

'A girl I was seeing found it and accused me of cheating,' he said with a laugh.

I laughed along with him, but couldn't help feeling jealous of whoever this girl was.

'What did you say?'

'That it belonged to an ex-girlfriend.'

He looked into my eyes, and I wanted him to kiss me, and wished that I could stay the night. How could this be happening?

'I have to go,' I whispered.

'Can't you change your flight?'

I couldn't be more thrilled that he wanted me to stay. Changing the flight wouldn't be difficult, but Harriet and Tarquin's engagement party was the following night.

'It's Harriet's engagement party tomorrow.'

'Harriet is getting married?'

I smiled. 'Yes.'

'She'd want the best for you.'

I bit my lip. 'Is it the best for me, though?'

'I think so.'

He put his hands on my waist, and I dropped the cardigan onto the bed. He kissed me, his tongue pushing against mine, and I wrapped my arms round his neck. He slid a hand under my jumper, caressing my back. How I wanted him to pick me up and put me onto the bed, and take off all my clothes – but I had to leave. Reluctantly, I pulled away from him. He picked up the telephone receiver on the bedside table.

'Why don't you call the airline?'

'What about the taxi downstairs?'

'I'll take care of it while you change your flight to Sunday afternoon.'

Two days and two nights with him. How could I turn down such an offer? I took the receiver. 'Okay.'

He left the room, his footsteps echoing around the stairwell as he went to the lobby. I'd never done anything so impetuous, and it was exciting. I got the flight details out of my handbag and called the airline.

Five minutes later, it was done, and I sat on the edge of the bed, wondering if I'd made the right decision. A giddy feeling told me the answer – I had absolutely made the right decision. I struggled to remove the grin from my face as Alessandro came back into the bedroom, took me into his arms once more and leant down to kiss me.

CHAPTER 64

JESSICA

'I have to tell you something,' Alessandro said.

His face was serious.

'What is it?'

We'd been lucky to get a table for brunch in the café at the Rockefeller Center after being very late getting out of bed. It was the kind of restaurant that had white linen tablecloths and napkins, and each table had a lamp. We sat by the floor-to-ceiling window with a view of the ice rink, where people skated in hats and scarves.

Alessandro pushed his fork into the potato hash on his plate. 'I was in Florence for a job interview.'

'Oh, really?' I wasn't sure I could take any more big news or changes.

'They more or less offered it to me on the spot.'

'Where is it?'

'It's at a small art gallery called La Galleria Antica.'

I had no idea what this meant for our future. I'd thought about going back to Italy, and had spoken to Teresa about submitting an idea to a publisher for a travel-writing book along the lines of *A Year in Provence*. She'd loved the idea and was going to put out feelers to a few people she knew in the business. Having read a few travel-writing books since returning home, I'd been thinking about renting a house in the Tuscan countryside and living there for several months while writing about the experience. Would this mean I could be with Alessandro? We couldn't live together, and that would be too much anyway, but we'd be close enough to see each other sometimes in the evenings and at weekends.

'That's funny, because I was thinking about going back to Italy.'

He smiled. 'You were?'

I told him about the book proposal idea.

'Well, imagine that. Within a few months or even weeks we could be near each other again,' he said.

I cut into my French toast. 'I know, it could be amazing, but I can't get excited yet. What if there aren't any publishers interested?'

'You could always rent a place there anyway and write the book and then submit it. Or stay at my flat in Florence for a while if you don't want to pay rent.'

These were both good ideas, and they gave me hope.

'Thanks, that's a nice offer.'

We ate in silence, watching the skaters through the window. He wiped his mouth with a napkin. The waiter refilled our coffee and Alessandro stirred sugar into his.

'Did you go up the Empire State Building yet?' he asked.

'No, but I walked past it on the way to the office.'

'Shall we go there after? It's only round the corner.'

'I'd love that.'

I couldn't think of anything more romantic that we could do together in New York.

. . .

The sun shone, the sky a deep blue with scattered clouds and I put on my sunglasses. High-rise buildings lay below, Central Park, a rectangle of white from the snow. Traffic moved along the gridded streets, the cars so small they looked like toy ones. The Hudson snaked round the island, spanned by the bridges leading in and out of Manhattan. Alessandro pointed across the river.

'I'll take you over there to Hoboken one day to meet my folks.'

That was a scary thought. What would his family think of me? I tightened my scarf.

'Do you ever wonder what happened to my letter?' he said.

I tapped a clump of snow with my boot. 'I think my mother did something with it.'

'She didn't like it when I visited.'

'It's not you, she was just trying to protect me.'

'The things mothers do. Mine packed me off to Siena to get me away from Gabriella, remember.'

'Imagine if she hadn't.'

He got hold of my scarf and pulled me to him, kissing me on the lips.

'If I moved to Italy, my mum wouldn't like it,' I said.

'Would that stop you?'

I shook my head. 'She's just opened a farm shop with a café, called Eleanor's, after Gran. It was always her dream to have a tea shop, and it gives Mum something to do.'

I asked a lady to take our photo with my camera. Me and Alessandro leant against the barrier with our backs to the view, his arm round me, our cheeks pressed together. A photo to cherish. I would send him a copy, and frame one for myself. We walked round the viewing gallery, arm in arm, me being careful not to slip on the patches of ice.

'So, you're definitely going to end it with that guy when you get home?'

Nodding, I said, 'Yes.'

Then it occurred to me that I'd never actually asked him about his situation.

'What about you? Please tell me you haven't been seeing anyone.'

He frowned. 'I've been seeing a colleague, but it's nothing serious.'

The thought of him being with someone else bothered me, but it must be casual otherwise he wouldn't have been looking for a job in Florence.

'What shall we do on your last night in New York?' he said. 'I can take you to a restaurant.'

'Something simple.'

'Like what?'

'A home-cooked meal.'

'Let's get down from here and go to the grocery store.'

We headed for the lift.

'What will you make?' I asked.

'The only thing I can make, pasta. What time's your flight tomorrow afternoon?'

'Six o'clock.'

He turned to look at me.

'Do you remember when I promised to take you to Pisa airport?'

I nodded.

'I felt bad about that,' he said.

I thought back to that day. I'd cried in the taxi to Siena station, then on the train to Pisa airport looking through the window at rows of vines and hilltop towns, unmoved by the scenery despite its beauty.

'It was a miserable journey.'

'That week in Siena with you gone wasn't easy. Me and Matt drank a lot of beer.'

It was good to hear that he'd been affected by how it ended between us.

'I'm glad you came to find me.'

We got in the lift and he took my hand in his.

'Me too, and I'm glad you came to New York. I'd given up on the idea of you visiting.'

'Will you be taking me to the airport this time, then?'

'Of course, how could I not?'

CHAPTER 65

JESSICA

LONDON, JANUARY 1996

I took the lift up to the second floor, then wheeled my suitcase into the flat. That morning, I'd taken a taxi to the office from Heathrow airport after spending all night on the red-eye. I was exhausted, but got myself a big coffee and did my best to catch up on work at my desk. After lunch, Teresa had called me into her office and said a publisher had shown a great deal of interest in me turning my travel-writing column into a book. The commissioning editor there was a fan, and she really liked my writing style. Teresa planned to put me in touch with an agent she knew. I couldn't have been more excited – this was the kind of opportunity I'd always dreamt of. Did it mean I might be able to go and rent a house in Tuscany, and spend the day writing, with a lovely view and lots of delicious food to eat? And see Alessandro, who would only be living down the road in Florence? I could take up the offer of staying in his flat, of course, but I didn't feel ready to live with him so soon. Besides, I really liked the idea of living in the middle of the Tuscan countryside, on the edge of some charming village. I'd spent some time searching online that afternoon for villas to rent, and they were quite reasonably priced. There was a strong possibility that I could make this dream come true! I just hoped the publishing deal would come off. But then again, even if it didn't, I could afford to rent somewhere for at least six months. Maybe I could teach English to make money, and I could still work for Teresa from Italy too while writing the book I so wanted to write. Perhaps Alessandro was right and I could get a deal when it was finished.

Drained from the jetlag and having to go to work from the airport, I sat down to summon up the energy to make dinner, hoping Sebastian had managed to at least keep bread and milk in the house. A decent cup of tea would be a nice start. But then I spotted a woman's shoe on the floor. It was red with a stiletto heel. The sight of it turned my stomach. A trail of clothes led to the bedroom: Sebastian's shirt, tie, trousers, and a black dress, and lastly a lacy electric-blue bra. Music – a ballad – came from behind the bedroom door. I got up and walked over, and braced myself before pushing it open. My expensive sandalwood candle, a Christmas present from Harriet, flickered on the bedside table. Sebastian and a woman, whom I assumed to be Emily, lay like spoons, her red hair spread over the pillow.

I switched on the light, and he sat up with a start.

'Damn, what time is it? Jessica?'

'So, I guess this is Emily.'

'I didn't think you'd be back until later,' he said. Of course, I'd forgotten to tell him my arrival time. On Saturday morning, I'd left a voicemail to say that I'd be back on Monday night, forgetting jetlag would mean I'd end up leaving work earlier than usual.

Emily pulled the duvet over her head, and I heard her muffled voice saying, 'I don't believe it.'

Sebastian put his head in his hands. 'I'm sorry, Jessica.'

Obviously, I had planned to finish with him anyway, but finding him in bed with Emily was still a huge blow. I didn't deserve to be embarrassed like that.

Wheeling my suitcase straight back into the hall, I pressed the button for the lift. For once, it came immediately with a clunk, and I stepped inside.

'Jessica, wait!'

Sebastian was standing at the door of the flat facing me, wearing boxer shorts, the yellow paisley ones I really didn't like. I pressed and held the button that was supposed to make the doors close more quickly.

'What do you want?'

'I'm sorry you found out like this.'

I shrugged. 'I was going to end it anyway. But it wasn't fair to allow me to find you in bed with her like that.'

'Have you been with the American?'

I nodded.

'You're no better than I am then.'

He had a point, although I might not have contacted him in New York if Harriet hadn't told me about Emily.

'I heard you snogged Emily in Covent Garden though before deciding to go and see him.'

He looked at the floor and then back at me again. 'Right, well... there isn't much I can say to that. Where will you go?'

'Harriet will hopefully put me up.'

'If you'd loved me more than that damn American, none of this would have happened.'

I doubted this was true. He loved Emily as much as I loved Alessandro.

'I'll be back for the rest of my things when you're out. Could you do me a favour and blow out that candle – it's very expensive and I'd rather it wasn't used while you're shagging Emily.'

I pressed G and the doors finally slid shut, providing a full stop to my parting sentence. Sebastian had rescued me after

Siena, and I was grateful for that. Sometimes people came into your life for a reason, and that was all I could put our relationship down to. We'd both been on the rebound from people we should have been with. What was done was done, and I couldn't be more excited about everything that was to come.

CHAPTER 66

ELEANOR

Mary cut the carrot cake into slices and placed it on the counter, next to the quiche. Eleanor's Farm Shop and Café had been open for a month, and takings were better than expected. Phil's friend had converted Manor Barn – where me and Jack had our wedding reception – for next to nothing, so outgoings had been low. Tom's mother, Patsy, had visited with a group to organise a coffee morning and she'd spread the word amongst her fellow churchgoers. Villagers had spotted Mary's postcard in the newsagent's window and had dropped in for chutneys and jams, then stayed for coffee and cake. Mary had selected a classical music radio station to create a relaxing ambience, and locals seemed grateful for a change from the tea shop on the village high street with its slow service and stale scones. Mary had all kinds of exciting ideas: a weekly supper night with candlelit tables and a local band, as well as hiring it out as a venue for parties, events, and perhaps even wedding receptions. Customers could bring their own booze so she wouldn't need to get a licence.

Mary was doing everything to make Eleanor's a success, and I was grateful. My daughter had helped me achieve my dream – the one that I'd talked about with Peter in Raymond's all those years ago. And he'd achieved his dream of writing novels. When Alessandro brought Peter's diary to the farm, he changed all our lives – and somehow, he woke us all up. It brought me closure at last. I only wished I'd known sooner that he was alive all those years while I'd been grieving for him – that way I could have got over it all. My marriage to Jack might have been more successful, too, if I'd been aware that Peter had known about Mary and actively chosen not to return. Instead, I'd always found myself yearning for someone else. But now, I was glad that Jessica was going to try to find him. It would be good for her to meet her real grandfather, and Mary was coming round to the idea of his existence, slowly, but she'd get there in the end.

CHAPTER 67

JESSICA

Alessandro had offered to drive me to Limone sul Garda, and we were on the autostrada. It was spring and the weather was warm. I was so excited about the prospect of meeting my real grandfather, but also nervous about his reaction upon seeing me. Rather than going to his house, I'd planned to go to the bar he frequented every morning, by the old harbour. Gran had written to Mabel, explaining that she knew everything and finally telling her the truth about Peter being Mary's father. But she also said I planned to visit him. Mabel had been glad the news was out at last as she'd told Gran she felt terrible keeping it to herself all these years, and she was delighted to find out Mum was actually her niece. And now she knew why she was Mum's godmother. She'd written to wish me luck, but also mentioned a place in Limone sul Garda, called Bar Luisa in case it would be less daunting than going to Peter's house. She said that he'd sit outside most mornings with a notebook and pen.

We drove along the road that followed the lake, passing through village after village. It was mind-blowingly beautiful, with an abundance of flowers in bright colours, and the lake was surrounded by what I'd read in the guidebook were the Dolomite Mountains. It was one of the most stunning settings I'd ever been in. There were boats of all kinds crossing the water – small passenger ferries, rowing boats, fishing boats, kayaks – and on the pebbly beaches there were umbrellas and people sitting in chairs and on towels.

Before long, we were parking in Limone sul Garda.

'Do you think he'll be here?' I said.

'If not, I guess we can try his house. You have the address with you, right?'

'Yes, I do, but that would feel like imposing. Approaching him in a café would be so much easier, given the circumstances.'

We found Bar Luisa, and it was in the most perfect setting, on the edge of the harbour. There were fishing boats in an array of pretty colours, and the tables outside had views of the lake and the mountains behind them. It was an idyllic spot, perfect for writing, and the kind of place where I would like to sit with a notebook and pen and draw in the inspiration from all around. I'd brought my copy of *Sporchi Trucchi a Lago di Garda*, and had studied the photo inside the back cover once again.

And then there he was. It had to be him. He was sitting alone, a cappuccino and a panama hat on the table beside him. He was writing in an A5 notebook with a fountain pen and he seemed to be in deep thought. I wasn't sure if we should interrupt his writing. It might not be the best way to approach him with the news we had to deliver.

'Shall we sit over here and get a coffee, wait for him to take a break?' I said to Alessandro.

'Sure, good idea. I'll go and order us something.'

I sat down a few tables away from Peter and studied him out of the corner of my eye. From the way he held himself, he appeared to be in good health.

Alessandro came back outside, and said, 'The barman will bring them over.'

Peter stopped writing, closed his notebook and picked up his coffee cup.

'I'm going over,' I said.

'All right, I'll wait here.'

I stood up and went over to Peter's table.

'Hello,' I said.

He looked up at me and frowned, then removed his glasses. He sat back in his chair, assessing me in the way a writer would. And then he inhaled deeply. 'I knew this day would come.'

'You did?'

'You have her eyes, the colour of emeralds.'

I remembered him writing about Gran's eyes in the diary. Nodding, I said, 'I know.'

'My mother wrote to say you and Eleanor visited, and she showed you my letter, written all those years ago. And Mabel called to say she told you I write here most mornings. It was only a matter of time before you found me.'

'Did you want me to find you?'

He seemed to be thinking about this carefully. 'I believe I did, yes. Until now, my life has been a novel without an ending. And now, you have come to complete my story. Your name is Jessica?'

I nodded and smiled, unable to believe this moment was actually happening.

'And your mother, my daughter, is Mary?'

'Yes, that's right. But my mother currently has no interest in knowing you, I'm afraid. She's furious with my gran for not telling her everything sooner. And she isn't very happy with you, either.'

He let out a sigh.

'I am truly sorry for what I've done to all three of you. It's no excuse at all, but war makes people act in strange ways. I went through a great deal, and Italy saved me, helped me process all of the horrific trauma experienced. I believe you have my diary?'

'Yes, Benedetto sent his grandson – Alessandro, who is sitting over there – to England with it on his deathbed.'

'Did he now?'

'And as he lay dying, he told Alessandro the truth – that Francesco had taken you to the countess's villa – about the possibility you survived that night.'

'Well, I'm glad he came clean. He must have felt very guilty about running off and leaving me with the Jerries like that, especially as I'd saved his skin on the day we met.'

He tore a page out of his notebook and wrote down an address and telephone number. 'I'm afraid I can't stay, but let's write to each other. I'd like to hear from you. I leave for a book tour tomorrow, but would very much like to meet again next time you're in Italy.'

Looking down at the address, I saw it was Villa Selva like in the letter he'd written to his mother.

'That sounds good.'

Standing up, he downed the rest of his coffee, placed the panama hat firmly on his head and picked up his notebook and pen.

'Do stay in touch, Jessica, and thank you for taking the trouble to hunt me down. I hope we can get to know each other better.'

He walked around the corner, and I watched him – my real grandfather, a novelist, a writer like me. He was quite sprightly for his age. I watched him get into a car parked next to the fishing boats. And then he drove off. I looked down at the piece of paper in my hand and smiled to myself. Corresponding with the man who'd written so beautifully in that diary would be a wonderful experience for me. I would write a letter to him as soon as I got home.

CHAPTER 68

JESSICA

TUSCANY, JUNE 1996

I pulled into the drive lined with cypress trees. At last I was here, living my dream, approaching the villa I'd be renting for six months, with the option to extend if I wanted to. It was called Villa Caterina, and was absolutely perfect, set on the edge of a vineyard, near to a farmhouse owned by what appeared to be a lovely Italian couple. I'd exchanged a few phone calls with Signora Fantini about all the arrangements, and it would be reassuring to know they were there at night, as the villa was in the middle of the countryside. There were other villas on the land, and Signora Fantini said everyone often ate together on the terrazza on summer evenings. Visitors would be welcome, and she had no problem with Alessandro staying over. I'd told her about writing my book, and she'd said I could get as involved in the vineyard as I wanted to in case it provided material. I couldn't wait to learn how to pick grapes and see how wine was made – right there on the property. I'd been exchanging letters with my grandfather since seeing him in Lake Garda. I'd told him about moving to Tuscany, and the travel-writing book. He was delighted that I'd be writing books like him, and he'd suggested that I visit him and his family. Alessandro would be most welcome too. I couldn't wait – and as soon as I was settled, I'd give him a call and fix a date.

The narrow drive was riddled with potholes and the ride was bumpy, but when I rolled down the car window all I could hear was the sound of cicadas and birdsong, and all around me were fields reaching as far as the eye could see, and neat rows of vines. Before me was the big old stone farmhouse where the Fantinis lived. Next to it were outbuildings. To my right was an olive grove, and a winding road to the left led to Villa Caterina – Signora Fantini had given me directions over the phone, saying there would be a key under the plant pot on the front step that contained pink geraniums. She'd come over later on to see how I was doing once I'd settled in, but I should have everything I needed.

A sign directed me to Villa Caterina, and I pulled into its drive. Like the farmhouse, it was made from stone, with a red terracotta roof. I got out of the car, too excited to carry anything in from the boot yet – I just had to see inside. I found the key under the plant pot and opened the front door, and it was just perfect. A huge open-plan room with a kitchen on one side and plush sofas on the other. There was a round table large enough for a few people and the floors were terracotta tiles. The windows had thin blue curtains and, when I went outside onto the veranda, there were chairs and a table and the most stupendous view of Tuscan hills. Right in front of me was a field of sunflowers, their cheery bright-yellow heads facing in the same direction. I just had to stand there for a moment and take it all in, and savour my new surroundings. And in the distance, there was Siena on a hill. The view of its red-brick buildings took me back to the journey I'd been on since Alessandro turned up at Birch Farm with the diary. It had been the best journey, and everything I needed, but also what Mum and Gran had needed.

That diary had transformed all of our lives. Before that we'd been almost stuck in time, not moving forward, all of us with dreams remaining unfulfilled. But now we were all on the right path and I was glad.

I went inside and opened the fridge. Signora Fantini had been kind enough to fill it with a few basics until I could get to the shops. There was butter and a delicious-looking Italian hard cheese, and then milk, bottles of water, tomatoes and salad leaves. On the side was a loaf of bread, fresh from the bakery, and a couple of bottles of Chianti from the vineyard. I couldn't be more excited about living in this place and writing about my experience. But for now, I was tired from the journey, and decided to take a look at the bedroom and perhaps take a nap. I went upstairs, where there were two bedrooms, again with magnificent views. I would use the smaller one as an office for my writing. The larger bedroom had a comfy-looking double bed and was made up with white linen, and there was a pile of towels on a chair in the corner. The bed looked so inviting that I just had to climb in and take a nap. Alessandro was due to drive over from Florence after work, and I couldn't wait to see him.

A knock at the front door, and the sound of Alessandro's voice calling, 'Jessica?' woke me up. Looking at my watch, I saw that I'd been asleep for two whole hours. I got out of bed, went downstairs and opened the front door. And there he was with a huge grin on his face.

'You're here!' I said.

'I'm here.'

He was carrying a brown paper bag that appeared to be filled with food. Beautiful yellow peaches and a cantaloupe melon peeked out of the top.

'I stopped at the grocery store and got us a bunch of delicious things to eat.'

'You'd better come in. I'm starving,' I said.

'Yes, but first—' He leant down to kiss me, and I wrapped my arms round his neck, breathing in the scent of him. Alessandro, my Alessandro. Finally.

He was right – first I did need to show him upstairs. We went into the kitchen, and he put the brown paper bag on the side, and then he picked me up in his arms.

A LETTER FROM ANITA

Dear reader,

I want to say a big thank-you for choosing to read *The Tuscan Diary*. If you did enjoy it, and want to keep up to date with all my latest releases, just sign up at the following link. Your email address will never be shared and you can unsubscribe at any time.

www.bookouture.com/anita-chapman

I hope you enjoyed *The Tuscan Diary* and if you did I would be very grateful if you're able to write a review. I'd love to hear what you think, and it makes such a difference helping new readers to discover one of my books for the first time.

And I love hearing from my readers – you can get in touch via my website, and follow me on social media to see updates about my books and everyday life as a writer.

Thanks, and best wishes,

Anita Chapman

www.anitachapman.com

KEEP IN TOUCH WITH ANITA

www.anitachapman.com

facebook.com/anitachapmanauthor
x.com/neetschapman
instagram.com/neetschapman
tiktok.com/@neetschapman

ACKNOWLEDGEMENTS

Thank you so much for helping to make this book happen:

My former editor, Jayne Osborne (recently departed for sunnier climes), who was an absolute joy to work with. Jayne gave me that first two-book deal with Bookouture, changing my life, and I shall miss working with her very much. Jayne did the structural edit for *The Tuscan Diary*, and after that my new editor, Lucy Frederick, took over the book, starting with the line edit. Thank you so much to Lucy for doing such a thorough and helpful line edit – I really felt it took this book to a whole new level.

Thank you very much to the rest of the Bookouture team, always so dedicated, efficient and friendly, and senders of beautifully-written emails. To see who has worked on this book, see the information in the following pages.

Special thanks also go to cover designer Debbie Clements, who has once again designed an absolutely stunning cover – what a beautiful Tuscan scene that you could just step into! Also thank you to copy-editor Jacqui Lewis, who has been so thorough and helpful, and to proofreader Anne O'Brien who picked up so many important things.

Thank you very much to readers who read advance copies via NetGalley and for the blog tour. I really appreciate you taking the time to read *The Tuscan Diary* and write reviews before publication day, especially those who have done this so soon after reading and reviewing *The Florence Letter*. I so appreciate all of your support, and it always gives me such a warm feeling to see your social media posts and reviews go up during launch week. I'd especially like to say a huge thank you to Anne Cater, Anne Williams, Barbara Wilkie and Karen Hilton who have read and reviewed advance copies of all three of my books! A special thanks here to my lovely publicist at Bookouture, Jess Readett, who has once again organised a wonderful blog tour, and who has given up her time to do an Instagram Live with me on publication day as she did for *The Florence Letter*.

To my social media followers, especially all those who continue to cheer me on and share news about my books.

To my family and those friends who always support me, and to my writing retreat pals: Jules, Donna, and Liz, who played a big part in me getting my books out there in the end.

To everyone who bought, read, spread the word about and wrote reviews for my debut, *The Venice Secret*, and my second novel, *The Florence Letter*. Thank you for encouraging me to write more books with your lovely words.

PUBLISHING TEAM

Turning a manuscript into a book requires the efforts of many people. The publishing team at Bookouture would like to acknowledge everyone who contributed to this publication.

Audio
Alba Proko
Sinead O'Connor
Melissa Tran

Commercial
Lauren Morrissette
Hannah Richmond
Imogen Allport

Cover design
Debbie Clement

Data and analysis
Mark Alder
Mohamed Bussuri

Editorial
Lucy Frederick
Melissa Tran